To Grake

Cynthea Gregory grew up   ie
taught in comprehensive schools before ....   :h
her husband. There she had three cookbooks published in
French by CPE Editions. She is the author of one other novel,
written under the pen name of Cynthea Ash, 'A little Slice of
Paradise.' It is also mainly set in the Caribbean. She currently
lives in East Devon with her husband.

Happy reading,

Cynthea

Mango Bay

Cynthea Gregory

For all the wonderful people of the Caribbean.

Many thanks to my husband Mike for all his patience and without whose help and encouragement my books would not have been completed.

Chapter 1

Zing

This was turning out to be another bloody awful day, Emmalyn told herself. One of those days your mind won't ever let you forget.

Scorching sand bit at her bare feet. Searing heat burnt her scalp. Sweat prickled her temples. Her heart was racing, her breathing shallow.

The shimmering dark canopy above her shifted in the breeze. Noisy grackles flew amongst the branches crying a harsh lament. A subtle fresh, briny smell hung in the air. Muttering and whispers came from the lingering throng around her, but her focus was on the dinghy heading shoreward, towing its burden. Her eyes did not leave its path for a moment.

'My God, how will I tell her if it's him?'

Her thoughts flew to her friend; and fear started to consume her. She felt a strong wave of nausea; her limbs started to tremble.

The driver cut the motor of the dinghy. He pulled his burden from the ocean's grasp. Strong sunlight caught on glistening grey skin as the body emerged. Salt water drained from a head of white hair—as white as the surf crashing onto the beach. Immediately, she knew.

For Emmalyn, the world paused.

Her mind emptied. Blackness. She fell against the person next to her; her legs crumbled, and the hot sand received her.

~ ~ ~

Just an hour before, the first slice of Emmalyn's day had started very differently. Stepping off the bus, sun beating on her skin, she'd felt she was entering a world of promise and expectancy. There'd even been a slight tingling of excitement inside her.

Approaching the road-side café, the first things she noticed were the mangoes. They were fighting for attention, stacked alongside some pineapples and golden apples on a table in front of the wooden structure. She focused in on the oval forms with their matt skins of green, tinged with streaks of crimson. She stopped alongside the stall and inhaled their mellow odours. Emmalyn could imagine the taste of ripe mango, orangey, honey coloured flesh cool in her mouth, the juice running down her chin. A large woman, with a cheery smile, emerged from the café's unlit interior.

'How much for the mangoes?' Emmalyn asked.

'Dey eight dollars mi dear.'

Emmalyn raised her eyebrows. 'What, for each mango?'

'Dey not in season 'ere—dey from 'nother island.'

'Yeah, I realise that, but I'm afraid I ain't got eight dollars for a mango. That's too much for me.'

The café owner cast her a sympathetic glance. 'De tourists, dey expects to buy 'em 'ere in Mango Bay.' She leaned across her stall and said softly, 'I don' says dey ain't from around 'ere and dey pays the price.'

'Sorry … not me … even though I love them,' she smiled faintly at the woman's commercial canny. 'I'll have just a bottle of Coke please.' The woman's hips jiggled as she disappeared back into her café.

Emmalyn walked towards the empty adjacent wooden tables and benches and installed herself at one of them. Her slim dark legs were swung over the bench, constricted by her knee-length pencil skirt. Her fabric bag was stowed alongside on the well-worn seat. She noted the grey flaking paint. Several large marks stained the furniture. Looking at the café building, it appeared to be in a similar state. Sometime ago, the cabin had been painted in vermillion; and the name 'Zing' painted on the side in blue.

Fierce tropical sun and lashing rain had faded it all to a weathered, sad-looking, pale red. The Zing was barely discernible.

Emmalyn twisted around to survey the beach. A wide strip of low vines edged the stretch of pale pink sand. The sea, unsettled after a recent storm, rolled onto the shore in large circles, each rhythm pounding and spraying up white foam. Mango Bay was popular with the islanders at the weekend, but today there were just a few tourists, presumably from the hotel, sauntering along—strolling after breakfast. There was no sign of Jeffrey.

She checked out again the state of the run-down establishment and wondered why Jeffrey had insisted they meet there. Surely, it would have been more appropriate, more business-like, and more pleasant, if they'd met at his workplace—Topaz, the hotel at the end of the bay. She'd never seen the hotel interior, except on the internet.

The café owner reappeared clutching a bottle running in condensation, an inverted plastic beaker balanced on the neck. Flip, flopping of her plastic sandals accompanied her amble towards the table. The bottle was plonked in front of Emmalyn.

'Dat three dollars mi dear.'

Emmalyn, unprepared, snatched up her bag and hunted. Folders with sheets of commercial properties were unceremoniously slung on the table. Her second-hand iPad was balanced on top. Next came the hairbrush. After a little more rummaging, her purse appeared.

'I need to get a smaller bag,' she confessed, 'I keep too much in this one. I can never find anything in it.'

'We'z all de same, uz ladies. We'z all too much in our 'andbags,' her full face, framed by a vivid-coloured turban, lit up. Emmalyn returned the smile and handed over the change. She watched as the cola glugged into the beaker—froth bubbled over the top.

'Ya works at de hotel?'

'No, I've come from the capital on the bus,' Emmalyn told her, 'I've arranged to meet a friend here. HE works at Topaz. Well, some of the time. He's a bit late I'm afraid.'

'He be along soon, for sure,' the café owner promised, before flip-flopping back to the welcome shade inside her café.

The cold drink vanished in seconds. The brisk walk from the bus stop had made her sticky and hot. She longed for a second, but knew she couldn't afford it. Hopefully, Jeffrey would buy a round of drinks when he arrived.

Minutes ticked by. Emmalyn became uneasy. She kept checking time and again in the direction of the hotel. The sun's glare off the water made her eyes squint—myriads of diamond flecks bounced off dark blue. Several brightly coloured boats patterned the bay, bobbing and rocking with the turbulence. On the beach, a solid dark row of bulbous boulders fenced in the territory of the affluent, but only to the high-tide mark—below that was public. Planted alongside was the security guards' white booth enforcing a caution. A few bathers were relishing the warmth of the sea. Jeffrey was not in sight.

She scanned the hotel buildings again at the end of the bay, climbing up the bluff. Most were camouflaged by soaring palms and other tropical vegetation. But she could just make out the few rooms which topped off the ridge, over-looking a vast expanse of turquoise sea. Her eyes ran back down to the beach. No, he still was not there. Emmalyn sighed.

She'd met Jeffrey through her friend. His offer of work had vastly improved her prospects for the future. Right from first meeting, they'd got along. They'd found plenty to talk about, both having worked in the same profession. Jeffrey was keen to start up a real estate office on the island. He was the one with the money. She, being an islander, had the contacts. She'd be the one who would do the running around, measuring up properties, taking photos and putting them on to a website. She was excited about it all and eager to get on with their meeting. Shame Jeffrey was very late. She was certain he had said ten o'clock.

She reached for the folder emptied from her bag. As a distraction, she thumbed through the information sheets. She had traipsed from realtor to realtor in Bourbon, giving them the spiel about starting up an office. Studying each sheet, she envisaged the commercial units available. To her, there was a firm favourite, but perhaps Jeffrey might have other ideas. They were to discuss setting up a business selling high-end villas and dealing with property management. It would be great to work in realty again. Her temporary job had become more than temporary. It exhausted her. Waiting tables, at forty plus, spending long hours on her feet, some days left her aching and miserable. She hoped this new prospect would turn her life around. Jeffrey was the chance she'd been waiting for.

She dragged her much-used bag onto her lap. Several seconds scrabbling exposed her phone. Emmalyn scrolled through her list of contacts. Pressed Jeffrey's number and listened. It rang continuously.

'Talk to me, talk to me. Pick up,' she mumbled. But the phone just switched through to the message service.

'Hi Jeffrey, its Emmalyn here. I'm at Zing waiting for you. Hope to see you soon.' She put her phone away and started to worry. Would he show up?

Once again, she scanned the shoreline, in both directions. No Jeffrey.

She'd have to move into the shade. She patted her braided hair; her head felt too hot. Emmalyn was beginning to wish she'd brought something to protect her head. There was no shade across the seating area—she could do without getting sunburnt.

A vehicle pulled up alongside the café. She half-raised herself in the faint hope it might be Jeffrey. But it was only a passing car, the driver wanting to buy fruit. Two pineapples disappeared

5

through the open window; the café owner pocketed the money. Glimpsing Emmalyn, she sauntered her way.

'Ya friend, he not come?' She smiled.

'He must have got held up somewhere,' Emmalyn made excuses to herself. 'We were supposed to have a business meeting this morning.'

'He often late?' She folded her arms across her ample bosom. 'Dere's some folks who'z always late, I'z got a friend ...'

A blood-curdling scream cut dead the conversation.

They looked at one another in silence and turned towards the outcry. A woman, in a vivid blue bikini, was emerging from the sea, stumbling up the beach. She stood shrieking hysterically, her arms flaying.

The howling was terrifying. Emmalyn's stomach instantly started to churn. Not really sure why, she was drawn to the woman—she had to know what was happening.

'Sorry,' Emmalyn put her hand out towards the café owner; 'I must see what the problem ...' she stood up and grabbed at her bag.

The commotion compelled her towards the waters' edge. The proprietress was left standing alone. Emmalyn's progress over the flowering beach vines was slow; it slowed even more as she reached the bare, dried out sand. She stooped to remove her thong sandals and shoved them into her bag, disregarding its other contents. People were sitting up on their sun beds. Books were being disregarded. Sunglasses removed. A few people approached the distraught figure. She was doubled over, her face in her hands. Her squealing hadn't stopped.

When someone reached her, she yelled, 'there ... there ...,' waving her hand vaguely across the bay. 'Oh God, I swam into it ... floating ... it was floating in front of me.'

The security guard had deserted the shade of his booth. His hotel uniform seemed to give him confidence to take control. The bikinied woman continued wailing, 'in the sea ... in the sea

… just there. You need to pull it out!' She indicated again out to sea.

'But ma'am, what is it?' Emmalyn heard the guard ask. The curious had started to gather. Emmalyn's gaze followed where the woman was pointing. She saw nothing. Nothing, except two bobbing boats anchored a little way out. She joined the gathering group of onlookers surrounding the security guard.

'Ma'am, ya needs to explain, den perhaps I can 'elps ya,' he said gently.

The screaming subsided and was replaced by gasping sobs. The woman's eyes were swollen; her face marked by tears. Her arm swung out again, indicating in the direction of the boats. 'By the boat,' she wept. 'A body … I swam right into it.' Her fingers swept under her eyes, trying to erase her tears and remnants of sea water.

'I hopes ya mistaken ma'am.' The guard directed a couple from the crowd to accompany the overwrought guest up to the main buildings. Her sobbing continued, fading gradually as she mounted the slope of the bluff.

'I calling for help,' the guard said to anyone that was listening. He keyed a number into his phone.

Emmalyn remained, hovering close to the group of onlookers. Her hot and sweaty hands clutched her bag tightly to her. Dumb struck, her anxiety mounting, a hollow sensation started to gnaw at her insides, a strong wave of nausea hung in her throat. She felt her heartbeat must be audible. Out of desperation, she kept looking along the beach. But no! Jeffrey was nowhere to be seen.

The guard took control of the growing number of observers. Waving his arms, he endeavoured to herd them a little further up the beach. They all stood there and waited. Minutes passed. Emmalyn sensed the air of suspense and curiosity amongst them.

Minutes later, four others from the hotel appeared on the beach—two more security guards and two who had a managerial appearance—white shirts and crisply creased trousers. They carried an air of assertiveness. They insisted the beach was cleared and sent the crowds to the top of the beach, next to the hotel's restaurant. Emmalyn stuck with them and drifted towards the stylish contemporary structure, set against a backdrop of towering mango trees. Like the rest of the group, she turned to stare at every move of the hotel staff; taking in all of their directives. Her insides were shrieking, as loud as the woman in the blue bikini had been, but not a sound escaped her lips. Emmalyn prayed.

The drone of a motor cut across the quiet. All eyes followed a small inflatable dinghy. It left the jetty at the base of the bluff. The whirring sound quickly died as it stopped behind the yellow form of the first wooden boat.

'De'z a body in de water Boss. I thinks it caught on de anchor rope,' shouted the driver. The unfolding tragedy created a murmur among the lingering audience. The dinghy driver bent behind the yellowness, but reappeared rapidly.

'It a man,' he called. 'I thinks I knows 'im.'

Emmalyn sucked in a lungful of air. She wanted to turn away. She wanted to walk back to the café. But she knew she would not, could not. She had to know; had to witness the whole macabre scene. She had to reassure herself it wasn't Jeffrey. Had to be sure the promise of a better future, for herself, for others, hadn't drowned behind that small boat. Jeffrey had told her he went swimming every day. He had boasted he was an excellent swimmer. So, why would it be him?

'De police's comin' sir,' one of the guards informed Boss. The heads of the staff came together. Decisions were made.

'Can you get him into the dingy?' shouted Boss across the water.

'No Boss, 'e a dead weight ... it overturn. Best drag 'im in de water to de beach,' he shouted back.

'Keep the guests away,' directed Boss. 'Please go back to your rooms,' he barked towards the waiting throng.

But the crowd had grown. The inquisitive had left their tanning stations to check out the drama being acted out before them. Real life theatre being played out on a normally quiet, paradisiac stretch of sand.

The morning heat increased. Emmalyn started to feel queasy. Without a hat, her scalp and face prickled. Her head became hot and dizzy, but her body shivered with fear.

The buzzing of the motor renewed. The dinghy crept towards the staff at the water's edge. As the motor was cut, some waded into the sea to help.

Emmalyn pressed her sweaty hands together and prayed— prayed the dinghy's burden would be nobody she knew; and the world would keep on turning as she'd imagined it would just an hour before.

Chapter 2

Topaz—Five years earlier

Miranda and her husband hung back.

Looking, seeking that familiar figure in the crowded dining room at Topaz.

Then she caught a glimpse of him: his tightly coiled, cropped hair, his coffee-coloured skin, his upright stature. Politely, she excused herself through the celebrating mass, zigzagging around the chatting groups. An automatic smile lit her face. She noted Jeffrey was not as gallant. He followed on behind, forcing his way between people.

'Antony,' she said as she reached her goal, kissing him lightly on the cheek.

'Oh, hi Miranda, Jeffrey. I'm glad you could make it,' Antony returned the kiss.

'Despite being on holiday, we wouldn't want to miss the celebrations. Independence Day is such a key day on the island.' She surveyed the balloons, bunting, and tropical flowers adorning the room. 'Antony, it all looks so wonderfully festive. The staff has done a great job.'

'Let me introduce you to Mr Magson. He's just telling us about the new supermarket he's setting up.'

Miranda shook Magson's hand. 'That's wonderful news,' she said, glowing with enthusiasm. 'The island needs more supermarkets. The existing chain monopolises the market.'

'You're right; I'll try to undercut them to attract clients. It's clear you know the island well Mrs Taylor.'

'Yes, you could say that. I've been coming on holiday to Antony's hotel for many years,' Miranda explained, 'I love the Caribbean, and of course, Sainte Marie.'

The conversation about promoting the new supermarket continued. She turned to glance at her silent husband. She sighed inwardly. One could see he was in another world, making it clear he was only there out of duty. After several minutes, the businessman mentioned his new store would be in Doublon d'Or.

'Do you know what is happening at the school there?' Miranda asked, 'I visited several years ago and found it so enthralling.'

'That's the man you want to ask,' Mr Magson pointed to the far corner of the room. 'Bates. He's your man—Minister for Education. He'll be able to tell you what you want to know.'

'Come on Miranda, I'll introduce you,' Antony offered.

~ ~ ~

Jeffrey barely listened to Magson's long discourse.

Instead, he watched his wife glide behind Antony. They wove across the room towards a stocky West Indian figure. He stood isolated, tucked away in a far corner, next to the row of shutters, diagonally propped open in an attempt to keep the room cool. Jeffrey had not been tempted to follow. He wasn't the least intrigued in island education. Equally, he didn't hold a speck of interest in Sainte Marie's supermarkets. Magson was a pain in the arse. Why did Miranda enjoy fraternising with all these tedious types?

Boredom led him to position himself so he could see what Miranda was up to. Jeffrey smiled mechanically and nodded at Magson, who didn't seem to notice at least one of his audience wasn't paying him very much attention. Jeffrey watched as Miranda was introduced to the politician, obviously not fazed by fraternising with the Minister of Education. In fact, she seemed to be enjoying herself. As was Bates. Jeffrey had come to learn she got on with all and sundry—she was lively and intelligent, but too bloody serious for his liking. The woman needed to lighten up.

11

After his first marriage failed, he had vowed he wouldn't get tied up with anybody else. But then he'd met Miranda. She had come into his estate agents to try and sell a property after her first husband, Bradley, had died. She was still cut up by his passing, but she'd looked appealing enough.

By chance, he learnt of her financial situation. Overnight, he saw her through different eyes—no longer just an attractive woman in her sixties, but a desirable creature he had to spend more time with. She had a substantial portfolio of properties and lived most of the year in a country manor in Lyme Regis. Perhaps he'd been wrong about not wanting to re-marry. If he played his cards right, Miranda could be his ticket out of a mundane retirement. It had been tough. He'd temporarily had to become a one-woman man; had to turn up the charm, pampering to her wishes, but all of it had worked. He'd hauled in a great catch. Jeffrey was still congratulating himself.

Antony came back to rejoin the dialogue about the new supermarket, which was still churning on. Jeffrey was glad to see him return, being almost desperate for a topic of interest. Antony mentioned to the group Jeffrey's proposed excursion in a couple of days—a flotilla around the Grenadines. Instantly, he stopped observing his wife. His planned trip to the Grenadines was far more engaging. Some of those gathered told him how fortunate he was. Did he realise how sublime the islands were? A real paradise. They wished they could join him. Jeffrey became all smiles and pleasantries. Miranda had painted an idyllic picture from her previous trips. Soft white sands. Vivid turquoise seas. Swimming over spectacular coral reefs. She'd sparked a longing in him to experience it all. Right from the day the tour was booked, he'd felt really fired up about going. He was impatient to board that cruiser.

One by one, the small group broke up: started mingling with others, or they left, in search of refilling their glasses. When a waiter approached sometime later, there was just Antony and

Jeffrey. Their conversation had shifted to a building plot Antony had sent him to see earlier in the week.

'Thanks for suggesting I go to Three Isles Bay. I found it interesting—well worth the visit.'

'Did you like the use of glass … those long thin windows on the side, which pivot? I was really impressed by the contemporary feel about the buildings. I've met the guy who designed them—an Italian. It's good to be getting away from the traditional Creole style building. It's been a bit over used.'

'Yeah, they had a real luxurious feel to them.'

'I believe that around half of the plots are already sold. I'll have to introduce you to the marketing manager.'

'Out of interest, how much are they going for?' Jeffrey said.

'Between one and a half and three million US.'

'Wow, you can get that sort of money on Sainte Marie?' The sum attracted his attention. Once an estate agent, always an estate agent.

'The market's still fairly buoyant for that sort of property. And Three Isles is one of the best locations on the island. Land there is at a premium, because of the superb view over the beach.'

'Interesting.' The information triggered a spark of excitement in Jeffrey. He wondered how he could turn up the charm to persuade Miranda to part with a mil and a half to buy them a secondary home.

'You might be surprised at the money that's around. As I told you Jeffrey, half of them are already sold, off-plan.'

'I wonder if Miranda fancies living here in the Caribbean,' he said, only half-jokingly.

Antony laughed. 'You'll have to ask her. Can you see yourself setting up a real estate office on island?'

'Why not, I love the West Indies. I'm still too active to just spend my retirement pottering about.'

'Perhaps you can see yourself living at Three Isles,' Antony probed.

'Too damned right I can, though I don't think my funds can stretch quite that far.'

'To tell the truth, I've kept an eye on the project at Three Isles. The reason being, I've been thinking of building some homes at the end of the bay here. I already own the land at the back of the tennis courts.'

Jeffrey's ears pricked up. He was always interested in talking shop. Could it be a project he could get involved with? 'Yes, I think I know where you mean. A brilliant place for villas— backing onto the beach—with great views. How much land have you got there?'

'Surprisingly, there's nearly three acres. Enough to build six to eight large villas, I would have thought.'

'That much! I'm surprised that some local builder hasn't wanted to snap up the plot from you.'

'Well, naturally they have, but I've always hung onto it, thinking I could develop it myself someday.' Their conversation was interrupted by another waiter offering more canapés.

Jeffrey glanced in the direction of his wife. She was still exchanging views with the politician, though they had been joined by other islanders. 'Have you had the plot surveyed though Tony? There could be problems with the terrain being so close to the sea.'

A very full round sound filled the room. The vibrations of a large gong resounded in everyone's ears. The tumult of chatter gradually halted. It was the signal. The start of the Independence Day speeches.

The Bishop of Bourbon moved forward. He withdrew his written speech from his jacket pocket. His beaming smile and voice filled the large space.

Jeffrey heard nothing of the speeches. His mind was busy sifting through the conversation with Antony. He could imagine himself based on Sainte Marie. The island had plenty of delights to offer. Life's is too damn short not to be doing what you love. He'd have to see what he could arrange.

~~~

The tree frogs' refrain accompanied their walk up the bluff.

The tantalising crashing of the sea drummed in their ears. Jeffrey was glad the celebrations had been wrapped up. He knew from Miranda's bubbliness, she felt differently. She seemed to love the banal chatter.

A gust of cool air invaded their suite as they entered. Silver flashes reflecting off the infinity pool momentarily illuminated the gloom. As he switched on a light, the electrical glare blotted out the patterns.

Miranda's heeled shoes clopped into the shadows of their room. Halfway, they were jettisoned from her hot feet. Meticulously, she snatched them up and stored them away. Returning to the living area, she weighed up the space. Instinctively, she was in organisational mode. Table lamps were turned on. Already tidy cushions were straightened. A spent bloom, fallen from the vase, was removed from the coffee table.

Jeffrey opened the room's small fridge to find a bottle of water, before throwing himself onto one of the settees to consume it. He enjoyed the palette of black out over the terrace, the aromatic sea air filling the room, the unceasing music of the ocean beating on the rocks below. But Miranda shut it all out— she didn't welcome the flying insects attracted to the light. He watched his wife flit around the room one more time. All this tidying and rearranging was getting to be a real pain. Staff came to service the room every day for heaven's sake. But Miranda liked things done her way. He'd leave her to it. Just so long as she didn't expect him to help. He'd get himself out of there as soon as he could.

'Before dinner, I think I'll try starting that novel I bought at the airport,' she said re-organising the pile of books and magazines on the coffee table.

'Mm ...' was all Jeffrey could muster as a reply.

This obsessive tidying irritated him no end, but despite this his marriage to Miranda had brought him many compensations. He was getting used to 'the good life' she'd bestowed on him. A deluxe suite in a five-star hotel in the idyllic Caribbean. Trips around the Grenadines. As well as living in an up-market country house back home. Not bad, especially when one didn't have to dip your hand too deeply into one's own pocket. But perhaps things could be even better. He thought back to his chat with Antony earlier, before those lame speeches.

To Jeffrey's relief, Miranda appeared to have finished her tour of inspection. She picked up a book and tossed herself into the soft white cushions of the large settee opposite.

'How'd you get on with that politician you were chatting up?' he asked.

'I was not chatting him up,' Miranda corrected, 'Mr Bates is an engaging personality.'

'Mm, perhaps. I'm not too keen on politicians. They're too egotistical.'

She looked at him with a flat stare. 'I don't know how you can make that judgement when you didn't even make the effort to come and meet him.'

Oh, touchy, he thought.

'Anyway, we didn't talk about politics all the time. I got to know a bit about him.'

Lucky you.

'I really wanted to find out about the project in Doublon d'Or. It's a school I visited several years ago. It was in a sorry state then. It must be even worse by now. Fortunately, the Canadians are paying for a new junior school to be built there.'

Jeffrey displayed his level of interest by taking his phone from his pocket. He sensed being watched as he trawled through his e-mails. His head moved half up, aiming to show he was able to concentrate on Miranda at the same time.

'So, why did you visit the school?' he asked after several seconds, more out of necessity than curiosity.

'I met one of the teachers and she asked me along to see what she did. I went with Bradley. We loved it.' Her lips curved upwards, remembering the visit. 'We felt we wanted to help them. We donated money for some school equipment. It was about five years ago now, I suppose. Because of what happened, I haven't returned. Anyway, I told Mr Bates, I'd like to go back and see the plans for the new school.'

'Will you donate again?'

'Probably, they'll need money for equipment in the new buildings. The children were so sweet too—lots of big, cheery grins. And the teachers were so dedicated. Each time we went, it was a really memorable experience. It did us good to see …' she hesitated. Jeffrey became aware Miranda was staring his way, as he tapped into his phone.

'Oh, yeah,' he responded, still scanning through the information on his mobile. He noted her silence, so filled it. 'So, when are you planning on going?'

'When we get back from the Grenadines, I'll contact the school. Would you like to come with me?'

Jeffrey stared at Miranda, his mouth turned down, 'No, I think I'll give that one a miss.'

Miranda ignored the rejection. 'Bradley used to really enjoy it. He loved seeing the little kids. Some of them were real characters, they would …'

'I am NOT Bradley.'

'Okay fine. I don't mind going by myself. I just thought you might enjoy seeing a bit more of life on Sainte Marie.'

He stayed silent and swigged from his bottle of water.

'I enjoyed this afternoon, chatting to Mr Bates, then Lydia, the Prime Minister's wife,' enthused Miranda.

'You're always talking to people, aren't you?' Jeffrey stifled a sigh.

'But of course. I have an innate curiosity about others, and the life they lead. You should know that by now. I just love learning about anything and anybody.'

'And has it always been like that in Sainte Marie? You socialising with people in the island's government and its notables.'

'They're only people, Jeffrey. Like you and I.'

Jeffrey left his thoughts unsaid.

'You know I've been coming to the island and this hotel for a very long time. Antony has introduced us to a lot of island people.'

'I like Tony, he's a good guy.' Jeffrey deflected the conversation in his direction. 'He's thinking of building some villas on a plot of land here. I told him we'd get together over a drink to talk about it.'

'I'm pleased you get along.'

He didn't mention the rest of the conversation he'd had with Antony. Jeffrey emptied his plastic bottle. He got up from the sofa. Time to do something a little more interesting than replay all the details of Miranda's tittle-tattle that afternoon.

'Think I'll go and get changed for my swim. Then we can think about dinner.'

Miranda surveyed him without a smile and made no comment.

~~~

Miranda tried to settle herself with the book, but she was distracted. The activities of the day kept replaying. The people whom she'd encountered. The proposed visit to an island school. Their sailing excursion in two days.

18

She knew from experience; Jeffrey would be a good half hour. Miranda had learnt that whatever happened during the day, Jeffrey's swims took precedence. Everyone else had to fit around him. He had to thrash through water morning and evening, regardless of what everybody else wanted. Miranda was never asked to join him. Not that she wanted to, she was not a water baby. She preferred to exercise with dry feet. Jeffrey's addiction to swimming hadn't been all that evident while he was working—even at home in Dorset. But on holiday, being together 24/7, proved to be an eye-opening experience.

She had been grateful when they'd started up a relationship. Life was so empty without Bradley. Not wanting to live out her old age alone, she'd been content when Jeffrey had suggested marriage. An existence shared was preferable to a lonely one. But after marriage, she'd had to face up to disappointments. Disappointments as she lived alongside her new husband and learnt more of his pattern of life. She knew Bradley could not be replaced. But very quickly, Miranda found out that second time around, was definitely not to be a repetition of the first time.

But she'd made her choice.

The marriage was only into its second year, their second holiday in Sainte Marie. The first, their honeymoon, had been a whirlwind of passion. It hadn't exactly been what she wanted, but it had been what she'd expected. They had spent much of the time shut away in the room. The sex was enjoyable initially, but she tired of having the 'Do not Disturb' notice hanging on the outside of their room door. She would have much preferred to be out there discovering the island and its people.

She put down her unread book. She'd got nowhere with it, so went to get changed for dinner.

True to form, Jeffrey returned after his prescribed lengths of the pool. Routine dictated he take a shower before preparing to go to dinner. Miranda was applying her make-up.

19

He exited the shower, a towel wrapped around his waist. 'I thought you'd like to dine out tomorrow. I've booked a table in Anse Argent as a bit of a surprise. I've reserved it early, as I know we have to be away reasonably promptly the following day,' he said.

'Oh Jeff, that's very sweet of you. But we could have celebrated my birthday in the hotel.'

'No my darling, it's not every day it's your birthday.'

She put down her mascara and turned to kiss him. At once, she regretted her action.

Jeffrey took her hand and pulled her towards him. Miranda looked fixedly at him. His head of strong, curly white hair. A tan which accentuated the lines of his ageing face. Jeffrey's damp hand slid up her bare legs inside her dress. He kissed her forcefully. She was reluctant to reciprocate.

'Bye-bye lipstick,' she smiled automatically. Inside there was no smile.

He ignored her remark.

His hands went further up her thighs. His towel dropped to the floor. She knew exactly where this was heading. Inwardly, she sighed. She had just spent time getting ready to go out. The evening was not going as she had hoped. But Miranda was getting used to Jeffrey, and his demands.

Jeffrey drew her towards the bedroom area and started to unzip her dress. Miranda was not going to assist him. Her dress fell to the floor. She bent down to recover it; smoothed it over the bedroom chair.

She tried to empty her mind of all that had happened that afternoon—of all the people, and all the conversations. She tried to derive some pleasures from Jeffrey's love making, though it was the second time that day. No, she thought, it wouldn't be the second time they had made love that day—it would be the second time Jeffrey had had sex with her. He was not at all like Bradley—they had made love. With Jeffrey, they had sex.

Unquestionably, he would expect the same performance again later. The man, despite his sixty-three years, had a needy appetite.

Miranda could not relax. She felt distant from the activities on the bed. She didn't really want any of it. Resentment crept into her. She didn't want this three times a day routine. It was always what he wanted. What Jeffrey fancied, when it suited him. He didn't even try to excite her. It was not like her to be so submissive.

This time, she would be compliant. Next time, she would not be. Things needed to change. She promised herself that they needed to talk about all of this.

Chapter 3

Bling

She loved every detail.

The sparkling of turquoise sea. The soft pink, beige curve of the sands, edged with an explosion of vivid greens—palms and tropical vegetation. At the end of the arc stood the ruins of a former hotel. Closed for many years. Windowless. A pile of grey neglect. It was a landscape Miranda had seen hundreds of times—each time, it stirred affection inside her.

Bradley and she had habitually walked up there. Up, and then back to the hotel. Each day had started early with their shared exercise along the shoreline. Year after year, during their holidays there. Those days seemed oh so very long ago.

She stood outside the hotel suite just contemplating. Her gaze dropped. Jeffrey came into her line of vision. She took in his confident style, rhythmic, forceful strokes across crystal waters. He progressed from the diving raft anchored offshore, to a jetty at the base of the bluff. He had told her, he loved to be enveloped by the ocean; swimming emptied his mind. Slicing through the water, he thought only of his weightlessness, and his next stroke forcing him forwards. As Jeffrey reached the white diving platform, he touched it, then flip-turned to follow the same path. His motivation driving him along. Constant. Back and forth. Back and forth. It would not be for her.

Miranda had no real interest in Jeffrey's worship of the ocean. He could be, and would be, there for at least another thirty minutes. She had recently adopted an indifferent attitude to all of it, but the indifference bothered her. Their marriage was still new.

She turned her back on the brightness and regained the shade of the room. Her laptop was flipped open. This day was a special one—her birthday. She needed to bring some recompense into it. Her family would be eager to greet her, even if her husband didn't seem to care.

'Hi Mum, happy birthday,' echoed out of the computer.

'Hello darling, just wait Ella,' she said to her daughter. She adjusted the settings, 'that's better, now I can see you. Oh, and Kloe, our beautiful Kloe. Hello my darlings. It's great to see you both. How are things?'

Ella had been left behind in Dorset with husband, Sam, and daughter Kloe. But Ella knew all about Sainte Marie. She'd told her mother fond memories of family holidays spent there were emblazoned on her mind.

'Happy Birthday to you,
Happy Birthday to you,
Happy Birthday ...'

Their voices rang around the room. Miranda's face lit up with their love and jubilation. Kloe flashed a card in front of the computer as their song faded.

'Look, on your card, it's a dog. It's saying, "Happy Birthday Grandma." Do you like it?' Her drawing blocked the image of Kloe and her mother.

'Wow, he's great! Thank you, my darling.'

'You opened my pressie yet?' Kloe asked.

Miranda held up the square box encasing a pair of glittering earrings.

'Thank you, my darling. I'll wear them today. I'll treasure them.' She smiled as she checked out the tiny, simulated diamonds illuminating the box.

'I bought them myself you know. Well, Mum helped me. We know how you like your bling.' Kloe cuddled up to her mother, a wide smile dominating her face.

Miranda saw Kloe wriggle from her mother, bounce up and dash from the room. 'Got something to show you. Back in a sec,' she called.

23

'She's so excited, bless her. Well, I hope you have a good day Mum.'

'I'm sure I will.'

With Kloe no longer in earshot, Miranda took the opportunity to ask, 'Ella, do you have a bank account that I could transfer money into for Kloe's future? I have been thinking about my finances recently.'

Ella was taken aback. 'Sure Mum, but I don't have the details to hand.'

'Could you find out the maximum I can transfer at one time? I was thinking of a few hundred thousand to be put in trust for her.'

'Wow, Mum! That's very generous. What does Jeffrey think about that?'

'Jeffrey? Well, it's not his money, is it? It was your father's money. I shan't ask him.'

The computer screen went quiet for a few seconds. A hint of awkwardness had crept over Ella's face. 'Well, I just thought … well … as he's your husband now Mum, don't you think … don't you think you ought to tell him?'

'Oh, I might tell him, but I certainly won't ask him,' she felt the smile drop from her face. 'You know Ella, Jeffrey has his own money from the sale of his business. He only sold it last year—he's got plenty. He has led me to believe that he got a very good price for it—though he's never told me exactly how much. And, as you know, he's got his own London apartment.' Miranda felt she could share a little of the recent indignation she felt about her husband, but not too much. The problems she'd been thinking through momentarily flashed before her. But this was not the time or the place to raise them. She needed a serious talk with Jeffrey, not Ella. A talk about their intimacy, about his reluctance to bring out his wallet, about her feelings of being used. About Jeffrey. But today was her birthday—not the best day to do it.

'I thought that Jeffrey was going to sell the flat and spend some of the money on improving your house in Lyme Regis,' Ella said from the computer screen.

'Well, I know he said that, but it hasn't happened yet. I must ask him. A new kitchen would be good,' she replied, trying to hide the discontent in her voice.

'Mum, for the bank details, can you wait until you get back from Sainte Marie? We can talk about it then if you still want to go ahead.'

'I won't change my mind,' Miranda concluded determinately.

'You okay Mum?' Ella asked.

The question was never answered as Kloe dominated the computer screen again. Dressed in something else. A newly acquired sweater. She whirled around in front of the laptop. Danced. Backwards and forwards; wiggling her youthful form.

'Rocking eh Grandma? Don't ya love it?' Kloe asked pirouetting. 'What's Jeffrey got you for your birthday then?'

'Well, my darling, as yet nothing. But I'm sure he's saving it for this evening. He's taking me out for dinner at The Water's Edge.'

'I'm sure he'll have a big surprise up his sleeve,' Ella tried to convince her.

'He'd better! Otherwise, he's a real meany!' Kloe said noisily. 'He does know that it's your birthday, doesn't he?'

Miranda nodded.

'You tell him from me that he's a real meany.'

'I don't think I can tell him that sweetie,' she told her gently.

'Well, I'll tell him myself when I see him next if he doesn't give you something outstanding,' Kloe informed the lap top screen.

~~~

They listened to the murmur of the sea.

Throughout the meal, its music rang in their ears, overpowered by the bass notes of the water lapping against the platform supporting the dining area. Its echoing dominated their silences. These were becoming more frequent. Miranda was struggling to find things to say.

Birthday joyfulness eluded her. The ambiance felt flat. And she didn't feel that Jeffrey was making much of an effort either. Miranda searched for a hint of affection in what he said; but his only topic of conversation seemed to be very matter of fact comments about the flotilla around the Grenadines. How things had changed. When he had been chasing after her, before their marriage, he had been so amicable and seemingly caring.

She stared out at the blackness, patterned by gyrating boats' lights. Normally, she would have been enchanted. Not that evening. Miranda didn't feel great. Her head was muzzy; she couldn't focus. Her limbs were heavy. Secretly, all she wanted to do was return to the hotel and go to sleep. Because of this, she was feeling rather irritated with Jeffrey. They were supposed to be celebrating her birthday. So far, it felt more like a wake. Jeffrey hadn't offered her a card, or a present. He wasn't making a fuss of her. What was wrong with the man? Sure, they had sipped pink champagne when they'd arrived, but that had been the end of his efforts. Unfortunately, the bubbles hadn't lifted things.

After their main course, she sensed Jeffrey was perhaps a little put out. She had only toyed with her food. But she had no appetite. She sat staring at her messy plate, not caring she had little to say; not caring that her meal didn't taste extra special.

She raised her head to see a glow of candles and sparklers moving across the restaurant. The restaurant proprietress, Chandra, escorted by two members of her staff, carefully carried a decorated cake. A very pink, very fluffy cake. They all sang 'Happy Birthday.' Jeffrey's discordant voice joined them. To her embarrassment, the restaurant was soon filled with singing clients; all politely wishing her well. She knew that she had to force her spirits higher. She fixed a false smile.

'Bring on the carnival,' Chandra laughed, placing the cake on their table.

Miranda dragged herself into acting through the pantomime. Blowing out her candles. Smiling as the clients and staff clapped their good wishes. The smile remained fixed. It almost made her face ache.

Miranda had known the restaurant owner for years. But she couldn't summon up more than a few words of thanks. The social chit chat didn't come. One of the staff sliced up a huge pink mound of cake. Jeffrey did the chatting to Chandra, mainly about his topic of the moment—the Grenadines.

Chandra admitted to dreaming of lazy days sailing around the islands. Like a child, Jeffrey displayed eager anticipation. He spoke as though the trip was his own idea—a present for his wife. A fact far from the truth. It had been at her suggestion. It had been her who paid. Just like the rest of their holiday. Miranda stared through them. All the talk about their excursion set doubt in her mind. She began to worry. Would she be up to sailing around the islands? In the full sun, possibly in slightly choppy seas. At that moment, it seemed unlikely.

The pink goo of the cake was too much for Miranda—sweet, fatty, and sickly. But her mask of pleasure remained. The chatter floated around her. The romantic coastal setting was lost on her, and the strong odour of the sea started to bother her. She needed to leave.

Chandra left their table, but Jeffrey continued to grin. A small package appeared from his pocket. It was pushed across the table. 'A very happy birthday my darling,' he said in a low tone. He raised his glass. 'Here's to a romantic few days in the Grenadines.'

Miranda was silent. She stared at the tiny navy-coloured box with a minute gold bow, then looked up at Jeffrey.

'Aren't you going to open it?' She noticed the hurt tone in his question, but didn't care.

Without a word, feeling zero enthusiasm, Miranda undid the doll-sized bow. It would be a small piece of jewellery. Something bought without much thought at the duty-free shops in Bourbon. Opening the lid, a silver tear-drop shape sparkled at her—several tiny diamonds flashed. She'd been right.

'Let me fasten it up for you,' Jeffrey offered. He stretched across the table and took the box from her hands. Miranda couldn't be bothered with all this. He left his seat and fastened the clasp at the back of her neck. She made no attempt to assist. The pendant fell at the base of her throat.

'Hope you like it. I know you like your bling.' Jeffrey kissed the back of her neck.

'Thank you,' she said flatly, 'Jeffrey, would you mind if we go back to the hotel? I'm really not feeling all that great.'

Jeffrey looked flustered. He gaped at her. She knew he had expected her to say the pendant was a lovely surprise. It was really pretty. She would not. Jeffrey emptied his wine glass; he placed it back on the table with a little more force than was necessary. He raised his hand to a passing waitress to ask for the bill.

They were silent during their return journey. Miranda was lost in another world, worrying about their proposed visit the next day. She was very aware Jeffrey was aggravated. By then, she felt so unwell, she didn't care one little bit. Ten minutes' drive and they were back at Topaz. A sigh of relief passed her lips on reaching the main entrance. She ached for the cool, white sheets of their king-sized bed.

In reception, they stopped to pick up their room key. The receptionist was all smiles. She handed over the key and wished them a good night.

It was clear Jeffrey had other ideas. 'Many thanks. We haven't seen you at reception before. You must be new here,' he simpered.

'You're right sir. I started today.' Her smile revealed a set of perfect white teeth.

'I thought so. And what's your name?'

Miranda had heard enough. Her tolerance had reached its limits. She flashed a cold look at Jeffrey. He stood, grinning from ear to ear. A white-haired pensioner flirting with an extremely attractive islander. She was at least half his age.

Stupid fool she thought. Anger boiled inside. Miranda snatched the key from his hand. It felt warm and sticky. She paced away. At the end of the reception area, she heard the name 'Tamara.'

'I'm going to bed,' she called towards Jeffrey and Tamara. She was ignored. It was clear his conversation with Tamara took precedence.

'That's an unusual name. It's very beautiful,' was the last Miranda heard.

Through the hotel gardens, her anger turned to fury. In addition to feeling ill, she became incensed by his lack of consideration! Miranda was aware her new husband was fond of the female of the species. But he'd never been as blatant as this before. Why did the fool delude himself? Why think Tamara's smiles were especially for him? He wouldn't dream that she might just be doing her job. Why would Tamara be interested in him? He was pathetic! Insulting too. Miranda slammed the door of their suite.

What kind of a man had she lumbered herself with? She snatched off her expensive Gucci sandals and slung them fiercely into the wardrobe. She struggled with the zip of her dress. It failed to budge. She tried again, her efforts were in vain, and she pulled the dress over her head, tearing it. Unusually for her, it was left, forming a heap on the tiled floor. A silky nightdress and dressing gown were snatched from behind the bathroom door.

Miranda stood in front of the bathroom mirror to remove her layer of make-up. She studied her tight mouth. Fury remained. Earrings, watch, and rings were then flung violently into their box. She caught the flash of Jeffrey's present around her neck and grappled with its tiny clasp. Her shaky hands fumbled—it was impossible to open. She fought for several seconds. It only made her temper and sense of feeling unwell worse.

'Bloody cheap thing,' she said to herself.

A tap at the door.

Miranda guessed Jeffrey had finished hitting on the receptionist. She ignored it and waited. More tapping. Reluctantly, she opened the door. Jeffrey smiled as he sailed past her.

'You looked very beautiful tonight, Miranda.'

Not a word. She slammed the door with force and headed for the bed.

'The restaurant certainly did a great job of the cake, don't you think?'

Silence.

Jeffrey edged towards his wife. 'My darling.' He caught hold of Miranda's arm.

She struggled to withdraw it.

'Don't touch me!' she hissed.

Jeffrey paid no attention to her warning and pulled her sharply to him. He tried to kiss her fully on the mouth. Miranda beat her free fist on his back with as much strength as she could find. He ignored her again and pushed her so she fell back onto the bed.

'You bastard! No,' Miranda shouted.

She grappled to escape his powerful hold. A scream escaped her, but he swallowed her cries with his lips. She contorted her mouth to try to avoid his.

'Go to hell,' she managed to utter.

She wrestled, but her strength failed her. She beat him with her free hand. Jeffrey was too heavy. Too strong. She felt tears of exasperation trickle down her cheeks. He sat astride her, pinning her against the white of the bed. He tore at the belt of her gown. She couldn't believe this was happening. This was worse than her darkest nightmare.

'Stop! No!'

She fought. Flailed. The affection she had had for his mass of white hair disappeared. The strong odour of his after-shave nauseated her. The saliva of his mouth repulsed her. She felt like a small, weak animal being preyed on by a stronger, more powerful predator. Her struggles were futile. She beat and scratched at any part of him she could reach, shrieking persistently. She saw him undo his zip.

Her force against him was useless. The conclusion was inevitable. Her mind screamed as he came inside her. She swallowed back sobs; her tears dampened the crispness of the sheets. Seconds crawled by. Quickly satisfied, he released his grasp on her. He rolled off her body and laid parallel on the crumbled linen. Shock and weakness kept her silent. Seconds passed, and a slight strength returned.

'Get out of my sight, you worthless bastard!' Miranda hated the sight of him. She couldn't tolerate to be next to him.

'Miranda, I ...' Jeffrey propped his head up on his hand, looking at her. She slid from the bed, her legs trembling as her feet met the cool floor. She crouched by the bed, head in her hands, still sobbing.

'You selfish bastard! You raped me,' she said towards the figure she could no longer see.

'No, of course not,' Jeffrey replied, 'you're my wife. You just looked so lovely this evening. I needed you so badly.'

Awkwardly, she pulled on the bedding and rose from her place on the floor. She could not bear to look at him. She felt broken inside. Her nakedness became hidden by the silkiness of her gown. Miranda sniffed, attempting to wipe away her tears. Her body ached, from him mauling her, from feeling unwell. Her head hurt.

'Don't give me that bullshit!' How dare he think she would believe such lies? 'You're a lying bastard. Do you think I'm some teenage moron?' Miranda shrieked at him. 'You had the hots for the girl in reception. As she was busy, you thought I'd do! Get out! I can't stand the sight of you. Don't bother to come back.'

'Quiet Miranda, people will hear you.' He eased himself off the bed and moved towards her.

'Do you think I care?'

She looked at the man in front of her. She hated what she saw.

'You can't have me just because YOU want it,' she cried. 'This is the bloody twenty first century. I'm not your property to do with as you please. Where's your bloody respect? I'd told you I didn't feel well. I'd told you several times.'

She bawled, 'I—do—not—feel—well.'

Jeffrey attempted to make sympathetic noises. 'Best get some sleep then Miranda.'

'I'm not sleeping in the same bed as you. I don't want you here. Get out! Go!'

'Miranda, don't spoil your birthday.'

A mock laugh rose from her. 'You have already managed to do that. Don't you understand what you have done? Just get out of my sight.'

'Miranda, do be …'

'You can take this with you, you arrogant bastard.' She snatched at the silver around her neck. It remained. Miranda fought against it, until the fine chain snapped. She felt it cutting her skin. The jewellery flew at him. 'You can keep your cheap bling. I don't want it! And I don't want you.'

He tried again to console her by putting his arms around her. She felt her hand sting as it hit his face. 'Leave me alone! Go see if Tamara wants to be Mrs Taylor number three. She won't want you either when she finds out what you're really like.'

'Please Miranda. I'm sorry, we need to …'

'Go to hell Jeffrey. I don't want you near me. You're a selfish, inconsiderate monster. Go see if Tamara can find you another room.' The name was shouted at him. 'And I won't bloody pay for it.'

She pushed him away from her, pulled back the screwed-up bed clothes. As she got into bed, she turned off the bedside light, leaving Jeffrey in the gloom.

'And you can forget the bloody Grenadines. Now, get the hell out of MY room!'

Chapter 4

Crisis

Thumping on the suite door.

Jeffrey stepped out of the shower, grabbed for a clean white towel, and wrapped it around his waist. He strode towards the noise. An impatient banging rattled the door once again.

'OK, OK, I'm coming,' he shouted, smoothing down his hair. Partially opening the door, he let in a slice of blinding sunlight. It confused his vision and his mind. The distinct silhouette of a male figure blocked the doorway.

'Yes, what's the problem?'

'I'm very sorry to bother you Mr Taylor. It's your wife,' said the stark image.

Jeffrey's eyes adjusted to the brilliance. He could just make out the features of Hubert, the deputy hotel manager. 'My wife? What do you mean?'

'One of the groundsmen found her. She seems to be rather unwell Mr Taylor.'

'I've just come back from my swim,' he told him, being rather sparing with the truth. 'Where is she now Hubert? We are supposed to be going on a sailing trip around the Grenadines later on.'

'I don't want to worry you sir, but I don't think that she will be going on any sailing trip today.' His face was grave. 'She was apparently wandering around the garden in her night attire. She's now in Mr Denning's office, sir.'

'Just give me a couple of minutes to get dressed. I'll go straight over.'

'Sir, she seems really ill—very confused. Not her usual self at all,' Hubert said anxiously.

'Thank you Hubert,' Jeffrey snapped, and started to close the door on the hotel employee.

But Hubert didn't give up. 'Mr Denning asked that you take some clothes over for your wife. And some shoes as well sir. He also said to say that it is urgent.'

'Of course,' Jeffrey closed the door forcefully.

Jeffrey's mind churned; his body tense. He started to bristle. It seemed Miranda was having a strop. She had decided, after last night's tiff, that she wasn't going on the yacht cruise with him. She was spitting blood about last night's behaviour. It was just too much. The tour was paid for. What was wrong with the woman? If she didn't want to go, perhaps he'd go without her. He'd been so looking forward to the visit. He could join the group and leave her behind. What a stupid, selfish bitch he'd married.

He dried and dressed himself in a fury.

All he could think about was missing the tour around the Grenadines. He grabbed at the first dress in Miranda's wardrobe and threw it into a beach bag. He bundled a pair of sandals on top. Next some underwear went in the bag—that would do. Stupid woman!

He heard the door reverberate in its frame as he exited. The warm, velvety tropical air enveloped him; even the sense of that on his skin heightened his temper. He was exasperated, blowing out deep breaths. He kicked his way across the tropical gardens heading for the offices. How could the woman behave so immaturely, be so inconsiderate? The row from last night flashed before him. He hoped Miranda hadn't discussed this with Antony, but he felt confident she wouldn't have shared the tale of their little domestic. She was not that kind of person.

At the office door, he knocked lightly, and entered without waiting. The room was empty. This added to his rage.

'Where the hell ...?' he grumbled, 'if it's so bloody urgent, where the hell ...?' He stopped mid-sentence, as Antony's assistant was framed in the doorway.

'Oh Mr Taylor, I'm so glad you're here. I'm really sorry your wife is so unwell. She's in the car with Mr Denning, just behind this office. He wants to get her to the clinic as soon as possible.'

Ignoring the woman's considerate attitude, he pushed past her. The running motor attracted him to Antony's car.

Antony leaned over to open the passenger door for Jeffrey to clamber in and greeted him with a nod. Before Jeffrey had time to do up his seat belt, the car sped off. Once he'd recovered his equilibrium, he glanced towards the back seat. His reason for being there—Miranda—clad in a bathrobe, sat, her head hung down. She seemed not to be aware of him. He checked her again; her dishevelled hair hid most of her face. Was that really his wife? She looked a mess.

'This will save time Jeffrey,' Antony said, still concentrating on his driving, 'I'll get to the clinic faster than calling out an ambulance. The clinic is expecting you. Doctor Rubens will see you immediately.'

Jeffrey was confused. 'I don't understand, what's the problem?'

'I don't want to alarm you Jeffrey, but I think the sooner we get Miranda to the clinic the better. She is totally disorientated. It's difficult to understand what she's trying to say, but she's been muttering about Bradley. Worryingly, she seems unable to comprehend what anyone says to her. She even had trouble walking to the office, despite being supported by a groundsman.'

'But she was fine last night. We went into Anse Argent to eat.'

'That may be so, but you can see, she certainly isn't fine now. I had to get one of the women from the spa to come and help put the bath robe on her. She wasn't able to do it herself.'

Fury and disappointment, in equal amounts, still festered inside him. Jeffrey didn't comprehend—from the little he could see, the person behind him didn't look anything like his wife. Rather like some old, ugly stranger. Hunched up in a murmuring heap. Muttering incomprehensible things. She looked nothing like the smart, lively woman he had lived with for the past twenty months. The interior of the car remained silent. Antony put all his efforts into getting his vehicle to the outskirts of Bourbon and the Health Clinic as fast as possible.

During the journey, Jeffrey was trying to adjust his thoughts. Bit by bit, he was coming to the realisation that perhaps his wife was in a dire state. The raw, savage rage started to dissipate. But the bitter disappointment didn't. He was drowning in it. This was all Miranda's fault. She'd known that he was so looking forward to their excursion. Why choose to be ill today? He didn't want to have to face the vile alternative she was forcing upon him. Looking after an invalid wife, visiting her in hospital—it could be the end of a relaxing, exotic holiday.

The car stopped. Without explanation, Antony leapt from the car. He dashed inside the large glass-fronted building in front of them. Seconds later, he returned with a uniformed nurse and a wheelchair. But, it was difficult, even with the three of them, as Miranda's limbs didn't aid in any way. They struggled to manoeuvre her from the car to the wheelchair. The nurse spoke reassuringly, in an attempt to calm her. After a wrestle, she strapped her patient into the chair. Taking control, the nurse whisked Miranda through the automatic glass doors. Jeffrey followed reluctantly.

Antony called out from beside the car, 'I have to get back to the hotel. I hope that all goes well Jeffrey.'

Jeffrey waved back, begrudgingly following the nurse straight into a consulting room. A label, on the door, 'Doctor Zina Rubens' caught his eye. Entering, he automatically pushed aside his reasons for being there. His first thought was that she was attractive—very attractive. As Dr Rubens ushered him in, Jeffrey was weighing her up. Forty-fiveish. Slim. Sexy brown eyes. She brought an instant smile to his face. He received no reaction.

There was no preliminary chit-chat or niceties from Zina Rubens.

'What age is your wife?' she asked sharply.

Jeffrey hesitated, 'err … sixty-one.'

'What medications does she take?'

'Don't really know, she takes tablets each day, but I don't exactly know what they are.' Dr Rubens threw him a cold, disdainful look. From then on, he was ignored.

Jeffrey half watched the doctor doing several simple tests on his wife, while evaluating her physical attributes. Miranda was asked to smile. She did not. To close her eyes and raise her arms—no reaction. She wanted her to repeat sentences—again no response. Within seconds, Doctor Rubens re-called the nurse and Miranda was wheeled away.

'Please sit in the waiting room Mr Taylor,' Doctor Rubens said from behind her desk. 'I've sent your wife for a scan. Let me explain,' she continued in a superior tone, 'there is a nurse at reception. We need as much of your wife's medical history as possible.' Dr Rubens went and stood alongside the open door, waiting for him to go. There was not a flicker of a smile on her full mouth.

'I will give you my diagnosis as soon as I have the results of the tests,' she concluded.

Reality was kicking in. Not only would he not be sailing around the Grenadines, but it seemed his holiday in Sainte Marie was about to be metamorphosed. He imagined his day being monopolised by that old woman, his wife. Caring for her every need; wheeling her about the hotel as an invalid. He didn't want to cope with that.

He dragged himself to the reception desk and gave the few details he knew about Miranda's health. The receptionist went on to explain that in Sainte Marie, all medical treatment had to be paid for. She asked for his bank details. Jeffrey was flustered. In the hurry to get to the clinic, he hadn't thought of bringing

Miranda's bank cards. Begrudgingly, he had to give his own. Things were getting worse. Not only was Miranda ruining his holiday, but he had to pay for the privilege. He returned to the crowded waiting room, still clutching the goddamned straw beach bag. Miranda did not come back.

A very long hour later, Dr Rubens called him to her consulting room. She indicated that Jeffrey should sit opposite her. He noted there were still no smiles.

'Mr Taylor, your wife has suffered a haemorrhagic stroke. I will explain more about that later. We have stabilised her. But firstly, I need your consent to send her to our hospital,' she said.

Jeffrey sighed in despair. The nightmare had just become real. 'You don't need to explain, I know what a stroke is,' he snapped. Doctor Ruben's cold eyes met with his. The look instantly made him regret his display of annoyance. 'Yes, yes, of course she must go to the hospital.'

'You understand, Mr Taylor, it is a private hospital. It is fee paying.'

'Yes, I do understand.'

'She will be taken there by ambulance, which is also payable.'

Jeffrey nodded, thinking only of his bank details left at reception.

Whilst Dr Rubens gave instructions on the phone, Jeffrey was calculating how much this could all cost. He decided it was necessary, when he'd located Miranda's credit card, to return to the clinic. He saw no reason why he should have to foot the bill.

After putting down the phone, the doctor continued, 'Your wife is still very seriously ill. She needs further tests to find out the full extent of the bleeding, and then, what therapy will be required. We'll need to keep her under observation. If surgery becomes necessary, we may need to fly her to another island.'

Jeffrey tried to concentrate on what was being said. Temporal lobes, limbic systems, modified emotions, and diminished memory. All the information sailed past him. He couldn't believe this was happening to him. He did not want to have to contend with all this stuff.

'I suggest you don't visit your wife at the hospital until this evening,' Dr Rubens advised. Jeffrey did not respond. 'If there are any dramatic changes in your wife's condition, one of my staff will contact you at the hotel.'

Following her previous pattern, Dr Rubens left her desk, opened the consulting room door and stood by it, waiting for him to depart. Jeffrey didn't bother to shake her hand or thank her.

Back at the hotel, Jeffrey headed straight to the offices. He knew Antony would want to hear the diagnosis.

'I'm sorry to say, I thought it was a stroke,' Antony admitted after hearing Jeffrey's news, 'she had lots of the usual symptoms.'

'It was such a shock,' Jeffrey replied for effect. 'I have to go and see her at the hospital this evening.'

'Do let me know when I'm able to visit her.'

Jeffrey grunted. 'I've now got the formidable task of letting her family know. Ella will be devastated. You know how close she is to her mother.'

Jeffrey left the office with a heavy sensation hanging in his stomach. There was now so much he needed to organise—stuff he definitely didn't want to be doing. All he wanted to do was wash away the nightmare of that morning—all the garbage Miranda had chucked at him. He'd like to be able to turn the clocks back twenty-four hours. Go back to the pleasant, relaxing holiday he'd been having. Sure, he had to contact her family, but he came first. All that could come later.

Back in the room, Jeffrey changed into his swimming gear. He always felt so much better after a swim. His head would be clearer. His body less tense. His plan of action could be formulated after that. Or maybe after asking room service to bring him some lunch. Then, he'd consider coping with the chore of phoning Miranda's children, Ella, and Craig.

Jeffrey smiled as he slid into the warmth of the terrace infinity pool. The silky water felt good. He lay still, supine, flicking his hands to stay afloat. He relished the hot sunrays heating his skin. He drifted for several minutes—let his burden of problems seep away into the water. Then slowly he turned and beat his arms rhythmically, pulling himself through the pool. This was much better. Several laps later, he hoisted himself out. Jeffrey sat on the pool edge, taking in the view. Small boats dancing on the water. The beach activities below him. The heat gradually drying his body.

A lobster lunch and half a bottle of sparkling French white wine later, Jeffrey returned inside the room. His plan of action established, he commenced a search—firstly, a search of Miranda's belongings, her phone to begin with. He needed the family's contact numbers. It all proved quite simple. He knew his wife was very methodical. Everything was tidily lined up in a drawer. The rummaging through his wife's affairs gave him a sense of satisfaction, a sense of power over her. He enjoyed that.

He briefly checked her phone and then her laptop. He already knew Miranda kept most of her confidential data and personal info on her computer; her phone was just for calls. He would have to scrutinise those more closely a little later. Next, he located her purse, cash, credit cards and keys. It was easy! He also unearthed their return flight tickets and insurance information. He'd had nothing to do with any of that. Jeffrey lined up his wife's belongings on top of the white bed linen. A smirk broadened his mouth. He'd only have to lay on the charm for a bit, and tell Miranda he'd handle all the finances until she felt well again. He'd be able to run things his way. Perhaps having a wife in hospital did have advantages after all. And it could take a long time to recover from a stroke.

41

Jeffrey glanced at his watch. He couldn't put off phoning Miranda's family any longer. Craig came first. He would be easier to deal with. As he guessed, Craig was working. Their conversation was short. He asked Jeffrey to send him daily updates. Then came Ella. She was going to be a totally different matter. He and Ella hadn't always seen eye to eye. This was a conversation he didn't look forward to.

'Hi Ella, it's Jeffrey.'

'Oh, hi Jeffrey. This is a surprise. How is the tour of the Grenadines going?'

'Unfortunately, it had to be cancelled Ella. Listen Ella … I'm sorry … but I'm the bringer of some bad news …'

'Oh no, please don't … please …' he heard the anguish rush into her voice.

'Ella, Ella listen … please. Your mother is in hospital in Bourbon. I hope that she'll be all right, but its early days. She has had a stroke. She'll …'

'Oh my God no! When did it happen?' Ella sobbed.

'Sometime this morning. I returned from my morning swim to find out about it. I've just got back from the clinic,' he lied; Ella didn't need to know about the swim and the lunch. 'They've told me that I can't go to the hospital until this evening.'

'Jeffrey, I'm coming out there. I'll have to organise things at home and at work, but I need to see her.'

'No Ella, just think about it,' he said, 'what good would it do? Wait a couple of days before you make a decision. At present, even I'm not supposed to go and visit her. She has to stabilise …' Jeffrey paused, '… plus you have all your own responsibilities at home. Think of Kloe.'

Their discussion lasted for several minutes. Jeffrey worked hard to persuade Ella not to fly out to Sainte Marie. He promised to contact her every day. He'd even said he'd take the computer into hospital. It might be possible to speak to her mother via the laptop. He would have to wait and see. He finished the call telling her things Doctor Rubens had not said—that she hoped Miranda would fully recover, albeit slowly.

Jeffrey sighed when the call was over. The last thing he wanted was Ella fussing around in the hotel. A hyper-anxious Ella would definitely get on his nerves. She'd undoubtedly be a hindrance to him.

Duty over, Miranda's mobile phone was placed at the end of the line. The line of belongings which were an entrance ticket into Miranda's personal life—a key to her assets.

It was several hours before he had to head off to the hospital. Visits would be expected of him. In the meantime, he'd use those hours profitably. His thoughts flew to that very pretty, lively receptionist he'd met yesterday. He'd go and see if she was around. After all, a man who had missed out on a tour of the Grenadines deserved some compensation.

Chapter 5

Willis

'Sneakers! Hell mother, where're my bloody sneakers? Geez.' Willis shrieked.

Tamara did not reply, but went along the corridor to find out what the problem was. Willis was lifting numerous things that were scattered around his packed bedroom, swearing to himself as he went.

'Shit ... stupid dork ... where's my asshole kicks? ... bloody things,' he said, throwing a pair of shorts back on the floor.

'Willis, it is not necessary to swear about ...'

'But I'm in a hurry mother,' Willis interrupted, slamming his hand against the wall 'I NEED my goddamned sneakers.'

'I am also in a hurry Willis. I have to get to work,' Tamara said, trying to keep calm, 'but I don't scream and tell the whole street my business. Think. When did you last use your sneakers?'

'Ohmygod, do be serious,' he shouted, 'I don't have a bloody clue.' She heard him sigh deeply. 'Shit, I can't do sport without them.'

'Willis, stop swearing, it won't help you find your shoes. I haven't brought you up to swear like that.'

'Effing hell, don't go on'

'Willis, that's enough.' Tamara could see by the state of the room what the problem was. 'I suggest Willis, you tidy up your bedroom. Put all your things away methodically, then you won't have this problem.'

Willis ignored her. Disregarding the fact he was in his school uniform, he threw himself onto the floor. His head disappeared under the wooden bed his father had made for him. Socks. Scraps of paper. Underwear. Doubtless used underwear. A book. All were thrown towards her.

She watched the lower half of her son as he writhed this way and that under the bed. 'Thank Christ,' she heard. A jubilant Willis wriggled backwards clutching a very muddy sports shoe.

'I must go, or I'll miss the bus. One sneaker isn't much good, is it?' she said to a beaming Willis. 'When you find the other shoe, you really must clean them before you leave for school.'

'Can't do that … ain't got the time … and don't know how!' he bawled, still searching for the other shoe. He picked up a rather dirty-looking T-shirt. It didn't conceal anything. In his frustration, he chucked it towards his mother, rather than back on the floor.

Tamara was put out by this. 'Willis, you are nearly 13. I am not your servant, your dogsbody. I will not be cleaning your sports shoes, or tidying your room, or organising your clothes.' She let out a deep breath. 'You have created your own problem here! Get yourself sorted. Be more organised. And you CAN get yourself organised. You have the ability.'

He grunted whilst continuing his search.

'Willis, I'm going. I'll see you this evening,' she said to his back. 'If I have time tonight, I'll help you to rearrange a few of your things.'

Tamara snatched up her bag from the kitchen table and pushed shut the glass louvres of the front windows. 'You find that other shoe Willis, I can't afford to buy you another pair,' she called in the direction of Willis' room. Without waiting for a reply, she slammed the door behind her.

Tamara zigzagged down the concrete path avoiding the cracks, her heeled shoes resounding as she hurried to the bus stop. She was unhappy about leaving Willis alone in the apartment, but there was no choice. She was working the early shift.

Standing alone in the shade of the bus-shelter, Tamara was turning things over in her mind. Willis was becoming more belligerent week by week—a real punk kid. A boy with a bad attitude. He pushed the limits too many times. She took on board he had too much freedom, especially in the school vacations. But she had to work—she couldn't supervise him the whole summer. Recently, he'd informed her that he would not go to his grandmother's this coming vacation. Grandma was too old fashioned. Her mother had been really upset by the news. She'd enjoyed looking out for him. But Willis didn't care who he offended, grandmother, stepmother, or mother. Willis would say exactly what he thought. Like many an adolescent of his age, he was kicking out hard and unfeelingly to be independent—to escape the rules laid down by adults.

He only wanted to be with his mates—trouble was, she'd met his mates, and Tamara wasn't happy about them. They were wasters, jerks and thugs in the making. She'd thought the loss of a male role model was the problem. Willis said no. He resented his father and refused to visit him anymore. He'd told her that he couldn't cope with his step-mother—he couldn't bear to see them together. Tamara knew the solution—stay at home. Stop her job and oversee him. But it just wasn't possible. She had to work. They would starve without. The occasional handful of fivers she got from his father wasn't even enough to keep Willis in shoes.

Despite her problems, Tamara felt privileged to have the job at Topaz. It was such a beautiful hotel. It was also quite close to home. She'd been without work for nearly two months. Her previous employer had had to make cutbacks. Being jobless had been tough. She'd had to borrow money to pay the rent; they'd lived on pasta and scraps she could cobble together; her mother had given her a few hand-outs; the washing machine had gone unrepaired. Life had been a real bitch! Things were still tight, as payback time had come around.

Her pondering continued on the bus. She barely noticed the bus driver's loud, discordant singing to his radio pumping out reggae music. She failed to notice the calm, joyful, sunny day beating down on the bus; the abundance of tropical vegetation, and the cattle tethered at the side of the road. Tamara was mentally sifting—sorting through possible solutions to Willis' no-good, hard-headed, rebellious attitude. She loved Willis, but he wasn't going to win on this one. She was hell bent on coming out with the top score. Losing would be detrimental to both of them.

She got off the bus just outside the towering wrought iron gates enclosing the grounds of Topaz. Tamara strode down the long roadway, pleased to have the shade from the line of palms on either side, and headed for the staff entrance.

'Tamara, how are things with you? You seem wrapped up in your thoughts,' a voice said.

She turned to see one of the guests, in swimming shorts and sandals, clutching a beach towel. Mr Taylor was off for an early swim.

'No, I'm fine sir. And how is your wife?'

'Still in the hospital, I'm afraid,' he walked towards her. 'They've told me she could be there for at least another ten days. She seems a little better, but her memory is shot to pieces. And she's pretty depressed.'

'I'm sorry to hear that Mr Taylor, but she is in the best place. I pray that she will make a complete recovery.'

'That's very kind Tamara,' Jeffrey turned to go, then paused.

He looked her directly in the eye. 'Dare I ask … when do you finish work? I wondered … I wondered if you would like to meet for a drink. I'm finding it very difficult not knowing anyone on the island. The only person I know here is your boss, Mr Denning. And he's always so hyper-busy. My wife being so ill, not knowing …' his voice broke up.

Hell, that was the last thing she wanted. 'I'm sorry sir; I really would like to help …' she landed on a good excuse, '… but we are not supposed to fraternise with the guests.'

47

'Oh, I understand.' He moved even closer to her and lowered his voice. 'I don't want to get you into trouble, but I won't tell if you don't.'

Jeffrey Taylor being so near to her, Tamara noticed the deep lines around his eyes, and the lines leading to his under arm. 'I sympathise Mr Taylor. I'm sure things are difficult for you. But when I finish work, I have to rush home to my son.'

Tamara considered the conversation had gone on long enough and continued her path towards the staff entrance.

'Does your son like hamburger joints?' Mr Taylor persisted.

She stopped walking. Silly question, Tamara thought, at Willis' age, he loved any fast food—possibly, because he rarely got any. She certainly could not afford to take him out to eat. She glanced at her watch. 'Yes, he does Mr Taylor, but I really must get to work.'

She'd reached the staff entrance, and hoped she'd be able to make a rapid escape through the door, but no.

'Tell you what, I'll meet you both at McDo's in Bourbon tomorrow night? You'd be doing me a big favour,' he said.

'That's very kind, but …'

'No buts. I'll see you both there around seven thirty.'

Once into the hotel building, she let out, 'oh for heaven's sake, what have I gotten myself into?'

Going out with a guest was the last thing she wanted. She'd got enough of her own problems and didn't want to be a shoulder to cry on. And she certainly didn't want to jeopardise her job. The best solution for her was not to turn up.

Tamara had no time to think about the conversation during the day. But back at home, the idea of the invitation sneaked back into her thoughts. She felt sympathy with Mrs Taylor, who was clearly very ill. She tried to empathise with her husband; he had to cope with a life-changing situation alone, away from home. By the end of the evening, Tamara had convinced herself it would be good to take Willis out. It would be good for him to meet with somebody like Mr Taylor, from the other side of the world. It would possibly help Mr Taylor too, socialising with a young person, who had a different view of things.

Willis listened reluctantly to her story about Mrs Taylor—about her stroke and how ill she was. It was clear though, he was uninterested. That was his mother's world, not his. When she mentioned a visit to McDonalds, his attitude changed. But the grin dropped from his face when he understood he'd have to hang out with two oldies. It took some persuading on her part. In the end, his stomach got the better of him. The promise of a large hamburger and fries proved too much for Willis.

Even on the bus into Bourbon, Tamara was still undecided about the whole thing—whether she should be going or not. But she didn't get off the bus before the capital. She convinced herself one hamburger could do no harm.

Just after seven thirty, as Tamara pushed open the door of the fast food restaurant, three things struck her—the nauseous smell of fried food, the ear-shattering noise of the very crowded place, and the picture of Jeffrey Taylor's white hair. He'd grabbed a table close to some boisterous adolescents. She didn't care but could see that Willis did. He looked around, presumably wanting to know if there was any body that might recognise him. It wasn't cool to be seen hanging around with has-beens.

Mr Taylor kicked off the introductions.

'Hi, my name's Jeffrey. Great to meet you.'

Tamara looked towards her son, but he said nothing. Willis just raised his hand in recognition of Jeffrey being there. His face remained sullen. She caught him looking Mr Taylor up and down as if he were an exhibit in a showcase.

Mr Taylor looked a little bewildered. As Willis had made no effort, Tamara introduced him. 'Hello Mr Taylor, this is Willis, my son.'

'Hi Willis. What're you drinking?' He pushed a brightly coloured menu across the tabletop, as they all sat down. 'Hospital visits give me a real thirst! I'll need another coffee.'

The eye-catching food photos brought a slight spark of interest from Willis. He scrutinised it with more than his usual enthusiasm whilst amidst adults. He checked out the glossy photos and opted for one of the most decadent looking drinks topped with a huge swirl of cream and drizzles of chocolate.

Jeffrey left to join the appropriate queue for drinks. 'I'll leave you to decide what you both want to eat.'

As soon as he was out of earshot, Willis erupted. 'Holy shit mother, this guy is really pre-historic. Oh man, all that white hair!' he hissed. 'Where the hell did ya find him? You sure he ain't after a bit of arm candy?'

'Shut up Willis,' Tamara seethed. 'Have a bit of respect. He's just lonely. His wife is very ill in hospital. He's worried and he's got nobody to talk to.'

'Bloody hell… that's a real good line!' he sneered. 'Ya gotta be kidding me—like mother, he's old enough to be your goddamned grandfather. He should be in a bloody museum.'

Tamara felt her anger pull at her insides. She looked sternly at him across the table, 'if you aren't going to show a bit of human decency and respect, we are going right now. No fluffy drink. No hamburger. We're back to the bus stop.' She looked towards their host, anxious that he hadn't heard the clash of opinions. 'Willis, I shouldn't have to treat you like a five year old. You've got to learn to fit into the adult world. You ain't going to get anywhere with an attitude like that.'

To Tamara's amazement, the get-together went all uphill after that. Willis relished his outlandish drink. He cleaned up a double cheeseburger and fries, barely pausing for breath. She gathered that Jeffrey understood it was a real treat for her son. He made a real effort to engage with Willis. In short order, he discovered the boy's interest in sport, and then told him about his own love for water sports. Jeffrey mentioned he was eager to check out paddle-boarding. Had Willis tried it out?

'Hey man, no I ain't tried it, but give me half the chance,' Willis said, enthusiasm bubbling out of every pore.

'How's your swimming Willis?' Jeffrey asked.

Wham, that was it! Change of attitude. Change of direction. Willis seemed to forget he was with has-beens; and that he was surrounded by his critical peers. Jeffrey was no longer treated like a museum relic. Tamara could see Willis now saw Jeffrey as a possible means to something he yearned to do—something his mother would never be able to afford for him to try. Tamara didn't contribute much to the conversation, but watched the pair with amazement. Where was the conversation she'd expected about his hospital visit? About his poor wife. About having to cope with a dramatic change in life.

After that, Tamara felt rather left out and on the side lines. She just sat amongst the rowdy clientele of the restaurant taking it all in. She wasn't interested in eighteenth century boarding in Polynesia, stories about the 1930s and making boards in Hawaii, the comeback in Los Angeles in the 90s, but obviously Willis was. At least, he made out that he was. Willis listened to the lot and asked appropriate questions. Not a yawn in sight. Then, before you know it, Tamara heard them planning to meet at Topaz the next evening and have a lesson together. They were both fired up by the idea, without as much as a by-your-leave from her.

Tamara left McDo's puzzled and rather exasperated. Mr Taylor had got her to meet him under false pretences. He didn't seem to want to talk about his wife, or about the island medical services, or anything like that. She'd virtually been ignored once he'd started talking about water sports. At least Willis was happy—one might even say ecstatic—about having a lesson at Topaz the next day. On their bus journey home, he chatted away like an excited five year old at Christmas time.

~~~

After work the next day, Tamara waited for her son at the staff entrance. She hung around in the shade of the building. Ten minutes late, Willis rushed up to her.

'Sorry Mom. I'm a bit late.' He kissed her on the cheek. Tamara was taken aback. He hadn't done that in a long time. 'It was the best! A-maz-ing! All good. Ricko said that I was a natural.' Willis was bubbling over.

'Ricko? Who's Ricko?' She started walking towards the hotel drive.

'Oh, he knows you, Mom. He's the guy who runs the water sports. He said he'd seen you on reception.'

'And where's Mr Taylor?' It was obvious the lesson had been a huge success. Tamara hadn't seen her son so thrilled for a very long time.

'Oh, he's still talking to Ricko. I went right across the bay. You should have seen me, Mom. I only fell off a couple of times. I got to stand up and paddle. And Jeff showed me how to improve my swimming stroke. He got me swimming to the platform and back. He's an ace swimmer.'

Tamara was dumb struck. Where was the belligerent and argumentative Willis of yesterday? His attitude problems seemed to have been washed away with the waves. It just showed what a difference a dream being fulfilled could make. Despite that, she still felt dubious about him associating with Jeffrey Taylor. She felt very vulnerable; worried about her new job, and associating with a client outside work. Especially as she was taking advantage of him.

As they walked towards the hotel exit, Mr Taylor dashed up to them.

'Just came to say good-bye. We had a really good time, didn't we Willis?' He was beaming.

'Mag-ic. Ricko is a hell-o'-a-good teacher.'

'Are we game for another lesson on Monday?' Mr Taylor asked.

'Al-righ-ty! Too damned right I am! Hell, yes please.'

'Same time. Same place. Monday then. That OK with you Tamara?'

'Fine,' she stuttered, surprised he'd actually noticed she was there. 'Thank you very much sir. How is your wife today?'

Mr Taylor paused and perhaps looked a little guilty. 'Eh … slightly better thanks … I'm just off to the hospital.' A serious expression descended. 'I take the laptop with me, so that she can talk to her children. Like me, they are naturally very worried. Tell you what though; the lesson took my mind off things.'

'I'm pleased for you sir.' It wasn't Tamara's place to say what she thought.

'By the way Tamara, I spoke to Antony, Mr Denning, that is, about the lesson. He doesn't see it as a problem. So, don't worry about your job being jeopardised.' She nodded and gave him a faint smile.

They carried on towards the bus stop. Willis turned to call after the receding figure of Mr Taylor, 'thanks again Mr T. See ya Monday.' Willis flashed his teeth, still grinning about his adventure.

What was she doing? Tamara asked herself. She'd agreed to another lesson. She was far from comfortable about the idea. It seemed abnormal. A man, who should be worried sick about his poor wife and her uncertain future, wanting to take paddle board lessons with a teenager. She tried to convince herself she was reading too much into it. She hoped it was simply as Mr Taylor had said—a distraction.

Willis' excited babbling continued during the bus ride. Midway through his narrative, Tamara interrupted him. She had to ask what was worrying her. 'Listen Willis, I know you really enjoyed this evening but … I'm not sure how to say this … Mr

Taylor... Jeffrey wasn't dishonourable, immoral ... I mean ... he didn't try to touch you or hold you during your lesson?'

He glared at her as if she was something offensive. 'Shit mother! You think I'm some sort of rug rat wearing diapers?' He thumped the seat in front of him with his fist. 'Ya think I don't know about this world. No mother, Mr T is not a perv. And no, HE DID NOT TOUCH ME!' he almost shouted in her face. 'He's a nice guy. He's weighed down with worries. He's just trying to forget them.' Willis turned away from her and pretended to look out of the window.

Shame, Tamara thought, shame the new version of Willis didn't last long. She'd obviously said the wrong thing. But she was glad she'd voiced her concerns anyway. Mothers have to be certain. They finished the rest of their journey home in silence.

Chapter 6

T. L. C.

Miranda struggled.

Sitting on the edge of the king-sized bed, she fought to put her clothes on. Her arms would not move into the right angles. They seemed out of her control and just didn't want to go into the armholes. One arm was worse than the other; it seemed to have a mind of its own. After a battle of a minute or so, the blouse was on her back. She then had to face the strife of buttoning it up the front. Her fingers were now so rigid. They didn't respond the way they used to. She tried desperately to master the tiny buttons, but failed. Exasperation bubbled up inside her. Ella hovered in the background, wanting to help.

'Don't worry Mum, I can do them,' Ella bent down and secured the mother of pearl fastenings.

'Perhaps a wraparound dress would have been easier,' Miranda admitted. Her mind flew back to when she had helped her daughter dress as a little girl. She chose not to reminisce with Ella. Since her stroke, her words didn't always come out the way she wanted them to.

'It's on now. There you go. Now for your hair.'

Miranda sighed. Everything took so long. Everything was so exhausting. She stared at the walking frame. It was so depressing she had to rely on it. She sensed Ella surveying every move; her face full of anxiety. She stood up and clutched tightly to the frame. Then she had to drag one foot after the other, feeling unsure about every step. To reach the dressing table took a supreme effort. She flopped into the seat feeling as if she'd walked miles. She stared before her. The mirror showed her an image she didn't want to see. What a mess! She looked at least ninety—so tired. Her hair was sticking out around her—like some witch in a horror film. Tears started to sting the corners of her eyes. How was she ever going to look presentable to go to the airport? Without any enthusiasm, she picked up her hairbrush, but to get her hand to her head was difficult. It hurt. She tried to get the brush to persuade her hair into its usual style, but it wouldn't do what she wanted. What a battle.

'Ella ...' Miranda resigned herself, she'd have to ask her daughter, 'could you help again please.' The hospital had told her that she had to try and do things for herself. But some things were proving too much.

Ella had been hovering on the side lines, while fiddling with the clothes that had to go into the suitcases.

'Would you like some help with your hair?' Ella took up the hairbrush. 'A hairdresser would have been a good idea Mum, but I'm afraid we don't have time for that today.'

Ella's attempts to sort out her hair also proved useless. Her hair was a losing battle. Her reflection told her not only was her hair in a state, but one side of her face was slightly distorted. Her mouth seemed to have dropped a little, giving her a permanent troubled look. It was all so scary. She looked like one of the poor souls you see on a charity poster. Miranda closed her eyes, not wanting to believe it was her in that mirror. Tears stung in the corner of her eyes.

'I hate looking like this ... feeling like this ... depending on others so much. There are some days ... there are days Ella when I feel like giving up ...' she sobbed, wondering if her words had come out correctly.

Ella laid the brush down, bent forward and wrapped her arms around her mother, hugging her tightly. She kissed her head.

'I know it's difficult Mum, but try to think positive. You're so much better than that first day I saw you in hospital. You heard what the therapist said. It can take a long time to recover.'

'There are days ... days I wish ... the stroke had taken me,' she slurred. She felt her daughter's arms tighten around her.

'Don't Mum ... we love you too much. We want you here ...'

That was it. The comment touched her and released the tears; they trickled down her pale cheeks. Miranda tried to choke them back.

'When we get you home,' Ella said, 'there will be somebody there to help improve your recovery even more.'

But Miranda could not take this on board. Her mind was too filled with sorrow: sadness because she was continually tired, always weak, and unable to do the simplest of tasks. She just didn't know who she was anymore. And this was all his fault. Jeffrey. She'd convinced herself; it wouldn't have happened if he hadn't treated her like one of his belongings. But Miranda had decided she could not share these thoughts.

Ella kept her hands on her shoulders and broke into her thoughts. 'Be patient Mum. I know, it's difficult; but things will improve. You'll soon be better at home amongst your own things and your friends.' She gave her a final squeeze. 'Come on, would you like your breakfast now? Then I can get on and finish our packing.'

Miranda gazed vacantly into the mirror. 'I don't know ...' she stammered. She hung her head, looking at her lap, '... I don't know what I want.'

'Mum, you have been very ill. You are still ill. Your mind is confused. Try not to get too upset about things. You are getting better every day. Just give it time.' She kissed her on the cheek. 'Let's put your breakfast on the table outside. You know how you love to watch the people on the beach. You won't be able to see that view tomorrow.'

'You're right Ella ... perhaps it'll be the last time I see it.'

'Mum, don't think like that. Think you'll be able to come back again in a few months for another holiday.'

Ella passed her a tissue. Miranda dabbed her eyes before letting Ella help her up. She started the shuffle to the terrace, trying to abate her tears; trying to look forward to going back home. Ella followed with the breakfast tray. Strong light invaded the mist of tears, and she saw the blur of the shaded table against the view that had become a part of her life.

'Would you like me to cut up the fruit and the croissants? Then you can more easily pick everything up with your fingers.'

Miranda didn't want to think about it. Her misery filled her being. 'Oh Ella, I don't know … I don't want you to, but I suppose you must.' She collapsed into the chair and regarded the tray of food with contempt.

Ella prepared the plate of fruit, Miranda taking in every gesture. 'Where is Jeffrey? Why isn't he helping?'

'Don't you remember, he has gone for a swim? He should be back soon.'

'Do you think he will want to share the same bedroom with me at home?' she asked her daughter. She hated the idea of sharing a bed with that man again.

'Oh Mum. I don't know. You really will have to talk to him about it. He is your husband now Mum. He will want to make sure that you are all right at night.'

Miranda took one of her daughter's hands as she rearranged the breakfast things. 'I don't sleep well when he is in the bed,' she mumbled, not looking at Ella. She paused, trying to sort out what she wanted to say next. 'You know … Bradley was so much nicer … I liked waking up next to him … with Jeffrey, it's difficult to go back to sleep.'

Ella was taken aback and leant towards her. 'Mum,' she whispered, 'Dad has gone. He died. We all miss him, but you can't have him back. And you chose to marry Jeffrey.'

'I know my darling … I know.' Miranda looked directly into Ella's eyes. The tears started again and traced down her cheeks. A droplet of regret fell on to the glass topped table.

Ella handed her the paper napkin from the tray of food, 'Come on Mum. Where is the dynamic get-up-and-go Mum I used to know? Sit and enjoy the view over breakfast.' She moved to the edge of the balcony.

Pull yourself together Mirada told herself. Concentrate. Concentrate on the aspect down to the beach. You loved that view. Beyond the hotel grounds, the wild and savage bay. Tropical vegetation cladding the rolling hills. Pale pink sand edging the transparent, turquoise sea. Erratic rows of towering coconut palms, flickering in the light breeze. You know you love it. Take it all in. Encapsulate it in your mind—perhaps it could be the very last time you'd see it.

'Look Mum,' Ella said, 'you can see Jeffrey swimming towards the diving platform. He'll be up soon to join you for breakfast.'

'I prefer to eat breakfast by myself thank you,' Miranda murmured almost to herself.

She saw Ella's smile drop and watched as it was replaced by anguish. But Ella remained silent and left to get on with the packing.

~~~

Ella stood in front of the office door.

She was hesitating, and still re-playing the events of that morning—what her mother had said and thinking through what she would say to Antony. She'd arrived at the island full of hope, so grateful that her mother was still with them. Even in her poor state, it was better than the alternative. Ella wasn't ready for that. Her mother was only twenty-three years her senior—far too young to go. For ever. Her mother's health had been a shock to her. Her mother had been transformed from the lively, bouncy personality into an empty shell of a being—so forlorn and indifferent to the world. A fraction of what she had been a few weeks before. Weeks that seemed like an eternity ago.

Ella tapped lightly at the door. There was no response, but she could hear the droning of the air conditioning, so tapped again. This time Antony responded. As she entered, she could only see the top of his head—his dark, tightly-coiled head of hair. Antony was concentrating in front of his computer. He looked up, taking off his glasses, and flashed her an affectionate smile.

'Oh, hi Ella. Are you ready for the journey to the airport?'

'Nearly,' she said, her mind still in a bit of a daze. 'I've done most of the packing. I've come to say good-bye and thank you for all your help, Antony. If it wasn't for your quick thinking, Mum could be even worse.'

'We can't be sure of that, but ...' said Antony. Ella knew of old he always liked to be precise. He indicated she should take a seat.

She shook her head, 'no thanks ... I came to ask if you can come and say goodbye to Mum as we leave.'

'Of course, phone me just before you're ready to go.'

'I feel really nervous about the actual flight,' she admitted. 'Jeffrey keeps saying that with the medical help available, she'll be fine. But even so, I'll be glad to get Mum home. I'm hoping she will feel better with familiar things around her.'

'I understand your concerns,' Antony moved around his desk and squeezed her arm. 'I think I'd be the same. It's a long flight, but at least you'll have somebody there to supervise her condition. Will there be somebody to look after her full time when she gets home?' Antony propped himself against his desk.

'Yes, I may stay there for a couple of days; but naturally, I have to get back to work and the family. I found somebody through an agency. On paper, they seem all right. I'm crossing my fingers Mum will get on with her ... and Jeffrey as well of course. It's not easy having a complete stranger living under the same roof.'

Ella hesitated, wanting to say something else, but held back. She clenched up her fingers nervously, moved her weight from one foot to another. She took a deep breath and went for the question she really wanted to ask. 'Antony, I'm going to be completely candid. I haven't had the opportunity to ask you before. We've both been so busy.'

'Ask away. If I can help, I will.'

She looked directly at Antony's kind face, 'what do you think about Jeffrey?' she asked bluntly, understanding that it was a question he may not wish to answer. 'What I mean is—how do you find him as a person? Do you find him sincere and caring?'

Antony pursed his lips, 'Ooh Ella, that's a difficult one. You have to understand that I haven't spent a lot of time with him to make a sound judgement.' He paused. 'Well … he's obviously an intelligent man. He seems to have been good at his job. But caring?' he said, looking down at his feet. 'Mmm … I believe that he went to the hospital every day. Thing is Ella … very importantly … it's strange that he wasn't around when Miranda was first ill. We just may have got her to the hospital a little quicker if he had been.'

'He told me that he was swimming,' Ella said, raising her eyebrows. 'Frankly, he seems obsessed about his exercise. It seems to come before everything else.'

'The swimming and paddle boarding you mean. Yes, I suppose they're distractions … to help him relax Ella.'

This didn't reassure Ella. It wasn't what she wanted to hear. 'It's just … this is a bit difficult … but since I've been on island … Jeffrey seems to have left everything for me to do. He doesn't seem to want to spend time with Mum—or show affection in any way … in fact, he doesn't seem to give a damn about her state—doesn't give a damn about anything, except his bloody water sports.' At last, she'd managed to say what she wanted. 'And … something that Mum said to me this morning; I wonder if she is perhaps a bit unnerved by him,' her tone changed, 'even a little scared—but perhaps, I'm just jumping to conclusions.' Ella bit her lip and waited for Antony to react.

'I don't know … I hope not. Before the stroke, they seemed fine together. Miranda seemed happy. Then … when it first happened, Jeffrey was distracted. In his own little world. But I put that down to worry. It was a big shock. I just imagined that he's the type that doesn't cope with illness very well.'

Antony hung his head again. There was silence between them for a few seconds. He shifted uncomfortably, as though he wasn't too sure how to tell her about something.

'I don't know if I ought to tell you this Ella …' he started '… it may be nothing … but,' he hung-back, 'but … the night of Miranda's birthday, Jeffrey spent the night in another room. He paid for another room in the hotel. He has never said anything to me. It was pointed out to me by the accountant. He asked if it was an error. I suppose he could have had too much to drink.'

'Oh! How strange! As you say though, there could be some explicable reason for it,' Ella said unthinkingly. Then the information gradually seemed to sink in, and it hit her rib cage, cramping it up with stress. What had Antony just told her? She dropped her head into her hands. Squeezed her eyes together, in a futile attempt to block out reality. What if …? The worry turned another screw, tightened up a bit more inside her. Pictures of how things could have been started to flash before her.

'But Antony … what you're telling me … Christ, no …' she breathed, 'Antony, if he had been in the same room … if he'd been there … perhaps …'

Antony stepped towards her and took her shoulders. 'Ella … Ella don't … don't go there. Don't even think about it.' He shook her. 'You don't know that the stroke could have been avoided if they had been in the same room. Don't torture yourself. Perhaps I shouldn't have mentioned it. Listen Ella, you can't change the past. What's done is done!'

After several seconds, she lifted her head and looked at him, 'No, you're right. Perhaps you shouldn't have told me. But I have to say, it puts a new perspective on things. I now see Jeffrey a bit differently.'

'Don't Ella. Don't put two and two together and make fifty. What's the point? It doesn't change anything. Just concentrate on getting Miranda home and trying to improve her quality of life,' the ever-sensible Antony told her in an authoritative tone.

Ella looked away from him and tried to push away the accusative thoughts she'd had about Jeffrey. It was best not to respond. She looked at her watch.

'Got to go. There's the last of the packing. The ambulance will be here soon. Antony, thank you again.'

She kissed his dusky cheek and left Antony to get on with his work. She'd gone to see him for reassurance, but she was coming away more stressed. He'd given her another perception of Jeffrey—one which made her feel even more ill at ease about him.

~~~

The list of tasks she'd been given seemed endless. Tamara was working hard and hoping they'd all be done before the end of the afternoon. In the middle of a call, she saw him—Mr Taylor striding across the lobby. It wasn't just his mass of silvery white hair and the expensive clothes on his back which made one look twice, but also his boldness and his air of ownership which made him noticeable. She wasn't sure she liked it. Since working at Topaz, she'd become aware the world was peppered with people like that. He seemed blind to the tall contemporary sculpture in the water feature, unaware of the huge display of tropical flowers which dominated the reception desk, and the other employees working at the front desk. It was clear to one and all, he was focused on only one thing. Her. He stood, the other side of the reception desk, smiling at her whilst she finished her call. His stare made her very self-conscious.

'I've come to say au revoir Tamara,' he said as she put down the phone.

'Good-bye sir, I hope …'

'And to say a big thank you, and to Willis, for being so kind to me during our stay,' he interrupted. 'I do hope we'll meet again in a few months.'

'It would be a pleasure to welcome you back sir.' She took in the interest her colleague was giving to the conversation. Tamara wanted to deflect the conversation away from herself. 'It has been a dreadful time for you Mr Taylor. I pray that your wife will continue to improve once you get home.'

'Eh, yes … thank you Tamara. Yes, she's already improved a lot. And with her daughter here, she has really bucked up.'

'That's wonderful news sir.'

'I thought I'd come and say good-bye and …' a wide grin spread across his face. Tamara thought he didn't look one bit like a man who was anxious about his sick wife's long journey home, '… there's something else …'

'Sir? …'

'If you could just spare me five minutes of your time Tamara,' Mr Taylor asked rather firmly.

Tamara smiled politely, but the mass of work she had to get through was uppermost in her mind. It was also clear her colleague was keeping an ear open to what was going on. Staff were instructed not to give preferential treatment to any of the hotel's clients.

'I'm afraid I have rather a lot of …'

'It will only be for a few minutes,' Jeffrey Taylor insisted. 'You don't mind if Tamara comes with me for five minutes, do you?' he said, addressing the other receptionist. She looked bemused and uncertain what to say.

As Mr Taylor was so determined, Tamara felt it easiest to accompany him and get it over as quickly as possible. She made apologies to her colleague and followed on after Mr Taylor.

'I said my goodbyes to Willis yesterday,' he explained.

'Yes sir, he told me. I'm very grateful for the time you spent with him.'

'I've enjoyed it. I'm going to miss Willis, and all that fun ...' he said as they walked through the hotel gardens. 'And all this.' He indicated towards the explosion of colour from the fuchsia-coloured bougainvillea, corn yellow and mauve orchids, and vivid orange lilies.

Tamara maintained a fixed smile, nodding at his comments.

'And the laid-back atmosphere, and the charm of the island. I do love it here.' He continued telling Tamara how he dreaded going back to the inhospitable weather of Dorset; how life was so different in Britain. They passed the enormous irregular shaped swimming pool, under the coconut palm fronds stirring and rustling above them, until they reached the beach. He continued across the sand. Tamara removed her sandals to follow. He stopped at the hut used as a sports centre.

'I wanted to show you this.'

Tamara regarded the blue pointed board leant against the wooden structure.

'A paddle board,' she said, not knowing what else to say, but guessing what would be coming next.

'Yes, I've bought it second-hand from Ricko. The point is I'd like Willis to feel he can use it until I return. Ricko has the paddle. It would be such a shame for Willis to lose his enthusiasm because he doesn't have access to a board ... for his interest to fade, because I've left.'

'Mr Taylor, I don't think he can do that. You've been very kind to Willis, but sir, I can't allow him to take advantage of your kindness ...' She felt uneasy about the situation, embarrassed by his attentions.

'Tamara, it's not taking advantage. I want him to use it. I got the feeling that he wasn't too sure which way his life was heading when we first met.' He moved right in front of her and looked confidently into her eyes. 'Now he knows he wants to spend most of his spare time doing sport. I'm right, aren't I?'

Tamara could feel herself colouring up. Redness burnt her cheeks. After all, Mr Taylor was a hotel guest, who'd gone to so much trouble for her son. 'Yes sir, you're right.'

'So, it makes sense he carries on doing something he enjoys—the board will ensure he can do that.'

'Oh Mr Taylor … I just don't know what to say.'

'Well, it's better he uses it, rather than it stays in some corner doing nothing.'

Tamara just gazed at the board. Inside, a muddle of emotions whirred around. Awkwardness, disbelief, but at the same time, appreciation.

'It's true, he's changed,' she said quietly, 'he's more motivated since you introduced him to paddle-boarding.' Out of nowhere, she felt tears welling up, making her feel even more ill-at-ease. 'He's basically a good boy, but …' she ran a hand underneath her eyes, '… he was becoming very troublesome, starting to mix with the wrong lot, a bunch of troublemakers.'

'Hey, what's up?' Jeffrey looked startled to see tears shining in her eyes.

'I'm so grateful Mr Taylor …' she sniffled. He put his arm around her shoulder and hugged it briefly. This unsettled her even more. And she wasn't certain she liked the way he looked at her, '… now he's got a real interest … thanks to you … and he's getting to meet a different set of people.'

'So, there's no reason to cry, is there?' You just tell him; I'll be back as soon as Miranda is well enough. And I'm expecting him to look after that board for me.'

'Thank you Mr Taylor, I'm sure Willis will be very excited.'

'He's helped me as well you know. I'll let you get back to work now Tamara. And I need to get to the airport.'

His last statement filled Tamara with relief. She wanted to get back to her long list of tasks for that day. It was certain Willis would be on cloud nine when she told him about the paddle board. As for her, she was thankful for Mr Taylor's departure. She couldn't cope with all his attention.

Chapter 7

Oakdale

Buzzing rang out.

Ella had opened the heavy oak front door. She scurried directly to the cupboard in the hall and opened the decorative wooden door. The droning stopped as she tapped in the code. With the quiet, she sighed. Four thousand miles. The journey to Oakdale had been a long and stressful one.

Her mother had coped satisfactorily with the journey—naturally, Jeffrey and a qualified nurse had been with her. But Ella felt she was the one who had carried the heavy burden of responsibility. The nurse was just doing her job. And Jeffrey gave the impression it was just another flight. He'd been next to useless.

As the private ambulance had crunched slowly down the long drive to her mother's home, she took in the trees edging it and the large garden. Her body had started to relax a little. The tensions and worries of the journey had started to drain from her, leaving her feeling exhausted.

Ella signalled to the nurse and ambulance driver—time to help her mother in. The heating needed to be sorted. Despite having organised with a neighbour that it should be switched on, cool air wrapped around her. But then, Oakdale was not your average home. It was substantial. Consequently, it was still chilly, especially noticeable after the temperatures in Sainte Marie. Ella battled with the thermostat. Jeffrey wasn't there to lend a hand, as he was driving his car back from the airport. Thoughts of him laid heavy on her mind. He was never around when you wanted him. He seemed to have taken a back seat in the organisation of everything. Much to her indignation and annoyance, she had done it all. Over the ten days she'd been in the Caribbean, a new opinion of Jeffrey had evolved. He'd come over as the type of man who didn't want to spend time with his ailing wife. Most of the time, he was off doing his own thing. His excuse had been that it was his way of coping with his anxiety. That hadn't washed with Ella. What was wrong with the man? She felt nothing but contempt for him.

'Home,' she heard her mum sigh.

Her mother shuffled her way up the steps, supported by the two medical staff, then gazed around the entrance hall—at the familiar bronze sculpture in the stair well, the curving staircase, polished antique tables, and the large gilt-framed mirror.

'It's all still there,' she said quietly, 'exactly as before.'

'But of course,' Ella said, hoping that she'd sorted the heating.

'I thought I might not see Oakdale again,' her mother confessed. Ella went to her and gave her a cuddle. 'Thank you, my darling. Thank you for getting me home in one piece.' Ella heard the slur in her speech.

'Mum, we'll help you upstairs,' Ella offered, 'so you can get some sleep.'

Climbing the stairs was an ordeal. They progressed at a snail's pace, even with the three of them assisting. It pained Ella to watch her mother drag one foot slowly after the other.

'I'll tell Jeffrey not to disturb you when he arrives,' Ella told her as they mounted the stairs.

'Mmm good.'

'But once Mrs Eavis arrives, I must get back home Mum.'

'But of course, darling. I'm sure they'll be so glad to see you.'

The main bedroom was filled with strips of light. Wintery sunshine filtered through the louvred shutters and patterned the herringbone parquet floor. Ella noticed the faint smile lifting her mother's deformed lips as she dropped onto her bed. It was clear, she was content. Pushing down the shutters, Ella caught a glimpse of shimmering silver. Reflections off the distant sea, blinking above the line of oak trees which fringed the sloping garden.

'I'll go and make you a drink Mum. Then you can get some peace.' She left the medical assistants to it. Despite her love for her mother, despite her weariness, she was impatient to get downstairs. Eager to have five minutes to herself and do her own thing—namely contact her family. She had more than done her duty by her mother, and longed to be able to drive herself home in just a few hours.

She bumped into Jeffrey in the entrance hall, as he manhandled a suitcase through the door.

'Hi Ella. Everything OK?' he asked. 'Why don't you head on home now. I can look after things here.'

'No thanks. I'd rather meet Mrs Eavis first,' she said briskly, thinking Jeffrey couldn't look after things at Oakdale if he tried. And when did he ever try? She disappeared into the kitchen to make tea. As anticipated, Jeffrey didn't come and ask how he could help.

Mid-afternoon, Ella spotted a small saloon car advancing down the drive. It parked in front of the house. After several seconds, a woman got out. Slim, with blonde, bobbed hair. Eye-catching, in bright red jeans and a neat, tailored shirt. Ella went to the front door imagining she might be one of her mother's friends—checking to see how she was. But on opening the door, the woman introduced herself as Mrs Eavis.

Ella hoped she didn't notice her surprise. From their telephone conversations, Ella had ascertained that Mrs Eavis was in her late fifties. The agency had recommended her as a very competent woman, medically well qualified. She'd imagined a conventionally clothed woman—somewhat rounded, with permed greying hair, her stereotyped image of a traditional older nurse. How wrong she'd been.

Mrs Eavis bounced into the house. In a flash, she was weighing up the interior, while Ella noted the stylish courtier handbag on her arm.

'Oh, what a beautiful home! Mrs Taylor-White was lucky to have found this.' Mrs Eavis shook Ella's hand enthusiastically.

'It's where I was brought up,' Ella explained, 'with my brother. We're all very fond of it.'

'I can understand why,' said Mrs Eavis, still scrutinising every detail.

Ella guided her towards the sitting room. 'Let's sit in here; I need to tell you a little about my mother. She's resting upstairs at present.'

Mrs Eavis skipped after her, still making admirative comments about the house. 'Your mother has very good taste. I love the Georgian style fireplace and the antique furniture.'

Ella shifted around a little impatiently in her chair and did not respond. She had no desire to further this conversation. She was keen to get straight to the point. Her home called.

'Well Ella, let's get down to business. It's just this is so different from my very functional flat in Bristol.'

The sad story of her mother's health filled the large room. Ella detailed all she knew about the stroke; and the progress that had been made so far. It was clear from Mrs Eavis' questions she understood her mother's condition. Ella felt satisfied she'd be leaving her in competent hands.

'Let me give you a quick tour of the house Mrs Eavis. Show you where things are.'

'Katie, please,' Mrs Eavis said, flashing Ella a friendly smile.

'You also need to meet my stepfather; naturally, he'll be in residence too. I think we'll do that first. He's taken his things to the down-stairs guest room. So, you live in Bristol,' Ella said, making small talk as she guided her down the long corridor.

'Yes, but I'm not at home very often, I mostly live-in. With this job, you get to see all kinds of homes and a great variety of folks.'

'And what about your husband?' Ella pried.

'Oh, we parted company some time ago. He's off to pastures new. I wouldn't have been able to do this work if I were still married.'

Ella tapped lightly on the double doors at the end of the passageway. Several seconds later, Jeffrey peered around the crack in the door.

'Oh, hi Ella, I was just trying to sort ...' he said in a flat tone.

His voice faded as he saw Ella was not alone. 'Oh, do we have a visitor?'

He stepped into the corridor and took in the figure of Mrs Eavis. Ella saw that his demeanour promptly transformed. She noted his false, smarmy smile and the unfamiliar light in his eyes.

'Not exactly a visitor Jeffrey. This is Mrs Eavis. This is Mum's carer. The nurse I hired from the agency in Dorchester.'

'Pleased to meet you Mr Taylor,' Mrs Eavis politely returned his smile. Please do call me Katie. Let's hope your wife will recover quickly and you won't need me here for too long.'

'Yes, let's hope so.'

Ella was exasperated by the tone of his voice. It oozed of insincerity. With the wave of a wand, Jeffrey had become attentive, affable. The more time she spent with him, the less she liked the man.

'I know you want to get home as soon as possible Ella. Now that Mrs Eavis ...' another smile,'... Katie is here, I can look after things. You get yourself home.'

'I've promised Katie I'll give her a quick tour of the house. Show her where things are in the kitchen and so on ...'

Jeffrey wasn't listening. Instead, he was taking in his crumpled attire. He put his fingers to his forehead and fumbled with his unruly hair. It was certain he was thinking about himself again.

Out of the blue, his right hand dropped onto Ella's shoulder.

'Many thanks for all you have done Ella. I'd have been lost without you.' More smiles.

The heaviness of his arm around her shoulder made her cringe. Ella avoided his gaze. She could only think how contemptible he was.

'She worked really hard to ensure that the return journey went smoothly,' he told Mrs Eavis.

Ella flashed him a look of distain. What a hypocrite. Why the hell couldn't you have helped out? But Ella politely kept her opinions to herself.

'Yes, you show Katie the ropes. Then get yourself home,' Jeffrey squeezed her shoulder. Ella squirmed again. This was a first. The first time he had expressed any gratitude towards her. But then, it was the first time that he had encountered Katie Eavis.

His affected charm annoyed Ella; she could do without his obsequious behaviour. Despite her tiredness, she picked up on the way he was checking out Mrs Eavis and felt sure she had noticed too. His leaning towards Mrs Eavis; the way he kept playing with his hair and his flirtatious glances in her direction. What a creep, a deceitful creep. Ella's opinion of him plummeted to zero.

~~~

Bloody hell, this is one hell of a home. I've really fallen on my feet here, Katie thought to herself. My own bathroom, a sea view, and a bedroom nearly as big as the whole of my flat in Bristol. She stood and surveyed the room full of stylish furniture and luxurious accessories; and glimpsed the enormous garden from the window. It was like living in a five-star country hotel—

73

so different from most of her clients, many of whom lived in musty suburban homes which smelt of urine and old age.

Great home, but the downside would be the husband. He was far too full of himself. He could be a problem. She'd sussed from his 'I fancy you' (and himself) glances and his constant cheesy grins, he would be hitting on her before too long. She'd met them before, though perhaps no one who'd been quite so blatant, so fast. She'd figured out the stepdaughter would have liked to slam him one, but she was far too well brought-up for that. Then there was her patient. She could be some whining, snooty, disagreeable soul. Katie decided she'd go and find out.

She tapped on and opened the door onto the darkness of Miranda's room.

'Ella?' she heard.

'No Mrs Taylor-White, its Katie from the agency.'

'Oh, come in … you can put the light on.'

The light revealed her patient half sat up in a huge bed, set in another enormous bedroom, even bigger than hers next door. 'I hope you managed to get some sleep after your flight,' Katie asked. Her patient nodded weakly and gave her a delicate smile. To Katie, she seemed like a thin, fragile, and neglected doll, drowning in the mass of white linen. She may be wealthy, but this one was not going to be snooty she told herself.

'Let's help you,' Katie said, striding across to her patient. Helping her to sit up straight, she felt her lean form, caught the white roots growing through blonde hair, saw the sadness in her lack-lustre eyes. The agency information told her this woman was only a couple of years her senior. At first glance, she would have given her at least twenty.

'Can I get you a drink?' she asked.

Her patient sat as if in a daze. 'Tell you what I'd really like—is a bath,' she said hesitantly after a few seconds, 'I feel really smelly after that flight.' They both laughed. 'And Katie, I'd rather you call me Miranda, not Mrs Taylor-White.'

'A bath it will be,' Katie told her. 'You'll have to tell me where everything is.'

After a long bath, Katie helped Miranda into a sophisticated dress and tried to untangle her dishevelled hair. She started to see what her patient must have been like before her stroke. As with many before her, her sympathy went out to her. But Katie knew that sympathy wasn't enough, she needed lots of care too. Her initial reaction had been correct. The only real problem in this job would be Mr Taylor. Why did this poor woman have such a swine of a husband?

~ ~ ~

Jeffrey was disappointed there were three for dinner.

He would much rather it was just the sexy-looking nurse and himself. It was not to be. Somehow, she'd convinced Miranda she was hungry, and they both came down for the improvised meal he'd cobbled together. To his wonder, they seemed to be hitting it off. Miranda even seemed a little like her old self. The conversation around the table flowed as readily as was possible, considering Miranda's speech difficulties. So, Jeffrey took a back seat and left the pair to get acquainted. He sat on the side lines enjoying his red wine and sizing up his dinner companions.

Jeffrey guessed Miranda and Katie were much the same age. Before her stroke, his wife and Katie could have been described as similar. Smart, attractive, and bubbling over with enthusiasm for life. But now—well, the stroke had transformed Miranda. She now looked haggard, thin, pale, and very plain. Her hair could no longer be described as blonde. She hadn't bothered to put on a scrap of make-up. Her affliction had remodelled her into something usually found in a care home. The fact that his wife didn't seem to want him anywhere near her, didn't bother him in the slightest. He didn't fancy her anyway in her new guise. But, on the other hand—Katie—well now, she was a totally different matter.

After dinner Jeffrey was delighted when Miranda said she still felt exhausted and would go up to her room. He planted a functional kiss on her rigid cheek and wished her 'sweet dreams.' He watched Katie fuss around her and help her up to bed.

Minutes later, Katie was back in the kitchen, as Jeffrey was unenthusiastically clearing away.

'If you could tell me where the drinking chocolate is, I'll make a cup for your wife ...' Katie said brightly, '... even though it's not the best thing to be consuming after a stroke, but I suppose one cup isn't going to hurt.'

He wasn't too sure himself, but helped her hunt through the kitchen units. When the carton was tracked down, she studied the instructions. 'Mm ... could be worse. At least, I can make it with hot water.'

'And what about you?' Jeffrey asked her.

'Oh no, I don't drink hot chocolate thank you,' she replied.

'I don't mean that,' he smiled at her comment, 'I mean would you like to share a drink with me after you finished helping Miranda?'

She glanced at her watch as she put the kettle on. He couldn't see much enthusiasm on her face. 'Yes, I suppose I could manage another one, but then I could do with an early night myself.' She flitted around looking for crockery and a tray, while he sized up her assets.

'Have to say your outfit really suits you—the red jeans make you look really...' He didn't finish the sentence. She cast him a look as if he had turned into some strange creature, and remained silent. 'Yes ... anyway, what's your poison?' he asked as she dashed off carrying the loaded tray.

'Another glass of white wine would be fine,' Katie said very matter-of-factly.

He eyed-up the red jeans clinging to her neat behind as she wound her way up the stairs. Jeffrey felt unsure about Katie. She seemed in work mode and not giving him the attention he would have liked. Nevertheless, he selected a good bottle of Sancerre, feeling sure it would impress. He dimmed the lights in the sitting room, turned up the imitation coal fire and put on some soft music—that surely couldn't fail to make the right impression. By the time she re-appeared, he was well down his glass of wine.

'Miranda's been telling me she's worried because she feels constantly tired,' she said as she installed herself opposite him. 'I tried to tell her that it's normal. Her brain and her body are trying to recover from the damage that occurred during the stroke.'

Miranda was the last person he wanted to talk about. He reached over to pour her a glass of wine and looked directly into her blue eyes. 'Let's talk about you instead, shall we?' he said passing her the glass. 'I'd like to get to know you better.' He regretted the statement as it left his lips. Whoops—too late. Her eyes turned icy, her expression frosty. Katie was not impressed.

'Mr Taylor, I'm here to help your wife recuperate to maximum health. I would have hoped that it would be important to you too,' Katie chided.

Knuckles rapped; Jeffrey hung back for a few seconds. He mentally reshuffled his plans for the get-together. 'Well, yes, but of course. Yes, I know she's very drowsy much of the time. I thought that maybe it could be depression.'

'You could be right. Stroke patients are frequently depressed afterwards.' She went on to explain about other stroke patients she'd nursed. Katie seemed to want to be taking control of the direction of their conversation.

Jeffrey waited for her to pause for breath and interrupted her story, 'tell me Katie, how long have you been employed as a private nurse?'

Katie started another rambling explanation. Jeffrey had to hear the tale of the breakdown of her marriage: being a live-in nurse had enabled her to get away from the marital home, and her husband had insisted on remaining there until the house was sold. She soon learnt to prefer private nursing, as working in a metropolitan hospital had been continually stressful and hyper busy. The story went on ... and on ... Jeffrey switched into snooze mode. He didn't get a look in for several minutes.

'So, whereabouts do you live Katie?' he asked, trying to get her off the job stuff.

He then had to endure another five minutes of hearing the history of purchasing an apartment in Bristol. How currently she had a tenant who shared it with her. She told him about her finances. How her tenant's rent paid for the apartment, so she could leave most of her wage in the bank. She even confided that she loved southern Spain and hoped to save enough to purchase a small property there.

Jeffrey became bored. He was yawning inside.

'It seems a great shame that Miranda suffered a stroke whilst on holiday. I imagine you like the Caribbean.'

He jogged himself out of his numbed state, 'Eh yes, I love it out there. I'm hoping Miranda will soon recover sufficiently, so we can go back again soon.'

'And the medical amenities on the island? How were they? I understand Miranda was in a hospital in Sainte Marie.'

Back to the medical stuff again! Reluctantly, Jeffrey explained a little about the private health care and how expensive it was. He detailed how he had had to pay for everything: ambulances, consultations, medications, scans, hospital fees. All of this at exorbitant prices. He endeavoured to give the impression he had personally paid for every cent and dollar. She didn't need to know that he had used Miranda's credit cards, and most of it would be reimbursed by her insurance.

Jeffrey inhaled silently. The conversation was going nowhere. The soiree was turning out to be a waste of a good bottle of wine. Katie looked appealing—a doll's body and a good face for her age, but that was where it seemed to end. Was she only interested in her work? No wonder the woman was divorced!

'And what about your spare time?' he threw into the conversation.

'Oh yes. It is usual that I have two days off each week. If that's okay with you?'

'Yes, of course, but that's not exactly what I meant.'

'Oh, hobbies and the like,' she said. He saw her first real smile as she scrutinised her drink. 'This is a particularly good wine. I appreciate its hint of gooseberry and the slightly acid, flinty aftertaste.'

'Let me refill your glass,' Jeffrey said, hoping perhaps another glass might improve her frame of mind. Let's go for it, he thought.

He smiled at her as he poured the straw-coloured liquid into the goblet, with his other hand, he lightly brushed her hand. Katie kept her head down but looked at him in an enticing way. There was a hint of a smile.

'Mr Taylor ...' she muttered in a very low tone—almost a whisper, while her eyes flashed him a flirtatious look. '... Mr Taylor ... I take my job very seriously ... I'd be grateful if you'd do the same.'

Jeffrey held her gaze. Her words were not a reflexion of her inviting glances. 'Of course, that's exactly what I expect you to do,' he said, though thinking the opposite. 'But we need to get to know one another much better, so we can work in harmony to get my wife back to full health.'

'Yes, naturally ...' she said, 'I'm certain, there's plenty of time to get to know each other very well.' She accentuated the 'very.' 'It's early days.' Kate raised her glass. 'Nice wine.'

Bloody hell, was his luck changing?

'Yes, it's one of my preferred wines,' he said, feeling pleased with himself. 'I've actually visited the vineyards of Sancerre. It was a memorable experience!'

He returned to his chair. Perhaps sitting through all that boring narrative might prove worthwhile after all. He could see by the way Katie was looking at him, he'd done it again. He'd scored. He tried hard to hide the smirk on his face.

'Now Katie—the shopping and cooking—what do we do about that? You have already indicated that Miranda should be following a special diet,' he said perhaps louder than was necessary.

For the rest of their evening, they discussed the full range of her duties while Katie would be working at Oakdale. He was pleased that the wine had done its job. It hadn't been a wasted expense after all. It seems as though Ella had definitely chosen the right person to look after his wife.

Chapter 8

Return

He slammed down the boot of the Mercedes.

The sound was swallowed by the thick, silky atmosphere. He immediately sensed the sultry breeze of the tropics brushing his skin as he wheeled his oversized leather suitcase towards the marble steps of the hotel entrance. Within seconds, one of the staff rushed up to assist.

'Please sir, let me help you. If my memory serves me well, you're Mr Taylor. I remember you from last year.'

'Spot on.'

'Welcome back sir... I hope that you very much enjoy your stay with us.'

Jeffrey followed his luggage up the path to the hotel's grand entrance. A huge, white pillared portico adorned with striking pinks and purples of hibiscus and bougainvillea. The palm fronds murmured a welcome to him in the breeze.

'I'll leave your bags here sir.' The hotel employee placed the suitcases in the lobby. 'Once you've checked in, I'll transfer them to your room.'

Jeffrey took in the familiar streaks of blue accessories and natural wood furniture as he strode towards the reception desk. He was greeted by the usual smiles from the staff. They told him they were pleased to see him back. He was certainly very pleased to be back at Topaz. He'd looked forward to being away from Dorset. He felt relieved at being a totally free man for several weeks, without the reins, the constrictions, he felt when in the same house as Miranda.

'Is Tamara working today?' he asked as the receptionist passed him the room key.

'No sir. I believe she will be here on Monday.'

'She was so kind to me during my last visit. And I got to know her son.'

Jeffrey had learnt that the people of Sainte Marie smiled very readily. The receptionist's face lit up and she beamed at him. 'Oh, you mean Willis sir. Yes, everyone here knows Willis. He's a regular visitor at the sports centre. He frequently helps out on the beach.'

'I look forward to meeting him again. And could you please inform Mr Denning that I'm here? If he's available, I'll go and see him once I've unpacked.'

'Certainly, sir,' the receptionist picked up the phone. She relayed the message that Mr Denning would meet him in the bar in half an hour.

Jeffrey watched Antony stride into the bar, his upright frame clad in his usual conventional manner. He thought the man looked tired and over worked, but then who wouldn't be with the responsibility of a five-star hotel on his shoulders. He noticed too that, out of habit, Antony eyed-up every aspect of the room—his role as owner never forgotten— constantly checking that all was as he would wish it. Here was the man who had invited him to return to the island. But he certainly wasn't the principal reason for being there. Antony's enquiry, about selling the villas being constructing next to the hotel, was the excuse he needed to get as far away from his wife as possible. For Jeffrey, the invitation had not come too soon.

Jeffrey had lined up two glasses of wine in front of him, and was already half-way through his when Antony arrived.

'Well, how was the flight Jeffrey?' Antony asked politely, shaking his hand vigorously. 'It's good to see you back, though it's a great pity that Miranda wasn't able to come along as well.' He installed himself opposite Jeffrey.

Jeffrey's face took on a down-cast mask. Privately, he was very thankful his wife was unable to accompany him. 'Yes, it's really sad, but she just wouldn't be able to cope with the flight. She's a changed woman from the spirited person I married.'

'Yes, I know. Ella has contacted me a couple of times. She also said Miranda isn't making the progress she had hoped. I know she left here feeling quite hopeful about her mother's recovery.'

'Ella gets very distressed about it all. We were all hopeful, but it wasn't to be. I've left Miranda in the very capable hands of a live-in nurse—a single woman in her fifties. Fortunately, they get on very well.

'Yes, Ella told me a little about her. It's an incredibly sad situation though Jeffrey. Miranda was such a bubbly, bright individual, living life to the maximum. She always had new projects on the go.'

Jeffrey did the done thing and explained about his wife's health in the most sympathetic voice he could muster. 'The specialist she saw in Dorset believes that the stroke may have been brought on because Miranda hadn't taken her blood pressure medication for some days. Also, she may have become stressed about something during the night,' he disclosed, failing to say that it could have been their 'little domestic' which had been the problem. 'The specialist has diagnosed the part of Miranda's brain that deals with social behaviour was affected by the haemorrhage. She comes out with some rather hurtful things sometimes.'

'I would imagine that's difficult to live with.'

'That's partly why I'm here Antony,' he admitted. 'Life is rather tricky at home some days. Miranda can be extremely ungrateful to those who try their hardest to please her,' he said, endeavouring to make the home situation sound as problematical as possible. 'We are no longer really a married couple, if you get my drift.' Jeffrey finished off his wine. 'Another one?'

'Please, yes, I'd like that. But let's go out on the terrace. It's perhaps a little more private out there.' Antony attracted the bar staff to order more drinks before they retreated outside.

In distinct contrast to the air-conditioned bar, Jeffrey was struck by a heavy blanket of silky, smooth evening air, the briny sulphurous odour of the sea, and the continuous refrain of the tree frogs. How he'd missed all that. 'What a wonderful evening after the weather in England. It's such a pity that Miranda can't share it,' he lied. 'Yeah, as I was saying, we are no longer truly man and wife. Some days, Miranda doesn't want me near her.'

'I understand. I suppose, that's why, when I asked for some help with marketing the villas, you volunteered readily.'

'I need a new project, Antony. I can't be staying at home all the time, trying to nurse a woman with dementia. It sounds cruel, I know. She's my wife, but I can't make nursing her my whole life. Nobody moves forward; there's no progress. On the contrary, according to the doctors we've seen, she will gradually get worse.'

'I sympathise,' Antony said, 'it must be extremely difficult. I'm sure I'd find it so. I'm like you. I have to be busy. I have to have challenges.'

They were silent for a beat. Jeffrey stared blankly out at blackness, assuring himself that he'd put across his situation admirably. Hunting bats sped a jagged trail across his line of vision. The garden lighting silhouetted the towering palms and the exotic flowers cocooning them. This was where he'd rather be—life here suited him better than being imprisoned in Dorset. 'I may be in my sixties, but my mind is still active. Don't just want to vegetate and be like some of the other retired people I meet in Britain. Some seem to just potter around aimlessly, waiting for their last days. I still want to discover and partake of an adventurous life.'

'Miranda used to be the same, didn't she?' Antony sighed.

'It's sad,' Jeffrey said, hanging his head, 'but all she wants to do now is tinker around in the house and garden. She seems to have lost all her confidence. We've talked it through … and well …' He knew he didn't need to say any more about the reason he was there. It was time to move the conversation on. 'Hey, what about Tamara's son? Is he still doing the paddle boarding?'

Antony laughed. 'He's a water sports expert now. He's on that beach nearly every day after school. Unofficially, he helps Ricko with the equipment. Water sports seem to rule his life. But he's a nice boy. I'm sure that you'll see a change in him.'

'I'm sure to bump into him on the beach. But Antony, we'd better get down to business and sort out how we are going sell these villas of yours. Are we going to empty another glass or is that it for this evening?'

The tone of the conversation changed. Ideas were swapped. Propositions noted. The dialogue become far more business orientated. Jeffrey was in his element.

~~~

The next morning, Jeffrey was thrashing through the clear, tepid water of Mango Bay. He hadn't let jet lag affect his daily exercise routine. After counting the designated number of laps, he pulled himself onto the swim raft anchored offshore. From there he was able to survey the beach. Hotel guests were starting to appear, roaming along the shoreline, venturing into the sea, or idling on the cushioned sun loungers.

The early sunlight touched his skin. Its warmth gratified his senses. He felt happy, the first time for ages. What ecstasy, compared to his miserable existence in Dorset. Away from the restraints of home, and the critical eye of Miranda. Away from the dreary atmosphere hanging over Oaklands. He revelled in his freedom. To top off his halcyon existence, he just needed to find himself an attractive young woman for his stay.

'Mr T, Mr T,' cried an excited voice.

A young male had swum up to the raft. He pulled himself onto the painted surface and sat next to him. Jeffrey stared at the adolescent; his muscles developed by exercising. A local youth shining with sea water, droplets glistening in his tightly frizzed dark hair. He exposed his gleaming white teeth with a cheeky grin.

'Willis, is it you? I don't believe it. You have grown so much.' Jeffrey's contemplative expression dissolved; he joined Willis in grinning. Time receded and he remembered the good times the two of them had shared during his previous visit. He wrapped a welcoming arm around the boy's wet shoulder.

'Great to see you again!'

'Hi Mr T. Man, I'm so pleased to see you back on island. My Mom told me that you were due in last night.'

Jeffrey leaned backwards to take a good look at the youngster sat next to him. Willis was transformed. The kid had metamorphosed into a young man.

'Wow, Willis. I almost didn't recognise you. You look so grown up. Look at these muscles!' He prodded a developed bicep playfully.

'I'll be fourteen next month.' Willis said proudly. 'I gotta lot to tell ya. And alot to show you.'

'I could see from the way you swam up to the raft, you're a great swimmer now.'

'Gee, fanks a bundle. Glad you noticed. Give me a five,' Willis raised his open hand towards Jeffrey's. His grin dropped. 'But Mr T, give me the low down on Mrs T. How's she been? Is she better now? Mom said to ask.'

'That was kind of your Mum.' His face dropped. 'No, I'm afraid not Willis. But, let me tell you about it over breakfast. Do you have a T-shirt, so we can eat at the beach bar?'

'Sure ... on the beach ... but I've already had breakfast. But I can just tag along as company.'

The odour of bacon cooking and the chance to eat in the smart, white beach restaurant was, however, too much for Willis. It didn't take much to persuade him to eat his second breakfast. They sat across the wooden table from one another, hotel life buzzing around them.

Willis gulped down a glass of juice. 'So, tell me what happened to Mrs T. Why isn't she any better?'

'During our stay here, she had a stroke Willis. Do you understand what that is?'

'Mom told me that, but no, I'm not a hundred per cent sure.'

'The night of the stroke, blood haemorrhaged into parts of her brain. It stopped parts of it functioning normally. Her world changed overnight,' Jeffrey told him.

'Hey, creepy. Scary stuff! What happened in her brain?'

'Yes, real scary. The blood from the arteries started flooding into her brain, probably because of very high blood pressure. The normal flow of blood to the brain is affected, and brain cells start to die off within minutes. There is no cure, Willis. That part of her brain is damaged for good.'

'Man, that's awful. And that's why she ain't with you?'

'Afraid so. She has a full-time carer at home now Willis. Life can be difficult for her at times—but also for her family. She is so different from the person I came on holiday with last year. You know what, I'm fairly certain she won't be able to do any long journeys again.'

'I'm real sorry Mr T,' Willis said quietly.

Jeffrey was touched by the sympathy on the boy's face. 'But that's life Willis. You never know, from one day to the next, what life will dole out to you.' Willis nodded. 'Now you tell me about what you've been up to since I was last here.'

The morning ticked by. To Jeffrey's surprise, they seemed to find plenty to talk about. Stories about using the paddle board tumbled out of Willis. He effervesced with passion for water sports. Much of their conversation circled around it. Jeffrey was pleased to see the boy again. He had a likeable way about him. But he would be even more pleased to meet up with that beauty, his mother, once more. He'd convinced himself she had the right qualities to play a role in the new life he'd planned for himself. When Willis mentioned a kitesurfing in the south of the island, straight off Jeffrey thought it could be the opportunity he wanted. Willis knew all about the wind direction and strength down there but had never been there. Jeffrey suggested a visit; and Willis jumped at the chance. So, by the end of breakfast, they'd organised to try out the school the next day.

'As it's a Sunday, do you think your mother would like to come?' Jeffrey asked.

'Dunno. Perhaps. I could ask her.'

'If I drive you home, then we could both ask her. Would that be OK?'

'Yup. Should think she'll be at home. Mom didn't say she was going anywhere.'

'You don't live far away, do you? If you wait in the car park, I'll go and get dressed and collect my car keys.'

As Jeffrey drove away from the hotel, his view of island life changed. Opulence and luxury were very rapidly replaced by the realities of Sainte Marie. Tropical vegetation abounded. Verges were high with weeds. Homes were generally small. Some still constructed of wood. Brightly coloured houses were planted along the edge of the road, without gardens, without pavements.

Willis directed and Jeffrey concentrated on the driving down the uneven roads. They ended up in the outskirts of Bourbon. Willis stopped him outside a large concrete apartment block. The sun had badly faded its original bright green colour. Paint was peeling off in places. The paving slabs leading to each door were cracked and uneven. The garden wasn't a garden, simply a patch of uncared for mud.

'I'll go see if my Mom is about,' Willis said jumping out of the vehicle.

Jeffrey watched him run towards an aluminium door with a mesh screen. In his absence, Jeffrey took in the neglected surroundings. He was definitely chasing the right woman. She'd jump at the chance to leave this. Willis was in the doorway again in seconds, beckoning to Jeffrey. He left the car, wondering about its safety, but realising it was inappropriate to even ask.

As Jeffrey approached the building, Tamara came to stand beside her son. Dressed in shorts and a T-shirt, she looked quite different than in her working clothes. But he didn't fail to note the shapely form revealed by her clinging top. Her coffee-coloured skin shone out from under a colourful scarf tied around her head. She smiled, but was perhaps a little embarrassed by her unexpected guest.

'Hi Tamara,'

'This is a surprise Mr Taylor,' she said, 'you were the last person I expected to see today.'

'Sorry to intrude on your day off. Bringing Willis home seemed to be the simplest solution. I suggested visiting the kite surfing school tomorrow. I came to check if it was okay by you,' he said in a warm and re-assuring voice.

'Well, I'm not sure ...'

'We had breakfast in the hotel Mom. It was real choice. Bacon, eggs, the works,' Willis cut in.

'Oh, that was kind Mr Taylor. As you've eaten so much, you won't need any lunch then, will you?' Tamara playfully punched towards her son's stomach. 'Would you like to come in for a minute Mr Taylor? Come in out of the sun.' She propped open the screen door.

'I don't want to take up too much of your valuable day of rest, Tamara.' Jeffrey said stepping into the small apartment. 'I just didn't think it was the 'done thing' to organise a trip without your knowledge.'

The room was what he'd expected. All was clean and tidy. But much like the rest of the apartment block, well-worn and out-dated. From what he could see Tamara would need him, just like he needed her.

'In fact, I did wonder if you might like to tag along as well. I believe there is a restaurant on the beach there. We could have a bit of lunch.'

'Cool plan. What ya think Mom?' asked an excited Willis.

Tamara considered the situation. Jeffrey watched her apprehensively. A day out. A free lunch. Surely, she couldn't say no.

'Well … I thought that I might visit a friend tomorrow … but why not? I haven't been down to Anse Anne for some time.'

'Gee thanks Mom!'

'But there's something I'd like to discuss with you Mr Taylor.'

'Oh really,' he flashed one of his good guy grins at both mother and son, 'please call me Jeff. I hope I'm not in trouble.'

Tamara's expression remained fixed. 'We can talk about things tomorrow.' She looked around her. 'If you don't mind Mr Taylor, I need to get on with my housework and cooking now. Thank you for the invite though. Willis will really look forward to it. So …' she said as she walked towards the door, '… I'll see you tomorrow morning … and you can tell me all about how your wife is doing.'

'Yeah, I've already filled Willis in. Anyway, I'll leave you to it. Great to see you both again. And enjoy the rest of your day.' He gave them a few more of his special smiles.

He walked into the blinding morning light and back to the waiting Mercedes car, feeling he'd had a good morning.

So far, so good he told himself.

Chapter 9

Emmalyn

She parked her car in front of the real estate office.

Emmalyn stared out of the windscreen, vacantly fixed on the brick building before her. The large sheet glass window filled with coloured posters. But, they might as well not have been there. Behind her the traffic thundered past. Her thoughts were elsewhere. She had just left her clients at their residence. The visit hadn't gone well.

She'd been convinced that during this second visit, they'd make an offer. She'd felt really confident about it. They had been so positive during the first viewing. The property and its garden had ticked all their boxes. They had been intoxicated by its architectural allure and layout. It was an inviting home. An important streak of white across the hillside of dark green tropical vegetation. Sleek narrow pillars. Long spanned arches. A large expanse of windows, whose reflexions brought the outside in. A hint of Spanish architecture, all facing out to sea. The interior sparkled with sunlight reflected from the large pool on the patio. To Emmalyn, it was a dream home.

All had gone so well on their journey that day up the coast road and through the prosperous development of imposing dwellings. They'd chatted casually about current island affairs on Sainte Marie. But almost as soon as they had parked outside the property; as soon as they recommenced a tour of each room, her clients' tone had changed. This time, they'd looked at the house with entirely different eyes, and the euphoria of the initial visit was not repeated—most comments were negative. They'd remarked on windows that needed replacing; bathrooms needing modernisation; and an area of the decking, which in their opinion had been attacked by termites.

Emmalyn's heart had sunk. She had reminded them of the property's reasonable price tag. She related how, in her opinion, with a relatively small amount of imagination, time and money, the villa could be remodelled into an exceptional address. But she failed. They didn't ask to negotiate with the owner; they didn't even ask to see comparable houses. Dismay had quickly descended. Emmalyn so desperately needed to sell something! But this had been the pattern of events for several months now. Her boss had sold a few small homes, but she, she hadn't come up with anything.

Each day, she was living with a sense of failure—she'd lost the ability to perform her job successfully. She usually had no problem convincing clients to buy. But now she felt useless. It all made her life gruelling. Things were tight without her commission. Existing on a basic wage was challenging. Surviving on a very tight budget, buying the cheapest of everything. Life was tough. She thanked her lucky stars that there hadn't been any expensive emergencies. When there were, she didn't know what would happen.

She leaned over to collect her bag and real estate agents' literature from the passenger seat. Sitting there, she'd been trying to summon up courage. The courage to go and face Mrs Leon, her boss. A downcast mood hung over her as she pushed open the office door. As anticipated, her boss was there to greet her.

'So, how was the visit?' she jumped in immediately.

'Not good.' Emmalyn placed her things on the desk where she worked. 'I just don't know what went wrong. They so loved the place the first time around.'

The spark in Mrs Leon's voice was dampened. 'Hell no! I was kinda banking on a sale there.'

'Sorry, Mrs Leon. I tried really hard. I'm getting a bit jittery and losing confidence in my ability to sell.'

'Seems like they were wasting our time,' Mrs Leon sighed. 'Oh, it ain't you Emmalyn. It's because of the bank cutbacks on lending and the damned government's new policies about not giving a tax-free period after purchase. I pray to the Lord that things improve soon.'

'I don't think He'll do too much about the real estate market Mrs Leon. It's a bit outside the realms of His powers.' She sunk into her chair. 'But no, it doesn't make life easy. It's all very well the government and the banks making all these rules, but how's anybody supposed to make ends meet and put a meal on the table every day, if you can't do your job properly?'

'We ain't the only ones,' Mrs Leon explained. 'I've been asking around; I've spoken to other agencies. They're finding it just as difficult. Nothing much is selling.'

'Thank the lord I don't have a mortgage to pay.' Several years previously Emmalyn had considered selling her traditional house and investing in a brand-new, well-equipped apartment. 'I really would be in a hole if I'd moved and taken out a home loan. I just couldn't afford to pay for that as well.'

'The situation's getting kinda worrying anyway. Can't carry on for too long.'

Emmalyn noted this last remark. It made her concern deepen. She would hate to lose her position at the agency. It was the one thing that made her life tolerable. Meeting folks from all over. Finding out about their worlds. Visiting fine, glossy buildings around the island. It was her escapism. Her means of dealing with the realities of her life—the veil which softened the sharp edges of the truth.

From behind the worn, wooden desk, she surveyed the things around her. It may be her flight ticket to elsewhere, but it really was quite run-down. It needed new flooring and the walls were desperately in need of brightening up. The only aspect that lifted the outlook was the glossy, colourful photos displayed on the walls and in the front window. From pocket-sized apartments to extensive mansions, all for sale. Or pictures of homes for rent. Even some of these images looked a little worse for wear, as they'd been displayed for so long. But she shouldn't criticise, her place needed a lot of attention too.

In the past, there had been periods when the housing market had been really buoyant. Despite this, Mrs Leon hadn't bothered to fix things up. She spent much of her day there, but didn't ever seem to notice the state of things around her. Emmalyn settled down to sending e-mails. Then to phoning, in an attempt to summon up interest amongst potential customers.

Emmalyn was physically occupied, but the afternoon dragged on. Her thoughts floated from one matter to another. The fluorescent strips soon bathed the space in a harsh, silvery glow, stripping away the disguise the fading and softening evening light had brought to the place.

'I've had enough for today. I've a viewing for a rental first thing tomorrow.' Mrs Leon switched off her computer; and then picked up her large faux leather bag. Emmalyn followed her example.

After an essential visit to the supermarket, Emmalyn headed for the outskirts of Anse Argent. She parked her precious, beat-up car next to her house. The lights shining inside and out gave the impression that Vinny was in. The small, wooden-clad square building that she called home had been painted a bright turquoise some years ago. In contrast, to complete the tropical image, the shutters and covered terrace were decked in white. The illuminations guided her across the garden to the side door. In truth, it was no longer a garden, just a patch of weeds. Weeds, now taller than a man. Vinny had promised to cut them all down many months before, but it had never happened. She'd have to do it herself.

'Vinny,' Emmalyn called, entering the kitchen-living room. Her voice resounded around the small room. No response. She dumped her plastic bags on the old wooden table. Threw her keys and handbag down next to them. All three rooms were brightened by lit bulbs, but Vinny was nowhere to be seen.

Anger surged in. Electricity was expensive on the island; and she was the one who paid all the bills. She did a tour to switch off all the unnecessary lights.

In the living room, it was obvious Vincent had been doing his usual thing. There were his belongings, or utensils he'd used, put down and left. There was no attempt to tidy them away. Emmalyn, still fuming, stowed away the perishable foods. The small counter fridge stood isolated in the corner of the living room which served as kitchen, dining and sitting area. Next was the exasperating chore of tidying all of Vinny's mess. Replacing each item made her level of irritation mount. Cup in the sink. Pick up the damp towel from the tiled floor. Empty bottle in the bin. The man was a fiend. She was treated worse than a skivvy.

Table cleared, Emmalyn meticulously wiped the patterned oilcloth draped over it, ready to start preparing the evening meal. Vegetables were chopped, tins opened, but cooking on the two gas rings was kept to a minimum. Their heat made the small space stifling, despite the main door being open—with its screen which kept out insects attracted to the light.

She rapidly concocted a functional meal. Annoyance with Vinny made her decide to go ahead and eat her own meal and not wait for him. She was halfway through it when he arrived, slamming the screen door behind him. Within seconds, Emmalyn realised from his gait, Vinny was returning from some bar or other.

'What ya eating?' he demanded as he slumped into the chair opposite her. Emmalyn took stock of his grubby T-shirt advertising local beer; the dishevelled, braided hair. He looked a flob out, a real slob.

'How you doing Vinny?' she said sarcastically, as he hadn't enquired after her. 'I cooked for you, but I'll need to cook you some more pasta.'

'What bloody pasta again! Where's de soul food?' he complained screwing up his face.

'There's a bit of yam. But pasta is cheap. You know things aren't easy at present.'

'Ya should ask ya bitch o' a boss for a pay rise.'

He was ignored. There was little point trying to reason with Vinny when he'd had a few. She left her meal and went to cook more pasta on the gas ring.

'Did you get any work today?' she asked. Vinny did casual work in the construction industry, or occasionally he went fishing with one of his mates.

'Nah, gonna try again tomorrow. Frankie say he might need me in Doublon.'

Emmalyn contained her exasperation. Vinny was unemployed more days than he worked. She didn't dare ask where he'd got the money to buy his drinks that evening. She calculated that the few dollars he had pocketed last week for one day's work would be long gone.

Vinny had come to live with Emmalyn not long after she had inherited the house from her mother. Things had gone well at first. Life had been pleasant when they had first met. Initially, she'd been attracted by his muscular form and his full, sensual mouth. They had been content with one another. He'd worked on a regular basis then; he'd patched up the leaking roof; he'd grown vegetables in the garden and even helped out with the household bills.

Then, the friend that he worked for had a bad fall. After the accident, his friend hadn't been able to work again. At first, Vinny had talked about taking over the enterprise. But, he never did. Since then, he'd only worked occasionally. He seemed to have lost all his motivation. Much of his week was spent in bars. Now, his full lips usually reeked of stale alcohol and the muscular body had turned to flab because he wasn't sufficiently active. He was content playing dominoes with other unemployed buddies. Not discovering anything new. Just throwing comments at one another; wasting each day; watching his life melt away.

Vinny had never suggested that they marry. As things had turned out, she was glad that they hadn't. She was also gratified they'd never had children. Kids would not have had an easy upbringing—with Vinny hardly working, not contributing to the bills, or helping in the house. Plus, he was wasted most nights. For Emmalyn, in her forty second year, it was too late to have children. Things were no longer easy between them. They argued, usually because he left everything to her. A lot of the time there just wasn't enough money to make ends meet. Their personal life had crumbled. He'd become a burden that weighed her down to despair. For Vinny, Emmalyn had become his meal ticket; she provided a roof over his head; a plate of food in front of him every day. For Emmalyn, affection had turned to resentment. She did everything. She paid for everything. Even paid for his few clothes.

Their relationship was just a habit. She had mentally sifted through their past few years and couldn't remember the last time they had shared happy times together. Vinny had become everything she didn't want to be. She felt that life was too damned short to throw it away day after day. To have no reason to get out of bed. She didn't want to hurt him, but God forgive her, she'd decided it was time for him to go. She'd be better off alone. At least, she'd have a few more coins in her purse. She didn't leave the lights on when the house was empty. She wouldn't leave a meal untouched. She'd made the decision some months before, but she'd not found the right words or the courage to tell him. It all added to the worry she felt about her vulnerable job.

Electricity for the room fan cost too much to have it on very often. So, working next to the gas rings, Emmalyn's skin shone with the heat. She re-heated the vegetables and tinned tuna, wiped a plate clean to spread it with cooked pasta, and then added the topping. She even collected him a knife and fork, standing up amongst the others in the large, recycled fruit tin next to the sink.

When she turned to serve up his meal, Vinny was fast asleep. Arms splayed across the table, his long braided hair fanning out over the plastic tablecloth, a faint snoring sound coming from him. Her anger climbed up another notch or two. She plonked the filled plate on an empty part of the table, and covered it with another.

'You can eat that god-damn meal tomorrow, you old juice head. I'm not paying to cook you anything different.' Emmalyn stored the meal in the fridge, slamming the door shut. It hummed at her. Emmalyn slumped into her chair, opposite her unfinished meal. Any appetite had vanished, just like her cool. She didn't feel one bit like clearing up, but dutifully did so, not wanting a draining board full of insects the next day.

Vinny remained supine, sprawled across the table, oblivious to the world around him. Determined she was not going to spend the rest of the evening in the same room as him, she picked up her work laptop, her headphones, a selection of CDs, together with a collection of magazines given to her by a friend, and lastly collected her handbag and purse. She needed to try and unwind. She installed the things in the main bedroom and turned the key in the lock. There was no goddamned way that Vinny was going to share the same bed as her that night.

Chapter 10

Kites

Tamara was confused.

The next morning Jeffrey picked them up and headed back in the direction of the hotel. She sat in the front of the hire car clutching her large straw bag. It contained all the things she had earlier bundled in for their day at the beach. Willis sat in the back of the Mercedes. It was obvious by his chatter, he was hyped-up. He wasn't used to going on jaunts out. He certainly wasn't accustomed to travelling in expensive cars.

Tamara was reluctant to comment, but thought she ought to say something about heading in the wrong direction for Anse Anne. 'Sorry Mr Taylor, but we need to drive through Bourbon to get to the kite surfing school. You need to be going in the opposite direction,' she announced rather quietly.

'If we are going to spend the day together, I insist that you and Willis call me Jeff. OK there?' He directed his last statement to the back of the car but carried on driving towards Topaz.

'Sure thing Mr T,' Willis called from the back.

'Jeff,' he repeated.

'Fine. But, you still seem to be heading in the wrong way,' Tamara repeated.

'Perhaps I should have said we are going down south in a water taxi. I organised one from the hotel yesterday,' he turned his head slightly and smiled.

'Wow, amazing! That's real awesome Mr T. Jeff. Man, high voltage!'

'I thought it was the simplest solution. It takes too long to drive down there because of the narrow roads and the hairpin bends.'

'Yes, it's almost a two hour journey. I know the roads aren't wonderful,' Tamara admitted.

'So, there you go. It's the simplest and quickest solution.'

Tamara cringed inside thinking how long she had to work to pay for such a journey. 'But, Jeff, this was supposed to be a simple Sunday ride out to the beach. You forget I know how much the boat trip costs. I book these water taxis working on reception.'

'I got a special deal from Ricko. It's all organised,' Jeffrey told her.

Tamara was dubious. As far as she knew Ricko had no authority to arrange special deals. 'This is really what I wanted to talk to you about Mr Taylor. It's about Willis really. It's exceedingly kind of you to lend him your board. To buy him a fancy breakfast. To take him down to the kite surfing school. I'm truly grateful. But … I don't want him to get grand ideas … about what he expects from life. You have to understand, I can't do those things. When you're not around, I don't have the means.'

'Mom, he knows that,' an exasperated Willis blurted, leaning towards the front seat. 'Don't talk about me like that. I won't get grand ideas. Chill out mother. Please don't go and spoil the day.'

The car had by that time reached the gates of the hotel. They glided slowly down the long driveway, shaded on either side by majestic, soaring Attalea palms.

'I hear what you are saying Tamara. I appreciate what you mean about spoiling Willis. But can we continue talking about this a bit later? The water taxi will be waiting for us.'

Tamara and Willis got out of the car. He caught hold of her arm while they waited for Jeffrey. 'Hell Mother, you're so goddamn annoying!' he hissed. 'Stop treating me like some little kid. Dial down the mollycoddling. Just take things for what they are. Just a pleasant day out. Some of us have been looking forward to this trip.' He scowled at her.

She wanted to respond, to correct his behaviour, but there was no time for discussion. Jeffrey was out of the car, and they were whisked through the hotel gardens and onto the beach. Within minutes, the water taxi was bouncing them over the waves. The breeze tugged at Tamara's hair. Spray lashed against her skin and dampened her clothes. The golden glints of sunlight patterned the ocean, as she watched the rugged coastline speed past. By the glow on his face, Tamara could see that Willis was thrilled. Never having been that enamoured by being on the water, she clung to the side of the boat with one hand and clutched her beach bag with the other. Jeffrey threw in an occasional comment, pointing out passing points of interest. She understood it was far from a suitable place to discuss the ethics of Mr Jeffrey Taylor spoiling Willis. Or him squandering enough money to feed her and Willis for at least two weeks on a boat ride.

But Tamara had to concede, Jeffrey had been right. It was by far the easiest way to get down to the south of the island. In addition, they had the opportunity to catch sight of the island's beautiful coastline. Sandy bays. Spectacular rocky cliffs. A couple of small fishing villages. The sea air was bracing. Neither Tamara nor Willis had seen their island from this perspective too many times before. Within twenty-five exhilarating minutes, the boat was slowing down prior to tying up at the jetty at Anse Anne.

Buzzing with enthusiasm, Willis hopped off the water taxi and jogged down the landing stage. He was too fired up to wait for the oldies. Jeffrey took Tamara's bag from her and jumped out of the boat. She sensed his eyes scrutinising her every move as he helped her onto the jetty.

'Well Tamara, wasn't that preferable to a difficult car journey?' he said, letting go of her hand.

'It was an experience,' Tamara admitted. 'I don't think I've ever reached the extreme south of the island so rapidly.'

'It's great! I love the speed over the water and the chance to take in the spectacular views.'

Tamara went to follow on after Willis, but Jeffrey grabbed hold of her arm, 'I know you want to talk to me. I haven't forgotten what you said about Willis. We must talk about it over lunch. You can see, now is not the right time.'

'Thank you, Mr Taylor. I know it's difficult when Willis is around. Perhaps we can send him off on an errand for five minutes,' she smiled at Jeffrey. 'So, tell me, how is Mrs Taylor White?'

They headed towards the brightly painted wooden cabin planted in the fine, cream sand. Jeffrey spelt out a few details about his wife's health—how much she had deteriorated. Tamara's sympathy went out to him. She couldn't imagine living with someone who had changed so much, so quickly. When they reached the kite surfing building, Willis was already chatting to one of the instructors sat on the sand outside.

Tamara loved it. The morning was filled with prime experiences. Before anything else, the first timers had to be tutored on the beach. The instructor had them lined up to teach them about the equipment. They learnt some of the terminology: the canopy, harness, heal side and board down wind. Motionless on the sand, they watched in awe. They beheld the kite surfers drifting across the bay. All this inspired her. She amazed herself by actually agreeing to have a go at the sport. She removed her shorts and large t-shirt self-consciously; wrapped her arms across her, trying to hide her dark clinging swimsuit. She was sure Jeffrey's eyes followed her every move. But there was too much to do, too much to think about for inhibitions. She inflated a training kite, strapped on the harness, and tried to get the feel of flying the kite from the beach. The thrill of the wind tugging at the canopy exhilarated her.

They all learnt the basics from the safety of the sand. There were screams of laughter, howls of elation. Yells of encouragement and shouts of advice came from the instructor— all their noise sailed down the usually quiet beach. She was pleased they were relaxed with one another. For Tamara, the three of them became the same age—young and with the same aims. They worked as one. Though they experienced differing levels of success; they sympathised in each other's failures. All were filled with camaraderie, full of joie de vivre. An incongruous phone appeared. Jeffrey insisted on taking photos of attempts to angle the kite correctly, as the wind pulled them up from a sitting position and dragged them a little way along the soft sand.

At the end of the session, they all chatted wildly, looking forward to a time when they could get a board onto the water. While helping to tidy the equipment, there were more selfies with Jeffrey. Tamara felt the kitesurfing had taken it out of her, but wasn't going to complain. Her body was not used to physical exertion like her son's or Jeffrey's. As she put back on her casual clothing, she was very aware of her already aching muscles.

'Are you beginning to understand? Understand why I immerse myself in sport?' Jeffrey asked as he placed his arm around her shoulder and guided her in the direction of the beach restaurant. She made no objection, still glowing from the morning's adventure. 'And why it's just so much more fun when you share the experience.'

'You do it to forget the rest of life? Let your mind unwind?' she said. He nodded in assent. 'Yes, I see that now.' She gave him a smile. 'Jeff, I had a phenomenal morning. Thank you so much. I know I was pretty useless, but I loved trying.'

'Perhaps you'll get the hang of it a bit better next time. There's a lot to learn, eh Willis. Tell you what young man; you did really well'

'It was mind blowing Mr T! Ridiculously amazing! Thanks a million.'

The restaurant was busy, but they managed to grab a table in the shade of a large bush. The worn, white plastic garden tables and chairs were embedded in the powdery, dry sand. Everything was very informal. The table was bare. No cutlery. No condiments. No table mats. No menu.

'I don't know if there should be a next time.' Tamara had seen how many dollar notes he had handed over to the instructor to pay for the three of them. Despite her reservations, she decided not to further this conversation. 'Man, do I feel worn out,' she admitted. 'My arms are not used to all that pulling and tugging …'

'Willis, can you run and ask one of the ladies what there is to eat please,' Jeffrey interrupted. Willis walked off and made his way towards the large wooden restaurant structure. She felt the weight of his arm drop on her shoulders and he turned her to face him. She looked into his smiling eyes.

'Look Tamara, did you enjoy this morning?' Jeffrey asked 'Yes, you know I did. But …' she paused, 'it cost you so much money. And the water taxi too.'

'But it was phenomenal…' Jeffrey argued, '… and without a doubt, Willis thought so too. And if you enjoyed it, then it isn't a waste of money, is it?'

'No, but …'

'Tamara. I have the money. I can't spend it on taking my wife on holiday. I shall be earning even more money when I start to sell Mr Denning's properties. I understand your concerns about Willis. But let's look at the positive side; you've confirmed that when I first met Willis, he was becoming a troublesome, bored teenager. I feel I've given him something to think about—an aim in life, a reason to get up every morning. For me, that's great.'

'I suppose …' Tamara agreed quietly. She was grateful for the change in her son. 'I'll always be thankful you introduced him to water sports. He has made new friends. He's much happier with life. He has more confidence; he's a more rounded personality. His negative attitude was struck by a bolt of lightning, and he now tries to be good at everything.' She looked towards the restaurant building making sure Willis wasn't on his way back with a menu. 'You are right … Willis was really heading in the wrong direction. Mixing with dropouts, troublemakers. Into booze, when he could get it. Drugs would have come next. He's gone from a raw kid skulking around dark corners, to a young man able to walk with his head up high. He's found he has more fun in and on the water. I'm real grateful.'

'Thanks … and I'm pleased for him … and I'm pleased for you. So, we don't need to talk about it again.' Jeffrey gently squeezed her shoulders.

Tamara pulled her mouth straight. She'd failed again. She hadn't said what she'd really wanted to say. She just hoped she wouldn't be expected to show her gratitude in the usual way.

'Here's the menu,' Willis said cheerfully. Tamara saw him weighing up the situation, her and Jeffrey still stood opposite one another, Jeffrey with his hands on her. He pushed a clip board towards Jeffrey. It held a rather crumpled piece of paper on it. 'Lady said she'll be here in a minute.'

'What are we having to drink then?' Jeffrey said, shuffling the chairs around the table.

'I'm as thirsty as a fish out of the ocean,' joked Willis, 'I'll have a kite surfers' cocktail.'

'I can't see that on the drinks list Willis. What's in it?'

'It's iced coke, served in a bucket,' Willis said, 'and I'd like a ham and pineapple pizza please. I'm as hungry as a lion.'

'Starving, as well as thirsty as a fish. I'll get a bucket full of coke for you, if you promise to drink every drop,' Jeffrey laughed.

As they seated themselves at the table, Tamara noticed Jeffrey gazing around himself. 'I really go for this place,' he said. 'I can't imagine why Miranda never brought me here. It all oozes "back to nature." It's truly exotic.'

Tamara followed his gaze across the fine, pale sand edging the glistening ocean just a few metres away from them. She took in the continuous sound of the waves heaving onto the beach, the overhead palms, the large wild bushes covered in small flowers sprouting up from the beach, the very few people dotted along the sand. Sea birds overhead. A couple of mongrel dogs hanging around hoping for scraps. A light, refreshing tropical breeze enveloping them all. Yes, she understood its appeal—it was so different from the more touristic north of the island.

'Mmm, it's really beautiful,' she said.

'I love it. It's a true paradise,' Jeffrey uttered.

Lunch was lively. Tamara appreciated every minute. She'd decided to drop her apprehension for the time being and just enjoy the meal for what it was. Waves of their laughter mingled with the constant melody of natural coastal sounds. They seemed to chat continuously. They interacted like old friends. Each of them learnt a little more about one other, even mother and son.

Their meal was simple, but it tasted like nectar after the energetic morning. Very quickly their plates were clean. The other restaurant clients drifted away, as did the afternoon. Far too quickly, it was time to go and wait for their boat.

~~~

The three alighted from the water taxi in age order. Each one cradled slightly differing opinions than when they had first embarked to jet down to Anse Anne.

Willis: he'd learnt his mother could be more adventurous than he had ever imagined. And Jeffrey, his view of him had matured. He had ascertained that Jeffrey's main aim was certainly not to endow his mother with ability in kite surfing. He'd studied the way the man looked at her. His eyes followed every move his mother made. He checked out every part of her body. And him? Was he being used as a stooge to facilitate some plan Jeffrey had cooked up? A plan to teach Mother new 'skills'—definitely not skills that were anything to do with water sports. Did he object? At present, he wasn't too sure. He needed a bit of time to mull that one over.

Jeffrey had done a lot for him. Perhaps he should continue to do so. He'd taken him from Dullsville to Adventure Land. He seemed to be mega rich. His wallet was always chockfull of green ones. And he wasn't frightened of blowing them.

Tamara: her thoughts were confused. As far as Willis was concerned, she believed that she understood why Jeffrey wanted to share his new water sports experiences with her son. She'd believed what he told her about the activities being an escape from his deteriorating home life. She'd always be grateful for Willis' change of direction. As for herself, she had been amazed at learning kite-surfing skills. She was flushed with a new-found confidence, and exhilaration. She felt real good, better than for a long time. She was grateful to Jeffrey for facilitating a chance to do this. To top it all, she wasn't used to being pampered. She didn't think she'd ever been as indulged, as she had that day. She was enjoying it—the whole visit had made her feel special. Perhaps this was turning her full circle. Did she want all of this to continue?

Jeffrey: he felt pleased with himself, he'd had both of them eating out of his hand. He felt the excursion had been a real success. Tamara had lightened up in his presence. She was warming to him. They made a great threesome. He was a large step nearer what he wanted—what he desired for his future. He was enjoying the pursuit, the game, as he had with Miranda. She hadn't been a walk over. But she was more serious—an intellectual. Nevertheless, despite her current state of health, she was proving very useful to him—or rather her money was proving very useful.

Now Tamara, she was something else. She had all the connections and attributes he was looking for. She was bubbly, lively and alluring. Most of all, she made him feel young. All he needed to do was keep showering her with attention and compliments for a bit longer.

~~~

The excursion was coming to an end. Jeffrey felt it was best to end the day on a high note and didn't ask the pair to join him for drinks at the hotel. It didn't seem appropriate, as Tamara worked there. During the drive back, they chatted amicably, replaying the exploits of the day. Jeffrey pulled up outside the apartment block.

'What about a repeat performance next weekend?' he smiled towards Tamara and turned to look at Willis in the back.

Almost immediately Tamara responded. 'That's very kind of you Jeff, but ...'

In the rear-view mirror he saw Willis' face sink. His mother was going to say no. '... but I'll need to check on my work schedule for next weekend. I think I have Saturday free. If that's the case, perhaps we could make it Saturday.'

'Yes,' squealed Willis.

To his surprise, Tamara leaned towards him and lightly kissed him on the cheek. 'Jeff many thanks for today—it was really great. I can't remember when I last enjoyed myself so much. I look forward to another try at kite surfing. I'll let you know about next weekend.'

Willis thrust his open palm forward to slap Jeff's raised hand from the front seat. 'Jeff, it was sensational. Off the scale! Perhaps, you'll be on the beach tomorrow. I'll be there after school.'

'Perhaps Willis, but I've got to get down to work. I need to start marketing Antony's villas. Don't forget though, you can still use the paddle board. Sharing today with you both was something very special to me too.'

~~~

108

As Jeffrey restarted the car, she took in his smile, his head of white hair. The Mercedes slowly glided off the piece of rough ground outside the apartment. She thought about Jeffrey returning to the five stars of Topaz, while she walked down the uneven path to the shabby apartment building. For once, she saw it objectively. She threw open their much-worn front door to the realities of her tiny home—to her life of eking out an existence on a developing Caribbean island.

'Mom, I was really surprised you said yes to next weekend,' Willis admitted.

'Why? We had an awesome time! You know I loved trying the kite surfing. And you were great, taking in all that information first time around. I knew you would want me to say yes.'

'Thanks a lot Mom.' He watched his mother as she went to the small countertop fridge. 'Mom ... you know that Jeffrey has got the hots for you, don't you? He's really struck with you.'

'I think you're imaging things Willis.'

Willis sniggered, 'Mother you only have to open ya eyes! He really wants to ...' he stopped, deciding it was not the best of ideas to say what he would to his mates. '... he's real hot and bothered about you. I've been watching him.'

'Willis would you like a drink?' She poured herself a cold drink from the fridge. 'I think you are fantasising. He only recently remarried.'

'From my limited experience, I'd say that never stopped most red-blooded males' His mother smiled at the observation. 'He may be an oldie, but he's still got the energy of a rocket—you could see that this morning ... and Mother ... his wife is sick ... and it seems she won't be getting any better.'

'Willis, we should not be having this conversation.' Tamara felt it was best to drop the topic right away. 'You're my son. You're not yet fourteen. You shouldn't be talking like this. Now, what about this drink?' Although she denied Jeffrey's interest in her, despite her dissent, she knew Willis was right.

Chapter 11

Diamonds

'You beautiful woman.'

Jeffrey ran his fingers down her cheek, sizing up her smooth coffee-coloured skin, stroking her wild, dark halo of hair. He lightly kissed her full lips again. This time she responded. She put a hand behind his head. She pulled him into a hard and searching kiss. Just for a few seconds, there were sparks of pleasure between them. She held his gaze for a beat. He ran his hand up her bare brown leg. Then the moment was gone. She pushed him away, and he heard a deep sigh pass her lips. She sat bolt upright in the passenger seat.

'Sorry Jeff, I'm not sure I really want this,' Tamara said in soft tones.

'What does that mean? What don't you want?'

'Doing it for five minutes in the back of the car somewhere.' She hung her head, and he noticed the straight line of her mouth.

'What? Quick sex in the car to say thanks for the kite surfing lessons and the lunch? Is that what you really think I want for us?' He'd predicted this. That she wasn't going to be a walk-over.

'It's what ninety-nine per cent of the male population want. They give you something and they expect one hell of a lot more in return,' she told him.

'Tamara, I want us to have a long-term relationship. Not just make out on the back seat and then dump you.' He ran his fingers down her face again. 'Let's get out of the car. Let's walk,' he suggested, unfazed by Tamara's rejection.

She didn't argue. They left the confinement of the car, and stepped out onto the sands, joining the rest of the world: groups of people on sun beds, or occupants of brightly coloured towels, zigzagged along the beach. Jeffrey guided the way towards the damp sand. His ears were assaulted by snatches of conversation in different tongues, and the screeching of children. After removing her shoes, Tamara followed. They needed to find their own private space. He led the way to the shoreline—to the idle waves in a tranquil sea. They left the gregarious, without speaking, without touching. Jeffrey reflected it was better that way. Perhaps sat in the front seats of the car, facing a brick wall and the restaurant bins, had not been the most appropriate place for a romantic tête-à-tête.

At the water's edge, he enjoyed the warm, shallow sea sploshing over his feet. He could see further along the beach there were far fewer people. They needed to find somewhere more conducive to play out the possible scenarios he'd already rehearsed, and his convincing responses. It was essential for him to come out on top in this debate—achieve a positive result. He'd spent a lot of time on Tamara. A lot of time, a great deal of effort and of course, plenty of money—on her, and her son Willis. She'd been the one who'd ticked most of the boxes on his list of requirements. She lived and worked in the right place. She had the contacts that he needed. And most importantly, he judged that she was of the right disposition.

He'd been on island more than three weeks, but the lunch had been the first time they had been alone. On every other occasion, Willis had been there. They had shared the kite surfing sessions. The delight they all gained from the activity stayed between them. On each occasion, they had eaten a casual lunch at the beach café afterwards. But this time, Jeffrey had opted to lunch with Tamara in Anse Argent. It was the same restaurant where Miranda had celebrated her birthday the year before. He'd felt the setting was romantic. The menu was more impressive. Seducing. The atmosphere definitely adult.

Over lunch, their conversation had been easy. They were relaxed together. Jeffrey had told her about his former business in London. About life in the capital. What he wanted her to know about his past—working in the property market. He'd embellished his stories where he'd thought it was necessary to impress. And avoided those that didn't. He gave an update on his progress with selling Antony Denning's villas. All that was explained—establishing an office, organising marketing publicity, on island and internationally. He said with pride he already had some interest in the holiday homes. Tamara knew, from working at the hotel, that one villa was already underway. She'd been keen to hear of his plans.

When it was Tamara's turn, she recounted her life before Topaz. She'd played on the changes she had seen in Willis since meeting Jeffrey; what she hoped for her son's future. Jeffrey had been very happy with the ambience between them.

They found a spot further down the bay. Out of reach of others' hearing. They sat on cool sand, in the shade of vegetation, about a metre apart. There wasn't a word between them for several minutes. Jeffrey guessed that Tamara was assessing the situation, considering the right things to say.

'We've had an amazing time since I've been on island,' Jeffrey said, staring out to sea.

'Yes, I've really enjoyed it, and I know Willis has loved it,' but then she returned to her contemplating, eyes fixed straight ahead of her.

Tamara's mouth pursed into a displeased scowl, 'look Jeffrey, we can't pretend, you're a married man. I've even met your wife for Christ's sake.' He was prepared for this statement.

'Tamara, you saw my wife when she was full of life, sparkly, bubbling over with plans— enthusiastic. She's not like that anymore. Her stroke changed everything. Miranda's a different woman. We no longer have a relationship.'

Still looking out to sea, Tamara smiled to herself. 'Jeffrey, I feel sorry for your wife. I would have thought you'd want to be with her whilst she's ill?'

'Tamara, she doesn't want me near her. I might as well be a lodger in the house.'

'Listen Jeffrey, don't you think I've heard similar lines before? Men who blame their wives. I've encountered so many males who subscribe to the "My wife doesn't understand me" network.' Tamara spoke softly, but firmly. 'Willis' father was one of them. "You're the one I want. I promise I'll look after you." And look what happened!' Her head dropped, so that all she was looking at was her knees. 'I don't know how you really feel about me Jeffrey.'

'We've only known each other for three weeks. But I knew from the first trip down to Anse Anne, you were for me. You're so much fun. You and Willis. We get along. We like one another. We work things out together. It's a great basis for a friendship. I could change your life. You could change mine. Tamara, what do you think?'

'You have changed my life. But that's because you've changed Willis' even more,' her head came up and she turned to give him a smile. 'I'll always be grateful for that. You gave him something to aspire to. I've told you before, he was heading to be one mean, bad boy. You sharing the water sports with him changed all that.'

'I'm real pleased.' Jeffrey gave her a smile, though she wasn't looking his way. 'You know, I'm very fond of Willis.'

'Look Jeffrey, I can't get away from the fact that you've got a wife in England. Frankly, I have a moral problem with you having a sick wife who needs you.'

'You would think Miranda would, but she seems to prefer the company of her live-in carer. I feel very sorry for her,' he said, though these were not the emotions he was truly feeling. 'But Tamara, she made no objections to me coming out to help Antony sell his villas. In fact, I think she was glad to see the back of me.'

She glanced at him disbelievingly.

'I need a new companion,' Jeffrey continued. 'Somebody who wants me with them. Unlike Miranda. It's lonely being just one most of the time. I need someone to share my life with— someone to love.' Jeffrey considered, if she was wavering, the last statement might seal the deal. He supposed she must be, otherwise she'd have upped and gone by now.

They sat. Tamara with her arms around her bent legs. Jeffrey wondering what objection she would come up with next. Several minutes ticked by. He gradually switched off; he listened only to the lapping of the waves, which gradually enveloped his thoughts. Tamara scooped up a handful of sand from next to her and watched it sieve through her fingers. Unexpectedly, she manoeuvred herself in front of him. Held her hands out towards him.

'Let's just try it. Let's see how things progress . . . what have we got to lose?'

'You amazing woman!' He wondered what had made her have second thoughts about a long-term relationship. Could it have been that love word? He grasped her hands. He kissed them both. 'You won't regret it, Tamara. I promise.'

He felt well pleased with himself. He could forget trying to find another candidate. The cost of an extravagant meal hadn't been for nothing.

~ ~ ~

Two weeks later, Jeffrey was scheduled to go back to England. He was returning to Lyme Regis. Back to Miranda and the constraints of her large country house.

The evening before his departure, a taxi picked Tamara up from work. It drove her to the most up-market hotel in Anse Argent harbour. Jeffrey had reserved a table in its fine-dining restaurant, together with a room for them to use for the evening.

It wasn't Tamara's first visit to the hotel. For her, the first visit had been awkward. She'd been ill-at ease, very self-conscious, still anxious. Anxious that the decision she'd made whilst they'd sat on the beach together had been a dreadful mistake. She'd been all smiles, but it wasn't how she really felt inside. That first time, before dinner, Jeffrey had taken her up to a sea view room. Her heart had hammered against her ribs as she ascended in the mirrored elevator. She worked in an up-market hotel, but wasn't accustomed to using their guest facilities herself. It all felt fairly foreign to her. She'd struggled to fully take on board what she was really getting herself into. She kept glancing at Jeffrey and kept asking herself if she really wanted what she knew was coming next. She had to keep focused on her secret decision—the decision she'd made while sat on the beach.

The glass of sparkling wine had been waiting for her. It had helped a little with her nervousness. As she finished sipping her first glass, she'd watched Jeffrey as he'd walked to the wardrobe and brought out a chic white dress on a hanger. He'd insisted she tried it on. She'd not been ready for that and went to change in the bathroom. Almost instantly, she appreciated that she was being naive. Jeffrey had purchased the dress, so he could observe her trying it on. He insisted she stay near him. He'd watched her every move as she'd undressed, then slipped into the satiny dress. Second glasses of sparkling wine were poured; and within a few minutes, she was naked, the dress thrown over a chair.

She had not been surprised by Jeffrey's performance, having seen his unbounded energy during kite surfing. He'd made every effort to make her feel special, but Tamara felt relieved when she was able to slip back inside the dress; and they'd made their way down to the hotel's restaurant. The place was crowded. The clients dressed up. The dress had given her a little confidence. She'd been fazed by the menu, half in Italian. That evening, she'd eaten foods unlike anything she'd ever eaten before. The performance in the hotel room, the exotic atmosphere of the restaurant and the wine had made her feel heady, but thankfully more relaxed. After dinner, back in the room, the dress had come off again.

The evening before Jeffrey's departure, Tamara was not as uneasy about entering the lobby of the same hotel, clad in the same white dress. She knew it suited her; made her look classy. The dress showed off her slim form; displayed her dark skin to advantage. Walking through the revolving door, she was certain that the very same dress would be on a chair in their hotel room within less than five minutes.

Her internal conflict about their affair was starting to subside. She was able to rationalise a freedom from an indoctrinated attitude. Fear instilled into her since childhood. The burden of sin was dispersing. She hadn't been struck by lightning because she had transgressed. The sky hadn't come crashing down on her, as she'd once been led to believe. Guilt was fading. That freedom lifted a heavy weight from her shoulders. The stinging of her conscience was subsiding. Saying 'yes' generated more good than bad. A better future for her, and her son. Company and satisfaction for Jeffrey. She analysed that their relationship created more happiness and contentment all round. How could that be considered a sin?

Tamara's life had changed so much. Her life had left the realms of being humdrum. Life was no longer entirely work, housework and looking after Willis. She was wallowing in a new world. There'd been two more weeks of water sports lessons, trips down the coast. A special celebration for Willis' birthday. Dinners in expensive restaurants. Presents. Jeffrey was treating her well. She'd never before been made to feel so cherished. She and her son were living a life that they'd never experienced before. Best of all, Willis had been transformed from a potential villain to a young man; one who was fired up and positive about life. Things were working out as she'd wanted. All because of her new sexual adventure with a man she knew little about.

Their evening together, before he left the island, had gone well. Dinner was over. Tamara lay next to him on the hotel bed. Jeffrey's lips played over her naked body. Then from nowhere he handed her a small navy-coloured box, tied with a gold bow. Inside, Tamara found a silver tear-drop shaped necklace. Several diamonds glistened. She squealed with delight. Jeffrey placed the pendant around her neck, kissing it as he fastened the clasp. She walked to the long mirror to admire its sparkle, Jeffrey watching every move of her naked form. He told her it was to assure her he'd be back. He would be coming back just for her. Tamara's taxi home was extremely late that night.

~~~

Jeffrey was fortunate that his present to Tamara could not tell its tale. It could not explain it had been worn by Miranda on the evening of her birthday—the night before her stroke. Its broken clasp had been repaired; and the jewellery shop had re-wrapped it in a similar little box to the first time.

~~~

The next day, Willis was already at home when Tamara returned from work. He had spent the previous night with his grandmother.

'Chicken for dinner Willis?' she asked.

'Sure. I saw Mr T today. Just before he left for the airport. He told me he hoped to be back in a couple of weeks. You have a good evening last night Mother?'

'We had dinner at the Harbour Hideaway.' Tamara went to their small fridge and took out the chicken portions. The meat was smothered with spices and set in a dish. Peeling onions came next. Willis stood watching. 'How do you feel about Jeffrey?'

'What do you mean "how do I feel about him?"'

118

'Jeffrey wants to move away from living in a hotel room. He will be trying to find an apartment to rent, so he can be more independent. He wants his work and home to be separate.'

'Holy shit Mother, you're not going to say what I think you're going to say?'

'Willis, I've told you so many times, it's not seemly to swear. It's just not acceptable.'

'Maybe not in your world Mother. But straight up, not a soul bats an eyelid in mine. What were you going to tell me about Jeff?' Willis asked.

'I asked you how you felt about Jeffrey, because he has asked me … us … to go and live with him when he returns.'

'Holy cow, that's what I thought you'd say. That guy don't let the grass grow under his feet. You must get on real well. I like him, sure. But, do I want to be with him twenty-four/seven?'

'It won't be all the time. He will go to work. You will go to school, soon to college. You have your water sports on the beach. You've friends that you kick around with. You won't be together all the time.'

'It's just that … well won't it be a bit difficult? You and him in the next bedroom. Me next door. No, don't think I want that Mother.'

'Willis, you haven't seen the apartment. It won't be a tiny apartment like this one.' Tamara left the vegetables and put down the knife. 'Listen Willis, would it be embarrassing if I were with your father in the next bedroom? You can't have it all. You love the kite surfing lessons, your lunches out, the presents. It isn't me that pays for any of that, is it?'

'No, but Jeff is so much older than you. He's like a grandfather.'

'Willis, you got your paddle boarding and your friends at Topaz. You were over the moon when Jeffrey took you for your first lesson, weren't you? He wasn't a grandfather then.'

'It's just that …' he tossed his head away from her and muttered, '… well it could be embarrassing.'

'You're not a child anymore. You should be able to understand. We've had it hard since you were born. Your father promised to help me out. And his promises were as empty as the wind. Many times, life has been a struggle, a real pain. I've had to work hard, scrimp and save to get you where you are today. Jeffrey can make both our lives a lot easier. I'm not doing this just for me you know.'

'Seems like you've decided anyway Mom,' Willis said into his chest. 'I'm just telling you, I ain't sure it's a good idea.'

Chapter 12

Lyme

They turned into the drive to Oakdale.

Miranda had eyes front, while Katie admired the gardens and the avenue of yew trees. A weak sun tore across the windscreen and slanted onto the extensive lawns, highlighting their emerald hue. The home stood boldly on the top of the slight rise, its stone façade catching the winter's light. Each time Katie drove towards it, she felt as though she was arriving at some luxurious country hotel. Each time, she appreciated the well-tended garden and took in the symmetrical architecture of the residence. Her work there was an experience she didn't want to end. She loved it. It was just so different from the environments most of her patients lived in. She considered herself very lucky to be calling it her temporary home.

Caring for Miranda had lasted so much longer than Katie had initially thought. Her patient had made progress, but not as much as she had hoped. Talking to her family members and friends, it seemed she was far from her original lively, bubbly character. Katie hadn't said so, but from experience, she considered that the stroke had been too extensive for Miranda to completely recover. The affliction had left great holes in her memory. Some days a lot of cajoling was needed to shift her out of her lethargy and depression. It was difficult to motivate her into doing anything. Her patient definitely wasn't ready to be left on her own for long. Jeffrey had stayed around at first. But frankly, he wasn't much help. She could see he played at being the dutiful husband. Her relationship with him proved he was far from dutiful. When he wasn't at Oakdale, which was the majority of the time, Miranda was more at ease.

Katie pulled up in front of the house. Miranda's car was tucked away in the garage gathering dust. She relied on others to

121

ferry her around, as had happened that day with their shopping expedition to Dorchester.

'There you go Miranda. Let's get you and your shopping into the house.' Katie retrieved all her patient's packages which she'd been clasping to her chest, and helped her out of the vehicle.

'Thank you my dear. I'm looking forward to getting these boots off. They're pinching my toes. My feet really give me problems some days,' she said handing over her parcels.

'Yes, we walked quite a way. I'll take these things upstairs for you. Then, I'll go and put the kettle on.'

Miranda relied heavily on others. It was even Katie who unlocked the house and stopped the buzzing of the alarm. She turned to assure herself Miranda had managed the front steps and was following on behind her. She was always the same when returning home, relief would be written all over her face. As usual, she stood stock still surveying her entrance hall, checking on every detail. Katie had learnt she was always happiest there. She'd also learnt it was best to not to fuss over her.

Katie had dutifully taken her to sessions with the occupational therapist and to the gym. But Miranda was still unsure of herself. She'd explained that sometimes her head buzzed and whirled. She frequently felt giddy and wobbly on her feet and found that so difficult to cope with. Katie left Miranda motionless in the hall and bounded up the stairs, carrying the shopping bags. Katie's eyes took several seconds to adjust to the poorly lit main bedroom. The internal shutters blanked out any cheer from the sun's rays. It seemed Miranda wanted it like this—Katie felt this was a reflexion of her state of mind. Hiding in the gloom, meant that she wouldn't have to face up to the realities of the world. Katie lined up the shopping bags on the huge white bed.

Leaving the room of shadows, she sped into her domain next door. Brilliant light blasted through the windows, highlighting every feature of the elegantly decorated space. Katie revelled in the vastness of her room, three or four times larger than the bedrooms in her own apartment. At top speed, all her things were stored away.

Miranda was still in the hall fiddling as Katie descended the stairs. She left her dithering and sped into the kitchen. As well as preparing tea, she took the ingredients she'd need for their evening meal out from the fridge. In moments, she was carrying the tea tray into the sitting room. There was no sign of her patient. Whilst waiting, she prised her phone from her pocket to scan her messages.

'Shit' she muttered under her breath. Her spirits sank.

'*Returning Sunday*' was all one of them said.

It was a message from Jeffrey. He would be back at Oakdale on Sunday. He always stated that he would be arriving a day later than his flight arrived. It gave them the opportunity to meet up the day before. Katie had stood firm that they only ever got together, outside of Oakdale—when she wasn't on duty. They met always at the same hotel—one rather tucked away, in the New Forest.

'Shit,' she repeated. She had been looking forward to a quiet weekend at her friend's flat. If it wasn't for the fact that she really wanted to keep her job in Lyme Regis, she would have e-mailed him back to tell him to sod off. Katie felt she'd landed a gem of a job at Oakdale. Financially, she was much better off. She was able to bank most of her generous wage. The tenant's payment, in her own apartment, paid for her mortgage.

Rather than write what she would have liked to say, she simply replied '*I'll tell Miranda.*'

Miranda appeared in the doorway. She had thrown on a thick old cardigan. Her feet were enveloped in some unflattering, stained sheepskin slippers. The get-up definitely added years on her, but she no longer seemed to care.

'My feet feel better out of those boots. I think they are for the bin,' she declared, flopping wearily into the settee.

123

'Let's give them to the charity shop, shall we? They're too good to just throw out.'

'I don't care what you do with them. They hurt like hell,' she paused, staring in front of her. She seemed to be trying to remember something. 'I can't remember … I can't remember … where I bought them … probably somewhere abroad.'

'It doesn't matter,' Katie told her, 'that's not important. Would you like a slice of the cake you made yesterday?' This was the result of one of the projects Katie had set her.

'It looks very nice, doesn't it? How did I manage to achieve that?' Katie cut two small slices of the low-fat carrot cake and placed them on plates, adding a dessert fork. She had learnt that Miranda would not eat cake without one.

'Mm, seems pretty good, I think you'll enjoy it Miranda,' she sampled a mouthful of the cake's sticky texture, and then held her mobile phone up towards Miranda. 'I've just received an e-mail from Mr Taylor. It seems he will be returning on Sunday.'

Miranda stared at her in silence. At first Katie thought she hadn't understood what she'd said. After several seconds, she asked, 'But why? Why is he coming here?'

'He doesn't say Miranda. It just says, "Returning Sunday".'

'Typical of him … to be as unhelpful as possible. I'm so much better …' she stopped, perhaps assessing that she shouldn't say what she wanted to. Katie was not part of the family.

'I presume he's flying back from Sainte Marie, so he'll have to drive back from Gatwick.' She paused to continue eating her cake. 'Therefore, normally speaking, he should be here sometime mid-afternoon.'

'Well, aren't we the lucky ones?' Miranda said in a flat, sarcastic tone.

'I'm afraid it won't be "we." It's Friday, Jayne will be here first thing tomorrow. I'm off to Bristol.' Jayne was the week-end replacement.

'Yes, I had forgotten. I prefer it when you're here. But I know you deserve some time off.'

In her line of work, Katie had discovered that living with people between the same four walls, it didn't take long for people's facades to crumble. At Oakdale, she'd grasped all too quickly Miranda had little time for her husband, and vice versa. They didn't get on at all well—they slept in separate rooms—neither of them could be bothered with the other. They were always cold and formal in one another's company. Katie had frequently asked herself why on earth they stayed married. She certainly wouldn't, but then she hadn't suffered from a stroke.

Katie had been involved with Jeffrey for some months, only conceding to his sexual advances to keep her very desirable job. She'd soon tired of him, and sure as hell wouldn't want to be in a serious relationship with him. Having weighed up Miranda and Jeffrey's relationship, she lost her initial feelings of guilt about sleeping with her patient's husband. All too quickly, Katie comprehended Miranda's sentiments—Jeffrey was a very selfish soul. He did not play the part of a husband, or even a friend. He was only interested in himself; frequently visiting the gym; spending time on the phone in the study; swimming in the pool; meeting his friends in London, or playing around (having sex with her), and she supposed, other females too.

'I shall be seeing a friend in Bristol,' Katie told her.

This was basically true. But what she didn't explain was that first thing the next morning, she'd now be heading for the New Forest. Visiting her friend would now have to wait until Sunday.

'I'm sure that you'll enjoy yourself my dear and I'll see you again on Monday. What are we going to have for dinner tonight?

'We're having that fish I bought in Lyme, cooked with lemon grass and ginger.'

Katie hadn't responded to the Miranda's first statement. Yes, she would enjoy the meal at the hotel. The restaurant there was always excellent. But as for the rest, she couldn't feel positive about meeting Jeffrey. It had become a grind. She'd much rather see her friend in Bristol.

Saturday morning, Katie arrived rather early in the New Forest. She decided to idle away some time by lunching in Brokenhurst before meeting Jeffrey. She'd done it before, and had enjoyed her window shopping afterwards. She was drawn to the old-fashioned fronts of some of the shops and cafes. She was amused by the occasional wild pony wandering down the main street, creating havoc with the traffic

Her chosen tearoom was buzzing with tourists, but she found herself a seat at a small table squeezed into a corner. Through the large bow-fronted window she was able to watch the world go by. She wallowed in the lively ambience around her, so different from her slow-moving, tranquil world at Oakdale.

Sipping her coffee stopped—she was shaken out of her people-watching—her cup hit the saucer with a clatter. Outside was a figure she recognised. Jeffrey! But it couldn't be. His plane had only set down less than an hour ago. Unblinkingly, she stared. Yes, it was definitely him. There were very few men of his age who had such a full head of curly, longer than average, brilliant white hair. It made him instantly distinguishable.

Katie didn't consider leaving her place to greet him. Jeffrey could get on with his world and she would get on with hers. Instead, she sat spying on her employee; watching as he walked on the opposite pavement beside a younger man. Both were clad in crisp, dark suits. For Katie, that gave another clue that he hadn't just got off a long-haul flight. They were deep in conversation for several minutes, virtually opposite the café. The younger man then put forward his hand to conclude their exchange. Jeffrey walked away from the tearoom. The other man turned into the shop behind him.

Katie tucked the event away, intending to see what she could discover about it later. He had obviously flown into the country the day before, or even earlier. Over lunch, Katie checked on her

126

phone. Yes, the flight from Sainte Marie had landed forty minutes previously, yet here he was in Brokenhurst. It would be impossible for him to get there in that time.

Lunch finished, she checked-out the establishment opposite. It was clearly an estate agent. Looking through the advertised properties in the window, she saw the same suited young man busy on the phone. Jeffrey had obviously been doing some sort of deal with him. She continued her tour of the town and the area. She was certainly in no hurry to meet up with Jeffrey Taylor. Nor was she eager to get into the hotel room. There, she couldn't do as she pleased.

In Beaulieu, it was no surprise to find Jeffrey had already checked into the room. He was working at his computer. As she wheeled her overnight bag into the suite, she noticed two distinct things about him. He didn't look in the slightest bit fatigued after an overnight flight. Whatever was on his computer was not for her eyes. It was promptly closed.

'Hi Babe,' he welcomed. 'It's been too long. I've really missed you. I've been so looking forward to seeing you again.'

'Frankly Jeffrey, it was rather short notice,' she hoped he noted the hint of irritation in her tone. 'I'd organised something else for today, but ...' He took her coat from her and put it over the back of a chair. She failed to finish her sentence, as instantly he forced his mouth over hers. He pushed her up against a wooden post of the bed and ran his hands down her hips and pulled up her skirt.

She sighed with exasperation. Katie would have preferred to take things a little slower. She gently pushed him away. She'd hardly had time to catch her breath after arriving, and he expected her to be taking her clothes off. Didn't the man know anything about romance?

'Let's have a drink first. I'd like to relax after the drive,' she suggested.

'We can do that later. I've missed you so much. You look so tempting.' Where did he get his corny lines from, she thought?

Indignation rose inside her. It was always the same with Jeffrey. He was a manipulator, a dominator. She'd learnt that he thought he could get what he wanted through his charms. Katie thought little of his charms.

The more she learnt about Jeffrey, the less she liked him. Staying in a first-class hotel, eating a superb meal in the restaurant was great at first. However, the novelty had worn off. The excitement had faded. Katie recognised that she'd put herself into an unenviable position. A situation, whereby he could threaten her into ceding to his demands. In hindsight, she guessed that this had been his reasoning for starting the affair in the first place. She was his contact to his wife. She would know who Miranda met, where she went and what she spent her money on. When his wife's mind had still been very confused, Jeffrey had even used her to trick Miranda into signing documents, which eventually gave him power of attorney. She despised him for that.

In the bedroom too, Jeffrey liked to get his own way. Despite his crumby complements, she gave in. It was easier that way. She wanted to keep her job. She wanted an enjoyable evening. Despite her resentment, very soon their clothes were strewn around the room. The last of the afternoon sun streamed through the leaded windows, soaked across the curtained bed, and dappled over the enfolding forms on it.

Duty over, Katie insisted that she was dying of thirst. Once Jeffrey had got his way, it was easier to convince him to go to the bar. Katie sat waiting in the plush interior, enjoying the ambience, and looking forward to her Michelin star meal. It was just a pity the company was so crap.

The first thing he said, as he returned with their drinks, was that they needed a serious talk. He needed Katie to do something for him. Anxiety snarled up her insides. Not again she told herself.

'I want you to get Miranda to sign another document for me. She won't do it if I ask her,' Jeffrey said as he settled himself next to her.

'What type of document?' she said warily. Katie had had enough. She no longer wanted to part of his scheming—to do more of his dirty work.

Jeffrey got straight to the point, 'Miranda has a property in Richmond. I need to re-mortgage it. She needs the money.'

'I don't understand. Why does she need the money?' Disbelief crept over her.

'You live at Oakdale Katie. It's a big house. It gobbles up money. I'm responsible for all the accounts, as you know. She needs money to keep living there; to keep it maintained. I shall be putting all my investments into starting up a business in Sainte Marie, so I can't help out.'

'Hasn't she got other money of her own?' Katie cast a look of distain at him. She didn't like the sound of his plan.

'She has a lot of property, but she needs to release some cash, Babe.' He leaned over from the seat next to her and kissed her on the nose. 'Do you think Miranda could cope with living by herself?'

'Hell no!'

'Well, you know that having a full-time live-in nurse soon gobbles up the money. If you weren't there, I'd have to pay somebody else. So, to keep things going in Lyme, I need to free up some cash.'

'I don't like this,' Katie said. She valued her job, but Jeffrey was getting too much. 'Jeffrey, why don't you explain to her? Why don't you explain you need to sell her place in Richmond? I'm sure she would understand. I know she has lost some of her faculties, but she's far from being a stupid woman.'

'Do be serious.' Jeffrey's face mocked her. 'Would Miranda do anything I suggested? I just don't want to upset her and worry her either.'

That she did not believe. She'd never seen Jeffrey openly show that he cared one iota for his wife. His proposed deceit was asking too much of her.

'No, I don't want to do that,' she declared. She did have some morals. 'Just tell her. Tell her you don't have an alternative.'

'This way, she can keep the rent she gets from it …,' he showed her one of his false smiles, '… and we won't have to sell it. Unfortunately, the rent isn't enough to cover all the growing debts either. It's her care—you know how much that costs each week. And you've just admitted she still needs individual medical attention?'

'Yes, she does, and I'm sure she would hate being in a care home.' Katie knew if she said anything different, she was saying goodbye to her work at Oakdale.

'Then, she needs that money for maintenance of the house and for her carers. I don't see any other way of paying for things. Her incomings don't match her outgoings.' He pulled himself towards her. Took her hand and whispered in her ear, 'If you're a really good girl and help me with this, I might give you a bit of a reward—something to help you buy that villa in Spain.'

She gawped at him. He was descending to open bribery now. The man was too much. Slippery. Detestable.

'I'm going have to think about this Jeffrey.' She hated being pressured like this. She was not going to do as he said every time. She sipped at her rose-pink cocktail, 'by the way, I forgot to ask you how your flight from Sainte Marie was.'

'Long and uneventful.'

'Your flight arrived on time today then?' she probed.

'Oh yes, and then I drove straight here, yearning to feel your luscious body next to mine.'

Katie said nothing. Why was she involved with this creep? Jeffrey Taylor was such a bloody liar—despicable, and a bit scary too.

Chapter 13

Villas

A hostile ocean thundered onto the forlorn sands.

Driftwood scattered the shoreline of the bay. Palms fronds shuddered in the strong gusts of wind above Antony's head. Remnants of a tropical storm swooped around him. It was the hurricane season.

He fought against syrupy mud. Clinging earth pulled heavily on his boots and his progress pulled on his calf muscles. The atmosphere felt thick to breath. It carried the odour of damp earth folded into the marine air. A mist of tiny insects followed his path. The previous day, the rains had descended. A violent storm had stopped work on the construction site. The dark, laden clouds carried on the strong winds had left the island a few hours before. Dawn had brought the sun to burn his skin, forcing perspiration to his forehead, and making his light shirt cling to his back.

Antony was checking for storm damage. His eyes ran over the exterior of the near-completed villa. Its black framed windows appeared to be untouched; as was the wood over the covered terrace. He peered through the large ceiling-high glass, trying to ensure that everything was intact inside.

'Mornin' sir.' He turned to see his site manager approaching.

'Good morning Henrick. Do you have the keys, so I can look over the inside?'

'That was sure some storm last night sir. These low-pitched roofs, they not like this weather. The rain find a tiny hole, and whoosh, the water start runnin' inside.'

Henrick felt inside the pouch attached to his belt and produced a bunch of keys. 'I thinks that the one.' He tried the selected key. The front door opened. Both men removed their filthy boots as the internal flooring had been laid.

'There's some debris on the foundations of villa three. Nothing serious,' Antony said.

'Yeah, I seen that. Seems all OK here boss. I go size up upstairs.' Antony followed behind his worker.

'Oh, my Lord! That real bad Mr Denning,' Henrick called.

The two men stood at the entrance of the large bedroom. Antony was surprised by the state of the wooden floor. Humidity had bowed it upwards in the centre. It has risen about twenty centimetres.

'Got to be re-laid for sure,' Henrick grumbled, 'but suppose it not the end of the world.'

The other rooms seemed unaffected. As they both descended the open wooden staircase, Antony's cell phone rang. Its melody echoed around the empty house.

'Yes Cuthbert,' he answered, '... yes, they've reserved the Surf suite and we have put the children in the one next door,' he paused. '... OK I'll be over in five minutes. I can call her then.' Antony stored away his phone.

'Henrick, I need to get back to the hotel. You'll see to organising some men to get the site cleared, won't you? We're working to a real tight deadline now.'

Back in his office, he was immediately bombarded by a horde of hotel problems. It was sometime before he returned the call to Europe—a call to Ella. Her image on screen told him a story; he could see she was tense.

'Hi Antony. I hear there was a storm last night. Cuthbert filled me in.'

'Apologies Ella,' Antony said, 'I've been rather tied up with problems because of it. I had hoped to contact you earlier. I have to admit, you look rather distressed. Is it Miranda?'

'Yes, I've been trying to contact Jeffrey. I haven't had any luck with his mobile. I presume it's turned off ... I've left him an e-mail.'

'Sorry Ella. I don't see him every day. He's not always in the Real Estate Office. He could be with a client. Let me try his phone.' He picked up his mobile. The number switched through to the message service. 'It's as you said—switched off. What's the problem?'

'I'm afraid Mum may have had another stroke.'

'Hell no. But how? I thought she had somebody living with her full time.'

'She has. It was Mrs Eavis that contacted me. When she went to wake Mum this morning, apparently she was behaving very strangely. Mrs Eavis called 999. Mum is in Dorchester hospital now. Jeffrey needs to fly back home.'

'Lord, I don't know where to start looking for him. You know he doesn't stay at the hotel now. He just comes to work here. It made sense for him to find an apartment. I believe he's near Anse Argent.'

'Yeah, he told me last time he was in the UK. No, I don't understand about Mum. She was doing OK. Not great, but OK. Her memory is a continual problem. She has good days and bad days. And her social skills, some days are non-existent.'

'She must be a real worry for you.' Antony knew how close Ella was to her mother.

'Yeah, it's a good thing I live fairly near, but Mrs Eavis is incredibly good with her. She takes her out as much as possible: for walks, to the shops, cinema and so on. She makes sure she eats the right stuff. Now all of a sudden, this happens.'

'Mmm,' he hesitated, uncertain if he should impart his next piece of information, 'Jeffrey confided that Miranda isn't too enamoured by him anymore. She doesn't seem to bother whether he's there or not.'

'Yeah, there's obviously some sort of problem between them. I really don't know what it is. I've asked Mum, but if there is something, she isn't letting on. But there's lots she doesn't remember. She's told me he was better off doing something positive for you, than moping around in Dorset. And around her, of course.'

Antony watched Ella's face on the computer screen. 'He has done really well out here,' he added. 'In the time that he's been here, he's stirred up a lot of interest and three of the villas are sold. We hope to have two of them completed by December. We'll be able start building a couple more once they are paid for. And Jeffrey, well he also seems to have fingers in other pies on the island.'

'What sort of pies?' Ella asked.

'Oh, all real estate ones I suppose. He doesn't tell me the details ... as I said I don't see him too often. But from what I hear, he's made lots of contacts on the island—on other islands too I believe.' He realised Ella would want to go to see her mother. 'Look Ella, I'm sure that you want to get to the hospital. I'll keep trying Jeffrey's number for you. I'll get him to contact you as soon as possible. And let me know about your mother.'

~ ~ ~

Jeffrey had left his mobile phone at home. It lay on the long contemporary dining table in the apartment he shared with Tamara and Willis. He'd left a newspaper on it to hide it from view. It had been neglected for the day, and work left with it. For Jeffrey, this was a special day. One he'd looked forward to for so long.

Jeffrey had told his new-found family, he wanted them to meet a friend. This was partly true. It was more a business friend. He had inferred that they would all be eating lunch with him at Three Isle Bay. This part of his story was not true. They were all going to see a villa. The villa he had craved for since seeing the plans. The villa he'd told Antony he couldn't afford.

They were all heading for Three Isles. During the short journey, Willis and Jeffrey heard about problem-solving. A task Tamara had been given the previous day as part of her training at the Business School. Jeffrey had suggested she give up her job at Topaz, and discovered she hadn't needed much persuading. The qualifications would mean she could have the security of a much better job and wage.

At the bay, the car park was virtually empty. It was a little early for lunch at the restaurant. The half-moon beach spread out before them, tucked in between gently sloping escarpments. Jeffrey stared out to sea. A view which would soon be his, every day. A little way offshore, three small rocky islands confined the bay. Their stark masses commanded the skyline. Each one topped with smudges of green vegetation. The ocean battered up to them, its murky waters tossing foamy white spray high up against their walls—a remnant of yesterday's storm. On their right, topping off the ridge, a little way in, some contemporary houses were under construction. This was what they had come to see.

'Hey Jeff, why haven't we been here with our kites? Could be good.' Willis asked as he got out of the car.

'Could also be dangerous,' forewarned his mother. 'There's sure to be a load of rocks in the sea. You can tell by all the dark patches.'

'Yupp,' Jeffrey agreed, 'I think this is a bay for paddle boarding and kayaking, in tranquil conditions only. Your Mum's right.'

As they left the car, a tall man, perhaps in his thirties, walked towards them.

'Hi, as punctual as ever,' Jeffrey called to him. 'This is Delan. I've told him all about you both.'

Introductions concluded, Delan looked at his watch and started his charade. 'It's good to meet y'all. It's a little early for lunch. Would ya like to check out one of my prime properties? I'm sure y'all will be impressed by the design. And y'all can see the views are stupendous. Yes sir!'

Jeffrey could see Willis wasn't too keen on the idea. He'd looked the real estate agent up and down as though he was some strange being. Perhaps it was Delan's accent that did it. Willis was under the impression they'd come just for lunch and Jeffrey was sure he'd rather head straight to the restaurant. Tamara, on the other hand, was always polite, and knew Jeffrey would be interested. She would agree.

Delan indicated towards the right hand ridge. 'The show house is just over there. It'll only take a hot minute.' Delan lead the way along the edge of the beach towards the path leading up to the gated community. Around a dozen villas crowned the escarpment. Most seemed completed. The buildings were low and sleek. Mainly white structures, partially clad in strips of timber. Passing through the wrought iron gate and nearing the first home, the layout became clearer. The dividing fences for each plot had not been installed.

'The show house will certainly give ya an idea of the wow factor the homes will have when finished,' Delan led the way onto a covered paved veranda. Large pieces of garden furniture had been installed.

'Wow, look at the pool,' Willis admired the large infinity swimming pool that bordered the terrace.

'Sure is mighty fine,' said Delan.

'And wow, look at that view,' breathed Tamara. 'You're right; it's really something from up here.'

'Yes'm, that sure sells these properties,' Delan started his sales patter. 'These here villas are better than any others on island. They's being snapped up real fast. The view that changes every day, and the continual sound of the ocean, it's what folks just love. Let me give y'all a quick peek inside.' Delan walked towards the wide expanse of glass backing the terrace. He slid back the folding window.

They wandered through the large living area. The place smelt of newness. Fresh paint. Recently polished floors. 'I like the kitchen Delan. The bright blue and white makes a real statement. Do you think the ones at Topaz will be as stunning?' Tamara asked Jeffrey.

'They don't have such a prestigious setting. But sure, the interiors will be as modern,' Jeffrey told her. He was grinning from ear to ear.

They completed their tour of admiration: the spacious bedrooms, tiled bathrooms with state-of-the-art accessories, and a minimalistic kitchen. And to top it all, the magnetic view. All four stepped back out onto the shaded terrace, to be met by a cooling wind.

'So, what do y'all reckon? Pretty cool homes, eh?' Delan beamed at them.

'Real fine,' Tamara said, 'thanks for showing us. Each time I come past Three Isle Bay, I'll now know what the houses are like inside.'

He threw her a smile and then looked towards Jeffrey. He gave him a nod. The agent drew something from his pocket. He put out his hand towards Tamara. 'Here ma'am, this here's for you.' He put a key into her hand. 'I believe y'all be living here in a couple of weeks.'

Tamara stared at him. Then she looked at Jeffrey. Her face was full of confusion. 'I don't understand Delan. I won't be moving in here.'

'Yeah, ya unit will be wrapped up in about ten days ma'am. Mr Taylor has bought the villa for ya both—and Willis of course. He didn't want me to tell y'all straight off. We wanted to give y'all one hell of a surprise.'

Jeffrey watched Tamara's jaw drop. He knew, she couldn't take it in—didn't know what to think. She was silent for several seconds, and then looked directly at Jeffrey again. He nodded slowly; his head filled with joy. 'We're going to live here?' Willis muttered, 'but how?'

'You'll be able to swim in the pool every day. Go paddle boarding in the bay as often as you like. I've bought it for us. For all of us,' Jeffrey said very proudly.

'I'll leave y'all to it then folks. I'll see ya again for sure,' Delan turned and moved away from them.

'But what about lunch?' Willis asked him. 'Aren't we having lunch together?'

'I gotta get back to the office,' Delan admitted. 'I'll leave y'all to celebrate over lunch. The security guard knows that yaz here, so ya can take another looksee around for as long as ya likes.' He proffered his hand towards Tamara. 'Enjoy ya lunch.' He grasped Willis' hand. 'Great to meet y'all. Thanks Jeff. I'll see ya next week.' He made his way down the path to the exit.

~~~

Tamara collapsed into the voluminous cushion on the garden sofa. Her eyes followed Delan as he walked away from them. Her mind in a fog. It seemed best to remain silent, like Willis.

'It's not like you to have nothing to say Willis,' Jeffrey draped his arm around his shoulder. 'Don't you like your future home?'

'I ... I ain't got a clue what to say. I'm all spinning. I can't get my head around it,' Willis confessed.

Jeffrey went to sit next to her. 'Say something Tamara. I thought you would be over the moon.' His tone told her he was expecting more jubilation and gratitude, not her muteness.

'I have bought it for us. It will be ours. Not just mine. It will be in both our names, he said, trying to explain his purchase more fully. 'I have set up a company in both our names to buy it. We need to sign the paperwork next week. The lawyer will explain it all. You've made me so happy. I wanted to show you how much I love you both.'

Tamara lifted her head to scan the view. Its unmistakeable beauty struck her. Jeffrey's words rang around in her head, but her mind was exploding with a hundred and one unanswered questions. Never in a hundred years had she expected this. She'd learnt that living with Jeffrey did have its moments—but this! She was finding it difficult to focus; her mind felt as though it had been struck by lightning. There was a flood of amazement, but also a whisper of uncertainty pushing in as well. She definitely needed time alone to think this all through. But there was one thing she could be certain of. Jeffrey certainly hadn't bought that villa for her, or for Willis. Jeffrey had bought that Hollywood-style villa, with a million-dollar outlook, for Jeffrey.

At last, she found her voice. 'Lord, what have I done to deserve such a wonderful place to live?'

Jeffrey took her face in his hands and kissed her fully on the mouth. The kiss was long. He pulled her to him. She felt his arms encircle her waist. After, Tamara noted that his previously grinning mouth had slipped into a thin, flat line. His eyes had grown cold and drilled into her. A muddled mind she may have, but she knew she had to react. It was expected of her. She had to play her role. She dropped her face onto his chest. All at once, the situation became too difficult to cope with. Her eyes began to glaze over. A large tear started a crooked path down her hot cheek. She was not certain why she was crying.

'Jeff, never in my life did I ever imagine …' she sobbed into his chest. 'I just don't know what to say. You have transformed our lives.' Tamara inwardly sighed and hoped that her performance had given Jeffrey what he'd expected from her.

~~~

Willis was also astonished, and unsure. He watched them in silence, seeking to find some truths, but what he saw only led him to confusion. He saw Jeffrey's hands caress his mother's body, touch her glowing face.

This man, he asked himself, this man with white hair, this man with a lined skin, this man, whom he had lived with, but knew so little about. Jeffrey had given him gifts, taken him out at

140

weekends; and had even taken him to other islands. This man who shared his mother's bed. Who the hell was he? He had appeared into their lives, from nowhere. They knew next to nothing about his past—about his life outside the island. And now this.

A huge villa. How had that happened? Where had the money come from? And how did he feel about it? Was it really what he wanted? His friends didn't live in villas like this. Only rich kids did, like in the movies.

Their entwined forms were mirrored in the backdrop of the villa's huge window. Willis saw he own image. A sharp silhouette observing. He watched and reflected. His mother, the person he knew better than anyone else in the world. What was she truly thinking? Did she really love this guy? Sometimes, he even thought it might be just his bank account that was the attraction. And Jeffrey—a foreigner, a clever foreigner. Did he really love her? Or was he using her; or both of them? He was learning that sometimes life was complicated. He wished he knew the answers.

He looked on and speculated.

Jeffrey grabbed hold of his mother and kissed her fiercely. For a minute or so, they were in their own world. They locked him out. Willis was forgotten. Jeffrey whispered something to his mother. It was inaudible. But he understood it clearly. He knew what Jeffrey planned for later.

Abruptly, Jeffrey left their intimate world. His eyes met those of Willis. He saw him studying them, and flashed a grin towards him.

'You ever drank champagne Willis?' Jeffrey asked, 'I think a bottle is called for.'

Willis didn't reply for a beat. His mind was still churning. But it didn't take him long to make a decision. He punched a fist in the air. 'Yeah!' he shouted jubilantly, 'today'll be a first. You reckon that restaurant got champagne? Let's get to it and find out!' He walked up to Jeffrey and gave him a light hug.

'Jeff … this place is totally off the charts … and the large back bedroom, with the A-1 walk-in shower, has my name on it … OK?' he said excitedly. His hug was returned. 'Ace!'

They ate lunch. Willis drank his first-ever champagne. Back at the apartment, their current home, the home Jeffrey paid for; a phone lay on the table. Another message was being left on its voice mail.

Chapter 14

Change

The folding doors were firmly closed.

The hum of an air conditioner broke the silence. Tamara stood with her back to the sitting room, gazing out—past the shuddering fronds of the palms and over the swimming pool. Three sepia mounds presided over her view—Three Isles. That day, they looked eerie and menacing silhouetted against a bleached sky, stormy, flat, and grey. The sea mirrored the mood. Dark greens, muddy browns, flicked with the white where the water lashed against the isles and the shore.

Tamara recalled what the real estate agent Delan had told them. It had been sales chat, but was true. The landscape from the villa was different every day. The light changed—an inconstant palette of numerous colours. The crashing tones from the sea. Sea birds floating above. She never tired of observing it.

Her eyes focused on the beach. Three young people, made miniature by the distance, were the only people there. Her son and two new-found friends—the children of a Canadian couple who had purchased the villa next door. Willis had promised to teach them how to paddle board. They had not been perturbed by the light rain and they'd all ventured to the shoreline. But the two boards remained on the sand. The waters were too choppy for a novice paddle boarder. Even so, they seemed to be enjoying one another's company.

Her son brought her joy. She'd watched him mature into a lively and intelligent person. Enthusiasm oozed from every pore. His world revolved around water sports, but he loved life in general. Willis' zeal seemed to attract all; and he established a good rapport with most. Tamara felt relief he'd been transformed from the belligerent rebel she had lived with before

Jeffrey had come into her life. Willis had been a bored, truculent adolescent, who'd formerly roamed the streets—drinking, shouting, being aggressive. That Willis had gone. His current friends came to use the pool, or they were boys who were also pumped up by water sports.

Willis' initial doubts about living with Jeffrey had faded. Repeatedly, they shared time together, nearly always in, or on the water. Their heads were frequently together conversing about some aquatic detail or other. Occasionally, she joined them.

Tamara's new job suited her well. In Sainte Marie, who you knew was always more important than what you knew. When her Business College course had finished, a friend had introduced her to the manager of a hotel in Anse Argent. He was recruiting staff. Very soon she'd become his events manager. She'd been over the moon. The job was very demanding, but she loved it. Her wage even gave her enough to buy a second-hand car, albeit in instalments. The events were chiefly weddings—big business in the Caribbean.

At work, she was always confident and lively. She could shine. Work became her distraction, a diversion from her private life. At home, she couldn't always be the same positive and assertive character. When she walked through the front door at Three Isles, she had to don a different garb, particularly if Jeffrey was at home. He had moulded her into what he wanted; what he expected from his partner. He dominated. He called the tunes, as he was the one who paid the bills. Tamara wasn't always happy about her new role, but she learnt to tolerate it. Tolerate it for the sake of Willis.

Bit by bit, Jeffrey's initial attentiveness had faded. The presents dried up; though there were sometimes off-island trips, chiefly when he went away on business. Jeffrey relished exploring the Caribbean, trying to establish contacts in the vacation home construction trade. He seemed to have built up quite an extensive address book. It became obvious to Tamara that his business deals were more important in his life than anything else. But details were never discussed with her. She was only ever given sketchy details of what he was working on.

It was the same with news from England. He went back to see his wife every two or three months. On his return, she was told very little about his visit. She'd been informed that Miranda's health continued to deteriorate after her second stroke. However, her poor health certainly didn't keep Jeffrey away from his work the other side of the Atlantic. Once Tamara and he had started living under the same roof, it had become clear that Jeffrey didn't consider her as someone to talk through life's problems with. Her function was to satisfy his needs, whatever he chose them to be.

From her observation post in the villa, she guessed that the paddle-boarding lesson was at a close. The three figures were attempting to drag a large piece of driftwood across the beach— a remnant from the storm. Their endeavours were short-lived. The wet sand clasped at the branch, making it difficult to displace. She speculated that fairly soon they would be back in the villa wanting drinks or a snack. On turning from the window, the image of the minimalistic style sitting area struck her, as it always did. It was all still a novelty. She lived there, but it was not truly her home. It was not as she would arrange it. There were no family photos on the wall. No little mementos that she'd collected. No bits and pieces belonging to Willis. It was still a show home. Her eyes roamed over the clean lines, the ultra-modern furniture. All was impersonal and clinical, exactly as Jeffrey wanted it.

It was a world away from the apartment she and Willis had shared. That had spoken of their life being a struggle—money always in short supply. Windows framed with cheap net curtains: broken screen door, fabric flowers in a Kilner jar set on a Formica-topped table, clothes in plastic boxes under the beds. She hadn't hesitated to exchange that for life in an interior design magazine setting. She'd always known that was why Jeffrey had selected her. But at least, her old apartment had felt like her home. She headed for the kitchen area and the large American style fridge, very unlike the inadequate under-counter model she'd been used to.

As expected, within minutes the three adolescents were there. They brought with them an atmosphere of chatter, bustle, and smiles.

'Any eats in the cooler Mom?' shouted Willis as he ushered his friends through the door. 'We're all hungry as wolves.' Tamara's peace was over.

'Hi Tammy,' called Madison, 'it seems like paddle boarding could be fun, but Willis advised against it today.' She strode into the room, her long, athletic–looking legs, protruding from denim shorts.

'No, the sea's too rough, we'll perhaps have a go tomorrow. The sea will be calmer then. What you got for us to eat Mom?' Willis asked again.

'I can heat up some patties for you. Okay? There's plenty of drinks though … help yourselves.'

'Thanks Tammy. What's in the patties?' Madison asked in her soft Canadian accent. She held out a glass for Willis to pour her a drink. For her sixteen years, Madison was tall, considerably taller than her elder brother, Nathan.

Tamara couldn't fail to notice that her son was very conscious of the fact that Madison was pretty. He took in every detail of her animated form. He tracked her long blonde hair, tied up high in a ponytail, as it swung from side to side. He took in every word she said, storing every scrap of information— constantly grinning.

'There's beef, potato, onion, and spices. That's about it,' Tamara explained.

'They're real lush,' interrupted Willis, 'yeah please, we'd like some of those.' He picked up his mobile phone from the kitchen work surface and trawled through his e-mails. 'Hey, listen to this. *"Get your carry-all packed Willis. We're going on holiday. Tell your Mom to take a few days off."* Wow! What you reckon Mom?'

'Yes, I got an e-mail too. I can try, but I'm not certain I can get the time off. Jeffrey comes home tomorrow, so, I suppose he means to go away in a few days.' Tamara put the patties onto a baking tray and pushed them into the oven.

'Any idea where you'll be going?' Madison asked.

'Knowing Jeffrey, it'll be something to do with work. Usually is. He's frequently jetting around looking at properties for sale or going to property fairs. If I go as well, he leaves me at the hotel to look after myself.' Tamara didn't want to seem as though she was complaining, so changed the subject. 'What are you planning to do during your vacation?'

'Learn to paddle board,' Nathan joked.

'I've got some schoolwork I need to do. We have exams after the holidays. Other than that, swim, and flop,' Madison sighed.

While they waited for their snacks, Tamara interrogated Madison and Nathan about their plans for the future. Madison bubbled over explaining her interest in becoming a sports instructor, or something to do in sports administration. She explained she wanted to follow a sports management degree. Nathan wasn't as forthcoming.

Willis was all ears. Tamara noticed how intently he listened. His face was animated; eyes gleaming as Madison's soft tones spelt out her master plan, the goals she'd set her sights on. She guessed what was going through his mind. She knew him too well. It was written all over his face. He'd fancy himself heading in similar directions.

Tamara didn't want to shatter any illusions, so said nothing to him in front of his new friends. But the idea bothered her. She didn't want Willis making too many long-term plans—to want the same as Madison—for two years down the line. Tamara had promised she'd see him through college, but as for a degree, she knew her wage wouldn't run to that. Madison's father was a lawyer. Rather different from her meagre managerial job in a country where incomes could be painfully low. Tamara was never sure how long her relationship with Jeffrey would last. Some days were difficult; she'd want to walk out, but she'd learnt to hold her tongue. But without him, their circumstances would dramatically change; even college for Willis might really stretch her financially.

'Hey, look Willis,' said Madison nudging his arm. She pointed towards the bi-folding doors. 'Look, the sun has come out. Look at it glistening on the sea.' The murky tints of the sea had been metamorphosed to gold by the reappearance of sunlight. The glint bounced off the large windows. 'What you say we all go to Anse Argent after lunch. Catch the bus. How's about kayaking? Our treat!'

'But the sea is still choppy,' Nathan said, 'we couldn't learn to paddle board because of it.'

'Where's your backbone Nat?' mocked his sister. 'That'll make it more exciting. Learning a new skill in rough water is different from performing one that you are already skilled at.' She pushed her brother on his chest with both of her hands, scoffing his timidity. 'You can wear a life jacket, can't you?'

Willis smirked at her bravado. As she walked in her bare feet to survey the ocean, his eyes were glued to her image, ponytail swaying behind her. Tamara took it all in. Her son was forsaking his juvenile ways and becoming a man.

~~~

The next afternoon, Jeffrey returned to Three Isles. He hoped the villa was empty. Tamara would be working, but Willis could be around. Wearily he slung his leather bag into the hallway and dragged his suitcase after him.

'I'm home.'

There was no response. He listened to the silence. He made directly for the main bedroom and flung the case on top of the neatly made bed. He returned to pick up his hold all and lined that up next to the case.

'Willis, are you in?'

He marched to the back of the villa, wanting to do a double check, and tapped on the bedroom door.

'Hi Willis.'

The room made no answer; silence still hung around him. Wanting to be a hundred per cent certain, he peered around the door. The usual clutter of clothes confronted him; belongings nonchalantly thrown down after use. A body board propped against the wall, an unmade bed, but no Willis. Satisfied, Jeffrey returned to the main bedroom.

Jeffrey flung open the glazed door onto the veranda. The ocean's music invaded the space, accompanied by a chorus of sea birds' cries. Jeffrey was fond of the roar of the sea, but that day didn't have time to relish it. He may have been tired, but he worked like a man in a hurry emptying his luggage. Garments, shoes, socks, and toiletry items were tossed out indiscriminately across the wide bed. From the very base of his cabin bag, he withdrew a bulging brown envelope. He placed it precisely on the bedside cabinet. The enactment was repeated with the suitcase. He tossed out more crumpled clothing, the pile mounting up around the cases. A second brown package joined the first. As Jeffrey emptied his wallet and pockets, and placed the contents into a third brown envelope, a satisfied smile flicked over his face.

Working in double quick time, Jeffrey opened the wardrobe door, snatched out several shoe boxes and stacked them on the woollen rug. A small security box was revealed in the floor. He punched in a code. Door open. All three packages were rammed into the safe. He heard a thud as the safe door hit the metal of the frame. Handle locked. Secrets tightly hidden. Shoe boxes were stashed back on top. His empty leather bag was rapidly stowed over the shoe boxes. Wardrobe door slid shut. It was a performance he has acted out before. He blew out a lungful of pent-up breath.

Despite the cool breeze accessing the room, Jeffrey felt warm. His hands mopped at the sweat trickling down his neck. He felt exhausted after the flight. Exhausted, but satisfied. He'd done it again. He'd succeeded again. All good so far. The packages stowed away, he could work at a slower pace. He grabbed at some of the garments stacked up on the bed, entered the bathroom and pitched the creased and dirty clothing into the laundry basket. Jeffrey caught his reflexion in the floor-length mirror and perceived his soiled shirt. Quickly, it was peeled over his head and joined the other laundry. The mirror saw him smile to himself. Back in the bedroom, he raked through the remaining clothes until he came across his swimming shorts.

Clad in swim wear, Jeffrey picked up his phone from the remaining clutter; and stood momentarily enjoying the coolness from the open window. His eyes narrowed to a squint with the glare. He was not inclined to appreciate the magnificent view— the isles emerging crisply and clearly from the grey blue seascape, the harsh sunlight illuminating their green crowns. Jeffrey didn't have time to waste on the vista. There was something more important to do.

Settled in the wicker effect armchair, he scrolled through his phone, neglecting to check his messages. He hit the dial button.

'Hi Herman, it's Jeffrey, yeah Jeffrey Taylor … I'm doing great. Can you do me another five hundred of those pamphlets? … Yup, exactly the same. Yes, I'm real busy … I need them on the double. Quick as you can! … Tuesday. That's amazing. Same price as last time? … You're a wonderful guy. I'll see you then.' He ended the call. Left the comfort of the chair and laid his phone on the glass top of the garden table.

Without hesitation, he dived into the turquoise of the pool and blew out the contents of his mouth as he came to the surface. Jeffrey started to thrash the length of the infinity pool, tearing at the water with each stroke. Ripped and clawed at it as if he were attacking his worst enemy. The end wall was kicked violently to change direction. Up and down, up and down the pool with force. The sun smacked at his head of white hair. Having beaten up his pool for a good ten minutes, he pulled himself out. Jeffrey sat on the edge drying off in the intense afternoon heat.

His aggressions and tensions left in the pool, he headed back to the armchair; sank slowly into the large, spongy cushion and picked up his phone again. He tapped in a short message. The appliance pinged as he sent it.

'Hi Babe. Hurry home, my beautiful woman.'

Chapter 15

Airports

'Come on Willis, shift yourself.'

Jeffrey called gruffly down the corridor, 'we're only going for seven days. You won't need too much.'

The door to Willis' bedroom opened. He exited carrying his sports bag and a backpack.

'That plane isn't going to hang around for us,' Jeffrey complained. Tamara asked herself why he was irritable, but there was no way she was going to ask him.

'We've got plenty of time Jeff,' she said trying to smooth over the situation. 'And anyway, you know the local airlines never run to schedule.' Tamara stood by her small wheelie suitcase.

Jeffrey picked up a package from the kitchen work surface. A colourful brochure was taped to the front of it. Printed on the front were photos of contemporary homes against a strong blue background. Jeffrey's name was superimposed over them in bold yellow letters.

'Can you push those in your carry-on bag please Willis? I'll go over my weight limit if I put them in my hand luggage.' He handed the package to Willis.

'Sure,' Willis shoved them into his burgundy-coloured backpack and zipped up the front.

'Got your waterproof and that book I bought you?' Jeffrey enquired. 'We might need that.'

Willis nodded. Tamara spotted he was put out at being treated like some little kid. 'In here,' he indicated towards his sports bag.

'Right, let's go. Don't want to arrive at the last minute,' ordered Jeffrey.

Tamara started to wheel her suitcase in the direction of the front door. 'Which book is that?' she asked, making another attempt at lightening up the atmosphere.

'Just a guidebook I ordered from the States,' he replied briskly. They were ushered outside and locked the front door with a very firm action. Willis and his mother took their luggage to the car. Tamara had gauged Jeffrey was stressed. She supposed he thought they might be late for their flight. Or perhaps she had said something he objected to—though she couldn't think what. She considered it was best to say nothing and just let him simmer down on the journey to the airport.

'You like me to drive?' she asked helpfully.

'No. Let's go.'

They arrived at the airport in with plenty of time, but Jeffrey was still in a mood. The journey had been a subdued one. Willis had made a few occasional comments. Tamara very little. To her, the ambience was so unlike people who were supposed to be going away for a good time. She had fought hard to get the time off work and really wanted to enjoy herself.

'Good morning, Mr Taylor,' the airline representative welcomed them as they reached the check-in desk. 'Are you off on another business trip? Going to Barbados?' She grinned cheerfully.

'No, this time it's a holiday. My family are coming with me. We are just changing planes in Barbados.'

Tamara stared at Jeffrey. The term 'family' was new to her, but she was aware he was prone to saying things for effect. Presumably, that had been said for the benefit of the young lady behind the check-in desk.

'Oh yes, I can see now. 'Their tickets and passports scrutinised; Jeffrey placed the first of the cases on the conveyer belt next to the attendant.

'That's terrific!' she said, 'wish I could join you. Well, you all have a great vacation.'

'Willis, like me, is a bit of a water baby,' Jeffrey explained. 'We're hoping to enjoy some snorkelling and surfing. Tell me, do we have to check in our luggage again in Barbados? Or is it checked through to our final destination?'

'Oh yes, it's checked straight through. There's no need to worry about any of that. You have to wait in the Barbados transfer lounge until your next flight.' She folded an identification label onto the handle of Jeffrey's suitcase. Tamara noted his gaze followed its progression along the conveyer belt, then out of sight behind the dark, flexible screen. Their other hold baggage was sent in the same direction, each piece scrutinised by Jeffrey.

'Your flight will be called in around forty minutes Mr Taylor. As you know, you can then go through security to the departure lounge. Let's hope those foreign waters are welcoming for you water babies.' She passed Willis a sunny glance. 'Have an extra cool time. Think of me working my fingers to the bone every day at the airport.'

'Sure will,' responded Willis.

The experience of air travel was still a novelty for Tamara and Willis. She was prepared to sit patiently and uncommunicatively next to Jeffrey awaiting their call. But not Willis. He wanted to investigate the few facilities in the small waiting area. Firstly, he went to converse with the person behind the currency exchange desk.

He returned to interrogate Jeffrey. 'We got some of the right currency Jeff?'

'Yes, I've American dollars.'

'But …' queried Willis.

'I know, Panama has its own currency, just like Sainte Marie, but US dollars are legal tender there too,' he snapped.

Willis' glance was diverted to Tamara. He looked at her quizzically, as if to say, 'What did I say wrong?' She raised her eyebrows and twisted her mouth. Willis was off again. This time, he sized up the magazine stall. He stood poring through most of the magazines on display—the agitated sales assistant studying his every move.

Willis returned. 'You got any loose change Mom? There's a magazine I'd like to have to read during the flight.'

Ordinarily, Jeffrey, who was never strapped for cash, would happily put his hand in his pocket. Instead, he spoke quickly and snappily, 'can't you just sit down Willis? Our flight will be called soon.'

'How much is it, Willis?' Tamara asked, ignoring Jeffrey's remark.

'Eight dollars.'

His mother handed him a note.

'Thanks a bundle Mom,' he pocketed the money. The magazine stall called him back.

'Why doesn't he just stop fussing around?' Jeffrey asked in an attacking tone.

Tamara glanced sidewards. What was up with the man? He was as keyed up as a chased mouse. Jeffrey was not his usual self. She'd not know him jittery about flying before. Unfortunately, the sense of agitation became contagious. Because he was like that, she started to feel uptight herself. She so wanted to enjoy their time away, but so far, things sure as hell weren't buzzing. A feeling of uneasiness soared through her— her stomach churning, her chest felt tight.

'Are you okay Jeff?' she chose a light, bright holiday-style voice to ask. 'You seem rather agitated with Willis. He's just a bit excited about the vacation. He's never travelled so far before.' She squeezed his hand.

'Yeah, I just slept badly that's all,' Jeffrey did not return the squeeze.

Tamara realised from her limited travelling with Jeffrey that Sainte Marie airport was tiny. All the modern security equipment had been installed like any other, but what was different there—

155

so different from the huge international airports—was the staff. This was Sainte Marie, and as with most of the population, they were amicable and chatty. That day, they were having a great time talking about the cricket match scheduled for the following week on island. She gaped at Jeffrey who momentarily joined their party. He dumped his previous mood and chipped in, professing to being a big fan of 'The Windies'. He even joked about who was going to get thrashed in the match. Tamara took this all in. As far as she knew Jeffrey wasn't keen on cricket and he was only joking around to draw attention to himself. She wished they'd stop the wise cracks about sodding cricket, so they could get through into the departure lounge. Her heart was beating so fast, she felt sure she had guilt written all over her face, and they would get stopped by security. But they weren't, and conversation about cricket carried on. Once through security, she thought she noticed a hint of a smile on Jeffrey's face. This made Tamara even more suspicious.

In the departure lounge, Jeffrey's improved temper led him to the tiny bar. He ordered himself and his 'family' a drink. Tamara was pleased to sit and allow her heart to get back to its normal pace.

~~~

Their arrival in Panama City would be one that would stay with Willis for some time. The weather demons fanfared their arrival. As they landed, the heavens opened. Thunder clapped. Lightning dazzled eyes. The rain was torrential, bringing an early dusk. With all the push and shove of descending from the plane, and waiting to board the terminal bus, they were drenched before they reached the arrivals area. Uncharacteristically, Jeffrey laughed at their sodden state. They jostled through the airport heading for the baggage collection area. But the airport shops' displays were a magnet for Willis. He was enchanted by their sparkle and bling.

156

'Hey, look at that Mom! That's really something. Love the shirt!'

'Let's get our baggage first Willis. The shopping is for another time,' Jeffrey pulled him away from a couturier label exhibit.

'Bags first, and then a taxi to the hotel.'

The taxi stand was swamped with local cab drivers all greedy for fares. Willis guessed that all three of them must have had tourist stamped all over them and were likely game. They were approached by a stocky driver, who in the blink of an eye, snatched for his mother's case. He sensed her confusion.

'We must take a yellow cab,' Willis dictated as they followed the cab driver, still clutching the case. The driver stopped beside a large grey 4X4 and placed the suitcase next to it to unlock the vehicle.

'No, it's got to be a yellow cab. Not this one,' Willis insisted. He grabbed his mother's case and started to walk away. 'The yellow ones are the only official drivers. The other drivers can rip you off.' The irritated driver shouted something in Spanish none of them understood.

'There's one,' Willis pointed out. Tamara looked at Jeffrey, raised her shoulders and they both followed on obediently. Willis took this to mean that he was in charge of the taxi situation. Porting his sports bag over his shoulder, he headed for the line of waiting cars. The disgruntled taxi driver chased after them, proclaiming loudly in Spanish. He was ignored by all.

'Hola,' Willis greeted the driver of a yellow taxi. 'How much to go to Calle Este?'

'Hola, Calle Este, thirty dollars.'

'That's OK. Is it OK by you Jeff? You have to agree the fare before you start.'

'I'm impressed Willis. Somebody actually read the travel guide which I bought. Great! I'm so pleased.' Jeffrey put one arm over Willis' shoulder, then ruffled his damp hair. Wide grins spread across both their faces.

The yellow cab sped away from the airport. Soon they were into four-lane traffic. Clouds of rain concealed any view of the city, until a streak of lightning gave them a momentary glimpse. In a flash, Willis caught sight of contemporary, smart show rooms and commercial outlets alongside the freeway.

'Man, this is really something' he gasped, his face glued to the car window. 'Look at all those cars Mom.' The highway was hugely different from the poorly maintained roads back home.

The rain teemed down, smashing onto the roof of the taxi, making it even difficult to hear the music on the radio. Windscreen wipers raced. The roads became awash— metamorphosed into rivers. A deluge of rainwater gushed from the guttering alongside the route. The cityscape was fleetingly lit up by streaks of electric charge, giving a flickering effect, like in old movies. Then all was black. Willis was the first to catch sight of the skyscrapers. Colossal fingers, dotted with tiny lights, grasping upwards.

'Wow Jeff, my first skyscrapers. That's a feast for the eyes. This visit is going to be really cool.'

The storm had made the taxi ride a difficult one. The driver had had to stop for several minutes because of the unbelievable force of the rain. Despite all this, Willis was enthralled. His excitement was amplified when they arrived at their high-rise hotel.

~~~

Tamara did not share her son's emotions. Privately, she sighed with relief when they reached the haven of their rooms. Concern about Jeffrey's behaviour had dragged her down. He still seemed a little edgy with her.

Almost as soon as the luggage was deposited in their contemporary sleek suite, Jeffrey left. Left making an excuse to go down the corridor—to check on Willis. He returned clutching his package of pamphlets and the travel guide. Trying to ignore him, Tamara busied herself. She didn't want to have to analyse what she thought was happening, what she thought Jeffrey was up to. She started taking a few things out of her case, whilst surreptitiously following his movements. Without comment, he went to the wardrobe, and punched a code into the door of the room safe. In an instant, the two parcels of flyers and the book were locked inside. She scrutinised everything he did.

Tamara felt tired. Tired, but also stressed and resentful that their vacation had started so badly. Bewilderment was then added to her list of concerns. Why did Jeffrey do that? Why put flyers in the safe? What was happening here? Jeffrey had not been all that approachable during the whole journey. She knew of old though, she was not expected to make any comment. Throughout her unpacking, she eyed up what her partner was doing. His activities at the wardrobe complete, Jeffrey stood weighing up the view from their fifteenth story window.

'Mmm ... quite a view from here!' he said, 'A great mass of illuminated skyscrapers.'

Tamara guessed it would be her turn next. She was right. He grabbed her from behind and planted a kiss on the back of her neck. 'I'll go and get Willis. Wasn't he great at the airport?' She was surprised by the lightness of his voice. Perhaps his unsociable mood had lifted.

Jeffrey pulled her around to face him and ran his hands down her body. His kisses became passionate, but Tamara's body couldn't relax into his. She didn't throw her arms around his neck. She was too busy thinking of other things; and remained silent. Jeffrey didn't even seem to notice her lack of interest. Her lips received his kiss, but behind her closed eyelids, her thoughts were escaping to the realms of doubt, the realms of suspicion. They were clicking through the unfamiliar images, the illogical little episodes that she had experienced during their journey.

Jeffrey's displays of agitation. Odd expressions which had flashed across his face. They all bothered her.

Jeffrey held her face between his hands, 'you beautiful creature,' he kissed her again. 'I look forward to later.'

He clutched her hand. 'Let's go. Let's go and get Willis. I think we all deserve a large drink,' Jeffrey beamed at her. The words that Tamara wanted to utter stuck in her throat; instead, she forced her lips into a curve. Despite the halo of uncertainty which hung over her, she made an effort to become someone beautiful for him to wear on his arm. The false smile remained during drinks in the bar and throughout the gourmet dinner at the twentieth-floor restaurant.

Chapter 16

Vacation?

Tamara needed to know.

There was urgency inside her. She needed to get rid of her mounting alarm.

Dinner was over. Willis' vivacity had kept the conversation going through three courses. Jeffrey and she had returned to the huge hotel bed in their room, fifteen stories up. Outside the sheet glass windows, the sky was inky black, splashed with a myriad of lights from surrounding skyscrapers.

She lay naked next to him. He was raring to go. Kissing her deeply, and clasping her to him, entwining his body to hers. But, passion did not rise in her body, her mind was still whirling. She felt cold towards the man clinging to her. She felt the creep of his hands over her skin. Her eyes focused on his lined face, his closed eyes locking out the world. She could not enter his domain of lust.

Tamara recognised she was expected to play her part—be there for his needs. But she couldn't erase the images of Jeffrey at the airport. His nervousness that had left her feeling agitated. His edginess and snappy attitude towards Willis. Dashing to secrete packages in the room safe. She'd had enough! She needed to know what the hell was going on. Tamara had convinced herself that Willis and she were being used as a cover for something.

Tamara wanted to scream at him. Tell him to stop, but the words were only in her head. She turned her face away from his kisses; and the wetness of his mouth left a trail clinging to her cheek. Determinedly, he pushed her head back with strength, so that he could continue his kissing and fondling. Her heart jumped in her chest; she must find the courage to confront him.

'Stop,' she tried again, as his mouth moved to her breasts. This time her voice was audible. She recoiled from his touch. But Jeffrey didn't seem to notice. He did not stop. He had her pinned to the bed. Determination strengthened her. She struggled to try and push away from his demands. When she was ignored again, she beat his back with her fists; disentangled one leg from his.

She became very conscious of his power and weight on her— very aware that she was helpless. A pawn to his will. He dominated her like a lord and master. She knew of old; her role was to be the compliant lover; but this time, Tamara wasn't going to act out her part. She swallowed hard. Rallying all the strength she could, she pushed at his shoulders. Jeffrey moved away slightly.

'Stop, no,' she cried, and broke away from his grip, but continued the hammering on his back. She was about to start kicking with her free leg when he actually paused.

'Please Jeff,' she said catching her breath. 'I need to talk to you. It's important.'

'Later Tammy, after,' his feelings were transparent from the scowl on his face.

'No,' she yelled again. Her distress had become insupportable. Tension rose inside, and with all her strength, she pushed him well away from her. Her vigour sent her backwards across the bed. She snatched onto the bedding to prevent herself falling. In a flash, she manoeuvred herself onto the tiled floor. As she stood facing him, Tamara gasped with relief to be out of his control.

'What?' he groaned, propping his head in a hand. Jeffrey didn't hide his annoyance. But she was annoyed too. He had been prepared to use his strength to dominate her.

'I didn't like that. I asked you to stop. You tried to bully me into having sex. Forcing me, using your strength to make me,' she said accusingly.

162

'Shit Tammy. I was all turned on. Of course I'm hacked off.' He threw himself flat on the bed. 'What do you expect? I'm a normal red-blooded male.'

'I expect some consideration, a bit of respect. I asked you to stop. I meant it.'

'Bloody hell, you never asked me to stop before. What's up Tammy, tell me. What the hell's the matter?' he growled in displeasure.

'I need to know. I need to know why we're together. What my role is for you. Why me? Why me and Willis?'

'Christ Almighty. I don't understand. Now you're really pissing me off. You stopped me midstream for that. You're not pregnant are you?'

'No. No, I'm not,' she looked him directly in the eyes. 'What are you doing Jeff? I need to know. Is there some hidden agenda here? Are you using Willis and me? Are we your cover? A cover for something that you are doing. Something you shouldn't be doing,' she blurted out. 'Why are we here?'

Jeffrey pondered momentarily, and then inhaled deeply. 'Why are we here? Shit, what's wrong with you Tamara? We're supposed to be on vacation,' he thumped the bed with his fist. 'I thought that you and Willis would like to see somewhere different. Widen your world. Willis seems to be enjoying the experience. I thought you would too.'

He pulled himself to sit on the edge of the bed as he suppressed another sigh. 'I was also eager to see Panama myself. The economy is growing really fast here.' He paused; and she saw him force a smile across his face. He put both hands forward to invite her to come towards him. His invitation didn't tempt her.

'And why you? Babe, just look at yourself. Go look at yourself in that long mirror.' His manner softened, but Tamara didn't move. She remained facing him, feeling the cool draught

163

of the air conditioning on her back. She knew what she looked like. She didn't need to look in any bloody mirror.

'I've told you before, I returned to Sainte Marie for you, nobody else. You're everything a man could want,' he continued, 'plus you have a great son who is as crazy about water sports as I am.' He gently drew her towards him and ran a finger gently across her lips.

Her confidence was faltering, and asked herself if she was seeing everything through a distorted lens. Was her imagination getting the better of her? It was clear his patience was wearing thin—to upset him too much was unwise. They had the visit to get through; and there was Willis to think about too.

'But the nervousness,' she said in a soft tone. 'You were as anxious as a turkey at Christmas when we went through security at the airport. And man, it was contagious; you even got me feeling all strung up too. I'm still strung up now.'

He kissed her gently. 'You imagined all of that Tammy. I don't do nervous.'

She was not going to contradict him, but knew this just wasn't true. 'But, the packages,' she insisted, 'the ones you gave to Willis. They aren't drugs?'

Jeffrey's eyes widened.

'No Tammy, they don't contain drugs,' he laughed at her, 'you've too active an imagination.' Jeffrey reached forward and cupped her face in his hands, then ran his fingers down the side of her face.

Tamara could have screamed all sorts of accusations at him, but didn't. She didn't want to get into a stand-up row.

'How can you think that of me? Would I put you and Willis in danger?' Tamara searched intently in his eyes. She noted the silkiness to his voice; she detected a hint of insincerity in it. He leaned forward to kiss a breast. 'There are no hidden agendas here, you should know that.' Tamara was certain she did not know that.

He pulled her between his open thighs and ran his hand down her spine. 'They are just as I've told you. Advertising flyers. I've told you, this country is developing fast. There's a lot of money here. Some inhabitants can now afford to buy homes abroad—in beautiful places like Sainte Marie.'

Tamara laid her head on his shoulder to avoid his eyes and thought for several seconds. She could see the logic in what he was saying, but was far from convinced.

'I don't want Willis mixed up with drugs,' she muttered, her courage waning even more.

'Too dammed right. I don't want him mixed up with drugs either. I love that boy,' Jeffrey said loudly. 'And think Tammy, I'd be taking drugs out of here, not bringing them in. You must have seen on the news, there's been a big crack down here. Things are not like they used to be. They've had a massive clean-up.' His mouth twisted into a smile. 'It's pamphlets Tammy, just flyers. I need them for a meeting I've arranged. I think you've been watching too many crime movies.'

'No, I haven't,' she said sharply, and smacked at his pale tanned body only half in jest. He encompassed her in his arms.

'You know what, you worry too much.'

'No, I get concerned about Willis. He's very precious to me,' she admitted.

'I know that Tammy.' He put his lips to her cheek and whispered, 'Can we get back to what we were doing? Come back to me Babe and make me happy. I want us both to go to sleep content tonight.' He guided her back on the crumpled bed cover.

Tamara complied reluctantly; sure she at least wouldn't sleep content that night. But she'd made her point and couldn't rock the boat anymore. For the time being, she'd go back to playing her role. With their first kisses, she decided she would definitely ask to see inside the brown parcels the following day. She heard Jeffrey sigh yet again as he pulled her closer. All too soon she was trying hard to forget the huge deluxe suite around her, Willis at the end of the corridor, and the sound of traffic far below. It wasn't easy.

~~~

Tamara awoke to find she was alone.

There was no sign of Jeffrey. The clock on the television screen told her that she'd slept in late. She bounced out of bed and dashed to the shower for a speedy wash. Rapidly, she went to select clothes from the wardrobe. Moving them along the rail, something shiny caught her eye. It was the silver buttons on the safety deposit box. Her decision of the previous night tumbled back to her. She turned to check she was still alone in the room. Cautiously, her index finger lightly touched the door. It moved slightly. Carefully, she pulled the door towards her. She stared in disbelief: the safe was empty, totally empty. She was too late. Jeffrey had already taken his packages to go to his meeting. She'd missed her opportunity. She could hardly ask him to show her over breakfast.

~~~

Willis was confused.

In the dining room, he walked slowly past the hotel buffet, weighing it up for his breakfast. He lifted up each of the silver-coloured cloches over the hot dishes. There wasn't much there that he was accustomed to. He's seen that there was a chef frying eggs, but where were the sausages. Where were the floats? Who eats stewed minced beef, meat turnovers, dough pancakes with corn rice for breakfast anyway? Corn tortillas or maple owners— what on earth was that?

He was startled as Jeffrey gripped at his shoulder. 'So, what are you going to try? Don't you think it all looks exciting?' Jeffrey jested. He was dressed in a short-sleeved shirt and tie; and was carrying a small case.

'Mmm, well …' was all Willis could muster. He screwed up his face.

'You have to think of it as all part of the adventure of travelling Willis? Your tongue gets to wrap around new exotic flavours. The food of a country tells you a something about the country's history and culture.'

'Suppose so …' but Willis wasn't convinced. He was still in a dilemma. His stomach told him he needed to pack away a huge plate full of something really tasty. Trouble was, he couldn't immediately see anything on the buffet that, in his opinion, fitted that criterion.

'Willis I'm just off to a business meeting. Hopefully, it'll only be brief. I should be back in a couple of hours. Can you keep your Mum company until then? I'm sure she'll be down in a minute. After breakfast you could go and weigh up the swimming pool on the roof. We're off to see the canal this afternoon.'

'Great!' Having read about the canal in the guidebook, Willis was eager to see it. 'Yeah, I can do that.' He sneaked another look towards the buffet. 'Jeff, what on earth are maple owners?'

'Not the faintest. It's probably a bad translation. Just go and try them and then you'll know.' He left an undecided Willis still standing alongside the breakfast buffet.

~~~

Downstairs in the lobby, a driver was waiting for him. The city traffic was gruesome, bumper to bumper. The car advanced at a snail's pace. There seemed to be lanes of thousands of irate drivers all in a hurry to go places. Every few minutes, there was an eruption of cars sounding their horns. But Jeffrey was too occupied in the back of the car to heed any of that, or the cityscape they were crawling past. He failed to see the confusion of buildings; glass fronted skyscrapers and ultra-modern, smart shops, alongside derelict ancient residences. He was also blind to

167

the pedestrians the other side of the tinted windows, proceeding along the uneven pavements. Most of the time, their progress was faster than the courtesy car.

On his knees, his case was open, packages unwrapped. Crisp grey and rose notes being withdrawn from each flyer. The glances, cast from the mirror by the disbelieving driver, were ignored. He worked at haste, transferring the notes to a large brown envelope. After checking each one, the flyers were slung into another. At the end of their crawling journey, Jeffrey was prepared for his meeting.

Around twenty minutes later, the car stopped. A doorman rushed to open the car door for him. Jeffrey stepped out confidently, thanking the driver. He looked up at the front of a grey mirrored building. It rose skywards. Numerous storeys glinted in the golden sunlight. A large plate door was thrown wide for his entrance as he mounted the shallow tiled steps. He felt himself swell up with pride as he walked into the state of the art, shiny interior. He had been making plans for this visit for some time. Everything had gone so very smoothly, all because he was just so damn clever.

An hour later, the meeting over, he left the air-conditioned comfort of the high-rise tower. Jeffrey declined the driver's offer to drive him back to the hotel. He preferred to walk the short distance alone, to wallow in his success. He was alight with pride and triumph. Jeffrey was on a high. The steep, broken, irregular pavements, the poverty of some of the buildings, or the traffic which continued to creep noisily along the congested city roads, barely registered. He passed the chaos of enormous contemporary constructions, which were sited alongside antiquated Spanish style creations.

After several minutes walking, he came upon the shell of a building, with scaffolding supporting the crumbling ancient façade. By its architecture, it appeared to be of eighteenth century origin. Jeffrey paused next to the jacked-up archway of a window. The structure was a desolate shell. Inside were mounds of bricks and rotting pieces of timber, all blackened by the tropical climate. It appeared that the premises were to be restored, but there was no sign of any recent work, or workers. He balanced his case on the disintegrating brick work and scanned around him. His head turned left then right. No one seemed to be paying him particular attention. Rapidly, he opened the clasp and extracted a large envelope. His fist pulled out a bundle of coloured papers. They fell, fluttering inside the old building, covering the years of decay. The envelope followed inside the squalid interior.

~~~

Out of his sight, one sheet of paper floated to the ground, next to his feet. In his haste to leave, the single piece of paper was left unnoticed on the pavement. A flyer covered in coloured photographs that bore the name Jeffrey Taylor in bright, bold yellow letters across the top. It was soon trodden underfoot; torn by passing, unknowing feet. Before long, it became indistinguishable from the other scraps of litter scattered along the bustling street.

Chapter 17

Hassle

It happened!

Emmalyn lost her job. Monday morning, she went into the office as usual. Mrs Leon greeted her, but said little else. She was sat in front of her computer, just fiddling. After several minutes she stopped. Emmalyn sensed something was wrong.

'I'm sorry, but ...' Mrs Leon started. Emmalyn guessed instantly what was coming next. '... I've kept you on as long as I could ... and I know you sold a town house last week, but ... I'm sorry Emmalyn, but I can't afford to keep you on any longer. I'm really struggling. If it weren't for the rentals, I'd go under completely. The bloody government, the banks, with their money-laundering legislation, and the problem with loans, have really dried up the market for the time being.'

Emmalyn went into a cold sweat. She cleared her throat, 'I have to admit Mrs Leon, I've half been expecting it.' Her heart was racing.

'I'll pay your wage for a month,' Mrs Leon seemed somewhat embarrassed. 'As soon as things pick up again, I'll have you back.'

Emmalyn managed a weak smile.

'I'll give you a letter to take to the Department of Employment, to keep things all straight. You're a good worker Emmalyn. You know how to sell property. Plus, you always look very smart and presentable.'

'Thank you Mrs Leon.'

'I'll write you a good letter of reference if needs be. But I'm not sure it will do you any good. Seems like everybody in real estate, they's all in the same boat.' She paused and hung her head. 'And Vincent? Is he working now?'

'Not really Mrs Leon. Just occasionally.'

'Oh, my Lordy!' she snapped, 'you needs to give him a right kick up the arse.'

Emmalyn knew Mrs Leon had the right attitude. 'I think you're probably right. Something's got to give.'

After a few seconds of reflection, Mrs Leon added, 'I know someone with a restaurant who might need serving staff. It would be better than nothing. At least, it'll put food on the table. I could put in a good word for you.'

Emmalyn quickly thought the offer through. 'Yes, that might be helpful. Could I drive over there now? Because, you know, the first thing to go will have to be my car. I won't be able to afford the repayments on that. And once it's gone, I won't be able to get around the same.'

'How much more have you got to pay? That's if you don't mind me asking.'

'No, that's OK,' Emmalyn said. She thought about her finances, 'about eighteen months I think. But I won't be able to pay for the gas and the insurance either.'

'That's a real shame. I'm sorry Emmalyn, I really am.'

'That's very kind Mrs Leon. But I do understand your situation. You can't pay me for not achieving any results.'

'Well, I hope I'll be phoning you up in a few months telling you to come back again.'

Emmalyn was silent: crumbling inside, she couldn't muster another smile. Her work was everything to her.

'Let me phone up my friend. I'll ask what the situation is in his restaurant,' Mrs Leon told her.

Emmalyn drove over to Anse Argent and Jacko's. Emmalyn had seen the fast-food restaurant many times, but had never eaten there. There were several circular tables on a rough piece of grass in front of the building. Wooden shades over the top and benches around. But as she entered, the interior struck her. Everything was plastic with a capital P. Plastic-topped tables. Plastic stools and chairs. Faux wood plastic counter. One entire wall was decorated with an enormous image of a paradisiac Caribbean beach transposed onto a shiny sheet of Plexiglas. Even the food was served in polystyrene boxes and the drinks in clear, rigid polyethylene lidded beakers. Emmalyn hoped that the things on the menu wouldn't taste like seasoned plastic.

She asked the young lady behind the counter if Jacko was available.

'You mean Mr Jackson?' she asked sharply.

'I believe so. Is he the owner of the restaurant?'

'Yeah, he through the back … in the office.' She didn't offer to show Emmalyn the way. She just pointed to an open door next to the menu covering the back wall.

Emmalyn made her way behind the counter and out of the café. A dark corridor stacked high with labelled cardboard boxes confronted her. Following her nose, she moved hesitantly towards the end. Sounds of something being dragged, guided her to another open doorway. The back of a solid, masculine form dominated her view. It was trying to lug a large piece of furniture between more piles of cartons.

'Would you like some help sir?' she offered.

'Well, hell …' The form straightened up. Emmalyn was addressing a rather bulky back. When it turned around, it seemed by the lines on his milky coffee-coloured face, he was perhaps in his late fifties. He slicked back his straight black hair and adjusted his gold-rimmed glasses before he continued.

'I think perhaps it should be me asking that question. Were you looking for the ladies' toilets?'

She smiled. 'Not at present sir. Mrs Leon has sent me sir—to talk about possible work.'

'Oh yes, Emmalyn.' He surveyed the large wooden desk. 'Yes. You could help me with this if you don't mind. I need it over there. Then, I can stack the cases all against one wall. The place needs a bit of organisation. There ain't enough room to swing a cat at present.'

'Sure, let's go then sir,' Emmalyn edged herself around the desk, hemmed in by the towers of cartons. She grabbed hold of the end of the piece of furniture. Together they manoeuvred it to the other side of the room. Within a few minutes, the room was transformed from a crowded stock room to a space that could serve as a tiny office.

Mr Jackson stood, hands on over-sized hips. He stared at the area where chaos had existed minutes before. 'Much better. Glad you came along just at the appropriate moment. That's me sorted out. Now, let's deal with you. You'd like some work. Can you do the late shift on Wednesday?'

'But, sir, Mr Jackson, don't we need to …,' she felt slightly awkward, '… discuss this a little more?'

They were interrupted by his phone ringing. Mr Jackson prised his mobile from his shirt pocket. 'If you could go and get me coffee and whatever you want from the front, we'll talk about it after my call.'

Emmalyn did as he'd asked, and returned with the coffee and her passion fruit, parsley, banana, and kale smoothie. Both in their plastic shiny beakers, hers crowned with a fuchsia-coloured plastic straw forced into the top. The owner had found her a chair. He propped his weighty figure on the top his desk.

'So, let's get down to details,' he said. 'You have to realise that you won't be getting the same rate as in a real estate office. I pay six dollars fifty an hour, plus a percentage of the service charge.'

'Six dollar fifty? Is that U.S. or island dollars sir?'

'This ain't no gourmet restaurant Emmalyn, serving Chateaubriand with red wine sauce. We're serving tacos and burgers at competitive prices here. And everything's in local currency.'

'I understand sir.' She instantly calculated that she would probably go home with around a hundred US dollars for a forty-hour week. But she had to survive. She possessed no savings and would have bills to pay each month. The restaurant was located

173

reasonably close to her home. She could try and find something more lucrative while waiting tables there. At that time, Emmalyn needed this job.

They negotiated for a few minutes more. The owner promised to feed her each evening. As she had already seen the menu, she wasn't that impressed by the offer, but accepted it anyway. As she was about to leave, Mr Jackson asked her a rather unexpected question. 'You don't know where I can get tomatoes, do you?'

'Tomatoes?' Emmalyn was puzzled.

'There doesn't seem to be a single one left on the island. We need them for the burgers. I'll pay twenty dollars a kilo for them.'

'I'll see what I can find sir.' As she left, crimson invaded her thoughts. Twenty dollars for tomatoes. She would have to work for more than three hours at Jacko's to earn that much. Her little grey cells were churning over an idea as she drove back to the real estate office.

Her intention was to thank Mrs Leon for her aid in obtaining a temporary job so rapidly. Some work was better than no work. On arrival, her former boss was entertaining a friend. A woman Emmalyn had met before. Someone who always seemed to be airing her grievances and dissatisfactions. Someone who seemed to only see the negative side of the world.

Emmalyn related to both of them the story of her bizarre parley with Mr Jackson.

'You know, he's an unconventional soul, but a good one.' Mrs Leon disclosed.

'Oh, don't delude yourself. I've heard some spicy stories about that one,' her friend said with a malicious smile. She turned and looked Emma directly in the eye. 'I thought about you the other day. I see that you've got rid of that guy Vincent you were living with.'

'What do you mean?' Emmalyn asked.

'I saw him the other day with that tramp Janine. I suppose he's hooked up with her now you kicked him out?' A perfected spiteful expression crept across her wide features.

Mrs Leon looked awkward and flustered. Her chin dropped towards her chest; eyes fixed on her desk. 'I think you made a mistake,' she muttered.

'Oh no, there was no mistake, it was him.' The friend looked at Emmalyn, who was trying to hide her shock. 'Whoops have I put my foot in it?' she asked feigning innocence.

'Sweet Jesus, this is turning into one hell of a bad day,' Emmalyn wasn't surprised by the woman's bitchiness, but it still cut her to the core. 'It's perhaps best if I go and try to achieve something positive now,' Emmalyn shrugged and gathered her senses. 'I'll be in touch Mrs Leon. Thank you so much for your kindness.' She nodded to the 'friend' and exited as soon as possible. She imagined what the two women might be saying about her after the office door had been firmly shut.

Emmalyn did as she had previously planned; and left to drive to an acquaintance's home—an acquaintance with a vegetable garden. She got there on auto pilot. Rather than her mind concentrating on how she could economise at home, it was full of Vincent. It was whirling with anger. He had given up on their relationship way back, which made her feel the malicious comments were true. It seemed he was hitting on anybody that would put up with him and his drinking problem. She was done. She couldn't suffer him anymore. Vincent had to leave. She saw no reason why she should put up with him and his selfishness a day longer. Life would be so much easier, more economical and calmer without him. The decision had been made by the time she reached her friend with the vegetable plot.

Emmalyn was hoping that they might have tomatoes. She'd also planned to worm out of them as much information as possible about growing vegetables. Emmalyn had a garden. She must use it. With a little work, she was sure she could cut down on her food bills. She left the vegetable garden with a large bag of tomatoes, sprouting yams, several plants, and a whole heap of advice.

'You wondrous woman! You've saved the day!' Jacko told her when she handed over the plastic bag swelling with tomatoes. 'I like staff who show a bit of initiative.'

'Comes with age don't you think. You learn you can't just be hanging around waiting for things to happen. You have to go out and make things happen for yourself.' As soon as she'd said it, she asked herself if that was really her philosophy on life—for sure, it should be.

'Good attitude to have,' agreed Mr Jackson. 'Whilst you're here, you should come and meet Krish, our chef. He'll be thankful to see the tomatoes.'

Krish, like Mr Jackson, seemed to be of Indian origin. Rapidly, it became clear his approach to people was nothing like his boss. As they were introduced, Krish eyed her up and down.

'An oldie then Mr Jackson,' he stated bluntly. He turned towards Emmalyn, 'you reckon you're up to the work?'

Both were rather taken aback. Mr Jackson moved up his glasses. 'Emmalyn will be fine. She's proved that she's a very fit young lady.'

'I may look old, but I'm probably only a few years your senior. I've still got a lot of pep in my step you know,' Emmalyn retaliated. Mr Jackson flashed a half smile and adjusted his spectacles again.

'I like 'em young and full of energy,' Krish grunted with a leer. 'This is tough work, best for the young.'

'Emmalyn found us some tomatoes,' declared Mr Jackson. 'I told her she saved our bacon.'

'Okay,' Krish stared at the large bag of produce being held in front of him.

Krish had started badly. Emmalyn could see working alongside him was not doing to be a breeze. The events of the day had devastated her, but anger and resentment were added to her list of emotions after meeting him. But, the bottom line was, that job was essential to her, if only for a few weeks. She held back her wrath and kept her irritation to herself.

With the money for the tomatoes, plus some petrol money in her pocket, she headed home determined. After her visit to her gardening friend, she'd made a resolution. She was firstly going to attack her own garden. It was going to have to work for her; feed her and perhaps others. Secondly, Vincent was going. Who's to say how long he had been shacking up with other women? He didn't make any sort of contribution to the household. She wouldn't tolerate his selfish attitude any longer.

Once in her garden, she used an old machete to cut down the grass and weeds. By lunchtime, she had cleared a small bed in a shady patch; and the plants had been installed. Her efforts had satisfied her, taken her mind off her problems, but she still felt down. While preparing lunch, she heard shuffling of feet coming down the garden path. Vincent was returning home.

'Why you not at work?' Vincent barged through the screen door.

He looked unkempt. His T-shirt was muddy. His jeans were developing holes. From where she stood, it was obvious he needed a shower.

'I've told you before about my job. Mrs Leon made me redundant today. I have no job.'

'The bitch! What's for lunch?'

'There's no lunch for you Vinny,' Emmalyn announced. 'I'm not cooking for you again. In fact, you can collect your stuff and go.'

'What ya mean? I starvin'.'

'That may be so. But I'm not feeding you. I'm without a job. I can hardly afford to feed myself. You're a good-for-nothing scrounger.'

Vincent lumbered into the room and watched as she put down her wooden spoon and turned off the gas ring. 'Please go and get your things, and then leave.'

Emmalyn gathered by his slow reactions his mind was fuzzy with booze. 'I not leaving,' Vincent said eventually. 'Who's he? The man you'z found to take mi place. You'z got another man?'

'That's funny coming from you! No, I don't have anybody else. But, it seems the whole district knows that you do. You'll go with anybody who's desperate enough to put up with you. I've had enough—just go.'

Vincent made a move towards Emmalyn. He raised his hand in an attempt to hit her, but drink had made him unsure on his legs. He stumbled with the effort and hit his hip against the table. He flinched at the pain. Emmalyn quickly shifted into the middle of the room to avoid contact with him. At a stroke, he turned and picked up the hot frying pan from the ring. He aimed it directly at her. Frying pan, plus bits of green banana, onion, salt fish, peppers, and cabbage, all coated in coconut oil, sailed around the room.

'Get the hell out of my house!' she screamed.

'Not your house, it our house,' he bawled. 'I lives here too.'

'Not from today! My mother gave me this house. I thank God you never married me. So, this is one hundred per cent mine. Now go.'

Vincent stared at her; surveyed the havoc he'd created, and moved towards Emmalyn again. She snatched up her large cooks' knife in defence. He had to admit defeat. With a sullen face, he turned and left the stifling, messed-up room. The screen door banged behind him.

'I'll put your things in a large plastic bag,' Emmalyn shouted after the figure staggering down the path.

Emmalyn checked he'd really gone and grabbed for her handbag. Leaving her filthy kitchen, she sped to the nearest hardware shop. She invested in several strong bolts and a screwdriver. Installing them kept her busy that afternoon.

Chapter 18

Burgers

'Good day. What can I get you folks?'

Willis surveyed the waitress. Then, he looked at the menu again. 'A chicken cheeseburger,' he said finally. The order was written on the pad. 'And fries,' he declared; 'please,' ended his difficult decision.

'And for you?'

'No, I'll just have a drink thanks. There's nothing on the menu that I want to eat. I'll go for a pineapple and mango smoothie.'

'I know what you mean,' the waitress said quietly, 'it's not my type of food either.' Her face displayed a shade of a smile for her clients. 'So, one burger with fries. Anything to drink young man?'

'Let's make it a Sprite … please.'

'Why is it the young love all this synthetic fast food?' queried Tamara. 'Give me a good plate of fish, plantain and rice anytime.'

'Oh, but I like that as well,' proclaimed Willis enthusiastically.

'That's a blessing,' smiled the waitress. 'Thank you. I'll go and get your drinks.'

'Well, what do you think Willis? Do you want to come with Jeff and me tomorrow?'

Willis screwed up his face. 'It's a bit of a drive Mom. Just to see a bunch of houses and then have lunch.'

'It's not too long a drive if you're going to the kite surfing school, is it? And that's about the same distance.'

'Yeah, you're right. But the kite surfing makes the journey worthwhile. Tell the truth, I'd rather give this one a miss. I can go and lend Ricko a hand, or I'll catch up with one of my mates. I'll leave you and Jeff to go by yourselves.'

'I suggested it because I thought perhaps you'd be interested in getting into real estate—as a job I mean.'

Willis' face dropped. 'Hell, no Mom, I know that with real estate you can potentially earn more bucks. But I don't fancy working with all that type of stuff. I've set my heart on doing something sporty, perhaps sports management, just like Madison. You know I'm good at all of that. I need to be happy in my work, not just counting in the dollars in some boring nine to five.'

The aroma of fried foods filled their nostrils; the clatter of the fast-food restaurant invaded their ears. While awaiting their order, Tamara's attention was caught by the culinary activity behind a clear plastic screen, defining the kitchen area. She half-watched the performance, at the same time, explaining to Willis yet again that she may not have the means to put him through university.

'Mom, I hear what ya saying. But, let's just wait and see. Our lives are all good right now.'

'Thanks to Jeff'

'Yeah, thanks to Jeff. I know. He's a good guy. We've got lots to thank him for. But I want to take things as they come. I just got this feeling Mom, things'll work out just fine.' Tamara wished she shared her son's optimism.

Their drinks arrived. Whilst sipping bright orange smoothie through a plastic straw, Tamara gave thought to the emotions she would have liked to share with her son. She wanted to forewarn him. Part of her wanted to tell Willis not to build up big plans—not to rely on Jeffrey for his future. She'd have liked to explain her unease and suspicions about him; and about what he really did. She'd like him to understand what their life, hers and Jeffrey's, was really like—the type of man she had to contend with. Explain all about the uncertainty and unpredictability of living with a person who needed to dominate. Tell him about the Jeffrey Taylor who was introvert, unforthcoming, but also very demanding and occasionally almost hostile.

She watched Willis' face broaden by his dazzling smile. He was still so young; too young to take it all on board. And a crowded burger joint certainly wasn't the right place to impart such confidences.

Her considerations were distracted as a drama seemed to have developed the other side of the kitchen partition. Their waitress seemed to be getting verbally beaten up by the man doing the cooking. A stark, angular figure, clad in black. His features were contorted; his expression emitting malice and rage. The sound of his fury was smothered by the screen and the chatter and commotion of the restaurant. But one thing was clear; his words were not kind or complementary. Light flashed on metal. A large knife was thrust forward, threatening the waitress. The woman hung her head, not responding. Her form visibly slumped as she continued her work. The scenario continued until she left the kitchen with her next order.

It was Willis' burger. His face lit up with anticipation as soon as he set eyes on his reward. The waitress gently placed his polystyrene food container in front of him and left to collect the condiments.

'I hope that you don't mind me saying, but you seem to have one mean son of a bitch as a boss,' Tamara commented quietly, whilst Willis grabbed hold of the ketchup. The burger was lavishly covered with a coating of red goo.

The waitress paused. Firstly, she surveyed the ketchup, then behind her.

'That's not my boss,' she replied in a flat voice. 'My boss, Mr Jackson, he's okay. Unfortunately, he's not always here.' Willis, oblivious to the spectacle which had been acted out behind him, continued devouring his lunch and took little notice. As far as he was concerned, they were talking women's talk.

'Is he always so wound up?' Tamara asked in almost a whisper. 'How long has he been like that? '

'Months and months. Seems like years and years.'

'You must sure need this job.'

'Sure as hell I do. Can't find anything better.'

'This is a real good burger Emmalyn,' Willis announced, reading from her name tag. 'The chicken ain't over cooked. It's all good, bomb!'

'Thanks my dear, I'll tell the chef,' Emmalyn managed a smile.

'Perhaps it'll put him in a better frame of mind,' Tamara added.

'No chance of that ... got to go ... thanks for the feedback,' Emmalyn made the last statement loudly. 'Is there anything else I can get you?'

'No, don't think so,' interrupted Willis, 'but we'll see you again. I tell you what, this burger is awesome sauce, the tops.'

'Thank you young man,' Emmalyn returned to her loathsome kitchen for her next order.

There the spectacle continued. Tamara's sympathy went out to her. Shock filled her. The waitress was still being bombarded with abuse. The chef's face remained twisted by his odious temper. He reminded her of someone from a horror movie rather than a fast-food chef. That poor woman seemed she was living one hell of a life.

'Poor soul,' she muttered, but it crossed her mind perhaps she was in a parallel situation. She put up with shit from Jeffrey to keep her and Willis in comfort and the hope of giving him a better future.

'Del-ish!' Willis licked his fingers oblivious of the theatre performed behind him.

~~~

Jeffrey said very little. He was driving the hire car with care. Concentration was essential. The road was potted with a multitude of holes; edged by deep storm gutters and contorted by frequent hairpin bends. The journey to the south of the island was not for a faint-hearted driver.

It was clear he was unable to appreciate any of the terrain. But Tamara, alongside, was in her element. She loved the rugged topography, the richness of the island's beauty and charm. Much of the interior was uninhabited dense rainforest-clad peaks. Huge tree ferns, stems of towering bamboos and giant elephant ear plants, occasionally invaded the route, their mass blocking the light.

The route they were following clung to the side of the mountains: one side was a steep wall of rock, dotted with clinging vegetation, the other, a sheer drop tumbling down to the valley floor. Tamara studied each aspect, the sharp contrast to the busy, commercialised north. She was enamoured by the lushness of the plant life, the diversity of colours and forms. Aware this part of the island hadn't changed much for thousands of years— and dreamed it would remain the same for thousands of years to come.

This visit was a first for Tamara. Unexpectedly, Jeffrey had asked her to accompany him to a business meeting. She supposed it was because he wanted her to navigate. Joining him for meetings had never been suggested before. During visits to other islands on business she was left in the hotel. Even telephone conversations about work were taken outside her presence. The car was heading for The Tamarind, a complex south of the capital. The management was looking for investors. It seemed the resort had fallen on hard times. It's location near the airport was advantageous, but the site was a bit off the beaten track for some tourists' requirements.

The track down to the complex proved to be even more of a challenge for Jeffrey's driving skills than the perilous roads. The vehicle advanced at a snail's pace, steering around the large stones and the deep ruts every few metres. Fortunately, the drive only lasted a few minutes. They soon found themselves confronted by some tall, majestic gates. A security guard exited his booth.

'My name is Taylor. We've an appointment to see Mr McCloud.'

The pair had been surprised by the resort's high wall and protective gates, but were even more taken aback by what lay the other side. The guard ushered them into another land. A curved row of cream-coloured villas lay in front of them, each guarded by a resplendent row of palms. Their eyes were attacked by a kaleidoscope of colour from the open gardens. They became engulfed in a riot of scarlet, vivid pinks, apricots, and mauves—bougainvillea, plumeria, hibiscus and lilies in abundance. Everything seemed to need a bit of tending, but this, in fact, gave it an attractive, natural jungle effect.

'Wow, what a sight,' breathed Jeffrey uncharacteristically.

'Not at all what I expected,' agreed Tamara. The botanical gardens effect continued to the reception building. A stocky man, of undetermined age, stood on the raised terrace awaiting their arrival.

'Mr Taylor, so good to meet you,' Mr McCloud put forward his hand.

'Please call me Jeff. And this is my partner, Tamara. I don't think I'd have got here without her.'

'Yup, it's a bit of a drive. Let's get you a drink.'

'We are very impressed by the gardens here Mr McCloud,' Tamara told him.

'Splendid, aren't they? Please, it's Jay, please call me Jay. The gardens are what make this place so special. The beach isn't too bad either.' Tamara confessed to never having visited the beach before.

In Jay's office, they cooled off with glasses of green lime squash, whilst he went over why the complex of villas had become rather run down. Each villa was privately owned. Unfortunately, many of the owners, over the course of time, had fallen on hard times. Some hadn't paid their condo fees in years. The debt owing to the condominium was mounting into millions of dollars. There were only just sufficient owners who did pay to finance the few staff to keep the place going. They were looking for an investor, an investor to buy the debt. With the funds the management would repair the exteriors.

'And how much is that?' jumped in Jeffrey. 'The current debt?'

'Coming up to four million US. There's nearly sixty per cent delinquency here. We survive on around forty per cent of the condominium fees. So, you can imagine, we don't have the funds for massive renovation projects.'

'So, you're looking for an investment of around eight hundred thousand, twenty cents on the dollar?'

'Perhaps a bit more,' Jay clarified, a serious look on his face. 'Firstly, you would get your initial investment back through judicial sales. It takes a bit of time, going through the island courts, but it works. If it goes through the courts, usually the sale prices are low and the owner receives nothing, as all their debts have to be paid off. Alternatively, we have been assured that some owners would be prepared to do a deal.' Tamara studied Jay's face. He appeared worried, eyes sunken, dark shadows under them.

'Let's give you an example,' he continued, 'a property has a hundred thousand debt. You do a deal with the desperate owner for twenty thousand. You pay the debt. You get the villa for a hundred and twenty thousand. We get the hundred thousand debt owing. Once the outsides are all straightened out, perhaps in eighteen months' time, and the market picks up, the villa is worth half to three quarters of a million US.

Jeffrey kept his eyes down, his mouth drawn into a straight line, and his voice flat. 'Do you reckon there are enough desperate owners?'

'Oh yes, quite a few. These people live in the States … in the UK. They just want shot of them. They don't have the funds to do them up themselves, so their values are currently low. And the thing is, the value of the properties won't go up until the whole resort is done up. Once it is renovated, we hope to be able to attract a marketing team to rent out the villas most of the year. Tourists like the proximity to the airport and the calm of the place.'

'And the gardens, I'm sure,' Tamara said.

Jeffrey made a few notes on his phone. His face was bland of emotion, wearing his business attitude, indifferent to Jay's feelings. Tamara sat sipping her fresh juice, silently calculating the deal. If her maths served her well, there was certainly some money to be made here. She didn't know too much about buying debt, but superficially, it all seemed like a good investment.

'Let's show you around,' Jay offered, 'give you an idea of the state of the interiors—see what you think.'

'I can tell you now, I think this place has the potential to be something really special,' Jeffrey said, still without a flicker of a smile.

'It used to be. But, the world turns every day, and things change,' Jay added, a faint curve on his lips.

Warm air struck them as they left the cool and calm of the air-conditioned office. Immersed in a blinding tropical light, they feasted on the vibrancy of the garden and its floral perfumed air.

Jay was prepared. He held up bunches of keys he'd collected. He aimed to show them each type of villa. Nearing the first property, it became evident that the exteriors desperately needed power-washing and painting. The sea air had tainted much of the cream rendering to an unattractive drab grey tone. Many pots of paint and busy arms would be needed to bring the buildings back to a four-star level. Close inspection exposed extensive metal corrosion. Metal railings were unsupported at the base— rusted away. The salt in the air had taken its toll. Light fitments were speckled with corrosion and decay. Some issues were partially masked by the ever-abundant vegetation festooning each construction.

The interiors yearned for modernisation, a few contemporary touches. However, their spaciousness and basic lay-out were appealing. Individual gardens, housing compact swimming pools, gave them the prospect of being very up-market holiday locations. But sadly, an air of neglect hung over the place.

During their exploration, they saw very few holiday makers, or evidence of them. The tour was functional and rapid. On the whole, the three of them were uncommunicative. There was little to say. The problem was the same, whatever the size of villa. Neglect. Money, in large quantities, was the only solution to lift the resort out of the quagmire. Tamara sensed that Jay may have done identical tours before. He spoke in a resigned, unenthusiastic manner. She surmised that, secretly, his fingers might be crossed. Hoping on each occasion, that he would find potential investors who would be the salvation of the resort.

'Let's go and get some lunch.' Jay directed them towards the beach front restaurant. The building was supported by pillars drowning in flowers of vibrant colours. Through them they caught glimpses of the beige sandy beach. Palms, their trunks angled haphazardly, spilled down to meet the sand. As they sat at a beach-side table, Tamara noticed how few tourists were scattered over the stretch of beach—so unlike the hotel where she worked.

'I told you the beach was not half bad. So, what are your thoughts?' Jay McCloud asked as he handed them the menus.

'Yes, I think it could be a very up market resort. Not sure three quarters of a million would do it all though. You'd be on a

188

tight budget. I'll see if I can get anyone interested. You understand that the decision is not mine to make.' His speech remained a monotone.

Jeffrey looked up from the menu, in the blink of an eye, his voice found some enthusiasm. Food, he could get passionate about. 'The spicy duck burger with banana chutney sounds good.'

'It is,' Jay aimed an amicable look towards him. 'So, tell me, what brought you to Sainte Marie to live? '

'The usual things I suppose. The relaxed way of life, the friendly, charming people, and the great potential of the Caribbean. It seems some islands are really on the up and up after the recession. When I retired from my agency in London, I didn't feel ready to lead a sedentary life.'

Tamara gave Jeffrey a sideways glance, whilst tapping her fingers on the table, one by one. This is more information than he's usually prepared to give away, she thought.

'I think I'm happier now than I've ever been,' Jeffrey continued. 'I can do a bit of work to keep the old brain cells ticking over. I've got lots of time to pursue my passion of water sports. And of course, I've Tammy to go home to. Life is perfect!' He gave her hand a squeeze.

She presented an uncertain smile. She stared at him wondering if he was lying—or if it had been said to back up his sales talk.

Jay went on to explain how he had been in the Caribbean for over thirty years. But Tamara couldn't focus on Jay's story. She was too busy mulling over what Jeffrey had just said. He had never openly expressed such emotions before. Not to her anyway. That he was "happier than he'd ever been." His ailing wife, in England, naturally wasn't mentioned. In fact, she was rarely mentioned in her presence. Tamara speculated if she knew the real Jeffrey Taylor at all.

Jay was easy company. Full of stories about the island. Tamara enjoyed being with him; and hoped Jeffrey would be able to help him and the resort. One way or another, the lunch passed harmoniously. Jeffrey's duck burger was declared a gastronomic delight and the caramel marquise exquisite.

They left Mr McCloud in the tropical gardens, Jeffrey promising he'd be in contact when he had some news. He negotiated the track back to the main road without a word.

Tamara left feeling pleased that she had shared the visit on her day off. Delving into new corners of her homeland and encountering new personalities had made it a special day.

'Well babe, what did you think?' Jeffrey burst forth in an eager tone.

Tamara reflected. 'Well, it sounds like a reasonable investment to me. But then, I don't know about recuperating debt ...'

'If I had the money, I'd invest in it myself,' Jeffrey confessed. 'With the villas for sale at such knock down prices, one could double your money in a few years—once the place is spruced up. A very interesting place!'

She realised Jeffrey wouldn't expect her to say anything about his business negotiations, but thought it couldn't hurt to comment about his enthusiasm. 'Why didn't you tell Jay McCloud that? You could have given him a little hope. Why weren't you as fired up back there?'

Jeffrey said nothing. The car swung this way and that as he manoeuvred the bends.

'Are you telling me how to run my business?' He snapped, and continued concentrating on his driving.

She'd been right: she should have kept her mouth shut. 'Of course not, it's just you weren't all fired up at the resort.'

'Hmm ... Babe, it's not up to me. I didn't want to get his hopes up.' His voice was assertive—telling her not to interfere. 'I have to convince investors, the people with the big bucks, or

190

companies with investment funds. You know, I don't have that sort of money to invest myself,' he said dismissively.

For several kilometres, the journey continued in silence. Tamara had been told to keep her opinions to herself, but judged that Jeffrey was busy calculating how much he could rake in from any investment at The Tamarind. Money seemed to be his main priority in life, more important than any human. She gazed out of the side window, pretending to be taken in by the exquisite scenery, but was mulling over their relationship and the comments he'd made to Jay.

The hair-pin bends in the road slowed down their progress; Tamara tired of silence between them. 'Jeff, did you really mean those things you said to Jay?'

'What things are you talking about Babe?'

'About being happier than ever before. I've never heard you say that.' As she said it, she knew she was pushing her luck and should keep her own council.

He turned his head slightly towards her, 'Tammy, don't you understand how I feel about you? I love our life together—you and Willis.' One hand left the steering wheel, and he grinned as he squeezed her knee. 'When we get out of these bloody awful tight bends…'

Tamara looked at him trying to keep blankness on her face. Did he really expect her to believe all that crap he told about caring for her and Willis? She was pretty sure he wouldn't know how to care for anyone but himself. She should definitely have kept her mouth shut, because she knew that hand on her leg was a sign.

'What's the matter?' she asked, knowing a hundred per cent what would come next.

'Not a thing,' he lied.

The car started the descent away from the steep interior. A tension started to pull in Tamara's stomach. Her thoughts churned; Jeffrey was going to stop the car. She knew. Her day was going to be ruined. She watched the landscape level out. They passed through a collection of small homes. Suddenly, he swung the car right onto a narrow track.

'This isn't the way we want to go,' Tammy told him, one hand seizing the door handle tightly.

'Yes, Tammy it is.' After a few seconds he stopped the car at the side of a trail. They were surrounded by dense undergrowth and lofty swaying trees.

Why couldn't he wait until they reached home? 'I think this could lead to a farm or ...' Tamara got no further. He leaned forward. He forced her head against the car seat. Instantly, she smelt his stale breath, tasted his pungent mouth, remnants of his recent lunch. He pushed his tongue into her mouth, whilst pushing a hand between her knees. 'I don't give a shit where it leads Tammy. I want to live a little wild and show you how I feel about you. Right now.' His hand searched up her skirt. 'In the back. Get in the back. I want you so bad, I don't care if the whole village sees how I feel about you.'

'Not sure it's a good idea here,' she said knowing it would be pointless. 'It's illegal to do this on the side of the road.'

'Hmm,' Jeffrey waved that away irritably: it was of no relevance to him.

Tamara pictured being caught by the police, or an angry farmer. And never mind what she thought about the matter. She could really do without this. If the truth be known, she'd rather be doing anything else but doing that in the back of the car. And she'd rather be anywhere else on island, than on that track. She glanced at his face trying to find any indication of the affection he'd just been talking about. She saw none. Instead, she noted flashes of hostility and surliness. A look that told her Jeffrey would not be dissuaded. But then she'd known that anyway.

He grabbed at her wrist. 'Get in the back. You know you want it as much as I do.' His voice reflected the glower on his face. He tightened his grasp on her arm and twisted it slightly, turning her skin. She flinched, any sexual desire that she might have had disappeared out of the open car window. Dumb struck she rapidly unlocked the passenger door.

Tamara stepped out amidst the undergrowth and took in a lungful of moist warm air. As reassurance, her head turned up and then down the earth track in the hope that nothing, nobody was travelling along it. Fantasies of putting a can of biting centipedes, or wasps down his boxers flashed through her thoughts. But she slipped onto the back seat, endeavouring to empty her mind to be able to cope with the situation. Routine dictated she must play the role that was expected of her.

He threw himself in after her, pulled her to him. Illegal or not, Jeffrey was going to get what Jeffrey wanted. He attacked her body, without inhibitions. Their bodies stuck together with the heat of the day, in the back of the stiflingly hot car. Tamara played her role, but could not feel emotionally part of the activity; and found it more and more difficult to put up with his dominance. It was all becoming too much She couldn't wait for the sex to finish.

'Babe, aren't we good together?' whispered Jeffrey into her neck afterwards. 'You and I are made for one another. How could you doubt that you don't make me happy?'

Tamara was lost for words. Where the hell did he get this garbage from? She replied with a forced half smile. Was he trying to convince himself that it was true?

'I haven't looked at another woman since I met you,' he concluded, as a final insult.

Tamara heard herself give out a deep sigh as he moved to the front seat. She straightened her clothing, and made a move to return to follow him. At first, she'd thought she'd be able to put up with his demands for Willis' sake. Now most of her emotions towards him were negative.

'Don't bother to get fully dressed again Babe. Stay in the back. I'll drive on a bit further and we can stop again,' Jeffrey promised.

God forbid, Tamara thought to herself. She would prefer to make her own way home, even though it would be one hell of a trek.

Chapter 19

Control

A tropical storm hung over Sainte Marie.

The rain bounced off the roads and pavements. Streamed down the windows. Willis ran, splashing through the puddles. He held the hood of his sweatshirt firmly over his head and scuttled from the car to the shelter of Jacko's. His mother, behind him, progressed at a more sedate pace, the frame of her umbrella brought down onto her soft, springy black hair.

Willis shook with laughter as he held the door open for her. 'Step it up mother! You been having exercise sessions with a bunch of snails?'

'Don't be cheeky,' she told him as she shook water from her umbrella. 'I was trying to avoid getting drenched. It will have to be a quick snack. I've got to go back to work.'

'Alrighty. Great place to come until the rain stops.'

'Obviously, not everybody thinks so,' Tamara declared as she installed herself at a nearby table. The place was virtually empty. Willis flung himself into the clear plastic chair opposite her. She reached over to brush away the shining droplets on his dark skin. As expected, Willis pulled a face telling her not fuss around him.

'I told you we'd be back,' Willis told Emmalyn as she approached their table. 'I've been looking forward to getting my teeth into one of your chicken and cheese specials.'

'I'll see what we can do for you. Is that with fries?'

'Please'

'And for you my dear?' Emmalyn asked Tamara.

Tamara scrutinised the black board menu. 'Me, oh I'll just have an iced café latté. And you, how have you been?' She addressed Emmalyn directly.

Emmalyn looked surprised that she should be asked. 'Me, I'm fine. Thanks for asking,' she flashed them a smile, 'that all then?'

'Oh, and a large Coke for me please.'

Emmalyn dashed it off on her pad. Tamara stared after her as the waitress headed towards the counter. Willis commenced a long yarn about somebody he had encountered at the kite surfing school, she fixed an interested expression on her face, but was only half listening to his story.

The memory of their previous visit to the café was still vivid in her thoughts. Tamara hoped she wouldn't witness a repeat performance of the chef's aggressive behaviour. She tracked their drinks being poured and then placed on the counter. As Emmalyn was about to carry them to the table, the black clad figure of the chef exited his kitchen area. He muttered something to Emmalyn. As she replied, he slapped her behind. To add insult to injury, he then pushed her in the back and mouthed something which could have been 'stupid bitch.' If it hadn't been for the plastic tops to the beakers, the drinks would have spilt across the floor. His spite vented; the chef returned to his work.

Tamara went to stand up as it all happened. Willis stopped his narrative and turned around towards the oncoming drinks. He had missed the incident—completely.

'I'll explain later Willis,' muttered his mother. She hesitated, wondering if she should comment on the drama to the chef himself. In a flash, she made a decision. She grabbed her handbag from the seat next to her.

'Thanks, that's great,' chirped Willis, as his beaker was placed next to him.

Tamara was searching for a pen in her bag. 'Don't go,' she said to Emmalyn. She snatched a paper serviette from the plastic holder on the tabletop. Her name and mobile number were boldly written on the soft paper. 'For heaven's sake phone me. I might be able to wangle you a job where I work.'

Tamara looked towards the kitchen screen. The chef had his head down concentrating on cooking. She folded the paper and passed it to Emmalyn.

'He's not looking this way,' Tamara said. The serviette was secreted in Emmalyn's pocket.

'What can I say?'

'Don't say anything, just phone me. You can't put up with this abuse, this sexual harassment. Behaviour like that should be reported. Have you told your boss?' Tamara asked in a low tone.

Willis was mystified. He looked at Emmalyn, then his mother, unsure of what was going on. But he was wise enough not to ask.

Emmalyn hesitated, 'It doesn't happen when Mr Jackson is here ... well rarely.'

'What's wrong with the man? Is he a misogynist? Is he the same with the other staff?'

'With Lara, he was worse. She left last week. Most staff don't usually last too long here.'

'Phone me on your next day off. I can pick you up from ...'

The sound of metal on plastic. A knife cracking the kitchen screen. The chef raised a beige meal box in front of the partition. The burger was ready. Dutifully, Emmalyn departed to collect it.

'Mother, what the hell is happening here?' hissed Willis as Emmalyn left.

'It really is better if I explain later, once we're outside. Finish what you were telling me.'

Emmalyn returned with the burger, 'I'm on the evening shift for the rest of the week. I don't start until four,' she said almost under her breath.

She went back to retrieve the condiments and placed them in front of Willis. Within seconds, a generous trail of glutinous sauce seasoned the burger.

'Phone me tomorrow,' Tamara instructed 'and we can arrange a time that's good for both of us.'

Emmalyn didn't hang around and went to busy herself at the counter. Willis continued with his story in between greedily demolishing his lunch. Outside large droplets of rain snaked down the plate glass windows of Jacko's. Umbrellas were still up. But the heavy nimbus clouds above were dispersing. Slashes of blue sky were visible.

~~~

They tucked themselves away under a parasol, avoiding the midday temperatures. A wooden shade topped with long, dried palm leaves which shifted in the breeze. Their voices were lost amidst those of other numerous clients. Noise from the main road swept around them.

Tamara noted promptly that Emmalyn was a different character away from the hell hole where she worked. She came over as a lively, far more relaxed individual. She even looked different. Her brown eyes had more of a sparkle, and she'd taken the trouble to apply a bit of make-up.

'Why the hell don't you slap his face, or knee him, or something?' Tamara asked.

'Can't do that, it would make him worse. You don't know him.'

'I bloody well don't want to. How on earth have you managed to tolerate such working conditions for so long?'

'You know what it's like on this island, things can be tough. I've been trying to find another job for too long. There's always a long queue of folks for every vacancy. With no social security, you have to work.'

'Do you have a man to help out?'

'Not now. It's weird; I kicked out my long-time partner because he was treating me unfairly and walked straight into a job with another insufferable man.'

'Was your partner aggressive too?'

'In the end he was. I put up with him living off me for too long. He thought it was acceptable to live with me for free. Work as little as possible, run after any skirt going and not contribute to the bills. And to boot, come home drunk every evening, and expect a free meal put in front of him.'

'Well, we all know there are a lot like that on island. Let the little woman do all the work, whilst he sits around doing sod all, or playing dominos.'

This was the prompt for an out-pouring of many of Emmalyn's woes: from losing her real estate position, chucking out Vincent, Mr Jackson, tomatoes and serving food she had a strong aversion to—the whole sorry saga. Emmalyn ended her tale of hardship by explaining that the other chef employed at Jacko's was no problem; and Mr Jackson had tried to help her in every way that he could.

'You ain't having much luck girl, are you?' Tamara sympathised. 'This Mr Jackson might be kind BUT, he should be doing something about that demon from hell that he employs as a chef. People can't put up with that sort of behaviour. It makes their lives a misery.'

'You ain't heard the half of it. Lara, the girl that left last week, she was only nineteen, a pretty miss. Cheeky sod, he was putting his hand up her skirt.'

'Oh, for heavens' sake! I can't cope with men who think they can treat females just as they like.'

'Lara told me that she had informed Mr Jackson. Naturally, I don't know if he said anything to Krish. You know what, working there, at Jacko's, has really opened up my eyes. You meet all sorts—the good, the bad and the downright ugly.'

'Seems like there's too high a proportion of the bad and the ugly.'

'Maybe, but then, I met you, didn't I? And you're in the first category,' Emmalyn said cheerfully.

'But it a bit much if you can't help someone out when they're having tough times. Cos, life's a bitch sometimes, isn't it?'

Emmalyn paused for a second and sighed, 'hell, you're right,' she admitted. 'What about you? Do you have a man at home?'

It was Tamara's turn to give her potted life history. Being very aware of Emmalyn's misfortunes, she tried to play down the style of life she shared with Jeffrey.

'And what about your son? What does he think of your partner?'

'Willis? Well, Willis and he, they get along just fine. They are both crazy about water sports. They go out together swimming, surfing or whatever, quite frequently. But Emmalyn let's get back to you finding a new job ...'

'I really appreciate your help.'

'You know I can't promise anything, but if you contact a Mrs Rosemund, she's the human resources manager at the hotel. They'll interview you. If they think you're suitable, the next time a vacancy comes up, they will let you know.' She passed a piece of paper to Emmalyn, who immediately tapped the number into her phone.

'That's very good of you. Ideally, I'd like to get back into real estate. But, I have to take what's available to eke out an existence. As you know, with over twenty per cent unemployment on the island, jobs are difficult to come by.'

'Just give me a call and come over to the hotel. I'll show you around. I'm the events manager there. It keeps me frantically busy.' Tamara silently felt grateful that her job was relatively secure.

'You know, I just might do that.'

'Can I give you a ride back home?' Tamara asked, 'you said you didn't have to start work until four.'

Emmalyn didn't take up the offer for some time. They found many other topics to chew over. Despite Tamara's need to get on with work, she didn't drop Emmalyn off outside her small creole cottage for some time. She rushed back to Three Isles fretting that she'd spent too long on her socialising. Her job kept her so busy, dashing from one thing to another; with never enough time to straighten out her thoughts, and her own life.

A dark turquoise, turbulent sea awaited her at Three Isles. As she walked up the inclined path, thoughts of Emmalyn's small wooden cottage invaded her mind. She'd grown to love the ever-changing seascape, framed by the rustling palms. That day waves lashed against the rocky isles; the inclement weather had rendered the beach deserted. The ocean and its moods seemed to have become a part of her spirit. She could do without the rest, though she realised it was what many dreamed of: the infinity pool, the spacious rooms, sleek contemporary furniture, and the artwork; she could do without all that, but Tamara adored living over-looking the sea.

The living-room doors were folded back, allowing the natural light, reflecting off the pool, into the space. Grabbing a drink from the large refrigerator before installing herself on the settee, she was straight into work mode—organising her next wedding. On her phone, she scanned through her list of suppliers. The florist was first on her list. The couple wanted to walk off the beach under an archway of tropical flowers. Vibrant coloured bougainvillea would embellish the tables at the reception. The bride would be clutching a bouquet of frangipani and ginger lilies. It was an important, costly order. It was her job to ensure the couple's dreams were realised—everything must run like clockwork. Her telephone conversation reassured her. The flowers were all available. The team from the flower store would be at the hotel bright and early the next morning.

She was so preoccupied, hunched over her phone she failed to notice a silhouette blocking the open doorway. The ocean's tumult had masked sounds of his appearance.

'Hi Babe.' Jeffrey surprised her as his shoes clicked across the wooden flooring and into the sitting area. 'I didn't expect to see you here. So, what are you doing home?'

'I could ask you the same thing. This is early for you. I've a few urgent calls to make before heading off to the hotel. I'll be late this evening Jeff. There's an important marriage ceremony tomorrow.'

'Shame, I've had a great day. I thought we could go out for dinner. It just might have to be with Willis when he gets back from college.'

'Sorry, there's no way I can fit dinner in. I have to be there to supervise the organisation of the reception room and check on a multitude of other things.' She watched Jeffrey head towards their bedroom. 'I'm sure it'll be pretty late before I'm home again.'

'Shame,' a faint voice called.

Tamara was in the middle of another call by the time Jeffrey re-appeared. He made an entrance unshod, in just his swimming attire. He bounced towards Tamara, disregarding that she was on the phone. While she tried to maintain a conversation about decorating the dining area, he showered the back of her neck with kisses.

'Yes, that's right. You'll need to be there by eleven o'clock,' she told the person online, pushing Jeffrey away with her free hand. He was not deterred. He persisted. His hands went down her blouse.

'No, they haven't said so,' Tamara said, desperately trying to continue her call. Irritated, she bounced off the sofa and walked away. She shook her head at him and pointed a finger at her phone. But Jeffrey was not about to take no for an answer. He advanced towards her again.

She finished her call as quickly as possible. 'Please Jeff. The call was important.'

'More important than me?' clasping her and kissing her face.

'No, of course not, but it's for work.' She wasn't going to admit that perhaps it was. 'I'm sorry I don't have time to spend on … ' she muttered, avoiding looking into his eyes.

'Tammy I won't be seeing you for at least three weeks.' His face carried a hurt expression. 'I just thought that you could show me how much you'll miss me whilst I'm gone. I've had a great day. Don't go and spoil things for me.'

'Sorry Jeff, but I have to get back to work,' she said, resentment mounting inside; tension knots forming in her stomach.

Jeffrey had decided exactly what he wanted. He didn't care too much about the rest. As was usual, the tone of his voice, his look, his gesturers, showed his attitude—he was in charge and should definitely achieve whatever he fancied.

'You're disappointing me Tammy. You won't say no? Just ten minutes together. You know you'll enjoy it too.'

Tamara was far from sure about that. She knew she would not relax; she had too much to think about. Her eyes were levelled at the floor not wanting to look at him. She was silent, whilst inside her temper was boiling over. Thoughts of all that she had to do at work kept on circling around her mind. It seemed Jeffrey could do exactly what he liked with his time, but her time wasn't her own—it belonged to him, when he wanted it. She badly needed to get on with her work. Keeping Jeffrey happy was the last thing that she needed. She was so pre-occupied, there was no way she could switch onto feeling passionate or sexy. Nevertheless, she turned off her phone and placed it on the side table next to her. Despite the resentment inside, she lifted her face towards him and summoned up a half smile. Reluctantly, she touched his bare flesh. The word 'no' didn't cross her lips. This wasn't the time to upset him.

He kissed her lightly on the lips and led her by the hand towards their bedroom. As Tamara walked down the corridor, she thought of Emmalyn. She was like her. Emmalyn put up with things she didn't like to keep her job. She did exactly the same with Jeffrey. But he was leaving the island tomorrow. Three weeks without him; and she and Willis would be left in peace. She didn't like admitting to herself that she was a coward, an avaricious coward.

Chapter 20

Finale

'Come on Miranda.'

Katie put her arm around her employer's shoulder 'you know you'll enjoy it when we get there.'

'No Katie,' Miranda said slowly, but determinedly, 'I really don't want to go. I'm not good at the games.'

'Do you mean the exercises? You are fine with all the exercises. They're nothing to worry about. Don't you feel very well today? Remember it's only for an hour. You always enjoy the chit chat afterwards.'

'Perhaps, but not today. No, I just want to stay at home.'

Katie was trying to persuade Miranda to go to the twice weekly exercise class. She'd noticed a downward slide in Miranda's well-being. Since her second stroke, she had become far less active. Much of her re-gained confidence and energy had evaporated. Even for Katie, Miranda had become a shadow of her former self. Her sparkle had been virtually extinguished. Katie had also reported other noticeable changes to Miranda's doctor. Her short-term memory had deteriorated even more. She frequently found it difficult to concentrate, or was looking for words she couldn't remember. Katie would sometimes watch her standing around, looking about herself and wondering what she was supposed to be doing. Both of them became distressed by this. Fortunately, there was one thing that hadn't got worse— the slight unevenness of one side of her face hadn't dropped further.

'Let's go for a walk then. You know that you enjoy that. We could just take a stroll around the garden. We could go and see what's new in the flower beds.'

Miranda hesitated, stared out of the window at the weather. Unsure what to say, seeming unsure what she wanted to do.

'I'll go and get your coat.' Katie dashed upstairs in search of outdoor clothing for both of them. When she returned, her arms full of garments, Miranda was still in the same spot, still gazing blankly through the sitting room window.

Katie helped her patient with her coat and wound a scarf around her neck, as though she were a small child. Miranda made no effort to assist. Katie's heart went out to her; she grieved for the mere shell of a person that was left of her employer—someone only a few years older than herself. To look at her now, you'd think her well into her eighties. Someone who just limped from one day to the next. Lacking motivation to live. The only people who brought a faint smile to her lips were her daughter Ella, and her granddaughter Kloe.

Katie linked her arm through Miranda's and guided her through the front door and out into the muted light bathing the garden. They crunched over the pebbled path, heading for the flower beds.

'Listen, can you hear it? It's a blackbird. I always think they sing so beautifully. It's astounding that such load music comes from such a small creature.' Miranda did not respond. They continued the stroll along the edge of the border, her head angled downwards.

'That auricula is the colour of blood,' Miranda said suddenly. Katie halted. She looked down at the pom-poms of flower heads standing proudly along the edge of the cultivated garden. Primulas of crimson, their centres painted with smudges of white and yellow.

'They are exquisite.'

'They have always been one of my favourite plants. But you know Katie, they aren't that easy to grow.'

'So, what's the best way to grow them?' Katie asked, surprised at Miranda's unexpected burst of enthusiasm.

'Well, the soil must be well drained, and they don't like the mid-day sun,' she explained confidently; then her speech dried up. She stood focused on the spikes of sculptural plants.

After several seconds silence, Katie tried to continue the dialogue. 'Can you remember anything else about them?' Miranda slowly shook her head. 'Never mind, we can look it up when we get back indoors. You did well to remember their name. I didn't know what they were called. Let's see what else we can find.'

The tour of springtime plants continued. They ambled from one point of interest to another, Katie trying hard to engage her patient in conversation about the varied vegetation, in order to keep her mind active. As they progressed around the flower beds, Miranda's mood seemed to lift a little, as she displayed her obvious enjoyment. Katie judged that it was perhaps an appropriate moment to broach something she'd wanted to discuss for several days.

'Miranda, I need to talk to you,' she stood alongside Miranda who was scrutinising a tall bush. With as gentle a voice as she could manage, she explained, 'it's about my job. I'm sorry, but I have decided that I should move on.'

'What do you mean?' Her lined face looked hurt. 'Move on? I don't understand.'

'I mean I need to find another job Miranda.'

'You want to leave Oakdale?'

'It's not you, or the house, it's ...' she broke off, trying to find the appropriate explanation. 'The thing is, I've met somebody. Somebody who lives in Bristol. I see him every weekend now. But I want to spend more time with him.'

Miranda stood motionless for what seemed like several minutes. She looked vacantly at the fading, marshmallow-coloured blooms of the camellia bush. 'What's its name? I can't think of the name.'

'It's a camellia. Do you understand Miranda? I've decided to find another job.'

Miranda gazed at her companion. 'It's a camellia,' she repeated, as though she hadn't taken on board what Katie had just told her. But slowly, she took Katie's hands in hers. Unhurriedly, she continued, 'Katie, you know, I don't want you to go. But I understand.'

'Thank you. It's been a long time.'

'Yes, I will really miss you. You'll come back and see me, won't you?'

'Yes, of course. I've really loved living at Oakdale. But it's just you don't get too many chances like this, when you get to my age.'

'Mm, I understand,' she said again. She let go of her hands and restarted her circuit of the garden. 'I hope it works out for you. I hope it works better than it did for me.'

'Miranda why ...?' Then she stopped. She did not have the right to question her about her relationship with her husband, especially considering her own connection with him. Her patient had never opened up to her about Jeffrey. She would have liked to ask her why she didn't divorce him. But she knew it was inappropriate. And Katie knew only too well, Miranda no longer had the mental capabilities to cope with such a major problem.

'Miranda, I will naturally stay on here until you find somebody to replace me,' she smiled at her, but Miranda was already distracted by something else in the garden. A flowering viburnum had caught her attention. She was pulling at its leaves to scrutinise its new growth. It appeared that the topic of Katie leaving Oakdale was already cast aside.

'Bradley planted these you know. He was so clever in the garden. He knew so much about plants. Jeffrey knows nothing about gardens. He doesn't even know ...'

Katie interrupted her, 'Oh something else Miranda, I'm sorry I forgot. Jeffrey will be returning this weekend. He sent an e-mail to say he's flying back from Sainte Marie, arriving on Sunday.'

Miranda stopped removing faded flowers from the plant. 'Two bad pieces of news in one day. I wish he'd stay out there. I'm sure he's more wanted out there.'

Katie's opinion remained unstated.

~~~

Katie had always admired the lounge bar of the Beaulieu hotel. She'd privately considered that whoever had done the interior design work had done an excellent job. They'd managed to combine nineteenth century elements, such as the wood panelling and the stone fireplace, with contemporary leather furniture, and had achieved a stunning effect. She felt sure that it would be the last opportunity she would have to see it.

Sun blasted through the arched windows. Katie found herself a seat next to one in order to admire the garden. The tailored landscape tempted her to venture outside. It looked to be an island of calm; enhanced by plants to suit every temperament; from rigid, spiky leaves mounting confidently, to soft, velvety ones, shaped like lambs' ears flopping over. She craved to immerse herself in its enchantment, but her watch told her Jeffrey could arrive at any time.

Time ticked by, but he failed to make an appearance. Katie checked her watch frequently. The minutes seemed to drag. She told herself it was because she was on edge about seeing him. As she left her seat, intending to order another fruit cocktail, she saw him. Jeffrey was making his way from reception, pulling his wheeled cabin bag behind him. His lightweight zipped jacket was open, revealing a fairly crumpled patterned shirt.

'Hello Babe, they told me that you were in here.' He approached her and kissed her lightly on the cheek.

'What can I get you to drink Jeffrey? I'm already on my second,' she said, continuing her path to the bar. 'Have a good flight?'

'A white wine would be very welcome,' his tired face opened up in a smile. 'Yes, fine thanks. Shall we take the drinks up to our room?'

She turned from her place at the bar. 'You can go and dump your luggage, whilst I get the drinks. But I will be staying down here. I thought I'd like to go and look around the garden in a moment.' Katie was determined that she wouldn't be going upstairs this visit.

Jeffrey's mouth turned downwards. This was not part of their usual routine. 'Oh, I thought you'd prefer to ... '

'No.'

He stepped even closer and took hold of her wrist. 'Aren't you pleased to see me? I thought that you would be eager to show how you've missed me,' he uttered, his voice barely audible.

'Yes, but no,' she prised his fingers from around her arm. 'I'll see you in a few minutes Jeffrey. I shall be drinking my cocktail down here.'

Jeffrey persisted, 'But Babe, it would be far more appropriate up in the room,' he ran his fingers up her arm, as the barman approached to take the drinks order.

'I've said no. I'll see you soon Jeff,' Katie stated emphatically. He made it obvious that he was disgruntled by her attitude, and his failure. He trailed his suitcase out of the bar. Katie's eyes followed, knowing he was having a sulk.

'So, what's the problem Babe?' Jeffrey asked when he came back down and installed himself opposite her. Katie noticed that the golden light from outside made the lines on his tanned face very visible.

'Why didn't you want to come up to the room? And I noticed your case isn't up there.'

'No, that's because I won't be staying for the weekend. I'll be driving up to Bristol when I've said what I want to say.'

'I don't understand. The room is paid for. What's so urgent in Bristol?'

'My life is awaiting me in Bristol. I will no longer be a part of yours Jeffrey.'

'But Babe, we've got a great relationship going here. I thought that you loved living in Lyme Regis.'

'I love living there and I get on well with Miranda, but I've come to my senses. I'm fed up of being used. Fed up with your demanding ways. It's time to move on,' she told him in a discrete tone.

'But Miranda needs you there, she relies on you.'

'I've told Miranda. I've told Ella. They'll find somebody else. I've asked Ella to make it as soon as possible. I can't go on like this Jeffrey. Your poor wife doesn't have much of a life as it is. I won't have to fool her any longer. I'm finished with you and your cheating.'

'What cheating? I don't understand. You mean because you helped with the money for the upkeep of the house and to pay for Miranda's nursing.'

'So you told me, she lowered her voice even more, 'but you know, I sometimes wonder if Miranda suffered her second stroke because she discovered that you had used one of her properties to release equity without her consent. I told you I found an opened letter from the equity release company in the sitting room the following day.'

'You don't know that for sure.'

Katie sipped at her drink, feeling pleased she'd found the wisdom to make her life-changing decision. 'You look tired Jeffrey. You should give up all your globe-trotting.'

He leaned in towards her, and hissed his reply, ignoring her comments about his looks, 'You were only too pleased to get that money to go towards your Spanish investment.'

'I was foolish to take such a chance—misleading Miranda into signing your forms. But Jeffrey, I'm sure that you have been only too happy to spend some of that money yourself,' she raised her glass to him.

'I shall inform your agency that you're dishonest. You'll never get another job,' his face sent a warning to hers.

'You can threaten me all you like Jeffrey,' she finished her drink, 'but I know plenty about you that certain people would love to hear.' She looked directly at him as she stood and retrieved her handbag from the window ledge.

'You'll regret this. I shall make sure that you do.'

Katie moved towards him and bent level with his ear. 'If you say so Jeffrey, but don't forget, you say nothing about me and I'll say nothing about you,' she whispered. 'You can't frighten me like that.'

Standing upright, she took in his waning looks and asked herself how she had put up with him for so long. She made for the door to the garden, and then turned towards him one last time.

'Oh, I nearly forgot—a message from Miranda. She told me a few days ago that she couldn't understand why you didn't stay in Sainte Marie. You might be of some use there,' she grasped the door handle. 'I think I'd agree with her on that one.' She threw him a fake smile. 'Unfortunately, I shall see you at Oakdale on Monday.'

Jeffrey was half out of his seat, a comment on his lips, but it was never spoken.

'As it'll be the last time that I'll be visiting Beaulieu, I'm going to have a walk around the gardens. Enjoy your weekend Jeffrey.' She pushed her exit ajar, 'oh yes, and one last thing. My name is Katie, not Babe.'

Katie didn't wait to see his reaction. As soon as she stepped into the bright light, she felt relieved. She moved towards the strong floral smell which assailed her nostrils. The exterior was bursting with colour. She delighted in the flowering bulbs, the flaming of the berberis and the soft pink of the clematis.

There were things she had failed to mention during their set-to in the bar. The recent events in her life which had brought about her resolve to finish with Jeffrey, Miranda, and Oakdale. She'd said nothing of the man she had she had met several months previously. Or their plan to head off to Spain as soon as the agency had found a replacement for her. Her spirits rose. She studied each plot of the meticulously cared-for garden, but her dreams were flying to the Costa del Sol and viewing small apartments for her new life. The savings she'd made during her time with Miranda, had made it all possible. She'd just taken the first step to moving on and blanking out the past. Katie yearned to start her new life in the sun.

Chapter 21

Entitlement

Thanks so much.

Just heard hotel has put me on their waiting list. Speak soon. Emmalyn

Mid-morning, Tamara was on her coffee break. She sat in the shade, on a plastic garden chair which had once been white. The noise behind her of spoons clattering against mugs spoke of colleagues also making coffee in the staff canteen. She read the message again and felt pleased that her efforts for her new-found friend had been successful.

Great! See you soon. T was tapped into her phone.

She'd gained distinct satisfaction from reaching out to Emmalyn—doing all she could for her. It was clear that she needed a bit of support. A sympathetic ear and a helping hand had changed many a life. She must invite her for lunch soon, now that Jeffrey was off-island.

Phone stowed away, zipped into her canvas bag, she rested her head on the warmth of the building behind her. Sunlight flooded into the yard at the back of the staff quarters. Tamara's mind was clogged up. She had too much to think about. Thoughts bounced off the glaring white of the painted wall opposite her—the cement block wall which kept the back-of-house area well out of sight of the hotel guests. Enclosing the powerhouse, laundry, staff not on duty and the mishmash of unused articles stacked in untidy piles awaiting repair. The hotel may have four stars next to its name, but those stars didn't shine as far as the staff facilities.

Her brain was still buzzing with the events of the evening before. Jeffrey's domineering and controlling behaviour had not left her. A new tightness had settled inside her. It clutched at her chest, like an over-tight corset. It had taken away hours of her sleep. She'd replayed every line of the scene that night, and those from other episodes.

She had taken exception to his possessiveness. Looking at things objectively, she'd come to realise he'd always emitted an air of entitlement. He'd always adopted a term of phrase intended to make her feel guilty. Guilty, if she didn't succumb to his wishes. And inferior—the inference being that he was far more important than her. Jeffrey should always come first—certainly before anything she wanted. Was it to do with his age, his sex or his race, or a combination of all three?

For Jeffrey, his work was his raison d'être. Real estate and property always came first. It was stamped on each of his bones. Everything else came second to that. But her job was not permitted to be as hugely important to her. Of course not. What she wanted didn't matter. She was good for being on her back for him; and looking after his every other need. His presence was beginning to make her feel tense, frequently ill-at-ease. She knew there was a cure which would take away these symptoms, but she wasn't certain she was ready to take it just yet.

Tamara needed her work. It had become her escape—a distraction away from Jeffrey and their relationship. She realised that she must never admit any of this to anybody. She had to play along with his game; be the woman that he expected. Demanded.

Now that he wasn't at home, life had become more straightforward, more manageable. She wondered if his legal wife felt the same way—that life was simpler, less stressful when he wasn't there. Tamara knew next to nothing about Miranda, only the snippets Jeffrey fed her. He'd told her Miranda had changed totally; she was a different person from the one he first met. She'd become very fragile for her years. Privately, Tamara held the view that the poor woman must be in a very bad state for her not to divorce him. It seemed there was no love left between them. She gleaned from comments about his travels,

Jeffrey was not often with her. She heard snippets about successful business transactions across Europe—the different countries that he'd flown to.

Nobody's life was ever perfect, and hers had compensations. She had to appreciate the positive side of being with Jeffrey: he had furnished her with the opportunity to achieve new professional qualifications, widened her and Willis' world, and their view of it. She lived in a stunning environment. To maintain this level of privilege, she had to develop a tolerance of his self-centred idiosyncrasies.

'So, who are the happy couple this time?'

Her inner monologue ceased abruptly. Tamara turned to see one of her colleagues addressing her. She stared back at her blankly.

'Sorry, I was miles away Creselda.'

'Yeah, you could see that. You seemed to be studying that pile of junk over there as though it was a priceless piece of art. Dreaming of that man of yours?'

'Oh heavens no, I was just thinking of a friend. Someone who life is doling her one hell of a time at the moment.'

'Well, we all have to live through that at one time or another, don't we?' she said, sitting next to her. 'No, I was asking you what type of wedding you are organising this time.'

Tamara explained it would be a second time around couple. There wouldn't be too many guests, but they were spending big bucks on it. She would be in rosewood pink, and he would be wearing electric blue.

'Wow, that'll be an unconventional combination,' Creselda grinned.

'Yup, but they're an unconventional couple. It takes all sorts you know.'

'Do all these nuptials give you a hankering to have your wedding?'

'Hell no,' Tamara laughed. 'In fact, it does the opposite. You see so many brides and grooms that you can tell are going to be together for no more than five minutes. It all seems such a waste of effort and money. Lots of folks seem to be in love with the idea of getting married, rather than being in love with each other. You need to be one hundred per cent sure, don't you? And I haven't found that perfect guy.'

'What about your current boo?'

'Jeffrey, oh no, we rub along okay, but he's not the love of my life. And I know for certain, I'm not his. Besides, he's already married.' As soon as it was said, she regretted it. She hadn't chosen her words with sufficient care. What had she just confessed? Was that the way she really felt? She swiftly reverted the conversation back to Creselda. 'You ever been married?'

'No. Thought we would, then like a lot of Romeos, he told me a lot of stories, gave me a couple of kids, a load of debts, and then pushed off to some other fool. It's now made me very wary of others.'

'I know exactly what you mean,' Tamara said. 'So, who looks after the kids whilst you're at work?'

'They're both at school now, but I've got a lodger who keeps an eye on them if I'm not around.' Creselda glanced at her watch. Without skipping a beat, she sprung up from her seat. 'Hey, we're doing too much chit chattering! You seen the time?' she pushed Tamara's arm. 'It's back to that Kids' Club for me. Good luck with those wedding preparations. See ya again.'

'Good to talk to you. Yeah, see ya soon.'

Creselda scuttled back through to the staff canteen. Tamara snatched her bag up from the dusty concrete floor. Clutching her mug, she aimed for the sink to wash it up. Her brain had to switch over to wedding organisation mode, but her confessions to Creselda had unsettled her. She regretted opening up so much. It had set her mind wandering, zigzagging around the realities of her world. Her mind was in conflict again.

She reached her office on autopilot. Getting there, she knew she had to shut out her problems. Put her private life on hold, just like she had done so many times before. The wedding scheduled for the next ceremony had to take priority. She fired up her computer. Opened up the file for the second time around couple's happy, happy day. She scanned her long check list. Double check on the officiant. Contact the videographer again for last minute change of instructions. Ensure that the sound system for outside music was A Okay. Discuss the cocktails and wines with the sommelier. Visit the hotel kitchen to finalise details of the small reception. Touch base with the spa to chat through the bride and her friends' beauty and hair requirements.

The list went on. She was going to be as busy as a hummingbird with two tails, and hard pressed to get through all the demands before the ceremony.

~~~

Tamara swung onto the small, pebbled lot next to Emmalyn's cottage and cut the motor. She immediately took stock of the organisation and structure of the plot in front her. It was in stark contrast to the wall of savage, tangled vegetation behind. Large stones, bricks or sections of timber encased a patchwork of greens against ebony loam. Beds neatly planted. Straight rows of what looked like vegetables and herbs. Bright green, frilly-edged pumpkin leaves, masking vibrant orange fruits beneath. She recognised those, but the rest was a mystery to her. The garden spoke volumes about Emmalyn.

She took in the entirety of Emmalyn's world—living a scaled-down life, in a meagre home on a small-scale plot—like many others on island. Until recently, she herself had been amongst their numbers.

Most things had been a struggle, especially the finances. Month end, she had had to economise, large-scale—counting the days, counting 'til that last Friday of the month. Pay day.

Dreading Christmas and birthdays. Praying that there wouldn't be any unexpected household emergencies. Hoping against hope that neither of them would be seriously ill; knowing that if they were, she would be unable to afford the medical bills. Taking on short-term loans to cover the problematic times. Short-term, but with high interest. Depriving Willis, or herself of any little extras that they might have craved for. Living in basic conditions; making do with second-hand clothes, furniture, and equipment.

She stepped out of her car feeling a little guilty, but also relief she no longer had to live like that. The screen door of the wooden cottage was thrown wide open, framing a beaming Emmalyn. Attired in cut-off jeans and T-shirt, so unlike her work attire. She waved a welcome.

'Hi darlin'! It's great to see you!' Emmalyn called from the doorway.

'You're looking altogether more chilled than at Jacko's.'

'I've had a good week. Krish wasn't working,' uncharacteristically Emmalyn almost skipped along the path.

'You should suggest he stays away for good,' Tamara waved a hand in the direction of the cultivated area of the garden. 'Hey, I've been admiring your vegetable patch.'

'Wanna come and take a peek?' she asked proudly, walking towards the fruits of her labour. She guided Tamara towards a bed of tomato plants.

'You like a few tomatoes to take home?' She removed a truss of cherry tomatoes from the stem. 'I have to water this lot morning and evening. They're real thirsty veggies!'

'Thanks a lot Emmalyn, but just a few. All this must take up so much of your free time.'

'Sure, but it saves a packet on my food bills. I can also sell some of the stuff for a few dollars. Mr Jackson, he frequently pays for my stuff. Anyway, how ya doing Tamara? How's your maker-of-memories job going?'

Tamara chuckled, 'Well, that's one way of describing my events manager position. Yeah, I hope most of the memories will be joyful ones. It's been super hectic, but good. I'm pleased to be having a day off.' She moved around the garden checking over each bed. 'So, what's this then?'

'Oh, those will be chillies—yellow ones—really hot stuff! They'll blow your mind!'

'Oh, not for me then. I detest the stingy pain in my mouth.' Tamara took in the vibes of the patch of ground. The multitude of different plants and the numerous scents they gave off. She moved on to another row of healthy-looking vegetation. A strong, herby smell invaded her nostrils. She breathed in the perfumed air. Instantly, a scrap of her past floated back to her— watching her mother preparing food at an old wooden table. 'Mmm, that smells so good'

'It'll be the thyme, or the garlic,' Emmalyn ran her hand delicately over the herbs.

'You love it, don't you—the garden and growing your own stuff?'

'It's my calm after a hateful day. I can get physical. Tear out the weeds. Chop up remains for compost. Pretend I'm chopping up Krish. No, not really. But I like the quiet, the sun blaring down. The plants sprouting up; imagining what they'll taste like,' she paused and turned away from her beloved garden. 'And what about you? How do you switch off?'

Tamara wasn't sure how to answer. She had been an avid reader, but that had been a long time ago, before Willis, before her very full-time jobs; before having to keep a home clean and tidy. She was ashamed to say that she really didn't have time, didn't make time, to have a past-time just for her.

'Not a lot. I suppose I should.'

'Yes, I can recommend it. All the aggro disappears. Gone in a few minutes, working out here.' She stooped beside a large-leaved plant which dominated the bed. 'The sweet potatoes are doing well.'

'Talking of food, lunch awaits. I thought we'd eat at my place and then we can lounge around the pool afterwards. Willis has gone out with friends, so we'll be by ourselves. Have you got any swimmies?'

'Yes, somewhere. That's real nice of ya Tamara. It'll be relaxing.'

'Let's hope so. By the way, how many bedrooms are there in your house?

'Two, why do ya ask?'

'A spare room can earn you money Emmalyn—even if it's only a few hundred bucks a month. Somebody at work talked about her lodger, and I thought of you.'

'You can come and see whilst I look for my swimsuit.'

They walked back towards the compact dwelling. As Tamara had figured, the house was spick and span, but most of the contents looked very well–worn. She was shown the two double rooms with a bathroom in between. The pink bath, pink toilet and even pinker tiles told her that the contents had probably been installed many years before.

'Shame that the second bedroom doesn't have an en-suite. You could rent it for more.' Tamara commented from the bedroom doorway, watching Emmalyn rummage through a cupboard searching for her swim wear.

'I've never seriously thought of renting it out. Stupid isn't it, having worked in real estate? I've always liked my privacy.'

'Mmm, but needs must when the devil drives. It could help you out. Pay some of your bills, help get your car back.'

'I really miss my wheels. Losing my car was like losing a part of me. It's your independence gone. Yes, I'll have to re-think it through. I could always go and see my old boss. She does rentals.' She pushed her swimsuit into her bag and started another search for a towel.

'If you choose the tenant carefully, it could work you know. Willis and I could help you paint the walls if you like.'

'That's very sweet. I just might take you up on that,' she glanced up at her bedroom, recognising that it was in need of some attention. 'These walls haven't seen a fresh coat of paint in many a moon,' she sighed. 'I'm ready. I've got my stuff—and your tomatoes.'

Emmalyn clutched the bag bulging with ripe tomatoes all the way to Three Isles. She chattered all the time, oblivious to the change of images they passed through. Busy urbanisation fell away; the number of habitations dwindled. The lush greens of vegetation became denser. The car swung them towards the coast. The road petered out into an uneven track. Tamara slowed the vehicle to a walking pace. Flashes of light off the ocean reflected onto the windscreen. As Tamara pulled into the communal car park and stopped, she noted Emmalyn's sudden silence—as if she had been struck by a thunder bolt. Emmalyn sat and stared. Gazed out across the fence, across the margin of buff sand in the direction of the turquoise sea. Angled palms framing the aspect. She took in the three isles, stark against a cloudless sky.

Then she turned towards Tamara, 'this is where you live? You sure got one mega view.'

'Yeah, I said I lived at Three Isles.'

Emmalyn stared back at her almost nonsensically. 'But on the beach. I didn't think … I don't know where I thought you lived. This is really something. This man of yours, he got a friend?' her mouth widened into a grin.

Tamara nudged her arm playfully, 'I'm not sure. I'll have to ask. Let's go get our eats.'

She walked Emmalyn up to the front entrance in silence. Inside, the internal shutters were immediately unlatched to let out the stifling heat.

'Would you like to change into your swim wear and have a dip whilst I heat up our lunch?'

'Good idea,' Emmalyn said quietly. She followed her host into the guest bedroom, still carrying her bag of tomatoes as well as her plastic beach bag. Several minutes later, she appeared in a black swimsuit, clutching her towel. She hesitated at the living area to study the large contemporary settees, the local sculptures on the glass topped tables and the semi-abstract prints adorning the walls.

'Lunch won't be long. You enjoy your dip,' Tamara said chopping up herbs.

'Thanks. I forgot to give you the tomatoes.' She placed them carefully on the quartz-topped work surface, letting a finger trail over its smooth coolness.

Tamara watched as she cautiously slipped herself into the pool. Slowly her body rose to float on the water. Her hands flopped slowly. It took her minutes to commence her passage of the length of the pool, back and forth. By the time Tamara went out to lay the table, she was sitting on the edge, peering vacantly in front of her.

'What's going around that head of yours then?' Tamara laid place mats and some shiny cutlery on the garden table.

'I was just thinking through your suggestion about getting a lodger. I think I should do it. I might even be able to afford to get my car back. I'll go and see Mrs Leon when I can and ask her advice.'

'I'll be back with the chicken in just a sec.'

Emmalyn wrapped her towel around her, sarong style, and seated herself at the table. Tamara returned bringing two laden plates.

'That looks good mi dear,' Emmalyn said, sizing up her lunch. 'You know, you're right, I really should try. Try to get a lodger that is. Wow! I'm getting spoilt. A glass of wine as well.'

Tamara poured a cascade of straw-coloured wine into the glass next to her. 'Thanks for the invite.'

'You're very welcome. Did you enjoy your swim?'

'Relaxing,' she put a forkful of chicken and rice into her mouth, then rested her fork on her plate with a clatter. 'Tamara, I don't know you very well, so I hope you don't mind me asking. But how in heaven's name did you come to be living here? It's like something out of the movies. I mean, your parking lot is worth more than my house. I don't know too many islanders who live like this.'

'It's not mine Emmalyn. It belongs to Jeffrey. Yes, I'm pretty lucky to live here. And Willis too.' She looked directly at Emmalyn. 'I don't want you to think I'm showing off. Flaunting what I've got. I just happen to live here because I'm in a relationship with Jeffrey Taylor. I don't pay for any of the bills. I just buy the food.'

'No, I don't think that you're boasting. I don't see you as that type of person. It was ...' she broke off a few seconds to eat more of her lunch, '... well, it was a bit of a shock. It wasn't what I'd expected. Having said that I think it's unbelievably beautiful here. And the house, boy, I just love it. It must be worth a few dollars.'

'I don't pry Emmalyn,' Tamara confessed. 'I don't ask how much he paid for it, or how he pays the bills. I just know that he does. I know Jeffrey had his own real estate offices in London. Apparently, he sold it at a very good price. Here, on island, he works for Mr Denning, at Topaz hotel, Mango Bay. He sells properties for him and others too, all over the Caribbean. And oh yes, Jeffrey has gotten involved in property investment as well. He's frequently doing deals. He's not short of a dollar or two. But I don't get involved. I don't ask any busy-body questions.'

'That's probably the way he likes it,' Emmalyn said recommencing her meal.

'You could be right,' Tamara admitted, whilst knowing that it was undoubtedly a major reason why she and Jeffrey were still in a relationship. 'As far as the house is concerned, all I know is that forty-nine per cent of it is in my name.' She noticed Emmalyn's eyebrows go up. 'I don't really understand the complexities, but when we went to see the attorney, she explained that. She also said that Jeffrey had taken out insurance for the villa. An insurance that would pay for it, should anything happen to him. Jeffrey's never really taken the time to explain all about it. And I've never asked him either.'

'I can perhaps help you out there. He probably set up a company to buy it. You own forty-nine per cent of the company shares. In Sainte Marie, it's an advantage. It means, if he sells it, you don't have to pay the government ten per cent of the selling price in tax. It also means if the company is bankrupted, his personal assets won't be affected.'

'Oh, so he's done it to protect himself. What'll happen if we split up? I suppose Willis and I'd be homeless.'

'Oh boy Tamara, I really don't know! Depends what the fine print says. Ya think that's likely?'

'Hell, I don't know. I just live from day to day. We get along okay most of the time. But you know what life's like, you get so intensely busy, you don't have time to think about anything too much.' She felt it was time, to get off this topic, so asked, 'Tell me, what did you do when you were working in real estate?'

Emmalyn's face lit up as though this was exactly the question she wanted to hear. This was a talking point dear to her heart. 'I've told you, I worked for Mrs Leon in Anse Argent. When times were good, she would sell a lot of property. She did most of the paperwork. Dealing with the attorneys. Trying to get folks their loans. I would do the viewings. I used to get a commission when I sold something. I picked up a lot of knowledge on the way. I keep hoping that things'll improve enough for her to ask me back. By the sound of things, your man doesn't seem to have problems selling property, so maybe they are. I can always live in hope.'

She went on to relate some amusing stories about properties she'd sold and the out-of- the-ordinary people she'd encountered. Tamara noticed that once she'd finished her lunch, Emmalyn started to relax. She sat in the chair in a slanting position, her bare feet stretched towards a patch of sunlight on the terrace. As she told her stories, her voice rose and became excited. She smiled frequently, her eyes squinting into almond shapes.

The afternoon advanced. The intense heat changed the colours of their view to sharp silver, electric blue and lime. The conversation flowed freely. There were confidences that Tamara would have liked to share, but their friendship was young. She felt wary. She didn't want to say anything inappropriate, as she'd done with Creselda. So, instead she told her about her visit to the Tamarind, where she was sure that Emmalyn would love the gardens, the beach, and the complex. The wine bottle was drained. Tamara was enjoying her afternoon. She found Emmalyn entertaining. They laughed about the same things.

The ringing of her phone cut their amusement abruptly short. Tamara studied the display—Jeffrey on his English mobile. A flash of irritation clouded her face. A finger briskly flicked it to the message service. She smiled at Emmalyn, and returned to their dialogue without comment. The phone was returned to its place on the table.

Chapter 22

Partners

D–Day at last.

After a countdown of three months, it'd arrived. As he walked from the bus stop, his mind was overflowing with one thing. One person. One image. Madison. She was back on island. Her family had flown in that day. He knew she was very near. Just in their neighbouring villa. During their social media contact she had encouraged his interest. Enticed him with promises of an unfolding of their friendship. A blossoming of their mutual attraction. From the solitude of their own rooms, more than five and a half thousand kilometres apart, they had exchanged ideas about how they could avoid Nathan. Her brother seemed to stick to them like glue when they were in Sainte Marie. They had planned how they could be alone.

Willis put his key in the lock and let himself into the villa. The closed external shutters made the house feel stuffy and uncomfortably warm. He was far too pre-occupied and neglected to open the shutters. Hurriedly, he crossed the ill-lit, shadowy sitting room, down the corridor to his room. His backpack was tossed onto his crumpled bed. He felt an excitement. Semester was over. A long vacation lay ahead. But, it was thoughts of Maddie which made his heart race. Impatiently, he tore at his shirt, cast it on the floor. His remaining clothes joined it. He dashed into the shower, shuddering at the shock of cold water hitting naked flesh. He fantasised another form was beside him. Her whiteness as he had never seen it—without a wet suit or one of her colourful bikinis. Wet blond hair adhering to her head. Her small breasts pressed up against him. Her mouth clinging to his. The picture was shattered as he grabbed for the shower gel. The indulgence of dreaming was no good.

He had to strive for it to become a reality. Willis was confident it would be soon.

Out of the shower, he scooped up a previously discarded towel from the tiled floor and flicked it over himself. Demisting the mirror with his fist, Willis surveyed his developing shoulders and muscular arms; ran his fingers through his recently cropped hair. He felt assured that he couldn't look any better than he did. He snatched up his favourite shorts from a pile of clothes decorating a chair. Rummaging in his wardrobe, he chose a shirt that didn't look as if it needed too much attention. Willis convinced himself he was ready. He looked cool. He swung out of the bedroom and collided—slammed into a dark shape.

'Shit,' he shouted at the obstacle in his path.

'For Christ's sake!'

'I didn't expect you to be ...'

'Don't do that again. You nearly gave me a bloody heart attack.'

'Sorry. I was ... '

'I was coming to see if you were at home. Obviously, you are.'

'Yeah sorry, I came out of there in a bit fast.' Willis composed himself and grinned, 'Hi Jeff, good flight back?'

'It was long ... very long ... so, where are you off to in such a blazing hurry?'

'Eh, Madison and Nathan arrived today. I was just going to see if they were at home.'

'Madison's the cute blond I've clocked a couple of times on the beach? No wonder you're in a hurry,' Jeffrey smirked, 'I think I'd be too.'

Willis wasn't certain if he saw a flicker of a leer pass over Jeffrey's face. 'I'll leave you to get yourself sorted Jeff. See ya later.' He started to inch his way down the corridor. He took one, two steps away from him.

'How's about kiting tomorrow?' Jeffrey started to unbutton his crumpled shirt.

Willis hesitated, 'Tomo could be iffy. I'd need to ask the others. Let you know later Jeff.' Step three down the corridor.

At first, Jeffrey looked a little put out. 'Your mates can come too. There'd be room in the car.'

The grin on Willis' face dropped as he turned away. 'Okay, gotta go. I'll ask.' He escaped.

~~~

Jeffrey watched his departure. Heard the front door close with force. Assuring that he was definitely alone, he zeroed-in on sorting out his luggage. First of his tasks was to unfasten the safe tucked away in the floor of his wardrobe.

~~~

She pushed the door open with her foot, struggling with the packages barely in her grasp, and made a dash for the kitchen worktop. Everything was dumped there. Illumination from the exterior lights cast shadows into the room. Flickering light patterns from the pool played across the ceiling. The sound of splashing water assailed her ears. Instinctively, she knew Jeffrey was immersed in his daily exercising.

Tamara tidied her gear in the half light and then went to the edge of the pool cradling a drink. She sat enjoying the cooling air and the prelude of evening sounds—the squawking of the grackles, the high-pitched tune of the mockingbird, the calls of tree frogs. All accompanied by agitated pool water. Jeffrey beat at its surface with his palms. He failed to acknowledge her presence and continued his flailing in the iridescent turquoise swimming pool. Tamara was used to Jeffrey's fitness obsession. She watched his systematic to and fro. She preferred a far more relaxed approach to the sport. Without warning, he stopped.

Stood up at the shallow end and pushed back his unruly hair across his head.

'Hi Jeff, had a good day?' Tamara sat forward, greeting him with a smile.

'Hi Babe. Yeah, I got back a couple of hours ago. Honey, you couldn't get me a glass of cold water, could you?'

A little miffed that they hadn't shared the usual pleasantries; 'How are you Tammy?' or 'Had a good day Babe?' Tamara left to get the called-for drink. Jeffrey was lording it on one of the armchairs on her return.

'Was it a good trip?' Tamara passed him the glass and sat alongside him.

'I'd say it was pretty successful. I had some very positive meetings. I'm ninety-five per cent certain I've an investor who'll buy the debt at The Tamarind. Jay'll be over the moon. I've a meeting with him to talk things through,' Jeffrey sat back looking pleased with himself.

'Oh, that's great! I'm so pleased for him. Well done, Jeff.'

'Yes, it's great for the resort, but it should be very good for me too. I've been thinking that I might even set up an office on island to sell some of those villas,' Jeffrey paused.

'And how's Miranda?'

Jeffrey balanced his glass on the arm of the chair. His self-congratulatory air dissipated, a serious aspect clouded his face. 'Not good. During my visit, her live-in nurse resigned. It was a blow. Katie and she were very compatible. She's a lively, cheerful type. I really didn't get on with the replacement.'

'Why was that?'

'The replacement ...' Jeffrey thought about the new carer for a few seconds, '... well, she's one of the old-school. Like one of those strict, dowdy teachers you'd be frightened of as a kid. She didn't seem to have a spark of humour in her whole body. I can't imagine why Ella chose her. I know that Miranda and I may not be close any more, but I felt sorry that she had to spend her days with this bossy, old governess type. Miranda's health seemed to have deteriorated so much since my previous visit. Sometimes she's OK, at others, she's doesn't know if it's day or night.'

'Oh, I'm sorry Jeff,' Tamara laid her hand over one of his.

'Yeah, it's scary. I know Ella is worried about her. Miranda is younger than me, but you'd think she's ninety. You know, she used to be so sophisticated. Now, she flops around the house in an old, worn out cardigan and grubby slippers,' he sighed.

'She seems to worsen each time you visit.'

'Too right,' he finished his drink. 'I'd like to take you out Babe, but after the flight, I think I'd be asleep before the dessert.'

'It's not a problem! Let me see what we've got in the refrigerator,' she stood, her ten minutes of relaxation over.

'Got any of those pastry things Babe? I'll go change out of my wet things, whilst you sort something out.'

Jeffrey returned sometime later. The outside world had been excluded; the shutters closed. The air con was gusting. The table tamps were lit up. A table for two was set and Tamara was dressing plates with vegetable salads.

'You fancy a glass of wine?' Tamara asked, noting how tired Jeffrey looked.

'Mm, why not.'

'I was thinking whilst you were getting dressed, you said that you were maybe starting up an office.'

'Yeah, thinking about it. Antony's shared ownership sales are virtually at an end, but there's a lot of potential at the Tamarind site. There are so many villa owners there who won't want to go to judicial sales. They won't get a cent if their properties are sold by the courts. They'll go at rock bottom prices. They are much better selling them through real estate agents. The money achieved will go to pay off their debts.'

'Has the market improved enough to sell them now? I know Mr Denning struggled to sell some of his villas.' She placed two glasses of wine on the table.

'I've found interest is really picking up. And don't forget, they'd be sold at bargain prices. Why do you ask?'

'I was wondering if you would need somebody to help you.'

Jeffrey sat himself at the table. He smiled broadly. 'Why, do you fancy the job? You reckon we'd ever get any work done?'

Tamara didn't smile. Privately, she wasn't amused by his attitude. She was trying to have a serious conversation. 'Not me. I love my job as events manager.' She placed their meals on the table. Jeffrey made no effort to thank her. 'It's a bit of a long story really,' she started.

Jeffrey started eating, whilst Tamara put him in the picture about Emmalyn. She explained about their meeting in the fast-food restaurant, the harassment she suffered at work; that she hoped to return to work in real estate and mentioned their recent lunch together.

'So, what do you think? Would you like to meet her?'

It became apparent to Tamara he hadn't been listening very carefully. He seemed to be in a world of his own.

'Sorry Babe, I don't understand. That pastry was real good.'

'It's a patty. It's called a beef patty,' she told him crisply, rather put out by his blatant lack of interest in what she had to say. 'I was asking if you might be interested in meeting Emmalyn.'

'Yeah, if you like,' Jeffrey said casually.

'It's not what I like, I'm asking you.'

'Why not, but can we talk about it some other time though? I'm eager to get between those sheets.' He finished off the last of his wine and set down the empty glass. Jeffrey pushed back his chair and stood up. Tamara continued to eat slowly through her meal.

'Don't be too long Babe. I've really missed you whilst I was away. We got a lot of catching up to do.' With that comment, he left the table.

She did not respond. Half angry, half upset, Tamara watched him exit the room. Knife and fork clinked onto her plate; her appetite having evaporated. What was up with the man? Leaving her eating at the table? Who does that? She certainly wouldn't be heading for the bedroom in double-quick time. Sure, he must feel tired, but he'd shown no interest in what she'd been doing whilst he'd been away. In fact, he'd shown no real interest in her at all. Surely, he wasn't usually as lacking in attention. And he expected her to join him to do what he pleased with her, to satisfy his sexual appetite. For a few seconds, she asked herself why she didn't voice her vexation to him. But then, she knew the answer to that one.

~~~

The herb bed needed weeding. It was becoming difficult to identify the plants she wanted from those that she didn't. Emmalyn was pleased the ground was fairly workable, as it was frequently watered. But pulling up weeds was still a hot and sticky job under the morning sun. She was satisfied that the pile of weeds was slowly growing into a sizeable mound. Doing it made her light T-shirt glue to her body. Emmalyn peered from under her cotton sun hat as she heard footsteps crunch on her pebbled drive.

A tall, slim figure strode towards her. 'Bonjou Emmalyn.' He raised his hand in greeting.

'Hi, how can I help you?'

The man smiled. 'Ya forgets mi already?'

The tone of his voice lifted the shroud of non-recognition. 'Vincent. Sorry, it was the hair! Or should I say the lack of it.' His dreadlocks were no more—the short, trimmed hair transformed him. He approached her, grinning like a Cheshire cat.

'What ya up to? I seez ya got yaself a garden.'

'I can't get over you. You just look so different.' She thrust her garden fork into the ground.

'Mwen twavay apwezan. I works now. Full time.'

'Must suit you. You look real fine. Say Vincent, let's get out of the sun.' A little reluctantly, she led him towards the covered porch in front of her home.

'Yeah, I meet dis guy. He install dem glass stairways. They real pro. I works for him now. I learns a lot. He a real good guy.' Vincent shuffled a little on the wooden porch. 'I'z come to ask ya some thin,' his grin didn't fade.

'Oh yeah,' Emmalyn said, half-expecting what came next.

'I hears ya a lojman, a room to rent.'

Emmalyn shook her head vigorously, 'Oh no Vinny, it wouldn't work out. It didn't work the first time around.'

'But no strings … I pays ya … I gives ya three hundred dollars a month.'

'Look Vinny. This ain't going to work. No, no. We'd best go in. I don't want all the neighbours to know my business.'

'I makes it four hundred, if I gets dinner.'

Emmalyn weighed up Vincent. Looked him up and down. She opened the door to let him inside.

Half an hour later Vincent left, still grinning. Emmalyn didn't return to her herb bed immediately.

Instead, she tapped a message into her phone.

Tammy. I got myself a lodger. He's paying me four hundred dollars a month. He promised he'll help to do up the second bedroom. Coming on a 3 month trial. It's Vincent. What do you think?

She didn't wait for a reply, but went back into the garden to add more weeds to the pile. While Emmalyn worked outside, a reply came in.

234

You want to know what I think? Crazy ... I think you're a crazy woman! You'll live to regret this.

Jeffrey says he would like to meet you. Will phone to arrange. See you soon. T.

Chapter 23

Shadows

Tamara was relieved.

There were no weddings for three days. She was in her customary break-time spot, clutching a mug of coffee, back-of-house, in the shade. For once, her head wasn't filled with a long list. The catalogue of numerous tasks which had to be done right away for the impending bride and groom. Life felt relatively calm.

'So, this is where you hide yourself,' a figure appeared at her side.

'Oh, hi Emmalyn, how you doing? And how was your first day? I should have phoned you last night, but never got the chance,' she immediately felt guilty that she'd forgotten yesterday was Emmalyn's first day at the hotel.

'I'm good. Yeah, it wasn't too bad. It's all very different,' Emmalyn flopped into the seat next to her, clad in her uniform of a dark pencil shirt and pink blouse. 'They put me in the beach front, Garden Terrace restaurant. The menu's more my style of food. It was a little confusing at first, but I coped.'

'Preferable to Jacko's?' she joked.

'That's for sure. The chef's a real Joe bossy, but at least he ain't a right male chauvinist pig. The clients are so different too. They seem so much nicer, much chattier.'

Tamara weighed up her friend. It had to be said, she looked a whole lot more relaxed than when she worked at the fast-food joint. 'Just you wait. They aren't all like that. There are so many who think they've paid their money, so they should get the moon and the stars.'

'Oh, I'm used to those! It was the same working in real estate. Some of them treat you like dirt. But ain't that the same the world over? I ain't got no time for folks who think that they are

236

better than anyone else.' Emmalyn turned to display an irritated look smeared across her face.

'You and me both. Hey, how you getting on with that lodger of yours?'

'He's been as good as gold. Not put one foot wrong,' she pushed forward her hands, both with two fingers crossed.

'Yet!' Tamara added mockingly.

'But don't you see, the four hundred dollars was too good a chance to miss. I might eventually be able to get my car back. He's even started work on building me a bathroom off the second bedroom. That was a good idea of yours.'

'Oh, it's worse than I thought. He's only been there a week and he's worming his way back into your good books.'

'I've got things all under control. He's just thankful he's got a meal every evening and a clean bed to lie in.'

Tamara shook her head, 'it'll change, just wait and see. He's a man, and I've known a lot of them. He'll be after more for his four hundred bucks.'

'Somebody's in a cynical mood today. You fell out big time with your man?'

'Oh no, not today anyway,' she said, not wanting to divulge any personal details. 'By the way, Jeffrey's suggesting we meet up for a drink this weekend to discuss his business venture. Okay with you?'

Emmalyn's face shone, 'that's great! Just let me know where and when.'

'I suggest we go out somewhere local, but quiet, so he can tell you about his ideas.'

'Fine by me.' Emmalyn smiled to herself, 'I must tell you. I got a surprise call over the weekend—Mr Jackson, remember, my old boss.'

'The owner of Jacko's?'

'Yeah, he phoned and said he missed me being there. He asked if we could meet up one evening. I thought it was a bit strange why he never asked before.'

'Perhaps he didn't know what he was missing until it had gone. Did you ever tell him your real reason for leaving?'

'Not exactly.'

'Tut tut, Emmalyn, you really should, for all the other women's sakes,' Tamara said in a raised voice. 'From what I've seen, that man's got a real problem.'

'When I see him again, I'll try to bring up the subject.'

'So, did you say yes to seeing him. Did you make a date?' Tamara asked inquisitively.

'Sure, he's a real nice guy—a bit disorganised, but friendly and chatty.'

'I'm pleased for you. I've found out it isn't easy to find reliable men, especially as you get older. Men that you truly want to spend time with.'

'I think it's a rarity anyway—it's got nothing to do with age.'

'Now who's being cynical?' Tamara vacated the shabby plastic chair. 'Let's get back to work. I'll let you know about the drink with Jeffrey.' She made her way back to her tiny, humid office.

~~~

The car manoeuvred the uneven surface of the driveway. Either side, the jungle of vegetation was awash with vibrant shades. The summer glare sharpened its intensity. Even to the untrained eye, the natural palette of dazzling blooms bought immense pleasure. In gloomy contrast, its backdrop was becoming a desolate scene. Jeffrey noted that the buildings seemed even more blackened by seasonal storms. The scorching temperatures had rendered the paintwork around the windows into a cracked and peeling calamity. All in all, it shouted an air of neglect.

Jeffrey was thankful he'd made the demanding drive to The Tamarind without incident. He was gradually becoming accustomed to the treacherous road system: the unexpected deep potholes, the numerous hair-pin bends, and the unpredictable, wild drivers of Sainte Marie. He was struck by the lack of guests on the site—the place was a bit like a ghost town. He left his car in the shade of an overgrown hedge and headed towards the reception building. There was a member of staff there who directed him towards the beach restaurant. Mr McCloud would be with him as soon as possible. Jeffrey decided he'd wait on the beach. He installed himself in the shade of a palm and sat gazing out to sea, across the deserted beach.

His wait was longer than he'd foreseen. He became lulled by the pounding and sighing of the surf breaking onto the shore. He half closed his eyes, a little sedated by the sultry heat, and took in the hum and swishing of the surrounding vegetation, the sunlight filtering through it. Jeffrey could not imagine returning to the cold, the commercial havoc of Europe on a fulltime basis. He had an aversion to the flat, dead skies covering Britain a disproportionate percentage of the year. The tropics were for him. You had to put up with a few inconveniences, but on the other hand, there were so many compensations; they presented so many possibilities. Jeffrey wanted them as his future.

He felt exhilarated by the probabilities which could transpire from his meeting with Jay McCloud. Behind him, in the restaurant, he heard Jay dealing out instructions to a member of staff. This was his cue to leave the sands and search out his client. Jeffrey strode across the restaurant towards him.

'Mr Taylor, a pleasure to see you again. I'm sorry you had to wait,' Jay held out his hand.

'It's good to be here. As I arrived, I could see that you are even more in need of financial help.'

'You should know by now, this fierce climate takes away your star ratings faster than you can turn around,' Jay sighed. 'Before we get down to business, can I offer you a drink?'

'Something cold please,' Jeffrey said.

'How's that beautiful lady of yours?' Jay directed him to a table in the empty dining area.

'Busy with a wedding today,' he explained, though he didn't really know for sure. Jeffrey took out a bundle of paperwork from his bag and laid it on the table in front of him. 'You know Jay, once you have splashed some cash around this place, that's something you should consider—weddings. They attract large groups of people, from all over. Tourists of all ages. The beach would be superb for the ceremonies, and you've got this beach-front area for a reception.'

'We've had a few in the past. Yeah, they're good money earners,' Jay's lips curled at the memory. 'We'd need a new management company to deal with the rentals first though.'

Jeffrey produced his wallet and withdrew a business card from it. He noted Tamara's name and number on the back. 'If you'd like some advice, I'm sure that she'd be only too pleased to help.'

Once their drinks arrived, Jeffrey revealed some details of who the investors were and the sum they were prepared to pay for Tamarind's debt. He provided Jay with a copy of the contract; and briefly went through the main elements. He made it plain that Jay would not receive the money until the contract had been checked over by both sets of attorneys, the investors' and Jay's.

'I'll let you sort through the specifics in your own time,' Jeffrey was eager to direct their dialogue towards the topic he was far more interested in. 'I've also found a company which may be interested in purchasing some of the villas—those which are not very delinquent.'

Jay looked up from scanning the contract. 'So, how would that work?'

Jeffrey would rather he didn't read all the small print in front of him; and directed the conversation towards the information he hankered after from their meeting. 'Well as you suggested, rather than the investors having to go through the courts to get the condominium dues owed, the company would pay off the debt and negotiate a small sum with the owner to buy the property. I think you said that there were some individuals who are desperate to get rid of them.'

'Yes, I did,' Jay said, 'so then the investment company would restore the interiors and sell them on, as I'd suggested.' His expression suggested he was mulling through suitable properties to put forward.

'Naturally, I'd need you to supply me with a list of people to contact,' Jeffrey said, trying to make the request sound as casual as possible.

'I can show you a couple of units today,' Jay said. 'I'm aware that both owners desperately want to get rid of their properties. They've become too much of a financial burden.'

'They'd be looking for units that don't have too much of a debt on them,' Jeffrey repeated, keeping his eyes on the notes he'd been making.

'Yeah, some of them owe over three hundred thousand dollars. But the units I'm thinking of owe under a hundred thousand. One of them has a bit of a termite problem though.'

'Bad?'

Jay sighed and tightened his mouth, 'One of them is. We've had it spayed. It'll prevent the termites spreading, but the floor and skirting board in the sitting area were a speedy snack for those bloody little vermin.'

Jeffrey had learnt how quickly termites can devastate wood and plaster parts of properties. 'Yes, it could be useful to see specific properties, take a few photos, and to know how much they owe.'

'So how did you find the company which could be interested?'

'Oh, whilst trying to find investors to buy your debt,' Jeffrey dropped his look and picked up his bag. He went through the motions of trying to find information about the company. Information he knew wasn't there.

'No,' he lied, 'can't find it. I thought I'd some information about them. I'll send you some of their particulars, if they are definitely interested.'

Jeffrey maintained his business face throughout the meeting. After viewing the villas and taking photos, he refused lunch. He had no desire to socialise with Jay. He was a nerd, a do-gooder. And he didn't wish to give Jay an opportunity to probe further into the prospective purchasing company. Jay McCloud was a professional contact only. A contact he could make money from—hopefully in abundance.

As he started the long drive home, his lips curved into a private smile. He glowed. He felt confident about convincing the owners of the properties to accept a cash sum. It was a minor hurdle for someone with his sales attributes. He could then triple or even quadruple his initial outlay in a relatively short time frame. Jeffrey felt sure he'd only need to lay out a relatively small sum to bring the villas up to scratch—and he knew people who could do that.

Yes. It had been a very productive morning. It was true what they said—that it takes money to make money. But, it also took the right expertise and skill, with perhaps a touch of cunning.

~~~

Shadows wrapped around the hotel grounds. Mysterious lazily moving shapes were cast around the gardens from the under-lit greenery. Gold light flooded out from the swimming pool. Tiny bats swept the starless, sultry night sky.

Emmalyn had always appreciated the setting of the Coco Palms bar. It was in the centre of town, but struck an extravagant, lush ambience. Its encompassing tall palm trees defended it from the commotion of urbanisation. Tamara and Jeffrey were a little late for their arranged meeting, so she sat on

242

a bar stool, toying with her drink. When her phone rang, she scrabbled around in her bag to answer it. The display told her it wasn't one of them calling to cancel the get-together. She was relieved.

'Hi Vinny, what's new with you?' she moved away from the bar into the gloom of the grounds. 'That's great. So, he's said that he will install the plumbing and the electrical cabling ready for the en-suite. When will he come? ... next week. Couldn't be better ... and what's he gonna charge? ... Man, that's good,' she laughed at Vinny's response.

'What you up to? ... Great! ... Me, I'm in Coco Palms. I'm meeting some friends. I'll tell you about them some time. Look Vinny, I've got to go.'

As she went back to the glow of the bar, she noted the man at the counter ordering a drink. Starting up top, she surveyed his shock of bright white hair, the tailored shirt and unconventional coloured leather shoes. His English accent rang out. She became aware of his gaze flicker over her pencil skirt, her bare legs, and heeled shoes. They exchanged smiles.

'Excuse me for asking, but are you Jeffrey Taylor?'

'Even if I wasn't, I'd say yes,' Jeffrey jested, 'just so I could chat to such a delectable young lady,' he took hold of her hand.

Though Emmalyn shook it enthusiastically, she felt taken aback. This was not what she'd expected from their business meeting. She wished Tamara was around.

'Do I take it you're Emmalyn?' Jeffrey Taylor's eyes smiled at her.

'That's right Mr Taylor, but I was expecting Tamara as well.'

'Oh yes, but you know Tamara, she'll be tied up at some wedding. She'll be along ASAP.' The smile didn't drop from his face. He still seemed to be making eyes at her. 'Let me get you another drink. Shall we move over there, away from the bar?'

Emmalyn would have preferred to stay at the bar, at least until Tamara showed up. But Jeffrey directed the barman to take their glasses to a poolside table—one enveloped by the shadows of the trees. Feeling a little uncomfortable, she was very aware of his arm on her back, guiding her to the table. Mr Taylor moved a chair for her to be installed next to him. They sat in the gloom of the trees marking the boundary wall. 'So, tell me about yourself Emmalyn.' Jeffrey leaned towards her, very close, perhaps unnecessarily close.

Emmalyn focused on the centre of the table, avoiding eye contact, and feeling self-conscious. This man looked sharp, though as yet she wasn't certain that she'd warmed to him. Her dialogue about herself was brief, unlike her usually talkative self.

'I understand from Tamara, you're keen to establish a real estate office on island,' she concluded, aiming to get straight to the point.

'Let me explain my situation. Before retiring, I owned several thriving estate agencies—real estate offices in London,' he said, in a tone louder than was necessary. 'Knowing I was no longer working in Britain, Antony Denning at Topaz, head-hunted me to market the villas he's had constructed on Mango Bay. I made a great success of doing that. But in doing so, I've come to learn of the real estate and investment potential in the islands, and of Central America. I'm not boring you I hope Emma,' he threw her another of his beams. 'Can I call you Emma?'

Emmalyn was flustered, her smile wavered. Nobody called her Emma, 'eh … well, I'm … oh why not? No, you're not boring me at all.' He hadn't explained things in quite the way Tamara had, but never mind. 'I believe you travel a great deal Mr Taylor.'

'It's Jeff to you Emma.' His mouth rose in another unnatural smile, exposing teeth as white as his hair. 'Yes, I think I can say that I now know the Caribbean almost as well as my native England.'

Emmalyn had made the mistake of leaving her hands holding her glass. His fingers brushed hers. Startled, she looked directly at him, and gradually withdrew them to her lap. She swung a glance towards the hotel entrance, in the hope that Tamara might be there.

'Let's have another drink, shall we?' Jeffrey said. 'In a moment, I'll explain exactly how I think you could help me.'

Before Emmalyn had time to refuse, he had pivoted in his seat, waved in the direction of the barman. 'The same again please,' he called. 'My drinking is only in the evening; I keep my shape by swimming every day. I'm sure that Tamara has told you.'

Tamara had not, but she wasn't too wild about furthering that topic. She was there for one reason only. 'Eh yes, I've seen your wonderful pool.' Emmalyn fidgeted in her seat. She'd hoped to be able to move their chairs further apart, while he went to fetch the drinks. But no.

'I prefer to swim in the sea of course,' he continued, 'when I'm on island, I try to do my laps across Mango Bay twice a day. I'm an excellent swimmer, but that's because I make sure I exercise daily ... '

Emmalyn fixed an interested, polite expression in his direction. She was not enamoured by the swimming saga—it wasn't her thing—but then her eyes were distracted by movement in the trees behind Mr Taylor. She tried to focus on the stirrings in the darkness. Could it be a figure? A member of staff? That was not very likely at that hour.

'Mr Taylor ...' she interrupted, thinking she'd mention her suspicions.

He seemed a little irked at being stopped in mid-flow. 'Ugh yes, I'm sorry ... the real estate office?' 'Yes ... my idea is that I need somebody to look after calls and viewings, look after the website, whilst I'm off island.'

This was what she wanted to hear. Her notions of a shadowy figure were cast aside, and she turned her thoughts to more important matters. 'So, you wouldn't anticipate being there yourself much,' she asked, half hoping this would be the case.

'No, not a great deal. In addition, I'd expect the assistant to supervise any maintenance of properties going up for rental, or purchase.' He detailed the situation at The Tamarind; and explained the likelihood of units needing to be spruced up before they could be resold.

'I don't see any of that being a problem. And what about transport? Would I get an allowance for travelling from an office to see premises?'

'Naturally, the level of your wage would reflect that. Your own vehicle would be essential.'

Emmalyn's interest immediately multiplied tenfold. 'And location of the office?'

'I thought that I could leave it up to you to find out what's available,' the volume of his voice dropping to a silky level, 'that's if you don't mind Emma. I'm a bit tied up with other ...' He was interrupted by a hand slapping his shoulder. They both looked up. Tamara was standing behind his seat.

'Hi, you two got everything sorted?' she asked. Jeffrey sprung up and kissed her mouth passionately.

'Let's get you chair, and a drink.' As he lifted his hand towards the bar, his phone rang out. He moved away to answer it.

'Sorry I couldn't make it on time,' Tamara said. 'The reception went on much longer than I had hoped. There were one or two hitches as well. How are you two getting on?'

'Er, ... yeah, just fine. We were just about to talk about an office to work from.'

'Judging by Jeff's usual roaming the Caribbean, I don't think that he'd be in it too often,' Tamara sat herself in the chair Jeffrey had vacated.

'Yeah, he's said as much. I'll have to think things through Tamara. I've only just started working at the hotel and ...' she stopped, noticing the expression on Jeffrey's face as he returned, without Tamara's drink. Still clasping his phone, his manner visibly changed.

'Ladies, I have to go,' he explained quietly. 'I've a lot to arrange.' He met Emmalyn's stare. 'Emma, we can sort things out when I return.'

'What's up Jeff?' Tamara asked.

Despite saying he had to leave, He stood stock still beside them. His face was drained of vivacity. 'That was Craig. I have to go back to England. Miranda has just died.'

Chapter 24

Shockwaves

The sea and the sky were ablaze.

Palms silhouetted against the fire. The image changed every second as the sun's disc dipped towards the horizon. Two dark figures progressed leisurely along the shoreline, each watching the fleeting spectacle marking the end of the day. Tamara clasped her sandals, enjoying the healing sensation of the spray as she splashed through the warm, lapping waters. Willis narrated his day. On an impulse, Tamara slung down her footwear away from the water's edge, and collapsed onto the heated sand next to them. She sat facing the gradual blackening of the ocean. The white spume of the breakers was slowly metamorphosed to glittering silver. The starkness of the three isles was smudged by the oncoming night.

'So, what happened to all those buddies from college?' she asked after several minutes.

'What do ya mean, what happened to them?' her son looked down at her dark shape.

'You seem to spend most of your days with Madison and Nat.'

'I can see the guys from college any time, Maddie and Nat will be going home in a few weeks.'

'And Madison is much cuter than the mates from college, eh?' Tamara laughed, but her eyes were fixed on the red of the sun as it rapidly slipped below the horizon. In moments it was gone.

'Hell yeah, goes without saying. Maddie ain't no basic babe,' He flung himself next to his mother. 'Mom, Maddie's already thinking about unis for next year. What am I gonna do?'

'I've explained before Willis, I'd love for you to go to university, but my wages don't run to paying for all of that.

You'll have to try for a scholarship.' Tamara was upset to have to tell Willis what the truth of the matter was.

'But, what about Jeff?' He has said he'd help me out.'

'Listen Willis, it'd cost around fifteen thousand dollars a year, you can't ask Jeff to shell out that sort of money. Anyway, Jeff and I might not be an item as long as that.' Tamara didn't want to reveal this confidence, but it had become a necessity.

Willis started kicking a hole in the sand with his heel. 'He did say Mom … do you think you could touch on the subject when he gets back?'

'We'll see Willis. Time to go and get something to eat.' As she sprung up again, her mobile rang out.

'Hello … yes, it's Tamara … oh hello Jay,' she said cautiously, 'er no, he's not on island. He had to go to Britain.'

She listened. Willis watched her in the meagre twilight as she commenced her stroll back towards the villa.

'Oh, I'm sorry Mr McCloud I really don't know anything about it. He told me he had found an investor and that was all. Have you tried his phone? … No, he had to go to help organise a funeral. It's undoubtedly why … no, I'm sorry; he hasn't said when he'll be back.' Her head hung down as she listened to Jay McCloud's grievances.

'But of course. Yes, I'll give him the message when I speak to him.' Tamara scrutinised her phone as she ended the call. She wondered how Jay had got her number.

'Who was it?' Willis probed.

'Nobody you know Willis,' Tamara continued her walk across the shadowy sand, but the conversation still rang around in her head. 'Oh man, he's one roiled guy. Is he bummed out? He's had a gutful of Jeff,' she said almost to herself.

'You'll need to explain Mom,' Willis walked alongside her.

'Well, in short, Jeff found some investors to buy the debt of a resort down in the south. Mr McCloud is the manager there, and wants the money to renovate the place. What he didn't realise was the hefty commission Jeff was going to charge him. Six per cent! Wow, that's big bucks. He's really rattled.'

'But shouldn't he pay Jeff for getting him the money? So, what's the six per cent?'

'Let's just say, it's at least twenty thousand more than it should be. McCloud is thinking he could do a load more restoration with that money.'

'Man, that's one mega commission. Mom, what'll you say to Jeff?'

They left the inky blackness; and let themselves into the villa. She re-played Jeffrey's conversation with Jay McCloud; recalled his attitude towards the resort manager. Tamara placed her phone on the kitchen counter and cold reality crept into her thoughts. She went to the refrigerator and got out a bottle of juice before she replied.

'Look Willis, I won't say anything to Jeff except that Mr McCloud phoned,' she said pouring out two glasses of juice. 'And you, don't you breathe a word of this to anyone.' She passed a glass to her son. 'It's Jeff's business, not mine, nor yours. Do you understand Willis? Mr McCloud should not have phoned me? And I perhaps shouldn't have said anything in front of you.'

'Mom, I'm not an ass—I won't say anything …' Willis looked somewhat baffled. 'I just thought …'

She looked directly at Willis, 'Let me give you a bit of advice,' she said in a serious voice, 'as far as Jeffrey is concerned, don't expect too much. Like when you asked me to talk to Jeff about your university fees—you need to understand my role here. I'm not Jeff's wife. We don't have that sort of relationship. Though his wife has passed away now—I won't be the next Mrs Taylor.' She breathed in deeply. 'We have an agreement, an unspoken pact Jeffrey and I. Do you understand what I'm trying to say?'

Willis hesitated, '… we ain't a normal family … we live here because …'

'Yes … because … yes, that, and well,' she wavered, '… other things … perhaps because I don't ask too many questions.' She looked at Willis soberly. 'And Jeffrey has actually told me, it's also because I don't demand expensive gifts, like a lot of women. I don't fool myself Willis, I just think, it's great while it lasts. Listen, you've got to be the same. You've got a lot to thank Jeff for—the visits, the watersports, the villa, the pool, your phone. Just be thankful for what you've got so far—you know we've got a lot more than some on this island. Just don't expect too much.'

'Sure,' Willis paused 'I was wondering … if … if you being here has anything to do with me.'

'Was that a question?' Tamara said. 'Willis, come on, let's get some eats. Tomorrow is another day.'

~~~

What the hell do I do now Tamara thought?

She had just received another call from Jay McCloud which she felt very uneasy about. She's taken the call at work, while trying to sort out a wedding problem. Though that had been explained to Mr McCloud he'd been insisted on continuing the conversation. He queried whether his message of the previous week had been passed on to Jeffrey. She promised it had. Jeffrey had said very little, but had told her he'd phone Jay back.

This seemed to accelerate Jay's annoyance—his voice turned to one of rage. And for some reason, he seemed to be mad at her.

'I'm sorry Mr McCloud, I really have to get on with my work,' she'd said. 'I don't play a part in Jeffrey's business affairs.'

'Now you know that's not true. You're a bad as he is,' he'd bawled down the phone.

'Truthfully, I can say, I know next to nothing about what he does.'

'You must do, your name is filed as one of the company directors.'

'What company? No, I'm not Mr McCloud.' As Tamara denied it, she knew, in fact, she was. She was a director of the company through which they had bought the villa they lived in.

'J&T Inc. So, you've never heard of J&T Inc.?' Tamara had been speechless. 'Taylor had the audacity to tell me he's a company interested in buying property at Tamarind … and fails to say, it's his own bloody company.'

'You'll need to talk to him about it Mr McCloud.'

'Too bloody right I do! He buys a villa at some bloody ridiculous price and has the gall to charge the owner a commission. Christ Almighty, you're a pair of lowlife bandits. You tell your swindling Romeo, I'm gunning for him,' he'd shrieked at her.

Uncertain how she should reply, she'd repeated yet again she had to get back to her work. She ended the call promising she would talk to Jeffrey about it that evening.

She was perturbed. The conversation had unnerved her. Her mind flashed back to her visit to The Tamarind. She'd liked Jay. He had seemed an honest soul, trying to do his best for all of the owners. She'd actually sympathised with him. There would be no way she'd tell Jeffrey, but she thought the way he was using Jay was scabby. It seemed what was bad news for Jay, was great for Jeffrey. All this said a lot about the real Jeffrey Taylor.

She gazed blankly at the wall in front of her. She didn't like this—her name being involved with Jeffrey's deals. Being tarred with the same brush as him. She needed to organise her life, once and for all, and decide what she should do about Jeffrey. First, she needed to find out as much as possible about his secret life. Finding the time to do so could be another problem; her days were always too hectic.

It took several minutes before Tamara felt controlled enough to make a call to the florist.

~~~

252

Four thousand miles from her, Ella was also perplexed. She was on her way to Oakdale. It was a home she'd always loved. But now that her mother was gone, it felt eerie. An enormous, very empty space. Oakdale and her mother, for Ella, had been one.

She hadn't asked Kloe to accompany her. She'd left her with one of her friends. It was too early for her to see the house without her grandmother in residence. Kloe, much like her mother, was still mournful, tearful. Ella's whole body still felt in shock. She was exhausted from lack of sleep. Images of her mother returning to her time after time. At work, it was difficult to concentrate.

But Oakdale had to be checked over. Despite its bleakness and sorrowful air, it still needed maintaining. Craig had contacted the workers, the domestic help, and the gardener, who had kept up the property, to tell them to continue.

The alarm rang hollow in the darkened hall. As always, she felt relieved when she'd stopped its wailing. Ella closed the concealed cupboard. She looked around her. The décor made the space look more like a mausoleum rather than a desirable family home. Pushing open the shutters, light invaded the entrance hall.

Ella squinted at the patchwork of greens shining in from the garden. That view was part of her life. She had played amongst the trees and shrubs as a child. She and Craig had chased each other around the lawns, shrieking with laughter. The family had eaten picnics together in the shade of one or other of the ornamental trees. Now, two of those picnickers, were no longer there. It tore at her heart. How Oakdale had changed.

Reaching the kitchen, a new message pinged onto her phone. It was tagged in red.

Dear Ella and Craig,
I'd be very grateful if you would contact me as a matter of urgency.
Best Regards, Thomas Keating

She'd been expecting contact from Mr Keating; he'd been her mother's solicitor. He was the executor dealing with the will. Ella opened the shutters in the kitchen before returning the call.

As soon as they started their conversation, she knew there was a problem. The tone of his voice was all wrong. It was clear he was finding the call a difficult one. This put Ella in worry mode. Just get to the point she wanted to say. When he did, she collapsed into one of the kitchen chairs. She asked him to repeat what he'd just said. For the rest of the call she was silent. Her eyes shut out the image of the kitchen. She was trying to sort out how on earth this had happened—even worse, how she was going to deal with it. Mr Keating had finished by saying he would appreciate a meeting with her and Craig in the next few days.

Ella carefully lowered her phone onto the marbled-topped kitchen table. This was all too much—her mother going. Now this. A pain tore at her insides. Large tears streamed down her cheeks. They fell to the shiny surface; sobbing echoed around the empty room. A wail, like a child imitating a howling dog, escaped her. She wailed until her chest hurt, her throat hurt. Until the tissue she clutched in her fist was sodden.

Ella couldn't hold back the tears. Several minutes passed. Her eyes started to sting. Her misted vision took in the details of the kitchen, so full of reminders of her mother. Little by little, her tears ceased, but the pain in her chest still gripped her. She decided to phone for support; she wasn't able to cope alone.

'Craig, how soon can you get to Oakdale? Three quarters of an hour? You'd best make it half an hour … I know you're at work … this IS an emergency.'

Next she called her husband, and Kloe's friend and told them she wasn't certain when she'd be home. Privately, she wasn't certain she was in a fit state to drive. She sat and passed her time staring at the walls of the large kitchen, trying to think through what she was going to do. The wait for her brother seemed an eternity.

~~~

Tamara had been very ill-at-ease since Jay McCloud's calls. Apprehensive about seeing Jeffrey that evening. She should confront him about J&T. Inc., demand an explanation; but she knew she would not. She needed to know the truth. More than the few scraps of info Jeff had deemed to dish out to her in the past. More about the man she shared a bed with; the man she gave her body to. The man she gave a lot of her time to. This problem had been pushed away from the confused muddle of her mind too often. It was time to deal with it. Her approach though, had to carry the 'With Caution' tag.

The expanse of illuminated windows in the villa told her Jeff was already at home. She closed the heavy front door with care. Repetitive lapping noises told her Jeff was, as usual, locked in his watery world, exercising in the pool. This was the opportunity to organise herself. Ten minutes later, dressed in shorts and flouncy top, she approached the pool carrying two glasses of wine.

'Hi. Didn't know you were here,' Jeffrey said, standing at the shallow end of the pool.

'I only just got home. How are things with you?'

'I'm still getting myself sorted after my visit to Dorset,' he stated vaguely. 'That glass of wine for me?' He stepped out of the water and wrapped a towel around his waist. 'You look real sexy dressed like that.'

Tamara made herself smile. She knew what would be coming next. She wasn't sure she wanted to cope with that.

'Is Willis in this evening?' he asked.

She had been right. She disliked the smile spread across his face. He wanted his way with her again. 'Yeah, he said he'd be back for dinner. I'll get something ready in a moment.' She passed him the glass of wine. She waited for him to start sipping it.

'I'm regretting you giving Mr McCloud my mobile number— He certainly doesn't want to discuss weddings.' She saw a frown wrinkle Jeffrey's forehead.

'Why? Did he phone you again?'

'Yeah,' she admitted, trying hard to sound casual. 'He seemed a bit irate that he hadn't been able to contact you.'

'It's possible. Phones been switched onto message service. I've been very busy. He should be happy; he's got the first slug of his funds.'

Tamara tried hard to hide her surprise: McCloud had signed the contract after everything he'd said.

'Today, he wanted to know something about the company which had bought a villa at The Tamarind,' she added, trying to be a vague as possible.

'Oh perhaps, I'll phone him sometime soon.'

'Is that one of the villas Jay showed us?'

'I don't know Tammy,' he said sharply, showing, for him, the subject was closed. 'Hey, what do you say if we go out for dinner when Willis shows up?'

That was it. Jeffrey was not going to tell her a thing about J&T Inc. buying a villa. Not a thing! It was clear he would not explain about any business dealings with Jay McCloud, or any other of his clients. Exactly the same as when he returned from England after the funeral—nothing about the family or the service. He'd told her everything went as planned. That was it. Jeffrey didn't seem to be grieving in any way.

At last, it was really sinking in what type of person she was living with. She watched him sip his wine, resentment towards him nagging at her. Her insides churned away. She was thankful that they wouldn't be alone at Three Isles that evening.

She left the veranda, on the pretext of phoning Willis about the meal. He seemed a little taken aback when she told him to be home as soon as possible, but she breathed easier when he promised he'd be home in half an hour.

~~~

He held her close. Craig wrapped his arms around Ella as she burst into floods of tears again.

'You have to tell me what's happened Sis,' he said disentangling himself from her. He held her at arm's length. She knew her eyes must be red and blotchy.

'It's Mum,' she gulped, 'Oakdale. It's everything.'

'Ella. You need to start at the beginning. Come and sit down.'

Craig guided her into the gloom of the sitting room. He unlocked one of the shutters and let in a river of brightness. Ella sat in a chair, staring at her lap, sniffling into a very soggy tissue.

'You know that …' Ella started, and then changed her mind. 'No, let me start at the beginning.'

'Should I find you a box of tissues or something?'

'No! Listen Craig,' she spat in exasperation. 'This is hyper-important. I received a message from the solicitors earlier. I phoned straight back and spoke to Mr Keating.'

'Yeah, the executor for Mum's will,' Craig leaned forward in the deep armchair.

'He had the bill from the funeral director and had to access Mum's account on the internet. He was surprised when he went into it. There was enough to pay for the funeral, but apparently not a lot else.'

'I don't really follow Ella. There's more than one account. And there are insurances too. Mum told me a long time ago.'

'Craig, you haven't heard the half of it. Mr Keating thought it was strange that the account should have so little in it. So, he starts looking at Mum's assets because he knew the will had to be read to us.'

'So, when will that be, it's a bit too early yet isn't it?'

'Let me just finish,' Ella was becoming a little agitated by Craig's interruptions. 'The bottom line is Jeffrey gained Power of Attorney after Mum had her first stroke. Do you remember? The accounts were changed to both of their names.'

'Yeah, I did know vaguely he had Power of Attorney. I supposed Mum didn't want to be bothered with all of that.'

'Yes, I knew too. I didn't really think much about it. The problem is Craig …' she faced her brother, 'he's emptied them. He's emptied each goddam account. Well virtually. That's what I think has happened.'

'The bastard! For Christ's sake.' His facial muscles contorted; his eyes narrowed.

'Do you remember, some years ago, Mum offered to bequeath several hundred thousand pounds for Kloe, and she was going to do the same for you?'

'Yeah, just before she had her stroke.'

'There had been a lot of Dad's money in those accounts. And money from the sale of one of those London flats. Afterwards, we both know Mum's main expense was paying for her carers; otherwise, she didn't spend a lot. But Craig, those funds aren't there now. Mr Keating said the accounts have been systematically cleared.'

'I'll kill him. I'll fucking kill him.' He sprung out of his seat with clenched fists. Craig stood looking at her.

'But you haven't heard all of it.' Ella let out another sob. 'The investments have been cashed in. And Mum's properties, Oakdale, and the others—he's re-mortgaged them. Mr Keating isn't sure there'll be enough equity in the properties to pay for the death duties. Craig, he's taken all Dad's money. Everything he worked hard for.'

'I'll bury that bastard. I'll slit his bloody …' Ella watched her brother pace the room. His rage had brought sweat to his brow. Craig removed his suit jacket and slung it into the chair.

'I know you never liked him, but this …' There was silence between them for a few seconds. 'He, Mr Keating, wants us to make an appointment to see him next week.'

Craig stood in front of her and inhaled deeply.

'Craig, whilst I was waiting for you, I was mulling things over. I've decided what I'm going to do. We'll go to the see Mr Keating next week.' She scrutinised her sodden tissue, realised the state of it and pushed it into her pocket. 'You need to tell me which day suits you. Kloe goes back to school soon, so I'll get a week off work. And I'll fly out to Sainte Marie. I'm going to confront Jeffrey. I'll ask what the hell he's done with our parents' money.'

Craig peered at his sister. 'That's not the way I'd sort things out,' he said under his breath. Ella was too upset to think clearly about what he'd said.

Chapter 25

Accident

It happened by accident.

At last, Madison and Willis got what they had both been hungry for.

They, together with Nathan, had been on the beach most of the morning. It was overcast; the sea was storm-tossed. Turbulence had transformed the bay's usual tranquil water into one with powerful, high, steady waves. The ocean struck the sand forcefully, the tumult echoing in their ears, exhilarating and exciting them. The confidence of youth plunged them into the wildness of those waters. On rented surf boards, they aspired to better their negligible skills. Firstly on land, trying to lever themselves up from a lying position. Next, unwatched, unattended, they threw the boards before them into the merciless Caribbean.

The ruling current directed them and their boards. It was a fight against an unstoppable power. The trio fell from the boards time and time again; and tired quickly. The adolescents needed to take frequent breaks—sit in a line on the sand to regain their strength. But that waned, as the morning advanced.

Whilst resuming their energy, Madison and Willis sat together, very aware that the sides of their wet bodies were in contact. They watched as Nathan chose to renew his battle. He launched himself flat on the board and paddled out to try and catch the surf. From their position on the beach, they followed his progress. Willis' arm reached around her; squeezed her shoulder. She welcomed it with a smile. Nathan succeeded in squatting up on the blue surfboard, as the roller bought him towards them. He attempted to rise up higher. He failed and slipped. In half a beat, a wall of water fell over him. And he was gone.

The dark seas swallowed him. The empty blue shape floated. Nathan didn't resurface.

'Willis,' Madison screamed. She shot towards the shoreline. 'Christ where's he gone?'

Willis ran after her. Without a thought, he plunged into the surging sea and forced himself towards the pitching board. Panic made his lungs feel tight. He had to find Nathan, find him in time. He had to save him. He knew he couldn't live with failing. He reached the surfboard leash. His eyes strained into the turbulence of the water. The leash was taught, but he couldn't see Nathan. He took in a deep breath and descended, hand after hand down the leash. The sunlight weakened.

~~~

All signs of Willis vanished. Madison ran against the weight of the beating surf. She heard a howl burst from herself. It was snatched away by the strong wind. The spray kicked up her body. Too many seconds seemed to pass. She became distraught, terror tearing at her insides. Feet in the pulling sand, she stared at the spot next to the tossing board. Her erupting mind told her this wasn't real. It couldn't be happening. This was only what happened in movies. Not to her. Please, not to her.

She stood alone. Desperately alone. Her wailing was replaced by a long 'No!' It was lost to the pounding of the breakers, thrashing against her helpless form.

Just as she was sure that they had both gone, Willis' head resurfaced. She saw him gulp for precious air. Almost simultaneously, he pulled Nathan up next to him. He dragged him in with one hand, the board following behind. Madison rushed forward to help heave her brother away. Away from the perilous surf. But Willis pushed her away roughly.

~~~

'Get out the way!' he shouted.

He hauled the limp figure towards him. Clutched the bent body against his legs. His fist pounded Nathan's back. And again.

'Come on Nat,' he shrieked. He thumped his back once more. A desperate Madison knelt beside them; her face contorted with terror.

This time, Nathan spluttered. Coughed. Spewed water. Vomited down Willis' thighs. Willis heaved him, retching and spitting, further up the sandy slope. Not heeding his friend's discomfort, Willis threw his arms around his torso.

'Thank the Lord,' Willis clung to him. 'Man, I thought I was going to have to give you rescue breaths. That board saved you Nat. I knew just where to look.' Madison joined the bundle of limbs.

'Give me air!' Nathan gasped, pushing them both away.

Willis stood up, but Madison still clung to her brother. He looked down at them, the reality of what he'd just achieved kicking in.

'Not sure, but I think you could have hit your head as you fell from the board. There're some large rocks where you lost your balance,' Willis told him. 'And looks like you've got a bump on your head' Nathan sluggishly put his hand to his head. Willis walked back to the shoreline. He let out several deep sighs, relieved, but with his heart was still pounding. He bent double to clean up his legs in the waves.

Madison's sobs continued, tears staining her eyes red. She clung to Nathan's arm. 'I thought you had both gone. Dead. Shit Nat, he saved your bloody life.'

Nathan leant his head on his bent knees. Still gasping. Slowly he raised his head. 'Think I'd better go back to the villa.' His voice was hoarse.

'Later, just get your breath back,' Willis tried to persuade him.

He watched as Nathan slowly gazed around himself, up and down the deserted beach. 'Don't breathe a word of this to the old man,' he told his sister, 'otherwise, we'll have to string along with them for the rest of the vacation.'

She nodded. They all sat waiting for Nathan to get back his strength and composure. It was clear the surfing was done for that day. Willis organised them both. Madison should return the boards, one by one, to the rear of Willis' home. He would support her brother back to his room.

After helping him slowly up the beach, they mounted the path back to the villa. Nathan was settled onto the sofa, with a towel around him, a glass of water beside him. The minutes ticked by, but Madison didn't appear.

'I think Maddie must be struggling. Best go and help with the boards,' Willis told Nathan.

He left by the back of the villa. Madison was waiting by his back yard, the gate wide open. Willis stepped inside to check the boards were all in place. In an instant, Madison flung the gate shut. Before he had time to think, she'd pressed him against the fence. Her mouth was on his, her hands tugging his head towards her. He was aroused in an instant.

'If he can't say thank you, I will,' she burst out, as she came up for breath.

Willis said nothing, but pulled her by the hand. With the other, he prised open the sliding door to his room. She didn't resist. The outside door was locked. The blind pulled down. Roughly, he forced his mouth onto hers again. Madison clung to him. They both know what would come next. Their sodden swimming things quickly formed a wet pile on the floor. He jerked Madison towards the unmade bed, and they fell onto its crumbled sheets.

~~~

The clouds were clearing. Sharp shadows returning. As he climbed out of his car, heat from the sun struck his mass of white, curly hair. Jeffrey noted the expanse of unsettled, murky water in the bay. The swell whipped against the three isles looming up out of the waters. The image told him he would be swimming in the pool that day. As he snatched up his bag, he heard the lively melody of his phone. Sunglasses propped on his head; he squinted to see the display.

'Hi Antony, how you doing? … No, I didn't do my swim in Mango Bay today—the sea's too rough. I'm hoping tomorrow morning, or the day after,' he leant against his vehicle listening.

'Yes, sure I remember her. She bought two months in one of the units. She lives in Hampshire, near Beaulieu. What the problem?'

He listened again for some time, in silence. The expression on his face changed. A shadow of concern dampened his expression. His bag was dropped on the ground next to him.

He punctuated his quiet, 'I don't remember the details. I'd have to check.'

He waited. 'Yes, I think she must have made a mistake. But let me look at the details. I'll come and see you when I've found out.'

I've got several meetings coming up Antony. I'll get back to you as soon as I can. See you in the next couple of days. I'll phone you.'

He ended the call and stood for several moments leaning against his car, looking blindly at the scene in front of him. Eventually, he opened the car again and sat in front of the steering wheel. Unmindful of the marine spectacle just metres away, he methodically contemplated information on his phone. Papers were extracted from his bag. Jeffrey scanned through some of them. Minutes passed. A decision was made. He went back to his phone, his fingers seeking guidance. He found what he needed. With help from his passport, he entered details into his mobile. Transaction completed; relief swept over him. It was plain to Jeffrey what came next.

~~~

They lay, their limbs entwined around each other. Their bodies sticking together from the heat of the room and their love making. Madison pushed away strands of her tangled hair. It had made a damp circle on the pillow.

'I hope you didn't do that because of what happened this morning—to thank me,' Willis muttered into her ear.

'Shit Willis, how can you say that?' She ran a finger over his full mouth; then started kissing and licking his chest. 'I've been hot for you for always. And boom, we've made it at last. You know, it's just been so difficult with Nathan clinging to us every second of the day.'

'That's the understatement of the bloody millennium. He's like a fucking leech. We've still got the same problem after today.'

'No, now we've gotten horizontal, I want us to keep on. You were the awesomist—real fun. I'll come to you at night. I can come to your room …'

Crash! They hear a bang outside the bedroom—the front door slamming. Willis shot up off the bed. He pointed a finger. Towards the shower room. As he rounded the bed, he grabbed at their wet things off the floor. He pulled the naked Madison behind the en-suite door, leaving it ajar.

'Jeff,' he mouthed, dragging Madison next to him in the gloom. Almost immediately, they heard the bedroom door open.

'You in Willis?' Jeffrey called. Stillness, then the door closed. Footsteps on the wooden floor. Faint noises from the next room.

'Shit, geez, that's a bummer!' Madison whispered. 'But hey Willis, this has been one astonishing day. So exciting!' she breathed into his mouth. Her fingers ran lightly over his shoulder next to her. She pushed the door shut with her body, as she crushed herself onto him, forcing her mouth onto his. Her tongue explored his mouth. She started to fondle him.

'Shit Maddie! Are you crazy?' He forced both hands against her, pushing her away. 'Your brother nearly died this morning. That ain't exciting!' he spat. Willis pulled the door open again. They could hear a subdued voice—presumably Jeffrey on the phone.

She traced a finger over his sweatiness, lightly moved down his muscular arms. 'You're what's exciting Willis. I feel hot for you.'

'Shit Maddie, Jeff is next door. My door isn't locked. Later.'

'Not too much later. Come and see how Nat is in an hour. He won't feel up to much this afternoon. We can find somewhere to get busy again.'

'For Christ's sake put this on.' He shoved her wet swimsuit into her hands and put on his shorts.

'Promise,' she said as she struggled against the wetness of the swimwear.

'Yeah, I'll come,' he sneaked a look around the door. Indicated she could follow him. Slowly, he slid the outside door open, just enough for her to squeeze through. He held the blind aside. Madison kissed him one last time, before he closed and locked the door again. Willis breathed easier. He stared at his room and saw it objectively. The scattered discarded belongings. The damp, rumpled sheets. His wardrobe door wide open. Clothes half off shelves. He slowly, silently, started to put things to rights.

Minutes later, he crept back into the en-suite. He splashed cold water over himself. He made every effort to calm his fired-up mind. What the hell of a morning! Willis dried himself down. His reflection in the mirror assured him that he actually looked no different after such a mind-boggling time.

Back in the bedroom, Jeffrey's muted voice could still be heard. His curiosity got the better of him. He shuffled to the door. The voice was faint. Taking great care, he pushed down the door handle and opened it a fraction. He concentrated, strained to hear what was being said. It was just snatches of words, all too indistinct. Willis guessed that Jeffrey was on the veranda. Back against the corridor wall, his bare feet slid over the wooden floor, he progressed towards the sitting area, the voice becoming clearer.

'That's right. I'm looking for something outside the city, perhaps near the beach.'

Willis saw Jeff's mop of white hair, with his back to him, seated on the outdoor furniture. The folding doors back against the wall. The sun had started to glisten on the pool. Its reflections played across the interior.

'I'll be there by the end of this week, so there's not much time. I could stay in a hotel for a few days, but I'd prefer an apartment.' Jeffrey listened. '...Yeah, that's a possibility. How much is that a month? ... Okay send me the details.'

Jeffrey went quiet, with his ear to the phone. Willis stayed rooted at the end of the corridor.

'That's very helpful. Yes ... I'll definitely check out your site. Thanks. I'll get back to you.'

Willis was intrigued. Why did Jeffrey want another apartment? Where was he phoning? Questions started to circle around his mind. He watched and waited while Jeffrey selected another number from his phone.

'Hi Delan, its Jeffrey, Jeffrey Taylor,' his tone was convivial. 'Yes, I'm good.' Willis immediately recognised the name. He listened more intently.

'Yes, it's great. Yeah, we love the villa. We love the view, but I have to move off island ... yeah, like yesterday, but don't make that public ... yeah, afraid so, it's like that. So, the villa—can you put it on the market?'

Willis heard his own breath, as he inhaled sharply. His hand felt sweaty against the wall. Tightness pulled across his chest.

'Yeah, I know I could, but I'm not going to be here, am I? Can you come and take some photos? Perhaps the day after tomorrow.'

Willis started to panic. Jeff was putting the villa on the market; he was certain he wasn't making a mistake. And what about him? What about his mother? They hadn't been mentioned.

'What do you think? To sell it quickly, I know I'll have to lower the price a bit. I was thinking one point two … Okay we'll try it at that.'

Steadily, his sweaty hands still against the smoothness of the wall, Willis edged slowly back down towards his room. He held his breath until he reached it.

'Yes, best with the furniture. We can talk about that when I see you,' was the last thing he heard as he eased his bedroom door open. Then the words become indistinguishable. He pressed himself through the gap. Placed his back against the closed door. Willis inhaled deeply.

He tried to reason through the information he'd just heard. Jeff was going. He wanted an apartment elsewhere. He was leaving Sainte Marie, in just a few days. Leaving for some time. He didn't want the villa anymore. Where on earth were his Mom and he supposed to go? Willis guessed they were not a consideration. Where had Jeff his friend, Jeff his mate, gone?

This was proving to be one hell of a day—one he felt sure would stay with him for always. Willis knew he needed to think fast. His mother needed to know. He felt certain she wouldn't be aware of any of this.

He studied his bed momentarily. The thrill of what had happened there flashed in front of him. Maddie's whiteness thrashing against him. Her nails digging into his back. Her whimpering of pleasure. Half an hour before, his life had been rocking and rolling.' Now his dreams were shattered. In minutes, his world had turned upside down. Jeffrey selling the villa sent his Mom and him back to their old life. Living in a tiny rundown apartment.

Yes. He knew what he must do.

He grabbed a T-shirt, found some sandals, and snatched up his bag. Carefully moving the clutter in his room aside, he searched for his phone. After several seconds, he saw a picture of it in his mind—on the kitchen countertop. He cursed. Cautiously, the blind was lifted and carefully dropped behind him as he left. It was with relief he heard the garden gate latch fall into place. Willis looked along the stretch of back fences of the villas. Madison was just a few metres down.

Music pumping from the television welcomed him. Nathan sat statuesque on the sofa, staring in front of him, towards the open window—the reality of the morning probably clicking into place. With glazed eyes, Nathan gawped out at the sea, at the ocean which had almost taken him. He was shivering slightly; cold fear had clothed his form. Madison had draped a sweatshirt around his shoulders.

Conversely, his sister was sparkling, full of chatter. Her face displaying into a broad smile as he entered. She was high on expectation. Madison flirted herself around him. Her hair was neatly tied up; she flounced around in a floral beach dress. Willis' eyes tracked her as she poured drinks for all of them. The situation was rather testing. It was clear that they were all realms apart.

'I have to go and see my Mom,' Willis said flatly after several seconds. 'I'll need to go there by bus.'

'Can't you phone her?' Madison beamed at him. Nathan seemed not to have heard.

'No. I have to give her something. It's important. She's got a wedding today, so she'll be real busy. You should stay with Nat, he's still in shock,' he told Madison, knowing that she wouldn't.

'What do you think Nat? Are you coming to the hotel?'

'What?'

'Do you want to come with us?'

'Where?' he asked his sister.

'Go to see Tammy.'

Nathan looked at her confused. She repeated the question. 'No, you go. I'm okay. The oldies will be back soon.'

'You sure? I'll phone them to say I'm going with Willis.'

'Don't tell them about the surfing,' Nathan insists. 'I'll just say I don't feel great.'

~~~

The pair crossed the vast expanse of the hotel foyer, bustling with tourists. Next to the front desk, the area was scattered with trolleys of luggage. The desk was busy assisting guests. Willis held back until a receptionist he recognised was available. Madison stuck very close to him.

'Hi. Do you think I could see my Mom for two minutes?'

'Hi Willis,' the receptionist smiled at them. 'She's real busy today; you know she's got a wedding.'

'Yeah, I know. Just two minutes. I only need to give her something.'

'Let's see if I can find her,' she went to the switchboard and picked up the phone. 'Hi Tamara. I've Willis here. Can you spare him two minutes? Yes, I'll tell him.'

'She's in the kitchens Willis. You know the way?'

'Thanks.' He turned to Madison. 'You wait here. I'll be back in five.'

Willis sprinted under the Spanish style arches: into the gardens, past groups of visitors, past the large swimming pool, through the open dining area to the stainless steel, sweltering world of the hotel kitchens. Pushing the swing doors revealed a domain of clatter and kitchen babble. He found his mother, standing in the middle of the kitchen, scanning a list on her phone.

'Surprise! Hi Willis,' she grinned at him.

Willis beckoned her towards him, 'ListenMomI'lljusttakeaminutecos ...'

'Slow down Willis, slow down. Now just start again,' his mother said.

Willis stopped and stared at his mother. He took hold of her arm and pulled her towards a quiet corner. He took a deep breath, lowered the tone of his voice, and started again. 'I know you're hyper busy Mom, but I've some news—real bad news. It's a big deal for us.'

Still clutching her phone, his mother's arm dropped, thrown by her son's attitude. Willis realised his news would be a shock.

'Mom, it guts me to be the one to tell you this, but its Jeff—he's leaving. I came into my room from the back yard ... I heard him on the phone ... he didn't know I was there. Mom ... he's looking for an apartment off-island ... he's putting the villa up for sale,' he still spoke so quickly, he could see his mother was having a problem following him.

He saw her take in a great gulp of air, saw her eyes widen. She said nothing for a few seconds.

'Selling the villa—you sure about this?' Her previous light-hearted expression disappeared. Willis nodded. Her eyes closed momentarily. 'Jesus, I didn't think it would happen like this.'

'Mom, he was on his phone to Delan. Remember, the guy who sold him the villa. They were talking about selling it. They even parleyed about the price and leaving the furniture. I'm sure I got the picture clear.'

'Hell Willis, it couldn't happen on a worse day. I'll be run off my feet until late this evening.'

'What can I do?'

'Nothing Willis, I'll try and sort something out,' his mother assured him. 'I don't know what, but ...'

'What do I say if he's in when I get back?'

'Oh Willis,' she grabbed hold off his arm and squeezed it. 'Don't do anything ... don't say anything about it ... try to keep away from him. I'll phone and see if I can get anything out of him. No, don't YOU do anything. Try not to worry. I'll try to sort it. Shit Willis. Thanks for letting me know.'

Willis looked straight at her, 'Mom, you've told me swearing is never necessary.'

'There are very rare exceptions,' she said without smiling. Her hand went to her forehead as Willis turned and left through the metal swing doors.

Chapter 26

Confrontation

The room was in chaos.

Summer clothes hung around the room. Ella sat on the floor with her head in the wardrobe, selecting which of her shoes she should pack. The havoc had to be put into some order in the next hour or so, otherwise, she wouldn't be able to sleep in her bed. The disorder must be stored in her suitcase. But she felt tired, and her insides were tense. She wasn't looking forward to going to Sainte Marie alone, and worst, confronting Jeffrey.

A pair of gold sandals were selected from the rack. She scrutinised them, then returned them to their place. They were not the right footwear to take. A thundering noise announced Kloe scampering up the stairs. Bursting into the room, she was stopped abruptly by what confronted her. She took in the disarray of her mother's bedroom before she spoke.

'Mum, Mum. Uncle C's coming over,' Kloe babbled excitedly.

'Err … what do you mean?'

'He phoned,' Kloe said not pausing for breath, 'you didn't hear your phone ringing, so I answered it.'

'Okay … so, he's coming to see us,' Ella said from the floor, 'but when Kloe?'

'Like now. He's on his way.' Ella sighed internally as she stood up. She loved him dearly, but really didn't have time for Craig this evening. Kloe selected one of her mother's dresses from the jumble sale of things on the bed. She held it in front of her. 'You taking this?' she asked screwing up her nose.

'What does my fashion advisor think?'

'Nah! Too formal. Not cool. You won't be going out anywhere Gucci. Back in the wardrobe.'

'Thanks Kloe!' she said tartly, snatching the coat hanger from her daughter.

'But Ma, you asked. Don't forget your gold sandals though. They're not too bad.' She pointed towards the base of the wardrobe. 'Wish I was going too.'

'Look Kloe, we've been through this before, this is not a holiday. Besides, you have to go back to school. Your Dad will be back tomorrow. He'll keep you busy and run you to school, 'til I get back.'

'I'd rather go to Sainte Marie with you. I wouldn't get in the way,' she whimpered.

'You are not going Kloe. The flights cost too much money.' The discussion was closed by the chime of the doorbell.

'I'll go, I'll go! That'll be Uncle Craig,' Kloe dashed out of the room.

'Kloe, tell him I'll be down in a couple of minutes,' Ella shouted after her daughter galloping downstairs. Ella snatched up the clothes strewn across the bed and threw them over a side chair. The gold sandals, a pair of trainers and a bundle of underwear were dumped into the open suitcase on the floor. She would have to get up extra early tomorrow to deal with the rest.

She went downstairs reluctantly, a little put out she wasn't able to finish her packing, 'Hi Craig,' she greeted her brother, reaching the sitting room.

'Look Mum,' Kloe shouted, waving a box in the air, 'Look what he's bought me! A neon sign! Wicked!'

'You spoil her too much Craig, but thanks a lot. I was trying to do my packing,' she kissed her brother lightly on the cheek.

'I'm going upstairs to find a place for it,' Kloe shrieked, darting out of the room, clutching her present.

'Well, that's certainly different. So, how's life treating you, Craig?' She looked at her brother, still dressed in his work clothes, before sitting on the sofa, leaving room for him.

'Fine. I thought I'd come over before you left to wish you luck.' Craig installed himself next to her. 'I thought I'd give you a bit of an update too. I've been trying to track down Katie Eavis.'

He explained that she no longer worked for the care agency. They had an address for her in Bristol, but weren't prepared to give it to him. He then remembered that she had said her apartment was in Filton. As her surname was not too common, he first tried the phone book and then social media.

'And I found her,' his voice lightened. 'Well, I thought that I had.' Ella could see from his face that in fact he hadn't. 'But guess what, when I phoned, the person who answered explained that she had moved to Spain. So, we're rather stuck.'

'It isn't that important,' she said. 'I just thought I could ask her if she knew anything about Mum spending large amounts of money.'

'Oh no Ella, Keating has now identified it was definitely Jeffrey who took out the funds from the bank, bit by bit.'

'The man's a crook.' Ella said with bitterness in her voice. Mentioning Jeffrey made her tension return. She wanted to erase him from her thoughts; what he'd done upset her too much.

'Strangely though,' Craig interrupted, 'the re-mortgaging application forms have Mum's signatures on them. So, she must have known.'

'Be real Craig,' Ella looked at her brother disbelievingly. 'Mum's poor mind was so confused. There were times when she didn't know what day it was.'

'Yeah, you're right,' Craig said, running his hand over his short hair.

'The man is such a liar; he could have told her anything about the forms. She probably didn't know what she was signing. I'm sure he relied on her confused mind.'

'So, you don't think we should read anything into Katie Eavis going to Spain?' Craig asked.

'Not at all,' Ella shook her head. 'Mum told me that she had met a new man and that's why she left. I liked her; I don't think she was part of the problem.' She looked down towards her pocket, as her phone rang out. 'Hang on Craig … Hi Antony.

Strange you ringing, I've been meaning to phone you all week, but I've just been so busy ... ' She stopped, mouth agape, 'Christ, I don't believe it. Antony ... Craig is here. Let me put the phone on speaker.'

She shuffled up nearer to her brother. 'It's about Jeffrey,' she mouthed, holding out her phone.

'Yes, it happened the day before yesterday,' Antony continued from the phone. 'I know I should have phoned before, but like you, I've been hyper-busy.' They heard him sigh. 'That morning, the sea was fairly rough. They think he got tangled up on some ropes, the anchor lines of the boats in the bay. One of my staff had to pull his body out the sea.'

'Oh God,' Ella's hand went to her face.

'Hi Antony,' Craig said, louder than was necessary. 'Where was this?'

'Unfortunately for me, right in front of the hotel. It was actually a female guest who swam into his floating body. You can imagine it caused a big upset amongst the guests ... the police and everything.'

Ella screwed up her eyes, imaging the scene, and sympathising with the guests and Antony.

'Yeah, not the best promotion for the hotel.' Antony paused, '... when he was on island, Jeffrey liked to swim across the bay every day.'

'I know,' Ella said. 'I remember when I went to Sainte Marie to bring Mum back home, he swam there twice a day. Listen Antony, I've been meaning to call you because I'd planned to fly out to the island. Now, I'm not too sure.'

'Ella, if you come, stay here, free of charge of course.'

'That's very kind, but I have already rented a tiny apartment.' She looked at her brother, eyebrows raised. 'We need to talk about it ... ' Craig nodded in agreement. 'Look Antony, I'll let you know tomorrow.'

'Yes, sure I ...'

'There's a lot to think about,' Ella didn't want to make an instant decision.

'I don't know when the funeral is,' Antony said in a flat tone, 'but I can find out.'

'Yes, there's that to think about too. Anyway ... I'll call tomorrow Antony.' She ended the call. 'Christ, what do I do now Craig?'

'What's happened Mum?' Kloe had come back downstairs and stood in the doorway.

'Look my angel, I'll explain later. I need to talk to Craig.' Her eyes left her brother to deal with her daughter. 'You go and get your pyjamas on.'

'But Mum, it's always the same ...' Kloe put on a fake sulk.

'Please Kloe. I promise, I'll explain in a few minutes.' Ella chased her daughter into the hall, flapping her hands to shoo her upstairs. She returned to the sofa and Craig. She held his gaze unblinkingly.

'I hate to ask this Craig,' she hissed, 'but you didn't have anything to do with this, did you?'

~~~

Why had she said it, she asked herself? But the words had rushed out before she could stop them. What had she been thinking? Accusing her brother of organising Jeffrey's death. But it all seemed so strange, so unlikely. Jeffrey was an exceptionally good swimmer. He could cope with swimming in the sea, even in fairly choppy waters. And it had happened so soon after her mother's death. The whole scenario didn't add up.

She could still see Craig's dead-pan face after hearing about Jeffrey. It was almost as if he was expecting the news. Ending the call, she'd scrutinise him. She had been amazed and shocked. But Craig's facial language didn't tell her any of that. His face bore no emotion, unlike his fury whilst at Oakdale—the shrieked threats about killing Jeffrey. After all, her brother knew plenty of

277

contacts on the island. It could have been possible for him to arrange it.

But Craig had been mortified because she'd added two and two together without caution, and come up with an outrageous solution. He'd really lost his cool with her. His shouting had brought Kloe back down to the sitting room and her presence had promptly calmed the situation. They both knew the argument couldn't continue in front of her. On telling Kloe the news about Jeffrey, her instant reaction had been that her mother no longer needed to leave for Sainte Marie.

But by the next morning, Ella had convinced herself, Craig, and Kloe, she needed to go. It was imperative to find out where all her mother's money had gone, though she told her daughter it was to attend the funeral. Kloe was too young to understand that her mother would also be fighting for her future and her rightful inheritance. For her and for any of Craig's future offspring.

She opened her eyes and struggled out of the memories of home. A slice of sunlight from the plane's window glinted across her face, forcing her to squint. She looked around at all the other passengers. There wasn't a single person she knew. She was alone—mid-Atlantic, dubious of what she was heading for. She'd refused the inflight meal; her insides could not have coped with that. Uncertainty told her she was heading for some sort of living nightmare. Who's to say what and who she'd encounter on island? She didn't look forward to any of it.

The flight arrived on time. Ella jostled at the baggage reclaim. It was packed with smiling holiday makers, selfie-takers, and residents eager to reach home. She wished that some of their positive vibes and cheerfulness could eliminate her cloak of qualms. They didn't, but calling home helped a little. She tried hard to sound lively and carefree. The time difference meant Kloe was about to go to bed. She blew her kisses; reassured her husband, Sam everything was famous. Her case bumping along the conveyer belt ended her call. She struggled to retrieve it, and told herself the extra luggage, thrown in at the last minute, had been a bad idea.

Ella gritted her teeth as she manoeuvred herself and too much baggage out of the air-conditioned arrivals building. Outside, tropical warmth breathed over her. She was confronted by a mass of human confusion: passengers, travel guides, porters, taxi drivers jostling for fares, all set against a blinding light. She scanned the agents waving paper with names on, but within seconds, a cheery-looking islander touched her arm.

'You Miss Ella?' he asked.

She read the square of paper he pushed towards her. 'Yes, that's right,' she said, relieved her journey to the north of the island was proving easier than she'd imagined.

'I thought to myself it were you. Mr Denning tell me you got long blond hair,' he beamed at her.

'That's wonderful. I thought I was going to have to fight in the queue for a taxi. Antony, Mr Denning, is a star.'

'Sure is milady. Let me takes ya cases. I'z Sylvester,' he said, pointing to his name tag. He took control. Sylvester relieved her of all of her luggage and led her proudly towards his splendidly clean Mercedes.

'Wow, I'm riding in style,' Ella watched as he stored her bags in the spotlessly clean boot.

'It always the best for the people stayin' at Topaz,' Sylvester flashed her another cheery smile, he as carefully lowered the boot, then held open the back door.

'I'd prefer to sit up front Sylvester, if it's all the same to you.'

'No problem mi lady,' he briskly marched around to open the passenger door.

Ella settled herself in the passenger seat. Already, the tropical welcome seemed to be unwinding a few of her knots—knots which had tightened whilst crossing the Atlantic.

'It from Mr Denning ma'am,' Sylvester handed Ella a letter.

Ella tore open the envelope. 'Aren't I lucky, Mr Denning has invited me to dinner this evening? He's just so thoughtful.'

'He a good boss ma'am,' Sylvester assured her.

Sylvester was only too pleased to chat. Ella was keen to wind-down. They talked about anything and everything. The long and difficult ride to the north of the island passed much quicker than Ella had imagined: they sped through numerous hamlets of small, brightly painted houses, past an abundance of lush vegetation, caught glimpses of the sea, slowed through the treacherous hair-pin bends, and glided past throngs of locals in bustling Bourbon. Two hours later, they stopped sedately in front of Topaz.

They were just in time to catch a fleeting glimpse of the sun as it dipped out of sight—tinting the turquoise overhead to purples, red and orange. Night comes early in the tropics. Sylvester carted all Ella's luggage to the reception desk. She tipped him well; and much to his pleasure, booked him for her homeward journey. His spirited small talk had dispelled some of her stresses; her smiles were more spontaneous after sharing his good humour.

Ella was shown to a room at the top of the bluff. Antony had done her proud, giving her one of the best rooms in his hotel. Opening the patio door, she was greeted by the music of the sea, as it beat against the base of the cliff. The shimmer of the rising moon mirrored off the small pool on the terrace. The seductive world of five star living beckoned to her. For a moment, she regretted her refusal to stay as Antony's guest for the whole week. She would be leaving the following day to go to the rented apartment.

Her huge suitcase was left at the edge of the room unopened, but she pulled her swimsuit out of her hand luggage. Escaping from her travel-soiled clothes, Ella immersed her weary form into the pool; and lay numbed, floating, barely stirring in the warm water. She soaked up the foreign sounds encircling her—

the battering of the waves, plants rustling, and tree frogs calling. It brought a satisfied smile to her lips. The visit had started well; it almost seemed like a holiday.

Seeing Antony again over dinner would be great, despite her fatigued body telling her perhaps eating a snack in the room, before going to sleep, might be preferable. However, Ella did not look forward to relating the sorry tale of Jeffrey's deception and fraudulence, or hearing Antony's side to the story.

Chapter 27

Lobster

As she got ready for dinner, Ella looked yearningly at the bed.

The journey, the time difference and the stress had drained her; she felt wiped-out. After her dip in the pool, the large, wide bed looked very tempting, but she knew seeing Antony was essential, even if only to thank him for his generous hospitality.

Making a supreme effort, she attempted to disguise her fatigue by cladding herself in her only vaguely dressy outfit, complete with gold sandals and a mask of make-up. Her damp hair was twisted up on top and clasped with a hair claw.

Leaving the isolation of her room, she descended through the illuminated calm of the gardens down to the beach front. A buzz of lively chatter dominated the bar, but she felt estranged to the revelry. Ella was pleased to see Antony turn up after a few minutes. He strode towards her, dressed in his habitual dark trousers and a plain cotton open-necked shirt. Ella had known Antony for what seemed like an age—she'd first met him as a teenager. He kissed her cheek and hugged her tightly.

'Great to see you, Ella. It's a real shame it has to be under such circumstances.'

'Let me get you a drink Antony. It's the least I can do after all your kindness.'

'Just a white wine thanks. Shall we go to our table, hopefully it'll be a bit quieter there.' He led her to a secluded setting at the far side of the open restaurant. It probably had the best outlook of the venue—the indigo of the ocean across the empty beach. They were followed by two waiters. Antony stood aside to allow Ella to be seated by them.

'I suppose, as the owner, you're entitled to have the best table in the place,' Ella joked.

'For sure.' He turned to address one of the staff, 'Good evening, Dell, you can leave us the menus, but is there anything you can recommend for this evening?'

'Good evening, madam, sir,' his head dipped in a very discreet bow, as he passed over the menus. 'For this evening, the chef is recommending the pumpkin risotto and the lobster and crab bake Mr Denning.' He unfolded the white starched napkins and placed them across their laps before leaving.

Antony surveyed his domain before giving Ella his full attention. 'First Ella, I must apologise for not being able to make it to your mother's funeral service. I really couldn't leave this place for long enough to get over to Britain. I had a lot of respect for your mother … your father too.'

Ella picked up her menu. 'I do understand Antony.' She studied his face in the subdued lighting. He looked as tired as she felt. Numerous lines fanned out at the corner of his eyes. Steaks of grey dominated his dark hair. 'I understand—the hotel's a great tie. It's very beautiful, but I know it takes a lot of effort to keep it in perfect order.'

'A lot of effort, but even more money,' he reminded her. Antony placed his closed menu on the table. 'Are we going for the risotto, followed by the lobster?'

'That sounds sublime.'

Ella took a deep breath and started her account of Jeffrey's double-dealing.

'Antony, there's a lot to tell you. I hardly know where to begin.' She fiddled nervously with her napkin while telling him that she and Craig were named executors of their mother's will. Apart from a small donation to the junior school in Doublon d'Or—they were also the sole beneficiaries, but this gave them a problem. He would understand why very soon. The call from the solicitor had rocked them both. They'd learnt Jeffrey had used his Power of Attorney to cash-in all Miranda's insurances; and he'd virtually emptied all her accounts. The extensive property portfolio had been re-mortgaged to the maximum. Their inheritance would be less than a quarter of what it should have been. The solicitor was concerned. He felt the money left may not be sufficient to pay the sizeable death duties. There would definitely be a large tax bill to pay.

Antony shook his head disbelievingly. Recounting the sorry tale, Ella had to concentrate to keep her voice level. Her insides felt mangled, and her heart hammered against her ribs. The whole affair of how her mother had been treated by her own husband upset her deeply. She detailed Craig's rage, and why they'd decided Jeffrey had to be confronted. She was thankful when she'd concluded; her unease settled a little.

But it was to be temporary. At first, Antony made no comment, his forehead creased into a maintained frown. She heard him sigh. 'Oh Ella, I'm so sorry. I didn't know things were so bad. It's all starting to make a lot more sense now. Things have not been easy this side of the Atlantic either.'

'I don't understand, what do you mean?'

Their conversation was interrupted. The risotto had arrived—portions of creamy rice, finished with tiny balls of bright orange pumpkin and fresh sage leaves.

'Would you care for more parmesan ma'am?' the waiter asked.

'Well, this was worth flying across the Atlantic for!' Ella jested, trying to lift her mood. 'No thanks, I'll take it just as it is. It looks delicious,' she turned her face to smile up at the waiter.

'Black pepper ma'am?' Ella shook her head.

Antony waited for the staff to leave before leaning towards her.

'Look Ella, I've never said anything before—perhaps I should have,' he said in a low voice. He lowered his eyes, '...but what should I say ... well—Jeffrey lived with a young lady when he was on island ... she's much younger than him ... in fact, he met her here.'

'Antony, I half expected as much. Nothing would surprise me of that man.' Ella tasted the creamy richness of her starter. 'Mmm, this is excellent ...'

'Tamara ... she's called Tamara,' Antony seemed rather awkward that he should be the one to tell her. 'You may even remember her. She worked as a receptionist here. Her first night was the night your mother was taken ill.'

'Yeah, perhaps I've met her. So, they lived together?' She ate another forkful thoughtfully. 'Antony, do you remember the night my mother had her stroke? You told me he paid for another room in the hotel. You don't think ...the affair could have started then?'

'It's possible, but I wouldn't have thought so. Not on her first night. She was a very good employee. And doesn't strike me as being the type to fool around with ...' Antony paused, '... go with anybody,' he said politely.

Ella stared vacantly, trying to imagine that evening. 'It's just that something happened during that holiday. I just have that feeling—but with them both gone we'll probably never know the truth. I have to stop myself from wondering.'

'You're right; it's wisest to do just that.'

'Mum never actually said anything, but when you saw them together, Jeffrey and her, the atmosphere was very frosty. After her stroke, I think she cursed the day she ever walked through his estate agency door.'

'Yes ... Miranda was a very private person. I'm sure she wouldn't have broadcast her feelings.'

The talk about her recently deceased mother became difficult. Grief tumbled back down inside her. Her eyes started to sting. Ella had to fight back her emotions.

'Craig, you know, never liked Jeffrey,' she started slowly. 'Not because he thought he was dishonest—he just didn't like the guy. But Mum was so pleased at first, she wouldn't have to spend her old age alone.' As she said it, she knew she shouldn't

285

have. Ella gulped back a sob, '... but she never even got to enjoy old age.' A large tear zigzagged down her cheek. 'Sorry Antony,' she sniffed, 'sorry, I'm getting over-emotional and talking rubbish.'

Antony bent over the table to squeeze her hand. 'Don't tear yourself up about it Ella. As I said, you just have to let the past go. You can't change it.' He waved to one of the staff nearby. 'Let me get you some tissues or something?'

'Antony, I'm so sorry ... I'm just tired,' she snuffled and ran a finger under her eyes. 'You're right, tears don't help. And there's a lot I need to ask you about. I need to pull myself together and focus. There are people I need to see—his solicitor—about the will. The police, I suppose. And this Tamara. And I need to find out where he's been stashing the money ... and there's the funeral.'

'Look Ella, would it be better to find time to talk to you about all of this tomorrow? You're obviously not up to it now.'

'Because I'm a weepy mess you mean?' Ella was embarrassed.

Their main course arrived. If Ella hadn't felt so out of sorts, she would have found her phone and taken a photo. With it came an extra silver tray holding a small pack of white paper tissues.

'Wow! Am I being spoilt?' she forced another grin and gawped at the huge plate set before her. A display of coral-coloured seafood. But her tears had washed away her appetite. Nevertheless, she found a few words which were needed to show some appreciation. 'That smells so yummy; and looks too good to eat.'

'The chef'll be very upset if you don't at least try it,' Antony told her.

'Antony ... tomorrow ... I don't want to take up too much of your time, but ...'

'Let's arrange to meet before you leave the hotel. Why don't you come to my office around mid-day?' He gulped down a mouthful of his wine.

'That's very kind,' Ella used one of the tissues and tried to wipe away some of her distress.

'Just a couple of things you should consider though Ella,' Antony said, perhaps trying to deflect away from her embarrassment. '… Jeffrey will not have deposited any large amounts in any bank on Sainte Marie. The banks on island are all paranoid about money laundering. It's even difficult to start up an account here. You have to answer so many bloody stupid questions. If he wanted to hide illegal earnings, he'd probably have to deposit them in some tax haven. And that could be really problematic for you. It means the money could be anywhere—anywhere in the world.'

'You could be right,' Ella forced a forkful of lobster between her lips. 'I haven't thought the situation through very well, have I?' Ella was beginning to feel perhaps she was not up to the task she'd set herself.

Antony glanced at her; his eyebrows raised questioningly at her comment.

'And the other thing?' she asked, so Antony didn't have to respond to what she'd asked.

'Tomorrow morning, when you surface, I suggest you get yourself to the car rental desk. Hire yourself some wheels. It'll save on having to keep paying out for taxis.'

'It's a good idea. Thanks for the advice. I will'

They sat in silence for several minutes, consuming their haute cuisine meal, Ella still feeling uncomfortable about her display of grief.

'So, what's this Tamara like?' Ella asked, trying to fill the gap in the conversation.

'She's a real looker. It's easy to see why Jeffrey fell for her, even though she must be nearly half his age. She's got a son,

Willis—a nice boy. He's water sports crazy, just like Jeffrey … sorry … like Jeffrey used to be.'

The comments about Tamara renewed the pain inside Ella. Jeffrey had married her mother. She had been attractive. He had no right to be messing around with other women, whatever age they were. Her misery wanted the evening to be over. She ate another mouthful of her lobster and crab bake. That was it. She could eat no more.

Antony however was determined to finish his. Ella waited for him to lower his cutlery, 'Antony, thank you again for your hospitality and the exquisite meal. I'll let you get home to your family … and I'll see you tomorrow.'

Antony scraped his chair across the floor as he stood up. He moved towards Ella and placed a sympathetic arm around her shoulder. She was guided to the exit. They stood studying the picture of the tropical night and listening to the beating of the waves.

'Things will seem better after a night's sleep,' he assured her.

'Hope so.'

'You go and crash out Ella. I'll see you tomorrow—I've loads of other things to tell you—all about Jeffrey.'

Ella kissed him lightly on the cheek, feeling relieved she would soon be able to close her eyes against the world, and sleep. As she climbed the bluff, Antony's words came back to her—"I've loads of other things to tell you." Despite her exhaustion, she was curious what tomorrow's revelations would bring.

The under-lighting of the plants and her gold sandals guided her. It was a relief to return to the isolation of her room. The digital clock told her it wasn't yet nine o'clock. Ella didn't care; it was nearly two in the morning in Dorset, and her family would be fast asleep.

Within seconds, her clothes were thrown over the upright suitcase, and she fell between the cool sheets. The last things she remembered were the hiss of the room fan and the faint sighing of the sea turning continually onto the shore beneath her.

Chapter 28

Police

Ella lay sprawled across the enormous bed.

A sheet was tangled around her, and she clutched at the softness of one of the pillows. Through half-closed eyes, in a semi-conscious state, she registered flashing patterns dancing over her. Struggling out of sleep she discovered the kaleidoscope was reflections from the terrace pool. Her body told her she needed to return to the arms of Orpheus; but little by little, the fantasies which had filled her sleep, drifted away.

Ella unwound herself from the mass of white bed linen; and shuffled into a sitting position at the top of the bed. Dropping her head onto her raised knees, she surveyed the day. The sun welcomed her through the veil of fine curtaining. A cacophony of bird song joined the greeting. Despite the glare, the air touching her skin felt heavy with moisture. Its warmth and stickiness irked her.

Gradually, thoughts of the previous day spilled back. The emotions of the previous night's dinner tumbled before her. It really hadn't gone well. Antony was a busy man. He had planned to impart all he knew about her former stepfather during dinner. And she had messed things up. Exhaustion and grief had taken over. Embarrassment still felt taut inside her. Antony had been right— if she was to achieve anything from her week on island, she'd need to toughen up, try and shut a door on the past.

She squinted at the clock beside her. Five forty-five. She had been dead to the world for nearly nine hours. There were still nearly two hours until the hotel breakfast. In Dorset however, the daily routine would have started hours before.

Ella wanted to unburden herself of the embarrassment and failure of the previous evening. A call home would bring her comfort. Familiar, loved voices always helped to put her uneasiness into perspective. Ella grabbed up her phone. Relief started to settle inside her after catching up with Sam. He talked her through the problems she described and told her Antony would understand. Of course, Kloe's constant enthusiasm for life lifted her spirits.

Next came a call to Craig, playing down the problem which meant the meal with Antony finished rather abruptly. Craig, being Craig, reiterated what he thought her priorities had to be during her visit. She listened, but considered his list far too demanding for her short visit.

'Not sure I'll cover all that. You want me to behave like some Inspector Maigret,' she laughed.

Craig ignored her jesting; and carried on doling out instructions. 'Look Ella, if Antony reckons that he could have secreted funds away, getting hold of his passport might help us. Despite what Antony says, there's probably only a few places he'd have an offshore account.'

'And how am I going to get that?' Ella sighed. It seemed like an impossible task.

'I suppose this girl friend would be the best bet, or the police may have taken it.'

Ella mentally marked the task on her list of priorities. 'I'd thought that I'd go to the local police later today, before I leave the hotel,' she told him. 'I hope to ask the questions we discussed. But listen Craig, I can hardly ask the girl friend. I don't even know how to find her.'

With the shower water beating on her head, she mulled over what her agenda for that day should be. Before eating an early breakfast and starting on Craig's list, she had time to wander down to the beach—time to renew her love of Mango Bay. Clad in shorts and a T-shirt, she closed the room door behind her and confronted the glare of the early morning sun. Ella started on the path leading down to the beach, but strayed from it to cut across to the edge of the bluff, guarded by a security fence. A little way along, a gate opened onto steps—steep steps, safeguarded by a railing, which led down to a wooden platform jutting into the sea. Ella recalled this was where Jeffrey habitually used to start his swims—doubtless his last one as well.

From her elevated position, Ella studied the sweep of the cove. The turquoise and teal, like a bold abstract painting. The crystal clear waters were breath-taking—a recompense for leaving her beloved family. Several small boats were anchored across the bay, leaving an unhampered passage between the platform below her and the swimming raft. Habitually, Jeffrey had swum between the two. She asked herself why a good swimmer would have any problems there.

Ella sauntered back to the path and followed the numerous steps towards the beach. At that hour, only a few staff were around—just a couple of gardeners. It proved too early for hotel guests. From her vantage point on the beach, she was able to check out the path that Jeffrey would have followed. She imagined him walking down from the top of the bluff, carrying a beach towel. At the base of the steps, he'd leave his towel and dive from the tiny wharf. An inflatable was tied up there. He'd swim across to the raft in the middle of the bay—about a hundred metres of unimpeded glistening water. Back and forth. She could almost see his progress.

The beach was deserted. Not a soul. Even the security guard, in his kiosk, wasn't visible—possibly having a crafty snooze. Ella could see it would be easy to get out to one of the boats anchored off the shoreline. The water was shallow; it would be possible to wade to the nearest craft. With no one around, someone could stand in one of the boats and attack a swimmer with an oar or something similar.

Ella stood on the empty beach, the morning sunlight warming her skin; and wondered.

~~~

Mango Bay police station was on the main road to Bourbon. Ella had passed it many times before. But during her holidays on island, she had never had the necessity to venture inside. Driving the hire car into the large car park, she noted the numerous cars. It was not like any police station she'd seen in Europe. The plot was fenced in by a jungle of tropical plants and flowers. A huge flamboyant tree, festooned with clusters of flaming-orange flowers, guarded the front of the low, once-white building. Its branches stretched across the roof. For several moments, Ella sat in the car, peering vacantly in front of her—trying to clear her mind, find some confidence, and home in on her reasons for being there.

She took a deep breath and left the car. She had to go for it. Ella manoeuvred around the sizable trunk of the flamboyant blocking direct access to the steps. Pushing open the main door, her ears were immediately assaulted by the sound of a sports commentary. The full car park had misled her. The foyer was not buzzing with people—there was no queue as she'd imagined. The wooden counter, at the end, was unmanned. She stood by the reception desk and looked into the small room behind. It was devoid of any sign of the local police force.

Ella coughed, hoping to draw attention, but the commentary (quickly determined as cricket) dimmed her efforts into insignificance. The seconds turned into minutes. An over later, and after some cheering in the next room, an impatient streak overtook her tolerance. Her knuckles banged onto the wooden surface, and she called out 'Hello.'

A very young, uniformed lady bounced into the reception space. Her straightened black hair was pulled sharply back exposing her beaming face.

'And what can I do for you then,' she grinned.

Ella cleared her throat. 'I've come to enquire about the death of Mr Jeffrey Taylor last week.'

The police constable's face dropped. In a flash, she seemed to recall the main purpose of her job. The rapture from following the cricket match dissolved from her features.

'You'z needing to see DI Hamity ma'am. I sees if they'z available. You can take a seat.' Her hand indicated the row of mismatching wooden chairs lining one wall of the foyer.

Ella did as she'd been instructed and sat uncomfortably on the edge of a chair. She misguidedly imagined that the volume of the cricket might be turned down, now the constable knew she was there. But not at all. The volume remained constant; and very soon there was more clapping and jubilation. Several minutes later, the policewoman opened a door next to the counter.

'Follow me please. DI Hamity'll see ya now.' She opened the door wider for Ella to pass. The pair were barely noticed as they crossed the large room behind the reception bureau. All eyes were glued to an over-sized flat-screen television suspended on one wall. The audience was at least half a dozen strong, and only two of them were uniformed.

'West Indies playing today,' the constable stated superfluously. Ella was directed to the end of a narrow, dingy corridor. The constable tapped on a door, before showing Ella into a tiny, cluttered office. The walls were empty apart for a large map of the island. Cramped behind the desk was a portly DI, clad in near-black trousers and a white shirt. Ella was a little taken aback by her formidable and serious manner. Her closely shaven head added to her severe facade.

'Good morning, ma'am,' DI Hamity said, indicating the chair opposite her.

Ella fidgeted in the seat, 'good morning. I've come to ask about my stepfather. I've flown from Britain for his funeral,' she explained rather timidly.

'Your stepfather being …?'

'Mr Jeffrey Taylor—he drowned next to the Topaz Hotel last week.'

'My sincere condolences,' the Inspector said gruffly. 'But how can I assist you?' she sat down and started to search for information on her computer.

'I just wondered what investigations took place after his body was discovered,' Ella asked quietly.

The Inspector's head came up; she studied Ella in silence. Her upper lip folded into her mouth as she next surveyed the screen of her desktop. 'That was Sergeant Lords. He went to the hotel when the head of security called. Apparently, one of the hotel guests swam into the body.'

'Did your sergeant retrieve the body from the water?'

The policewoman's eyes narrowed. 'I don't understand ma'am. Why do you need to know?'

She looked down at her bare white legs protruding from her shorts—knowing she was not appropriately attired for this. She swallowed strongly. 'What I really want to ask is, if the police considered the death to be in any way suspicious?' she said, grabbing hold of her tenacity.

'No ma'am. Mr Taylor's passing is not being treated as being in any way suspicious.'

Ella stared at the stern face before her. She must get a grip and ask the questions that she had planned. 'It's just that …' she started. Detective Inspector Hamity's eyes looked at her coldly. She tried again. She really wasn't doing very well … another deep breath, and this time she went for it.

' … I need to be blunt. My stepfather was not the most popular of characters,' she began. 'To the family, my mother's family that is, his death by accidental drowning seems extremely …' Ella paused, '… what can I say … unlikely, because Mr Taylor was an excellent swimmer.'

'That may have been the case ma'am, but I reiterate that the death is not being treated as suspicious.'

'Can I ask if a full autopsy took place?'

The DI sat bolt upright in her chair, protruding her white shirt. 'Ma'am, I'm not at liberty to discuss what happened at an autopsy. The body was taken to the main hospital in Bourbon. The doctor there signed the death certificate.'

'The cause of death being …?'

'Accidental drowning,' she said rather crisply.

'But what did … ' insisted Ella, her insides reeling—it was obvious the DI was irritated by all her questions.

Ella heard DI Hamity inhale deeply. 'Ma'am, I must say that there are factors here that you seem to have dismissed,' her tone was unfriendly to the extreme. 'Firstly, there's Mr Taylor's age. He was an old man. He was nearly seventy.'

Ella gaped. Jeffrey would not have liked that description. He'd still considered himself active and very fit for his age.

'Secondly, and very importantly, the sea was rough that day. There had been a storm. He should not have been exercising in such conditions. Next, every year people are killed along our coast because they misjudge the force of the seas.'

Ella didn't dare utter a murmur.

'And finally, ma'am, this is not England. We have two doctors who perform autopsies on Sainte Marie—two doctors for the whole island. We do not have the facilities, or the capital, to perform a full autopsy for every sudden death that occurs.'

Ella froze on her chair, her eyes still fixed on the Detective Inspector. Damn, she had hoped to find out if Jeffrey had any bumps on his head, or bruises on his body, but could feel her confidence drifting away, being replaced by self-consciousness and awkwardness. Ella had not wished to cause offense. But obviously had. Humility descended instantly. There was no way she wanted to give the impression she was criticising—finding fault with the Inspector, or the island Police system. The policewoman's last statements had put Ella firmly in her place. Had made her remember exactly where she was. Sainte Marie was a world away from Dorset. Ella obviously had a lot to learn about life in the Caribbean world.

'Is there anything else I can help you with?' DI Hamity asked with exaggerated politeness.

'Eh ... yes,' Ella took on board she wouldn't be able to return to the police station. She needed to try her hand, 'Eh ... I wondered if the Police have Mr Taylor's passport. And also, I'd be very grateful, if you have a record of my stepfather's last address?'

The computer screen was employed once more. After several seconds, the Inspector's hostile eyes were directed towards Ella again. 'Mr Taylor resided at Three Isles. If you have adequate identification, the constable who showed you to my office, may be able to help you with the passport.'

'That's very helpful. Thank you.' It was time to leave. Ella cast a final eye around the minute and disarrayed room, its only window of frosted glass, near ceiling level. She stood up, eyes fixed downwards, and held out a hand to DI Hamity. 'Thank you for your time and patience Detective Inspector Hamity.'

The policewoman shook Ella's hand; and her head dropped in a nod. The door closed with barely a sound as Ella left the chilled atmosphere of the office. She walked down the corridor wide-mouthed. Not once had the Inspector's lips flickered into a smile. It was clear, the DI took her work very seriously; and plainly knew just how to deal with difficult people. Ella figured the policewoman had probably come face to face with some hard cases in her time.

Passing under the parasol of the flamboyant tree, Ella tucked the late Mr Jeffrey Taylor's passport in the depths of her handbag. She felt proud of herself. Her visit had been a moderate success. The young constable had been far more forthcoming than her boss. A letter from her mother's solicitor and her own identification had not only obtained the confiscated document, but a more precise address for her late stepfather.

There were still two hours before her meeting with Antony. She had time to try and find Jeffrey's home. Driving along the coast, the morning's exploits spun around in her mind. She was sure the memory of meeting DI Hamity would stay with her for always. In a way, she felt privileged to have had that insight into island life. But she was still amazed—amazed that Jeffrey's death had not been investigated. Was she the only person who was sceptical about the accidental drowning verdict?

The coast road was full of enchantment: glimpses of island life and exotic vegetation. As a child she'd learnt to love Sainte Marie; she loved it still. Three Isles had always been a favourite family destination. The name summoned up cherished images of Craig and her playing wildly on the stunning beach. Activities all hemmed in by the three stark pillars of land reaching up from the sea.

She stopped at the car park next to the beach. Her memories of the bay were jolted. The basis was still there, but the once natural cove had the addition of a smart-looking restaurant and homes which had been built on one side, commanding the top of the ridge.

Ella left the car and drifted towards the sands. Apart from a couple with their children, the scene was deserted. She took out the crumpled note she'd been given by the constable and approached the seated adults.

'Excuse me,' she asked the man, 'Do you know where this address is?'

He took the paper. 'Yeah ... you ain't got to go too far ... that just there.' His index finger pointed upwards.

Her eyes followed his indication, 'Thanks for your help.'

She smiled at the couple and walked on a little further towards the shoreline. There, she turned, and her view of the villas became enhanced. A group of a dozen or so buildings topped the ridge: sleek lines, a mass of glass, and contemporary cladding; all high-end residences. For the second time during the visit so far, her heart lurched, and her insides were shaken.

Chapter 29

Fraught

Willis slammed his hand on the inside of the bus.

'Next stop please,' he called to the driver and stood up. The vehicle started to slow. 'See ya man,' he said, tapping the shoulder of the passenger he'd been next to, and squeezing past his legs. Willis manoeuvred into the aisle of the small bus, smiling at his fellow passengers. The chatter amongst the occupants continued until the bus halted. His exit was blocked. It was necessary for those in his way to get off. Once done, he could alight. At the door, notes of hip hop sang out from the driver's radio.

'Just gonna stand there and hear me cry,

Well, that all right, because I love the way you lie,' the driver sang, accompanying the hit.

'Thanks bud,' Willis grinned.

He joined in the chorus, 'I love the way you lie, I love the way you lie.'

'See ya,' he waved as the passengers climbed back on, returning to standing in the aisle. But Willis' cheerfulness and high spirits remained with them. Alone at the bus stop, a darkness descended on him, like the gloom of the evening. The noise from the Mango Bay bus faded in his ears. The visit to Topaz had been a good idea. Ricko had kept him busy. Willis had been occupied instructing beginners with hotel paddle boards. He'd helped to get things sorted with people who wanted to kayak; and chatted to the water sports staff.

But it was over. All the buzz and activity of the afternoon had dropped away. His pretence of good humour and liveliness deserted him. A black mood rushed in to replace it. Walking towards the villa, he kicked at stones which lay in his path; kicked at the problems he'd lived with for the last week.

Madison had gone. She and her family were currently flying northwards. She'd left a big gap in his life. Whilst on island, Madison had kept his outlook positive. She'd help push his worries aside. They, together with Nathan, had been active during the day, mainly in the water.

At night, she'd come to his room and left with the dawn. The excitement of their secret times together had pulled a veil over the crap that Jeffrey's death had dumped on him. Their nights under his sheets, had been like unearthing a precious jewel. Exciting, exhilarating for both of them. Madison made him feel like a king. She was gutsy and a bit wild, eager to explore every aspect of Willis. Every tiny part of his body. Discover the depths of his desires. Learn of his inner most thoughts. Willis had been dazed by her attentions, in awe of her boldness. Struck dumb by the extent of their intimacy. But Madison had flown. She'd be away from the island for three and a half long months.

They had promised the liaison would continue when she returned for the Christmas break. In his heart, he knew it wouldn't. The months ahead were doubtful. He had no idea where he'd be living on island. No idea how long they could remain at Three Isles. Without him living in the villa, Madison and he would become a universe apart.

As he turned off the main road, Willis smashed his fist into a bush which was in his way. He thrashed out, hitting out at the memory of Jeffrey. He was the reason why his life, his mother's life, had been tipped upside down. Why their futures were so uncertain, and everything was in a mess. He had trusted Jeffrey. He'd thought they'd had a good time together; he'd even deluded himself that Jeffrey liked him. He'd believed Jeffrey when he said he would help him to go to university. But he'd lied. Jeffrey had turned out to be nothing but a cheat and a liar. Jeffrey had planned to high-tail it far away, dumping them like an out-grown garment. The villa was on the market without a word to them. They'd be without a home. The bastard! And he would have to forget university. He detested Jeffrey, hated him.

A hazy circle of light from the streetlamp guided his way, but illumination on the road melted away as he tromped into blackness. Nearing the end of the track, the breathing sounds from the ocean assailed his ears. They failed to smooth out his gloom. Willis kicked out again and trudged through a pothole attacking a loose morsel of tarmac. The windows of the restaurant on the beach sent spears of light and muted notes of table talk across the car park. He despised the invisible people he could hear laughing.

Willis started up the slope towards the villa. Mom would be home soon; he hoped there wouldn't be the same emptiness between them, as on previous evenings. Mom just wasn't the same: she hadn't been right since the evening he'd visited her at work. She barely spoke to him. Sure, she'd been busy, but it was more than that. Did she really miss Jeffrey so much? It seemed she was loaded down with troubles; her sparkle blacked out, constantly as though her thoughts were many miles away. He'd wanted to ask her about their future, but she was in another land, or deep, deep in the sea.

Willis fretted about not discussing things with her and being blocked out. It made him feel so low. All his hopes; his life had been reduced into worthless pieces. And tomorrow, would be the funeral. He was supposed to pay homage to Jeffrey Taylor, but felt freaked out by it. He'd be glad when the whole farce was over.

Like his mood, the interior of the villa was gloomy and dark. The shutters, which had kept out the heat from the day, remained closed. He made no effort to let in the cool of the evening, but headed straight to the refrigerator to snatch a chilled beer. Next, the air con was switched on. Knowing that the villa would soon be somebody else's home, made it feel strange, almost eerie. He sat at the kitchen counter, glugging back his drink; and feeling thoroughly miserable. He couldn't forget the stories the staff at Topaz had told him about finding Jeffrey's body floating in the sea. He played them over and over.

~~~

Ella scurried up the apartment block staircase clutching two plastic carrier bags—her food for the next few days. She was late, much later than she'd hoped. She'd spent a long time with Antony. Afterwards, she had to pack up the hire car with all her luggage. She was content to have taken his advice by getting her own transport. Next, she'd had to contend with the supermarket. Not knowing the store, it had been a struggle to find what she needed. There was so little choice in some sections. It certainly wasn't like shopping in her High Street supermarket back home. Apart from the locally sourced products, yams, bananas and so on, everything else—all the imported stuff—had seemed extortionately expensive. Ella was aware wages on the island were generally low, and couldn't imagine how the local inhabitants managed.

At the top of the steps, the bags were dumped on the floor. Ella wrestled to find the apartment key. Barging through the opened door, the stifling heat took her breath. The shopping was flung on the countertop. Next stop the windows. She sighed as the evening air immediately cooled her face and her haste.

She swiped her phone—nearly six o'clock. The video call with Craig was long overdue. In England, it was bedtime—she supposed he'd be in his pyjamas. But when she tapped his number, she saw he wasn't.

'Hi Craig, I'm sorry, it's rather late. I'll be very quick. I just thought I'd give you a bit of an update.'

'Hi, so, how's the apartment?'

She turned her phone to give him a shot of the main room. 'Its fine,' she said, 'unfortunately, there isn't air conditioning in the main room, just the bedroom.'

303

Ella started emptying the plastic bags as she talked, walking to and fro to the fridge with her purchases. She brought her brother up to speed with her day: her visit to the Police Station, her amazement that DI Hamity hadn't considered the death suspicious, and she'd considered Jeffrey old—something he certainly wouldn't have been very happy about.

'Next, I went to Three Isles. I thought I'd go to see where Jeffrey used to live. Shit Craig, that's some pad.' Her grief and anger were reflected in her voice. 'According to Antony, Jeffrey bought it. He didn't rent it. Apparently, it was Antony who showed him the development in the first place.' She watched as Craig's forehead creased with disbelief.

'When was that?' Craig asked, '... when did Antony show him?'

'Before Mum had her first stroke. Apparently, he fell in love with the place at first sight. Craig, when I looked at it, I wanted to cry. We all know whose money paid for that.'

'The bastard!' He closed his eyes and paused. 'Ella, you'll need to try and find out who it's willed to ... find out who his solicitor is?'

'Antony thinks it could be Munday and Munday, an attorney in Bourbon. But we hope to find that out tomorrow ... at the funeral.'

'That'll be some ordeal.'

Ella inhaled deeply, 'too damned right. Fortunately, I'm going with Antony, otherwise I don't think I could cope. Even Antony has admitted it's the last thing he wants to do. But he knows his presence will be expected by the islanders,' she explained, putting the last of her purchases in the fridge. 'Let me tell you about Antony ... I'll be as quick as I can. I know you want to get some sleep.'

Her flow was interrupted by Craig's land line ringing, 'sorry Sis, I'll call you back when I've dealt with this.'

'Fine, I've got plenty more to tell you.'

~~~

The click of a key in the front door lock wiped out Willis' reflections. His mother struggled into view, laden with bags. He noticed the forced smile she threw him as she slung her burden on the countertop.

Willis uttered a muffled, 'Hi Mom. Had a good day?'

'Busy.' Her voice was flat.

'You have a wedding?' he asked.

She looked at her son with disbelieving eyes. 'No Willis. I had the last arrangements for the funeral to organise. There's a lot to do, you know,' she sighed again.

'The guys at Topaz were telling me all about last week, Mom,' Willis said, impatient to share what was on his mind, 'about how security cleared the beach, thinking the cops would check up on everything. But they didn't. They just ordered the body ... Jeffrey, straight to the offices. Ricko said the folks at the hotel are still talking about it all. Ricko, he's real wound up, cos, for sure, he knew Jeff quite well.' The events of his afternoon spurted from him. Suddenly he looked up and met his mother's dark, worried eyes.

'Mom, we've got to talk,' Willis said, 'there's lots we need to ...'

His mother stood rigid, her forehead wrinkled in a frown, anxious eyes glaring at him.

'Yes Willis. We do need to talk. There's things you gotta tell me ... but not now ... I just want to get tomorrow over. That will be one big problem out of the way. Yes, there're things we need to straighten out ... but, after the funeral.'

Willis' most intimate moments with Madison flashed before him. It seemed like their secrets behind locked doors may not be secrets anymore. Somehow, it seemed, Mom had found out. There was so much he didn't want to share with her. His temperature rose.

'Yup, okay, after the funeral,' Willis agreed. His mother's face remained perplexed. 'You okay Mum? You been kinda strange since …'

'Yeah Willis, I've been trying to untie the knots in my head. I've been real uptight, unhinged about it all … and worried about you. I'll be real thankful when tomorrow's over—when Jeffrey's gone,' she let out another long sigh.

'We can start over again Mom—when all this is sorted. Things'll be just fine. I'll get a job. I can help with the rent.'

Tamara stared at him. 'I don't understand … I thought you wanted to go to uni!' her voice raised.

'I do, but Mom, I know you can't afford it.'

She sat herself opposite Willis, and paused, as though she was trying to sort out what she needed to say, 'Don't ask me about it now, but if you still have your heart set on uni, there'll be money for you to go.'

After all his anxiety, Willis looked at her in disbelief. Elation rushed into him; his senses reeled. 'That would be off the scale brilliant—amazing!' He left his stool and threw his arms around her, being conscious the hug was not returned.

'When all of this bloody nightmare has faded. I hope I can tell you what's happened; what I've done,' Tamara said in a monotone, speaking into the side of his face.

She pushed him away and picked up one of the bags littering the work top. 'I guessed you'd need a new shirt and tie for tomorrow. Go try that on.'

Willis was flying high: perhaps the whole of his life was not in ruins. He peered into the bag grinning and drew out a packaged, dazzling white shirt. It was laid on the countertop; he then extracted a matt black bow tie, displayed in a box.

'Gee thanks Mom. You're the best! You've really gone to town. I'll go and try on the shirt.'

Willis headed for his bedroom, his mind spinning like a top: one part of him was elated—university may not be out of the

306

question, another was distraught, thinking through the things his mother had said. "I'll tell you what I've done … I'll be thankful when tomorrow's over … when Jeffrey's gone."

He stood in front of the mirror and pulled off his top, he felt sweat streaming down his back, but was cold with fear.

~~~

Ella had just finished making her coleslaw when her brother phoned back.

'Sorry about that,' Craig said, 'a friend phoned about our plans for the weekend.'

'Okay, I was just about to tell you about Antony.'

'Don't tell me, he's been ripping off Antony too,' Craig said.

'You don't know the half of it broth,' Ella left the kitchen area to sit on the sofa. 'Not only Antony, but other business people on the island. You know how news travels like wildfire on Sainte Marie—especially bad news. To keep it brief, Jeffrey was working on commission when he was selling Antony's villas. But, the cheating shit decided to take his own extra commission from some of the clients. It wasn't until recently Antony happened to discover it. He'd trusted Jeffrey, and hadn't imagined he would con him.'

'I don't believe that man.' On her phone Craig's face distorted with fury. He shook his head slowly. 'Antony treated him like a mate … and what about the other islanders?'

'Yeah, seems like he's been lying and cheating all over. I'll fill you in on all the details another time … but Craig … this is hyper important … Jeffrey was planning to leave Sainte Marie. Listen to this … Antony found out … on the grapevine … things were hotting-up for him: he'd put the villa on the market, he planned to leave the island the next day—the very day after he drowned,' Ella said.

'Holy shit! That man sure knew how to make enemies. And you're telling me, the police didn't think his death was worth investigating?'

Ella shrugged, 'really Craig, I got the impression there wasn't much of an investigation. The DI told me, in no uncertain terms, Sainte Marie doesn't have the resources—the finances just aren't available to be doing full autopsies—or follow up on them supposedly. I imagine they have to pick and choose which crimes they should investigate.'

'I wonder if the police now know about Jeffrey's double-crossing?'

Her eyebrows went up. 'Guess we'll never know. Antony inferred that folks on Sainte Marie wouldn't let on, even if they do know. They wouldn't want to get muddled up with a murder investigation. They'd maybe think he got what he deserved.'

'Yeah, we know from the past, the islanders stick together,' Craig added. 'And Ella … it sounds like there are a few people who'd be glad to see the back of him—possibly even his lady friend—if he was planning to bugger off and leave her in the lurch.'

'Mmm … I hadn't thought of that.' Ella was silent for a moment, 'Well, if there IS a guilty party on island, they'll be able to breathe a lot easier after tomorrow. Jeffrey is being cremated … leaving no incriminating evidence.'

The phone line went quiet at Craig's end. Ella saw her brother's head drop, no longer looking directly at the screen. Her suspicions about her brother having something to do with Jeffrey's death niggled at her again. She had to push the thoughts away. 'By the way Craig, I managed to get his passport from the Police station.'

'Oh well done. And what did you discover?' Craig asked.

'I haven't had time to study it yet. I'll do that after I've had something to eat. I'll send you an e-mail if I find anything relevant—suppose you'll be fast asleep by then.'

'Well, I hope you get a good night's sleep after your hectic day,' Craig gave her a wave as they finished the conversation.

Ella ended the call with regret. She was tired; and the evening alone stretched out in front of her. It was only the first evening in the apartment, and Ella now realised staying alone in an apartment really wasn't for her. She'd have been much better off in a hotel, where there was the possibility of mingling with people.

Thoughts of the following day made her nervous and worried. Since arriving on Sainte Marie, the idea of going to the funeral had troubled her. Any funeral was an ordeal—but going to Jeffrey's sent a shudder down her spine. Ella guessed she'd be in for a restless night.

~~~

'Oh my God, I got him all wrong.'

From his bedroom, Willis heard his mother shout. His trembling fingers were struggling with the tiny buttons on the dress shirt. He rushed out, the cuffs still flapping over his hands.

'What's the problem?'

'I got him all wrong,' his mother repeated. She was a picture of anxiety. 'Look,' she thrust the handful of papers towards him.

Willis grabbed at them; he turned two slim booklets over in his hands. 'Holy Jesus ... Christ Mom ... Panama. One-way tickets to Panama City.' He checked the tickets again. 'One way for both of us. Hell Mom, he wanted us with him. Holy shit.' He noted his mother failed to reprimand him for his swearing.

'I picked the letters up from the Post Office box when I was shopping,' she muttered. 'I was so busy, I stuffed them into my bag and didn't give them a thought.'

Tamara's hand went over her face. Willis wasn't sure what to say, what to do. He thought back to the day after Jeffrey's death, when they had found his flight tickets—tickets for the very next day, secreted amongst his belongings. They'd also discovered e-mails on his computer to the real estate agent in Panama City. Found communications he'd made to Delan, concerning the sale of the villa.

'Whatever you do Willis, don't breathe a word of this to a living soul,' she pleaded with him, through her hands.

Willis was alarmed. Ideas why she might say that started to click into place. The previous excitement he'd felt about university vanished. His heart dropped to his stomach. He now knew what she must have done.

His mother raised her head, a tear trickling from her blotchy eyes. 'Go and finish trying on the shirt and tie,' she sniffled, 'the worst'll be over after tomorrow, Willis.'

Will it, Willis thought? The black mood. The things she'd said. The tears. They all screamed guilt at him. Christ mother! I pray to God, you haven't done what I think you've done, he said to himself as he walked slowly back to his bedroom.

Chapter 30

Ending

Tapping.

Ella awoke suddenly to a sound she didn't recognise. A continuous tapping, beating sound. Her hazy mind listened, forcing sleep away. Struggling eyes told her that she was already living the next day. Soft light filtered through the flimsy curtains. Oppressive hot air clung to her. A lethargic hand groped for the square of the travel clock.

Five thirty-seven.

The drumming, pounding became louder. Reluctantly, she dragged herself from the sheets and padded through the thick warmth towards the window. Drawing aside the curtain, a cool dampness splattered the warmth of her face. The thundering of rain on the corrugated metal roof drowned out the noise of the drip, drip, drip from the lintel above. Large droplets of rain invaded her space. Outside, everything was covered in a glassy sheen. Greyness pressed down from a heavy sky. There was no promise of sun. Ella closed the window and let the drenched curtain fall from her hand.

The noise was only the torrential rain on a poorly insulated roof. It seemed like Jeffrey's send-off would be a wet one. Another day, but her feelings of incertitude were still there—still unsure if she wanted to be part of the celebration of his life. A loathing of him festered within her. He had treated her mother so badly. She could not, would not, personally honour him at the service. That would be hypocritical. She would be present, and that would be all. Ella was grateful that she would have Antony to prop her up. She hadn't the confidence or courage to cope with it alone. Being a stranger and wondering if anyone around her would know the real Jeffrey Taylor—a man who cheated on his friends, and even his own wife. An evil person, whose cold, selfish heart only cared about himself. How many would actually be mourning his passing.

A heavy rain continued as she drove to Topaz. Antony was waiting for her. His attire shouted out where he was heading. Dark trousers, a crisp white shirt, and a sober black tie. He stood under a large golf umbrella, clutching another for Ella. She smiled weakly as she approached him, hunkered underneath her small collapsible brolly.

'Hi Antony. Thanks again for taking me. I confess I'm not looking forward to it.' The wind tore at her clothes pulling them tight around her body.

Antony opened the car door for her, ran around the vehicle, put down his umbrella and threw himself into the driver's seat.

'Why would you Ella? I share your feelings of animosity towards the man, treating people the way he did?' Ella took in the tone of his voice—full of hostility—and turned to see an expression of bitterness across his face.

'Okay Ella, let's go get it over with,' Antony said, starting up the car. 'Like you, I'm going because it's expected. The islanders like people to do the done thing; and one does the done thing because you never know whose help you're going to need on Sainte Marie.' The rear-view mirror was adjusted. 'I believe a few of my staff will also be present. Apparently, he used to treat them very well. He used to be good hearted towards them. They thought he was a great guy! Well, you can afford to be a great guy and generous, when it's someone else's money, can't you?'

As they started their journey, Ella sensed his resentment filling the confines of the car. Privately, she had already calculated Jeffrey's greed must have gobbled up at least a six-figure sum of Antony's money. It wasn't surprising he felt bitter. He'd confessed he hadn't had time to fully investigate the extent of the fraud. She remained silent for a few seconds, before asking a question which had been niggling at her.

'Antony, have you thought of going to the police?'

'I had. But then he died,' Antony said as he craned towards the windscreen in an attempt to see through the deluge of rain.

'But …'

'But? But what Ella? Take him to court posthumously?'

'Yes, why not?'

'Because, my naïve little friend, it would cost me more than he owes me.' He glanced at her again, 'good attorneys everywhere cost a fortune you know. You only take someone to court after their death in very exceptional cases Ella. It just costs too much. I'm not even certain I'm going to waste my money on getting an accountant to go through all the figures to find out how much he ripped me off.'

Ella made no reply—there didn't seem anything appropriate to say. To detract her thoughts, she studied the scene outside. The storm thrashed against the windscreen, invaded regularly by the swish, swishing of the wipers. All was murky with the relentless flood of rain. Unclear pictures of people sheltering at bus stops; drenched pedestrians with their heads down, scraggy, bedraggled dogs on the perpetual hunt for food. Torrents roared down the road, filling the deep storm-drains to over-flowing. Ella started to think to herself. Perhaps her vision was much like that outside. Cloudy. Antony always seemed to see things so objectively, unlike her. The reason for her being on island was becoming less obvious. What was she hoping to achieve?

'So,' she asked, a surge of self-doubt descending, 'you don't think contesting Jeffrey's will is possible?'

'Ella, we don't even know if there is a will. If there isn't, you might stand a chance. But if there is, I sure hope you and Craig have plenty of money to pay for the legal fees.'

'We don't have … have plenty of money that is.' She regretted embarking on that topic of conversation as well. Her mind was muddled. She tried to shift to another topic which wouldn't make her feel inadequate. 'Er … last night … yes …

last night, I was looking through Jeffrey's passport. He certainly got around, didn't he?'

'I believe so,' Antony said, still struggling to see through all the rain.

'He liked Barbados, Panama and the Bahamas.'

'There's plenty of money there, I suspect he was trying to find prospective clients, or investors. You know that he became involved in property investment.'

'I wondered ... well ... if he could be stashing money away in offshore accounts,' Ella said.

'In the Bahamas or Panama, you mean? It's possible. But how does knowing that help you?'

'If you know where his money is, you stand a chance of being able to access it ...'

Ever-logical Antony interrupted her, 'it's only the executors to his will who can access his bank accounts Ella. So, it's back to the problem, we don't know if there is a will. And if there is, any details of offshore accounts may not be included. It's best to wait and see if his attorney can help you. I suspect someone from their office may be present at the crematorium.'

'Mmm....' was all Ella could muster. She wanted to say, so you think I'm wasting my time here, but didn't.

When Ella had first decided to visit Sainte Marie, Jeffrey was still alive. She'd planned to confront him, challenge him over the disappearance of her mother's assets. Initially, she had been spurred on by strong feelings of anger and retribution. But after his death, it was now becoming clearer that she hadn't thought through the situation enough. Maybe she'd been too impetuous—too eager to defend her mother's memory. Before dashing off across the Atlantic, she should have considered the situation more logically. But doubtless it was for the same reason Antony had failed to find out about his losses—their lives were always just too dammed busy.

314

~~~

Ruminating, Tamara stood alone in the lobby of the crematorium.

Her thoughts were sombre. She was not feeling her usual sociable self. Never in a hundred years, had she imagined organising Jeffrey's funeral would be her responsibility. People had said her spirits would lift once the funeral was over, and her anguish and vexation would gradually diminish. She wasn't so sure. Anger still festered. She felt resentful about the way he'd treated her: planning to sell the villa, arranging to leave the island, without a word to her about it. Then he had expected her to drop everything and fly off to Panama to join him. Theirs hadn't been the greatest romance of the twenty first century, but they had been together for nearly four years. He should have treated her with more respect and consideration. Then Jeffrey had seemed indifferent to the rest of the world. It all left a very bitter taste in the mouth. It left her feeling miserable: uncertain about her future, her son's future, and where they were going to live.

Worry made her body tense, but nothing like the panic she was drowning in because of Willis. She felt terrified, her nerves raw. Day and night, it gnawed away at her. Nights had been the worst. The dreadful intuition that he was somehow implicated in Jeffrey's demise would not leave her. Her son had been so secretive, avoiding her. Tamara was convinced Jeffrey's death was no accident, and Willis knew something about it. She studied him the other side of the crematorium lobby—talking to Ricko and other friends from Topaz. She'd been so proud of him; content he'd have a promising future. Now all this. He just wasn't the same. Not since the evening he'd been to see her at work. The evening before Jeffrey died.

Her line of sight was distracted as the silhouette of Emmalyn appeared at the entrance. Tamara watched her, as she hesitated, surveying the lobby, and then advanced directly towards her.

Her wide brimmed black hat seemed to have suffered a little from the humidity. She knew Emmalyn hadn't been the same either since the day of the drowning—on edge and anxious. She still seemed to be reeling from the fact that Jeffrey wasn't going to provide her with a better future. Tamara sympathised, but wondered if he had ever intended to meet up with her that day.

'How ya coping?' Emmalyn said, as she took Tamara's hand.

'Coping. Just. You look very smart Emmalyn.'

Emmalyn squeezed her hand and her mouth turned up in a slight smile. 'Do ya have to return to work tomorrow?'

'I've a wedding tomorrow afternoon. Frankly, I'll be glad to be kept busy,' she said, though her thoughts could not focus that far ahead.

'Yeh, I know what ya mean,' Emmalyn said, glancing at her watch. It was almost time for the service.

'And what about you? Is that lodger of yours still behaving himself?'

Emmalyn paused and sighed. It took her several seconds to find a response.

'Oh, Vincent you mean. Oh, I haven't seen him for a bit. The work on the shower room hasn't advanced. You were right, his reformed self didn't last very long,' she said in an undertone. Emmalyn looked up again, as a figure she didn't recognise joined them.

The woman smiled at both of them and put her hand out to Tamara. 'My condolences for your loss Tamara. You may not remember me, Mrs Munday.'

'Yes, yes I do,' she said, 'we meet when we signed the contract for the villa.' Tamara, remembering her friend, introduced her to Mrs Munday, 'Let me introduce my friend Emmalyn—she works at the same hotel as I do.'

'It's a pleasure to meet you,' she said, shaking Emmalyn's hand. Then in a much quieter voice, 'Tamara, I wonder if could ask you to come and see me at your earliest convenience.'

316

Tamara guessed why Mrs Munday was making the request. 'Is it about the villa?' Nerves sent her hands to fidget with the neckline of her dress.

'Yes, you could say that—about the villa.' She smiled and seeing other people waiting, 'I'll leave you, as I can see there are others wishing to express their sympathy.'

As the attorney left, she met Emmalyn's eyes for a moment. From the sympathetic look on her face, she judged they were both thinking much the same thing—Mrs Munday already knew some of the answers to the questions Tamara desperately wanted to ask.

~~~

The car had been stop-start through the capital—a city dimmed by rain. Ella considered that the weather conditions must have brought every car on the island into Bourbon. Amidst the chaos of klaxons, flashing of lights, traffic congestion; she became fidgety—sneaking a glimpse at her watch. She didn't want to attend this funeral, but she didn't want to be late either. Relief descended as they left the choked-up city.

Antony drove them to the outskirts of the capital. Tucked away in quiet semi-rural location, he stopped his car outside the crematorium. A long line of parked cars announced that most mourners were already inside.

Ella demisted the inside of the window to look over their destination. A simple, brick-built rectangle, its walls enhanced by small open squares in the form of a cross. A stark white building, sharply defined against a mass of dripping tropical vegetation catching the flat light. A continuous stream running from the leaves; huge puddles on the path leading to the entrance.

Ella snatched up the borrowed umbrella from her side, 'Let's get this over with.'

'I'll buy you a long, cool drink when we get back to the hotel,' Antony promised.

'I'll keep you to that. I'm sure as hell going to need it.'

They slammed the car doors and scurried through the puddles. The circular torrent teeming from the edge of the umbrella, changing direction with the driving wind. It was clear Ella's open-toed shoes hadn't been a good idea, but she'd had no choice, being the only black pair in her suitcase. She was relieved to reach the protection of the building—despite the umbrella, the lower half of her was extremely damp.

As they reached the open glass door, she turned to see the hearse stopping outside the building.

'We cut that fine Antony,' she said in a whisper.

'No Ella, that's what's called good timing.'

The umbrellas were forced into a stand, as they looked around the large entrance hall. The gathering was larger than she'd imagined. The only person she recognised was Tamara. Somehow, she stood out from the others. She had the type of beauty even woman admire. Ella wished she could look as good in a simple, black straight dress. Tamara's untamed, frizzy hair was crowned by a matt black trilby. How on earth had Jeffrey managed to ensnare such a stunner? Ella asked herself. She was sure it would be by the same method as he had used to become her mother's second husband—by deception and lies.

Antony touched her elbow, 'that's Tamara,' he said, nodding his head towards Tamara.

'Yes, I remember her now. She's a beautiful woman.'

He smiled, and then started discreetly pointing out other individuals he knew. 'That's Willis her son, and Mrs Munday, the attorney. But we'll have to wait to introduce ourselves until after the ceremony.'

A hush fell. Heads turned towards the lobby door. Two figures moved to stand each side of it. The pall bearers approached supporting the coffin. Four stern, strong faces, running with rain, shuffled into the hall supporting their burden. All eyes followed the dark, shiny casket, as it was carried across

318

the room. Then, out of the corner of her eye, Ella noticed that they hadn't been the last mourners to arrive. At the entrance, stood a high-heeled woman, sheltering under a black umbrella. As she put it down, it revealed a rival for Tamara, another stunning Caribbean beauty, in a navy blue lace dress. She was the focus of everyone's attention for a few seconds. Then the coffin moved forward.

The chapel doors were swung open.

A wall of song escaped the main room—slow, loud notes accompanied by a guitar. Ella's jaw dropped. It was not what she had expected. The song was foreign to her.

> 'Take me to your river,
> I wanna go,
> Oh go on
> Take me to your river,
> I wanna know ...'

Like a sleepwalker, she followed the mourners. At the front, three women vocalists drew the attention of all. Their powerful voices, crooning the blues song; voices that charged the entire space. Ella was hardly conscious of the sheet of paper that was thrust into her hand. Antony had to guide her towards a rustic wooden seat along the back row.

> 'Tip me in your smooth waters
> I go in
> As a man with many crimes
> Come up for air
> As my sins flow down the Jordan...... '

The words of the song echoed through Ella. As the music faded, her attention was then captured by the celebrant, who stood on a dais welcoming all present. It was at that very moment, Ella noticed. The head end of the coffin was open. She could just make out Jeffrey's features. Ella shivered and the hairs

319

on her arms stood up. She looked up at Antony. His eyes were front. She touched his arm.

'The coffin is open,' she mouthed; he nodded in silence. The celebrant's stream of words flowed over her, failing to penetrate into any crevice of her mind. She was numbed. The image of Jeffrey had caught her breath. A wave of resistance shot through her. This quickly turned to revulsion. There was no way she would be walking up to the open coffin to pay her respects.

It wasn't until the second piece of music, a hymn, that her emotions ebbed, and Ella took in the piece of paper in her hand—a ceremony script which others were following. They were singing a hymn she recognised, but failed to find her voice. Instead, she listened to the continual splattering of the rain, slashing against the building, through the small areas of open brickwork.

In what seemed like a few minutes, it was finished. The hymns, psalms, readings, poems, tributes, R and B songs, were all over. Everything was ended for Jeffrey Taylor. There was no wailing, no crying, and no tears.

Ella watched as a few mourners approached the coffin. Tamara touched Jeffrey's hand. Her son, with lowered eyes, simply nodded. The stunning woman in navy lace kissed her fingers and placed them on his lips.

Ella and Antony stayed firmly in the back row. As the trio of singers hummed through an old Ray Charles song, the celebrant drew a semi-circle of curtain around the wooden casket. Tamara started to lead the gathering back towards the lobby.

'You go and introduce yourself to Tamara. I'll go and talk to the attorney,' Antony suggested.

Ella was a little taken aback. 'Yeah … yeah, I suppose so.'

In the lobby, Tamara was surrounded by those offering condolences. Ella stood on the edge of the group. Waiting. Not daring to say a word. She listened to the chatter for several minutes. Comments were made about the choice of music.

Compliments about the service. Talk about the flowers. Invitations to go to the wake at a nearby hotel. Gradually, the people dispersed.

'I think we've met before,' Tamara said directly to Ella, her manner cold and off-hand.

'Er yes, several years ago.'

'When I was working at Topaz,' she did not offer her hand to Ella.

'That's right. I went there to take my mother home after her stroke.'

'I remember. So ... Jeffrey was your stepfather,' Ella noted the lack of a polite smile, as Tamara's icy eyes caught Ella's. She offered no condolences to Ella for her mother's recent death.

Resentment descended on Ella because of it—bitterness towards Jeffrey's mistress— who doubtless had benefited from her parents' money, thanks to Jeffrey. The anger at this made Ella's courage return.

'Tamara, I want ...' Ella corrected herself, '... no, I have to talk to you about Jeffrey.' Ella put as much authority into her voice that she could raise. Tamara stared at her with startled eyes.

'I don't think I can help you in any way.'

Encouraged by the force of her own voice, Ella continued, 'I leave the island in three days. I'd appreciate it if we could meet in the next couple of days.'

Tamara searched in her bag and handed Ella a small business card. 'Call me later. Perhaps we can fix up a time before you leave.' As the card was received, Tamara turned around and showed Ella her back and commenced a conversation with another woman. Ella was decidedly excluded from the exchange.

Ella clutched the card in her hand, indignation brimming over. She glared disbelievingly at Tamara's back. The air of resentment between them did not bode well for a successful future dialogue. Ella sighed deeply and walked slowly towards the main door. Tamara's comments replaying in her head.

There'll be no 'perhaps' about a meeting, Ella told herself determinedly, we as sure as hell will get together before I leave this island!

Chapter 31

Revelation

Tamara had barely slept.

She had tossed and turned most of the night. Fear about the future clung to her. Normally, she wouldn't have described herself as a worrier. But this was different. The previous day, after the funeral, she had arranged an appointment with Mrs Munday. She prayed this meeting would alleviate some of her concerns, straighten out her life, even if only a little, and unwind some of the knots in her stomach.

Despite her early start, the traffic into the capital was heavy. The attorney's office was right in the centre of Bourbon. Tamara's agitation made the drive difficult, her concentration level being rock bottom. A sigh of relief escaped as she swung into the small car park close to her destination.

'Can you find a corner where I can leave my car?' she asked the attendant, his head constantly nodding to the music on his earphones.

'Anything for ya mi beauty. I thinks I can squeeze it in just over dere,' he directed her to the far end of the parking lot.

'You're a star. I'll only be around an hour. I'll pay you later,' Tamara said.

'No worries. Sees ya soon mi lovely.'

During the short walk to the attorneys, Tamara was preoccupied and barely noticed her surroundings. She strode along the high pavement, shaded from the searing heat by a covered walkway. Like many of Bourbon's older buildings, the attorney's office had jutting first floor balconies, supported on the far side of the pavement by elegantly slim pillars. This was the old part of town—a jumble of architectural styles, a hotch potch of brightly painted constructions.

At the office, Tamara found the reception area empty, perhaps it was too early for all the staff to be there. Bur as Tamara approached Mrs Munday's office, a refreshing breeze escaped through the half open office door. She knocked.

Mrs Munday was behind her desk, piled high with folders, her head in some document. An oscillating fan intermittently lifted some of the papers around her.

'Good morning, Mrs Munday.'

'Hello Tamara, please do sit down. I can only give you a few minutes I'm afraid. I have to work on court preparations, but it should be enough.'

Tamara sat opposite, in a well-worn traditional leather chair. She gazed across at the bespectacled attorney clothed in white and black, ready for her forthcoming court case. In front of her lay a file—presumably Jeffrey's last will and testament.

'Many thanks for seeing me so quickly Mrs Munday,' Tamara managed a smile.

'Well, I realised you must feel rather unsettled, not knowing where you stand as far as Mr Taylor's estate is concerned. Firstly, can I say that I thought yesterday went very well. It was a memorable service.'

'Yes,' Tamara whispered. Despite the fan, Tamara could feel sweat running down her neck and back, her clothing sticking to the chair, her heart thumping against her ribcage.

Mrs Munday removed her glasses and laid them amidst the documents littering her desk. 'There may be a few things that you're not aware of. I'll quickly run through everything; you'll just have to be patient if you know some of this information already. To save time, can you keep any questions until the end?'

'Yes, of course.'

'Firstly, when Mr Taylor set up a company to buy the villa, I suggested every eventuality should be covered. As you know, he had to have insurance for the mortgage he took out.'

Tamara looked on. No, she hadn't known. Jeffrey hadn't said. Mrs Munday continued, referring to the file. 'So, the remaining payments for the villa will be covered. He also wrote a will with an executor. Do you understand the term executor?'

Tamara shook her head slightly. She was fairly sure, but wanted to be one hundred certain.

The attorney hastily went on to explain the role of an executor; then topped it by stating that Jeffrey Taylor had named her in his will as the executor. She would have to ensure that all the property, owned by the deceased, was secure. She would have to pay, from his assets, any debts, or taxes, and make sure that the remaining assets were directed to the beneficiary. If she needed any help with this, she could ask for help from any attorney.

Tamara sat confused. This was not the news that she had expected. She didn't see how she'd be able to deal with all of the work. Her uncertainty must have been written across her face.

'Don't look so startled,' Mrs Munday said. 'As I've explained, you can always pay for help. In this case, it shouldn't be too complicated. As you may, or may not know, there is no death duty on Sainte Marie, any taxes to pay would only be income tax. In addition, there is only one beneficiary to deal with.'

'Oh really,' Tamara said, holding her breath.

'Well, it's simple for you, because the sole beneficiary is your son, Willis.'

Initially, Tamara thought that she had misheard. 'I don't understand—Willis?' The attorney nodded. 'What! I don't believe it!' her shriek rang around the room.

Mrs Munday stayed silent for a few seconds whilst the information sunk in. 'Yes, your son inherits the fifty-one per cent of the company. The same share, fifty-one per cent, of any other assets of the company, any monies in Mr Taylor's accounts. Any investments bonds, shares and so on.'

'Oh, good God!' What a revelation—it was too much for Tamara to make sense of all in one go. She felt herself freeze, trying to catch her breath. Rather than jumping around with joy, tears started to run down her cheeks, 'Oh, Mrs Munday, this is a real shock!' The attorney smiled sympathetically.

'I feel ... I feel like ... I don't know ... there's been an explosion inside me. My heart's ... I just don't know what to say.'

'Mr Taylor obviously was very fond of your son.'

'Yes,' Tamara muttered, searching in her bag to find something to wipe her wet cheeks, 'but this ... I never expected this. He'll be amazed when I tell him.'

'Naturally, the other forty-nine per cent of J & T Inc. will still remain with you. This means that the plot at Three Isles, two plots at The Tamarind, here on Sainte Marie, one in Barbados and one in Santa Clara, will belong jointly to you and your son.'

'Santa Clara, on the Gulf of Panama?'

'Yes, I believe so,' Mrs Mundy looked again at a document in front of her. 'Yes. This of course means that you are able to stay in Three Isles,' she paused, 'Tamara, do you have any immediate questions?'

Tamara sniffled and wiped her face again.

'The funeral Mrs Munday,' she said, trying to compose herself, 'can I pay for the funeral from the account? It's actually a joint account, mine and Jeffrey's, though I ...' Tamara was about to say never, but changed her mind. '... though I rarely use it. It was Jeff's account really.'

'Yes, of course,' Mrs Munday stopped to look at her watch. 'There are other details that need to be explained. Documents you'll require. But, I'm afraid I'm running out of time. If you could make an appointment to see my legal assistant before you leave—to discuss things further. She will be able to answer any queries that you have. There should be somebody in reception soon.' The attorney stood. 'Next time, please bring Willis along with you.'

'Yes, of course,' Tamara pushed her soggy tissue into her bag, and prised herself out of the chair. It felt sticky from her clamminess.

Mrs Munday closed the file to indicate that their meeting was concluded, 'Go get yourself a cup of coffee somewhere Tamara. You don't want to be driving home in a state.' She held out her hand to wish her client good-bye.

Tamara was still trying to catch her breath, but managed a smile. 'I just might do that Mrs Munday, and thank you so much for your time.'

Two cups of cappuccino later, she ventured back to the car park.

'Hi there mi beauty, ya havin' a good morning?' the attendant said, his head still bobbing to inaudible music.

'One of the best!' Tamara flashed him a smile. 'How much do I owe you?'

'Dat three dollars mi darlin'.'

Tamara handed over a twenty dollar note. 'You keep the change.'

'Hey, thanks mi angel. Ya wins de national lottery?'

'Yeah, something like that. See you soon.'

~~~

Tamara stopped the car in her designated parking space. Lights were shining from the villa. Willis must be home. She'd texted him earlier to ask if he could be there.

Her head was still spinning from that morning's revelation. During her drive, she'd been sifting through her time with Jeffrey. Things hadn't been easy. She's had to become obsequious—not her style at all. But she'd been rewarded extremely well for it. It was certain it had happened by fortuitous timing. Jeffrey would unquestionably have changed the legalities

327

of her owning nearly half the company's assets, if he had lived to start a new life in Panama. She knew his departure from the island had been organised in great haste.

Tamara wasn't sure how she'd managed to supervise the wedding that afternoon. Her mind had been all over the place. Wisely, no word of her good fortune was mentioned to her colleagues.

Opening the front door of the villa, a strong odour of spices hit her nostrils

'Mmm, what's that smell?' she called out.

'Oh, hi Mom. I'm glad you're here. I was getting a bit worried it'd all overcook.' Willis was busy in the kitchen area, cooking something up, 'chicken stew,' he explained.

'Willis, that's so thoughtful. We were scheduled to have patties from the refrigerator—again. Chicken stew will be much better.' Her bag was flung on the countertop.

'And coconut rice,' he boasted.

'Just let me change out of my work clothes,' Tamara headed for the bedroom.' Mmm, smells real good ... I'm so hungry, I could eat a horse.'

The meal was on the table when Tamara returned. 'This smells delicious. Thanks for cooking it, Willis. It's well timed, because we have a lot to talk about.' She sat opposite her son testing a forkful of spicy chicken. 'That's good.' She sat for a few seconds, relishing her son's cooking, and thinking through what needed to be said. There was so much to tell him.

'We should have talked before Willis. I've already said, but ... well, the thing is ... I've been very worried.' She took another forkful of stew. Willis waited eyes wide. 'I just wanted to get the funeral over before we had a serious talk about ...'

Willis thumped his fist on the table, 'but Mom, I was worried too ... about you. You've been so distant—since the night I told you about Jeff leaving.' He dropped his fork on his plate noisily.

328

'I thought that you were mad about Madison ... about Madison and me.'

'Madison?' Tamara wondered why she should be angry about Madison. Then it hit her. Willis and she had become more than friends. She smiled to herself. She'd been too busy to even notice them. 'No, I'm not upset about Madison.'

Willis just stared.

'The chicken is good,' she said. 'Willis, you're not far off eighteen. I'm not surprised. She's very pretty—a bit wild, but very pretty.'

'I like wild Mom,' he said, and averted her eyes.

Tamara judged it best to make no comment. 'No, that wasn't what I've been cracking up about. It's you ... that evening ... the evening you came to see me at work ... you left raging about Jeffrey ... about him abandoning us ...' Tamara paused, realising she needed to phrase what came next very carefully.

They stared at each other for a beat or two.

'Listen Willis ... we both know Jeffrey was an excellent swimmer ... the sea was a bit rough ... but ... he could look after himself in the water. What I need to ask ... you didn't take your anger out on him, did you?'

'Shit!' Willis jumped up from the table sending his chair backward. 'Shit Mom. You really think I could do that?' He gaped at her, eyes narrowed, his forehead furrowed.

'I just had to ask because you were so secretive ... so edgy ...'

'I was pissed off with him, sure, but Mom...' he looked her straight in the eyes, '... I ain't a bad guy!' he shouted. 'How could you ... I've been trying to tell you. I was with Madison. When Jeff left for Topaz to go for his swim ... when you left that morning ... I'd been locked in my room with Madison.'

She sighed and relief rushed in. Why hadn't she guessed about Madison? It all added up. She left her plate, went to him, and threw her arms about him. 'Thanks be to God. I was so worried.'

But she'd upset Willis. He pushed her away. 'How could you think …?'

Tamara's arms fell from their embrace and looked down at her son, one of his hands clutching his forehead. Her words hadn't been chosen well after all. But what do you say to someone you suspect has bumped off your partner?

'Christ mother, how could you?' Willis mumbled. 'After all those years you took me to Sunday School … after all your strict up bringing … after sharing so much time on the water with Jeff! Kill him—hell no!' He slumped back into his chair.

Tamara touched his shoulder. 'Sorry … sorry Willis, but I just had to ask.'

'So, that's why you've been so distant—you thought I was involved. He pushed his half-eaten meal away and sat staring at it, a sulky expression across his face. After a few seconds, he turned to look at her again. 'And that's why you wanted the funeral over—so I couldn't be accused.'

She nodded, and waited; looking for his face to relax, and his anger to ease.

'Shit. How could you?' Willis thumped the table again with his open palm. He pushed himself up, shoved his mother aside, and left the villa, slamming the door behind him.

Tamara considered it best not to follow him for a while.

~~~

Willis kicked his way down the steps towards the car park, cut up by his mother's accusation. It hurt. Surely, she knew him better than to think he could murder anyone. But, hey, Willis thought to himself, all the swearing, sulking, and shouting, creating a stink—he'd thought exactly the same thing about her. He'd thought his Mom had something to do with killing Jeffrey. Shit, what a mess!

He sat on the car park wall staring towards the pillars of rock rising out of the ocean, the moon's light illuminating their eerie forms. He listened to the surf breaking onto the shoreline, trying to work through the problem. If his mother was under the impression he'd been involved with Jeffrey's death—she could not be guilty. But everybody who knew Jeffrey, his Mom, the workers at Topaz, Ricko all thought the same—Jeffrey had been such an excellent swimmer— the drowning was suspicious.

At least, his mother's frame of mind seemed to have improved since the funeral. He presumed it had been worrying about him and thinking he was involved with Jeffrey's death. He would be pleased when he could get away from all this—living with his mother—being affected by her moods, having to live by her rules. He wanted his independence. He prayed what she'd told him about being able to go to university would be true. He was ready for it. He must ask her when his temper had chilled.

~~~

While Willis was outside cooling off, Tamara thought through the mass of information they needed to discuss. She'd go after him once she'd cleared up. He'd been such a treasure preparing the meal—tried so hard to please her, and she ruined it all by accusing him. She picked up the half-eaten meals; rather than throw them away, they were put in the fridge. She stood and took in the mess in the kitchen area. There was a lot Willis had to learn about organisation.

Tamara went in search of her son, guessing he wouldn't have gone far. The outside lights of the restaurant showed him sat on the wall of the car park, staring out to sea. He must have heard her descending the steps, but he didn't turn to acknowledge her.

She sat near to him on the wall, waiting for the right moment to speak.

'Sorry. Sorry I just had to know,' she said to his face in silhouette.

331

He didn't move for a moment, 'I kind o' understand, everybody thinks the same. It's strange, it's suspicious. The guys at Topaz wondered if he had a heart attack.'

'Guess we'll never know,' Tamara said. "Accidental drowning" was stated as the cause on the death certificate. The police seemed to be satisfied with that decision.' She joined her son's focus looking out to sea; and listened. The restaurant must be quiet as all she could hear were the waves, breaking onto the shore. It was a good place to tell him the news.

'Willis, I've some news,' she heard excitement in her voice. 'I went into Bourbon this morning. I had to see Jeffrey's attorney.' Her words almost ran into one another.

'About the villa?' he asked flatly.

'Yes ... about the villa. Mrs Munday... she told me about the will ... Jeffrey's will ... she said. I'm the executor ... I have to make sure that all his finances are put in order ... pay any debts ... and then ... what remains goes to his beneficiary,' she gabbled.

He looked at her, probably because of her excited babbling, 'so, who did he leave it to—you?'

'No Willis,' she got up and stood opposite him, grabbing at his shoulders, 'no ... no, he left it to you ... to you Willis!' She shook him. 'You.'

The light from the nearby building was low, but she saw Willis' mouth drop open, his face change. He peered at her.

'What ... you sure? Holy shit!' he mumbled.

She shook him again. 'Just think, fifty-one per cent of the company shares, Willis—the shares of the company he set up to buy this villa ... but he's bought four other properties through the company too ... and the rest of his assets.'

Willis was dumb struck for seconds, frowning. 'But how could this happen?' he said at last.

'I thought you'd be overjoyed,' Tamara leaned forward, so her face was close to his.

'But I've gone from trying to fathom how on earth I was going to find a job, to this—all that wealth! How could it happen?'

'It was the attorney, when Jeffrey bought the villa; she insisted he had all the ends tied up. It means we can stay in the villa Willis.' But he didn't seem as though he was listening.

Willis stood and gently pushed his mother aside. He walked away from her down the beach. Into the gloom. Tamara scurried down the sand after him.

Willis stopped. 'Listen Mom, think about it. Where did all that money come from? Where the hell did all the money come from to buy that lot?' he hissed at her.

'Well, from what he sold, from his deals,' Tamara tried to reassure him.

He grabbed at her shoulders. 'Listen Mom—five properties. Where did he get all that money? Remember...' he shook her again, '... remember you told me some guy was riled up and giving you grief because of a huge commission Jeff took.'

'Jay ... Jay McCloud you mean.'

'Yeah, that's him. And Jeff was leaving because things were getting too hot for him. Somehow, he'd stolen a stack of someone's dough ... that's it ... and they finished him off in revenge!'

She looked at her son in the blackness and turned cold. 'You mean we were living with a crook, a criminal.'

~~~

Oh man, this was turning out to be one hell of a day. His heart was still thumping a pace from the news about the will—as far as he could make out though, it dumped a whole heap of problems on him. And now his mother was real uptight. Get me out of here, Willis thought!

He heard his Mom let out a long, low sigh. For once, he felt sorry for her.

'We don't know for sure he was murdered,' she said unconvincingly.

Oh Lord, she was still going on about that. 'Look Mom—think about it—you thought he was murdered. I've told you, the guys at Topaz do.' Willis looked at her. This just was not the right place to be talking through this—in the dark, on the beach, right near the restaurant. 'Let's go ... go back to the villa. We can talk about it seriously. Come on.'

He led her towards the large, illuminated windows. She'd gone from being in a state of euphoria to one of shock. There was a heavy silence between them as they walked the short distance, up the beach, through the car park and up the steps back to the living area of the villa. It was time enough for Willis to think through what to say.

He noticed the meal he'd made had disappeared. All looked trim and tidied up. He said nothing about it. His mother slumped into the nearest chair next to the table, her eyes glistening with tears.

Willis cleared his throat, 'Mom, this will ...' he stopped for a moment, '... who knows about it?'

His mother stared at him for several seconds, seemingly taking in what he'd asked, 'eh ... you and I ... oh and Mrs Munday.'

'Mom, we need to get out of this villa. Nobody must know we own all this stuff. Maybe, they'll want to take their aggro out on us too.'

'Willis, I think you're over-reacting,' she said, but he could see by her face, she kind of believed him.

Willis flung his head back and rolled his eyes. 'Mother think!' He paced the dining area. 'We can't ignore the possibility! We can't take that chance. Listen, we can sell this and get something nearer to your work. It's great living here, but fancy homes take fancy money to maintain.' He stopped walking back and forth and stood in front of his mother. 'Listen, if we can stay here, we run the risk of somebody taking out their vengeance on us, because we're living off Jeff's ill-gotten gains.'

'I thought that you'd be on cloud nine,' she muttered, disappointment in her voice, 'all our problems sorted.'

'Sure, it's really bomb ... but it ain't as simple as that ... there's the other side of it ... it ain't all good Mom. All that money! I just said, where the hell did it all come from? You don't earn that sort of money just selling a few villas. We know how much this place cost. But four other places too! That's megabucks.'

'They'll be investment properties Willis—one's he'd bought on the cheap. I've seen the ones at the Tamarind. They were cut price, as they're run-down ...'

He stopped her mid-sentence. 'Don't make excuses, it still takes a pile.'

'I suppose, you're right.'

'Can you swear you knew Jeff well enough to say he was a hundred per cent honest? That he wouldn't dream of making off with somebody else's cash if he got half a chance.'

She shrugged. He could tell by her expression that she couldn't.

'It's great living here, but look ...' his hand swung indicating the things in the villa, 'is it worth putting your life at risk for this? Look Mom, having all this ain't gonna make you happy— not if you're always scared stiff, looking over your shoulder to see if someone's going to take it out on you.'

Her eyes followed his hand. He knew she loved the villa, but it had never really been theirs. It was always Jeffrey's.

'You're so right,' she looked around her. 'Do you think this made Jeffrey happy? He didn't seem content—he always seemed to want more. What he had was never enough for him.'

'And look what happened to him,' Willis added. The truth was coming out about their relationship—about Jeffrey and her.

'Yeah, Willis you're right,' she said again. 'The villa is too big for just us, especially when you go to university.' She looked downcast and depressed. 'Willis, all this, it's too much like a nightmare—Jeffrey has left us all this fallout to deal with.' They looked at one another across the table. Willis could see the tears were about to start again.

He went to the fridge, took out the remains of a bottle of wine, and poured out a glass. 'Drink this. We can sort this out ya know,' he said dutifully, putting the wine in front of her. 'Once this place goes on the market, people will think it was left to somebody else. Nobody needs to know it belongs to us—except the attorney of course—and she ain't gonna say anything. Try not to worry.'

'Yeah—easy to say Willis,' she said sniffling.

He noted her fake smile, and the constant fiddling with her top. His Mom was in a state, but he decided he'd ask his question anyway. It was the right time. 'Mom, there's something that has been puzzling me. The day before the funeral, why did you say, I'd still be able to go to uni if I wanted? You didn't know about the will then.'

Willis watched his mother sitting there quietly, presumably thinking through how she was going to reply. 'Well ... there's a simple reply. I was at the bank.'

If she'd been at the bank, she definitely, hadn't had anything to do with the death, Willis told himself. 'Yeah, so why was that a problem? What was all the secrecy about?'

She hung her head. It was clear she felt awkward about something. 'Thing is Willis ... when you came to tell me Jeffrey was leaving ... I saw us being left high and dry—without a home. I worried about it all night; and decided to take some money out of the joint account—to tide us over—Jeffrey's money.'

'And you thought he wouldn't notice until after he'd left, because he'd be so damned busy.'

'Yeah, something like that. I feel ashamed now,' she closed her eyes as she said it.

Willis dragged a chair from under the table and sat opposite. Silence . Willis wasn't sure what to say. He understood why she had been so cagey, so unapproachable. She'd been swiping Jeffrey's dough.

'How much?' he asked eventually.

'Enough to see you through the first year of university,' she muttered.

'Look Mom, it doesn't matter now. It's our money anyway? What did you do with it?' He wondered if she would tell him.

'It's in the safe.'

'What safe?' It was the first he knew about a safe.

'There's a safe on our... my bedroom. I think Jeffrey thought I didn't know about it. After he died, I got a locksmith to come and open it.'

'Holy cow!'

'It's under the shoe boxes in his wardrobe. And Willis ... there was something else.'

'What?'

'Details of a bank account in Panama.'

'Holy shit mother—this gets worse. Five properties and an offshore bank account. This man really was stashing away the dollars.'

'Who were we living with Willis? It makes my blood run cold.' Her tears recommenced.

This was all crazy. Willis looked at his mother, hunched up at the table, her face blotchy, eyes red from crying. He sure as hell didn't want to be living off stolen money; constantly fearful. They had to sort this one out, and fast.

Chapter 32

Panic

Crisp patches of shade played across the decking.

Bright-coloured parasols were shading clients outside cafes. An isolated figure was under one. She sat clutching her drink, gazing towards the landscape mounting above the lavish yachts moored in the marina. She was contemplating, and not seeing any of it.

Ella's mood was as dark as the shadows. A sense of failure had spread through her; she was at a low ebb. Whilst on island, all her discoveries had been negative ones. Her appointment at Jeffrey's attorney that morning hadn't brightened her prospects of a legal success—being able to recuperate some of her parents' assets through the courts. Her hopes had been dashed.

At her appointment with Mrs Munday, Ella had explained her reason for being there. It was clear the attorney was sympathetic, but seemed rather bemused. She appeared to be taken aback Jeffrey Taylor could treat his own wife the way he had. She had expressed surprised that his legal wife had only recently died. Incredulity was written across her face, but her opinions on the matter were not voiced. In contrast, her judgements about contesting Jeffrey's will were prolific; but were weighted towards the 'far from hopeful'. Jeffrey had definitely been of sound mind and body when his will had been made, making any challenge tremendously difficult. Mrs Munday asked if he'd had been awarded power of attorney over her mother's affairs. Ella told her he had. There was a sharp intact of breath and a shaking of her head. At this, Mrs Munday told her that fact made her scale of success sink even further.

The attorney reiterated what Antony had told her—they would also need substantial funds for such a court case. It may even be difficult to find an attorney who would take on the case.

It would have to be fought on Sainte Marie, as the will had been registered there. Finally, despite Ella's forthright questions, the attorney would not divulge who the will's beneficiaries were.

Ella had floated out of the attorney's office—disbelief wounding every pore. At that point, she was unsure where she would find the strength to explain to Craig. She'd driven out of the capital in a daze. All of life had been continuing around her, but it became a blur. Not part of her world. Ella was trying to come to terms with the fact, despite all her efforts, she would be unable to reinstate her parent's honour—recuperate a single penny that Jeffrey had stolen from the family. None of it seemed real. The only thing which did was her week on island had been a waste of her time and money.

She'd driven to the marina. Being alone in the apartment was too depressing. She sat, having finished her drink, trying to bring back some composure to her thoughts. Ella was flung out of her pondering by a waitress asking if she wanted anything else. She dragged her mind to take in the chatting tourists around her; the palm trees fringing the commercial area, and the spangled water slapping against boats moored within sight. Her time on island was slipping away. There was only one more day before she flew home. There was one important chore she had to cross of her list before she left. Confront Tamara.

Ella felt reluctant, remembering the wall of hostility she had been met with at the funeral. Tamara's cold and disdainful stare. But she was her last chance to find out about Jeffrey's will. Her hopes of achieving much didn't run high. But she had to try. She had to steel herself for the encounter. Come on Ella, she told herself. Focus. She grabbed the moment and took out her phone, and then foraged for the business card.

As expected, Tamara was at work. Ella was amazed at her response. She agreed, without an argument, to seeing her during her lunch break, at the hotel where she worked. Ella stored away her phone, thoughtfully. That had been too easy. What had happened to the contemptuous Tamara she'd met at the funeral?

She'd never visited the hotel before, but found it easily. Unlike everything else about the hotel, Tamara's office was cramped. There wasn't really sufficient room in it for the desk, chair, filing cabinet and two adults. As Ella was shown in, she noticed it was also extremely warm.

Her first thoughts were that Tamara looked worn out. 'Thank you for agreeing to see me,' Ella started off, wondering where she was supposed to sit.

'I don't know how I can help you really,' Tamara replied. To Ella's surprise her tone was sympathetic. She even managed a smile. Tamara seemed to have softened. She lifted her chair over the desk and held it towards Ella.

She grabbed the chair, and sat feeling very self-conscious, and extremely warm. 'There's only a small chance that you will be able to, but I thought I had to ask. First of all, I'd like to explain several things to you about my stepfather before I ask.'

'I don't understand,' Tamara said.

'You will, if I could just start by telling you a little about my mother. I believe you met her.'

'Only briefly. In fact, it was the evening before she had her stroke. I remember Jeffrey going to see her in hospital.'

The discussion was progressing far better than Ella had anticipated. She had imagined unfriendliness and antagonism from the start.

Ella had worked out what she needed to say. 'The story starts with my father really. He had to work extremely hard for his money. He had a great deal of responsibility; frequently away from home, leaving my mother to take care of my brother and I.'

'I don't really see why ...' Tamara interrupted.

'As I said, you will,' she looked towards Tamara propped on her desk, 'please, just give me a few minutes of your time,' Ella

340

insisted. 'My father had to earn all his money, none of it was inherited, given or stolen.'

Did she see Tamara flinch at the last statement? She couldn't be sure.

'He lived in an era when people invested their money in properties. Most were in London. They became very profitable investments. When he died, he left all of this to my mother. One day, she had the real bad luck to walk into the wrong estate agents, real estate office—Jeffrey's office, when she was trying to sell one of the properties to pay off death duties. I believe you don't have to pay those in Sainte Marie.'

Tamara eyes widened. She didn't answer. Her amiable expression seemed to have slipped a little.

'Somehow, a relationship started between Jeffrey, and my mother. Anyway, to cut a long story short, he seduced her into a marriage. I don't think she wanted to live out her old age by herself. Then, as you know, she passed away fairly recently.'

'Yes, I'm sorry for your loss,' she uttered, almost under her breath.

'What you won't know Tamara, is that during the last four years, since Jeffrey had chiefly lived in the Caribbean, he had virtually emptied her accounts; re-mortgaged all her properties to the maximum and cashed in most of her insurance policies. Jeffrey took all of it—a very sizeable sum—running into millions of pounds.'

Tamara caught her breath. Ella watched her. Panic visibly aged her stunning features. Her eyes went down and then her head.

As Ella had related the story, she could feel herself filling with rage. Here was a woman who had profited from Jeffrey's criminal activities. To enforce the gravity of it, she added. 'Unfortunately, our solicitor ... our attorney ... doesn't even think there are now sufficient funds, or equity in the properties, to even pay the death duties—the taxes, on my mother's estate.'

341

The silence between them was heavy. Ella felt unbelievably hot. She noticed beads of perspiration forming on Tamara's brow. Her hotel uniform looked as though it was starting to cling to her.

'Tamara, can I suggest we go outside? It's so hot in here,' she said as much for herself, as for Tamara. She felt no sympathy for her.

It took several seconds for Tamara to react to the suggestion. She seemed confused and distracted.

'Er, yes, why not? I'm sure we can find a place in the shade.' They left the stifling, claustrophobic box room of an office. Tamara found them space on a bench in the shade of the hotel building.

They sat either end of the bench, each of them staring downwards. Ella was calculating which blow she was going to dole out next.

She glanced towards Tamara. 'You worked for Mr Denning at Topaz,' she said struggling to control her voice. 'You may, or may not know, that your partner owed him a considerable sum too—from the fractional sale of his villas.'

'Mr Denning,' she exclaimed, 'No, I didn't know.'

'Didn't you wonder Tamara?' Ella said brimming over with anger. 'Didn't you wonder where all the money came from?'

It was time for Tamara to defend herself. 'You don't have to believe this, but I didn't see great extravagance or riches. Jeffrey was frequently away working. He didn't shower me with expensive jewellery, fine clothes. That wasn't like him. I'm even buying my own car.'

Disregarding the denial, Ella continued her rebuke. 'But there are other people too Tamara; Mr Denning has told me there are others on the island, who are really unhappy about Jeffrey's dishonesty and greed. Essentially Tamara, whether you realised it or not, you were living with a crook.' The final word was said with force. Ella doubted that she was telling her something she didn't know already.

Ella noticed Tamara's hand as it went up to her face, it was trembling. She took in the trickle of sweat which ran from her forehead. Bewilderment kept her silent.

'I visited Jeffrey's attorney this morning, Mrs Munday. I went to ask about the will—Jeffrey's last will and testament. She refused to tell me who the beneficiaries were. My main reason for coming to see you Tamara is to ask you. Ask you, if you know anything about it.'

Tamara, it seemed, was still in shock. Ella waited.

Then it came. Tamara opened up. She confessed to guessing about Jeffrey, after Mrs Monday had told her about the will.

'Then you do know about the will?' Ella exclaimed. She felt relief she was getting somewhere.

'I was stunned when Mrs Munday told me about it. She'd agreed to see me because she knew I'd be worried about living at Three Isles. Afterwards, when I talked to my son about the will, together we guessed. I feel so ashamed.'

Ella was stunned too. She hadn't expected Tamara to open up. But she hadn't told her yet what she really needed to know.

'You know what things are like, when you're working, you're looking after a house, looking after a child, you don't get time to think thinks through.' Tamara seemed to be talking to herself. Her mouth went straight, and she inhaled deeply.

Ella was losing her patience. The woman was exasperating. Why didn't she just get on and tell her about the will and who had inherited the assets? 'But what does it say...' Ella interrupted.

'It says there are five properties, bought through Jeffrey's company.'

'Five. My God.'

'Three on Sainte Marie, one in Barbados, and one in Panama.'

'Barbados. I kind of knew about that one,' Ella burst out.

'Do you, I don't.'

'The woman at the funeral; the one who followed the coffin in. Mr Denning made it his job to find out about her. Apparently, she lives in a property which Jeffrey owns in Barbados. And according to Mr Denning, it seems like they were more than just friends. You had a rival Tamara!'

Unexpectedly, Tamara reacted, 'not at all!' she said forcefully. 'I came to learn that I was a convenience for him, we were not true companions.'

Ella knew exactly what she meant. Her mother had been the same to Jeffrey. She doubted if he'd been capable of true affection. She decided to say nothing about Tamara's remark. She needed to play her cards right and find out who inherited all these properties. She started to look around her: the vibrant well-tended tropical gardens, coconut palms, and beyond the enormous pool, the pink sand of the beach. She inhaled the scent of the exotic plant growing behind her.

'You're lucky to work here. The setting is magnificent. I understand why my mother loved the Caribbean,' Ella said, for something to break the silence.

Tamara eyed Ella, whilst nervously twisting her hands.

'He left his assets to my son,' she blurted out. 'Willis inherited it.'

Ella shook her head to clear it. It was her turn to be surprised. Astonished, more like, that Tamara had told her; and taken aback that someone so young should inherit so much. 'What does he think of it all?'

'Jeffrey had always said that he would help him study at university,' she replied, avoiding the question. 'Hopefully, now he will be able to go.'

'My brother and I had hopes for our children too, instead of which we'll be faced with an enormous debt.' Bitterness still consumed her, but she was starting to view Tamara as being rather different from Jeffrey; and perhaps different than she'd imagined. She lived in different dimensions; not eaten up by the same immoral avidity.

'I'm not an unreasonable person. I think I can vouch that my son isn't either. I must ask him first because we're talking about his money as well as mine, but I'm sure that we can come to some arrangement here.'

Ella's felt her eyes widen, her brows rise involuntarily. She held back attentively.

'I'm sure that Willis would prefer that some of your mother's money was returned. We will need to talk, but I think that some funds from selling the house at Three Isles should be transferred to you. I need to talk to the attorney as well of course. Then, there's the villas at The Tamarind. They need renovating; but afterwards, you should be able to sell them for a good profit.'

Ella's mouth dropped; she felt her heart start to pound. This is not at all what she'd expected to hear. Why had Tamara's attitude done an about turn? She'd thought she would have to fight, argue, and pressure her to achieve anything. It took her several seconds to recover her composure.

'You can see Tamara, I'm really taken aback.'

'Even if Jeffrey was dishonest, it doesn't mean that I am.'

'I've never thought that,' she lied.

Tamara sat for several seconds as though she was thinking something through. She turned and looked directly at Ella, 'Now it's my turn,' she said, 'it's my turn to explain my story—tell you why I became involved with Jeffrey —it was all for my son.' Her voice was neutral and flat. 'Willis was becoming a real punk kid, a tearaway. I could see he was heading for trouble, towards a callous life of not having empathy with anyone. Then Jeffrey came into our lives.' She stopped and sighed remembering. 'Jeffrey gave him something I couldn't. I didn't have the cash. He opened up another world to Willis. Gave him aims for the future, a reason to live.'

'You mean the watersports?'

'Mm, he's so into sport, it's taken over his life. I'm hoping Willis will follow a career. And will be lucky enough to lift himself out of the continual grind of need, lack of money from the cradle to the grave. Whether by accident or not, Jeffrey did that for him.'

Ella said she understood, but was still agitated—eager to get to the specifics. A vague promise of a transfer of funds was not enough.

'Tamara, I fly home the day after tomorrow. How can we move forward with this?'

'I can phone my son and Mrs Monday's office this afternoon. I suppose, you could come to the villa tomorrow evening and we can talk things through with Willis. Get down to the essentials.'

'Sounds like a good plan,' Ella agreed.

'I do have to return to work now,' she said as she got up. Her hand was not offered to Ella. But she did manage a half smile, 'until tomorrow then. I get home around six.'

Ella remained on the bench for several minutes, a smile on her face, her spirits high. Her efforts had not been in vain.

~~~

The hotel car park was not the most alluring part of the hotel, but Ella sat in her hire car just gazing through the windscreen, taking in what was around her. She saw the brightness highlighting glowing colours, the flowers on a frangipani tree and the smart hotel building. A few hours earlier, her mood would have only seen the weeds in the gravel of the parking spaces, the pile of rotting vegetation waiting to be removed, and the hotchpotch of vehicles (some very tired looking) around her.

It was strange how just thirty odd minutes could turn everything around. She had really thought her meeting with Tamara would be fruitless. Full of animosity. She didn't comprehend why Jeffrey's mistress' approach towards her had turned around, but it certainly had. Now, just sat there, she was

346

filled with euphoria; overflowing with hope. She was yearning to give her brother the positive news and put Antony in the picture. However, as she'd left, Tamara had asked that she said nothing of their conversation to anybody else—it was too soon, she had to talk to Willis first. Ella had agreed; but was just about to break her promise. She pulled her mobile out of her bag.

'Sam, I know you're still at work, so I'll be quick. I've done it Sam!' she babbled excitedly into her phone. 'She's agreed. Tamara. She's agreed to return some of the money invested in Jeffrey's properties. I'm seeing her and her son tomorrow evening to work out the details.'

Her husband told her to slow down.

'Isn't it great? You never know, we might even be able to save Oakdale.' She had long envisaged her family living there. Bringing up her daughter in the home where she had grown up herself.

Sam told her not to be too hasty and to take one step at a time.

'Well, I can dream, can't I?' she said; and promised to phone him again later, when he'd be at home.

Chapter 33

Confession?

It had been a good evening.

One of the best evenings she'd had in a long time. It had done her good. Her date with Mr Jackson had really lifted her spirits. As she slammed his car door, after saying good-bye, she felt more valued and comfortable about herself. As expected, she'd been treated with respect. He'd asked her about her new job and how she was coping—managing after witnessing Jeffrey Taylor being dragged from the sea. It seemed most of the island knew about it. It did Emmalyn good to talk it through and reveal the distress she'd experienced at the scene; how she felt depressed afterwards. He was sympathetic—not only about witnessing the drowning, but also that her hopes for a better future had disappeared in a trice.

Emmalyn asked about his fast-food business, even broached the subject of Krish. She suggested perhaps he should observe the chef's behaviour around women. Mr Jackson acknowledged her warning and asked for details of problems. Emmalyn played down the abuse she'd had to contend with, but passed on the stories which other staff had related. He promised he'd look into it.

Mr Jackson (he told her to call him Samir) also seemed to have appreciated the evening. He'd been full of smiles; and asked if she'd like to go out again the following week. The invitation was accepted without hesitation.

Emmalyn's heeled shoes bounced up the path to her front door. The light thrown through the windows warned her Vincent was at home. Strangely, she hadn't seen him for days. His mate had come to install the plumbing in the half-built en-suite shower room. But afterwards Vincent hadn't made the progress he'd promised. Emmalyn's mind had been on other

348

things: the shock of having to tell Tamara about Jeffrey, talking to the police, going to the funeral, as well as trying to do her full-time job, had more than occupied her days.

The kitchen was empty; there was no sign of Vincent preparing food as she'd expected. She sighed. The door to his room was ajar, more light filtering out. Ever vigilant, she nudged the gap wider, intending to turn off the light. The sight of him sprawled out on the bed stopped her. His T-shirt and trousers were crumpled and stained. Filthy boots marking the bed clothes. An empty alcohol bottle lay horizontal next to the bed.

She wanted to wake him to complain about his shoes; about the wasted electricity, but then thought better of the idea. It was simpler to just flick the switch. It was clear, all those promises about staying sober; and helping to build the shower room, had been forgotten. Emmalyn should have known better than to give him a second chance. People had warned her, the reformed Vincent wouldn't last. She left him in the dark, snoring lightly.

Emmalyn woke with a start, thinking she'd heard a noise. In seconds, her eyes adjusted to the gloom. A very pale light filtered through the curtain. The dark shapes of her belongings in the room were just visible: her clothes hanging from the hooks on the wall, the chair next to them. Then a form that shouldn't be there.

'Vinny,' she said in a loud whisper. Her heart started hammering. Who else could it be?

Nothing.

She reached to the side of the bed and snatched up the torch left there in case of power cuts. The finger of light illuminated the still figure at the end of the bed. A figure clothed in a dirty t-shirt and dark trousers. She pulled the sheet aside and got out of bed.

'Vinny, what the hell are you doing in my room? You woke me up,' Emmalyn shouted, walking towards the light switch.

Vincent didn't move. It was clear from his bloodshot eyes he was drunk, or high on something.

'Vinny,' she'd prodded his senseless bulk, 'get the hell out of my room.' She threw the door wide open. 'Go back next door.'

Everything changed.

He lurched for her—one hand grabbed hold of her nightdress neckline, the other her upper arm. His eyes narrowed; forehead dropped. Emmalyn's body stiffened as she thumped at his chest with her free arm.

'Stop, for heaven's sake Vinny…' she tried to prise his fingers off her clothing. He dragged her through the door into the living room. Emmalyn kicked at his leg as he stopped to turn on the light.

'Comez to bed.' Pulling her towards his room, the fabric of her nightdress tore with a ripping sound. He stopped to look for a moment; then tightened his hold of her arm. 'Ya got jus' mi now.'

'That hurts,' she shrieked, 'go to hell.' The old Vinny had returned.

'I sees to ya fancy white guy. 'E gone.' he dragged her across the lino, Emmalyn protesting loudly. 'You'z got me now.'

'Like hell I do, you bastard,' Emmalyn screamed again. 'What the hell are you talking about?' She foresaw what was going to happen. She pictured herself being hauled into his room and being raped. It would be too much. She'd never want to see him again; he'd have to leave. Didn't he realise?

As he turned to throw open the door to his room, his grasp slackened slightly. She brought her arm up, lowered her head, and bit his hand with all her might. Vincent freed her arm instantly. Emmalyn crumpled in a heap.

'Ya bitch!'

Vincent's movements were slow, as he brought his hand to his face. She struggled across the floor. One of his boots went out, aiming for her. Emmalyn scrambled out of his path. She knew of old, threatened violence was needed against his drunken might.

Emmalyn half crawled towards the kitchen table and pulled herself up, grabbing for the tabletop. Vincent was there at the same time. Gnarled hands went for her exposed breasts. Emmalyn's arm's flayed, smacking at his head with force. He flinched at her repeated blows, defending himself with one arm, trying to grab hold of her with the other. She kicked. She scratched. She screamed.

'Ya ugly bitch!'

His hands went for her neck. Strong fingers pressed hard to the side and front of it. He pushed her against the table.

"E gone, yur uder man, 'e gone,' he slurred, 'Ya got me now,' his foul breath reached her nostrils, repulsing her.

Emmalyn panicked, gasping for breath, her energy failing. Desperate, but determined she was not going to die because of this bastard, she found some adrenalin. Using the rigidity of the table as support, she launched her knee upwards to his crutch.

Vincent howled; his fingers released her neck. He doubled over, head down.

'Ya cow, Ikillya,' he groaned.

Emmalyn struggled for breath. This was her chance. He was shoved out the way. Edging along the table, reaching the end, she lunged for the knife box. Trembling hands fumbled through the utensils and grabbed for the handle of her largest knife—a cooks knife. She seized it with both hands, holding it before her. Vincent's body was still folded over. That man was capable of anything. What had he told her about a white man? It didn't make sense. Could he mean Jeffrey Taylor?

Emmalyn's back went up against the draining board. She shivered from fighting for her life; breathed deeply to try and level out her nerves. If he came for her now, she'd have to attack him. Slash out. Stab at him. She hated the idea, but she hated him.

Vincent started to straighten and moved towards her; arms stretched forward. Seeing the glint of the knife, he stopped in his tracks.

'You bastard, get the hell out of here,' Emmalyn shrieked. 'Vincent, you are evil. Debauched. You've sold your soul. You come anywhere near this house, or near me, I'll go straight to the police. I'll let them know what you did. To me … and to Jeffrey Taylor.'

'Ya whore, I kill ya.'

'Just like you did Jeffrey Taylor,' she screamed at him. Vincent was capable of it.

Vincent stared; said nothing. Emmalyn gaped at his vile form. Fear ran through her, reading her suspicions as correct. His body slumped. She heard a sigh as he turned and made for his room.

'I'z got ya now,' Vincent snarled again.

'You're not sleeping in this house tonight, or ever again.'

Emmalyn picked up a plate from the draining board and threw it at Vincent's bulk. It missed his head and smashed against the wall.

'Get out! I never want to see you again. You'll end up in prison if I do.'

His body was reluctant, it was clear his mind was functioning slowly. Vincent shuffled towards the door, crunching over broken pottery.

'Go,' Emmalyn wailed. 'You come back here, and I'll tell everyone you killed him. You drowned Mr Taylor, didn't you?'

Vincent looked with bloodshot eyes. Sluggishly he tried unlocking the screen door, his fingers slipping, finding it difficult. Emmalyn sure as hell wasn't going to help. After several long seconds, the screen opened. Then the main door slammed into its frame. She rushed forward; and slid the bolts in place. Her strength gave way. Emmalyn slid and sat, her back against the screen, her legs folded before her. Fear and fury erupted as tears spilling down her cheeks, onto her bare chest.

She wept for herself. Life had been too tough for too long. And she wept for her friend Tamara.

How could she tell Tamara she suspected Vincent of murdering her partner? Her heart told her Vincent was involved. She replayed the evening at Coco Palms when she'd first met Jeffrey Taylor. Vincent knew she was there. She saw Jeffrey's hand on hers. How he'd sat so close. Then the figure she thought was in the shadow of the trees. The idea had gone straight out of her head, as Tamara had arrived. It could have been Vincent. He may have misunderstood Jeffrey's flirty ways and thought his days were numbered living under her roof.

Vincent hadn't been at the house for days—she couldn't remember the last time. For sure, he wasn't there when she returned from Mango Bay after seeing the body hauled out of the sea. Was this because he felt guilty? Did he decide not to return until the dust had settled?

Emmalyn touched her neck, still feeling the pain of those hideous fingers around it. Vincent, it seemed was capable of anything, especially when driven by drink or drugs. His brain became scrambled, not seeing things as they really were. It could have been the same when he encountered Jeffrey Taylor—he'd put two and two together to make far too much. She wouldn't put anything past him. And Vincent hadn't denied any of it.

Her head ached with confusion. She must unravel her thoughts. Sort out what to do. Go to the police—about his attack on her. The police weren't always good with domestic incidents. Tell them her suspicions about Mr Taylor's death? What proof did she have?

And Tamara? How would she tell Tamara?

Chapter 34

Secrets

Vincent arrested. Drugs charges. Tell you more tomorrow.

Emmalyn gaped at her phone. The text had come from a friend. At last, they had caught up with him. Relief ran through her. Vincent hadn't been seen since that dreadful fight. But each night she lay awake fearful. This news would help her to sleep easier; and reinforced her decision to go to the police about him—not only about his abuse of her, but also about her suspicions. The belief he was involved in Jeffrey Taylor's death.

She was on her way to see Tamara, intending to share her doubts about her former lodger, and to warn of her plan to notify the police. Any police enquiry would undoubtedly involve Tamara. Emmalyn owed it to her to forewarn her. It was her duty. Tamara had been so good to her. And being thoughtful had got her partner killed.

From her cramped place, Emmalyn looked through the smeary window. Her stop was next. The bus was crowded. The usual inescapable routine had to be followed to alight; some of the other passengers leaving their seats for her. A cool breeze blew over as she reached the open door. The smell of ozone gusted in from the shore. The bus stop was next to the track leading down to Three Isles Bay. The path was obstructed by the tangle of vegetation invading the route. Brushing it aside, Emmalyn advanced slowly, being in no hurry to reach the villa. With each step her heart seemed to become heavier. Telling Tamara would not be easy, but sharing her suppositions might lighten the weight she'd been burdened with for too long.

Emmalyn kicked through the stones of the unmade road; the images of that day surged back into her mind yet again—the morning of Jeffrey's death. It was one which would stay with her for always. None of the raw details could ever be eradicated from her distressed mind. The staff at Topaz hotel had been very thoughtful when she'd collapsed on the beach. They'd escorted her to the hotel and looked after her well. Later the police interview had been a trial. Subsequently, she'd had to phone Tamara to break the dreadful news. But all of that had been well before Vincent's attack.

~~~

Tamara sat on the patio waiting—watching the spectacle—bands of sunlight cutting through the clouds. Golden light splattered across the water, contrasting against dappled indigo of the heaving waves. It held her attention. She would miss it—the daily changing view of the bay. There was an emptiness, a sadness inside her at having to leave. But she'd always known living at the villa couldn't last for ever. It had become too difficult; Jeffrey had wanted to change her too much.

With Emmalyn's visit, there was a lot to tell her. Events were moving rapidly. A real estate agent had already surveyed the property. He'd assured her the property wouldn't be on the market long. It was very desirable.

When Ella came to the villa, Tamara had been filled with pride by Willis. He'd been so mature in agreeing that initially two thirds of the value of Three Isles should be transferred to Jeffrey's stepdaughter, together with the villas at the Tamarind. Ella had been delighted. They'd agreed everything would be done through their prospective attorneys. Willis had also told her that he would review the situation again, trying to reimburse her family further; and perhaps some of Mr Denning's losses. Willis had been adamant everything should remain confidential: as few people as possible should know about their arrangement. She was not to inform Mr Denning as yet. He didn't explain why, and Ella didn't ask. During that visit, none of them even mentioned Jeffrey' demise.

Tamara had been spooked by Willis' anxiety; and lived under a cloud of fear. Her thoughts dominated by suspicions that someone out there would take revenge on them as repercussion for Jeffrey's life of fraudulence. Panic had gnawed at her. There'd been days when she thought her sanity was unravelling, and became fearful of her own shadow. Sleep deserted her many a night; she would thrash this way and that, her body constantly tense. Worrying about what might happen to her or what might happen to Willis. A slight sense of relief settled inside Tamara once the sale of the villa was advertised. It gave an indication that it didn't belong to them. However, not all her anxieties had been discarded; and she had tried to alleviate them by keeping busy. Surreptitiously, without even a word to her son, she had registered a new company to transfer assets from J&T Inc. As an executor, she had contacted the bank in Panama City and informed them of their client's death; and who was to inherit his money. The funds there were more than enough to pay for Willis' university fees; and plenty to start him up in his chosen career. Trying to sort out the other properties, she had even bought flight tickets for herself and Willis to Barbados, then on to Panama. The visit was planned for the college vacations.

Her phone, laid on the table, pinged. Tamara lifted it to look at the e-mail. Out the corner of her eye something flashed across her line of vision. Automatically, her body reacted. Lit from behind by the bright sunlight, a dark figure stood before her. She shifted in her seat. Instantly, her heart was in her mouth, jumping to the conclusion it was one of Jeffrey's associates coming to take revenge. Realising who it was, her heart rate slowed a little.

'Don't do that! You frightened me to death,' Tamara gasped.

'Sorry,' said Emmalyn, 'I thought it was easiest if I came around the front. I'd guessed you'd be by the pool.'

'You really made me jump Emmalyn. Didn't you see me fly in the air?' She exhaled loudly and found Emmalyn a smile.

'Anyway, sit yourself down and let's get you a drink.' Emmalyn was left sitting by the pool.

Tamara returned with a tray of drinks and nibbles. Snatching a look at Emmalyn, she noticed the strong light made her friend look as tired and worn out as she felt. Could her new job waiting tables and being on her feet all day be taking its toll? Or was there something else?

'So, what's this news you've got to tell me?' Tamara asked, pouring the drinks.

Emmalyn's face had been serious, but there was a sudden quick grin. Her face lit up. 'Yeah, we don't get much opportunity to talk at work, do we? It's the best news I've had in months,' she grinned. 'Mrs Leon has asked me to go back to work for her. Only three days a week, but that's three days I won't have to wait at tables.'

'Oh Emmalyn, I'm so pleased for you,' Tamara shrieked. Her spirits rose. At least, the world was doling out good will in some quarters.

'She's going to loan me the deposit for a car too, and take it out of my commission bit by bit.' Emmalyn's face shone with pleasure.

Tamara grabbed her hand across the table and squeezed it. 'You've had to wait such a long time. At last things are going your way. Oh, I'm really, really happy for you. It was dreadful your plans with Jeffrey never came to anything.'

'Listen Tamara, that wasn't your fault. You were so kind. You got me my hotel job anyway, which is far preferable to Jacko's.'

Tamara stopped for a moment. 'I was thinking about you when I met Jeffrey's stepdaughter—Ella. I recommended you to her. She'll want somebody to supervise the renovations of the properties she's inherited—at The Tamarind. I thought that you might enjoy that.'

'Wow, I certainly would.'

'You could earn a bit of money from it too.'

'There you go again, always thinking of others,' Emmalyn said gratefully.

Tamara had distorted the truth, but it seemed an easy solution to some of her problems. The invented story that Jeffrey's family had inherited the villas seemed an easy solution. It avoided telling anyone about Willis' legacy. The villas, in the south of the island, would need doing up before selling them at a good profit. Emmalyn was capable of helping there. This was just a part of the list of half-lies Tamara told her friend: saying the Three Isles villa was being sold on Jeffrey's family's instructions, and she'd be searching for somewhere to live near her job, the implication being she'd be looking for somewhere to rent.

'So how did you get on with Jeffrey's daughter?' Emmalyn said.

Tamara didn't correct the mistake. 'Okay, but some of the time, I felt she treated me with contempt. I got the impression that she thought I was some sort of money grabbing hooker. Ella seemed to think Jeffrey showered me with expensive gifts— you know that was far from the truth—and it was me who started the relationship, wanting to get my hands on as much of his money as possible.'

'Well, if you'd been like that you wouldn't have worked all the time, would you? So, that wasn't true,' Emmalyn sympathised.

'To be honest Emmalyn, at first, it was the other way around. Jeffrey was the one who chased me. I've now realised, he wanted to give the impression that I was the reason he was on the island. And in fact, it wasn't that at all,' she paused, 'he wanted someone to deflect attention away from what he was really doing. Jeffrey must have thought I was the type of woman who fitted the bill.'

'What do you mean—deflect away from what he was doing?' Emmalyn looked puzzled.

Tamara pretended to study her nails and ran her fingers around them. She was giving herself a few seconds to decide just how much to open up to Emmalyn. She looked directly at her, lowering her voice, 'Emmalyn, I think I can trust you not to breathe a word of this to another soul.'

'You know I won't!' she promised.

'It seems that Jeffrey was leading a double life,' Tamara sighed. 'You can never know what's going on in someone's mind can you Emmalyn? Well, I certainly didn't know what was going on in Jeffrey's world. For sure as hell, he didn't want me to know about his other self.' She lowered her voice even more, 'Emmalyn, I've found out Jeffrey wasn't always honest in his dealings with people.'

'You don't have to explain to me Tammy if you don't want to.'

'Frankly, it will help to share it. Truthfully, I never really knew Jeffrey. He never opened up to me Emmalyn. He gave me all the spiel about me being the only person he needed. Of course, he never actually said what he really needed me ... and Willis ... for.'

'Mmm, it's a dammed good thing you can't read another's mind,' Emmalyn muttered across the table.

Tamara took no heed of her friend's comment, wanting to complete her own story. 'You know, Jeffrey even used my bloody bank account, for heaven's sake. We put it in joint names. You know how dammed difficult it is to set up a bank account on this island, without dozens of references, the banks being paranoid about money laundering. He'd used my name for setting up a company ... and for getting a mortgage too.'

'I didn't know that.'

'Well, no, you wouldn't. It's kind of personal,' she sighed again. 'To start with, I thought he wanted me because he found me attractive, but then ...' she put her face in her hands, '... but then, all the sweet talk stopped.'

Emmalyn touched her arm, 'You are attractive Tamara, a very attractive woman.'

Tamara managed a weak smile, 'Not at the moment though eh? I'm just too tired.'

'That'll pass.'

Tamara regarded her friend. 'He just wanted someone to look after his every need—and look after his villa of course. I Know now, he just used me.'

'There're people who think nothing of using others. '

'Jeffrey soon realised I needed help with Willis,' Tamara inhaled deeply. 'He knew I wasn't going to say no to moving into a fancy villa. He'd bloody well seen where I lived before for heaven's sake.' Tears started to sting her eyes. 'His money bought me Emmalyn, so Willis could have a decent future. But in return, I had to look after him like a lord. Clean the house, cook his meals, do his washing, ...' she sniffled and hung her head, '... as well as put up with his excessive sexual demands. The man wanted it all.'

'And not ask too many questions,' Emmalyn added.

Tamara nodded her head, 'Yes Emmalyn, you're right. Perhaps he thought I wasn't very bright.'

'No, I'm sure it wasn't that. He saw you as the type of person who's continually busy—too busy to want to interfere in his world.'

'Perhaps. I suppose you could say I used him too—him and his money. But I never guessed it was dishonest money.'

'Try not to upset yourself,' Emmalyn told her, whilst looking worried and concerned herself.

'I should have left him, you know Emmalyn.' She closed her eyes, trying to prevent the flow of tears. 'I should have left him ages ago, but I kept on in there for Willis.'

'Look Tammy, millions of women stay with men to give themselves an easier life. Don't beat yourself up about it.'

But Tamara wanted to expose all her misery. 'He turned me into somebody I wasn't. I had to give in to every demand—totally submissive,' she revealed. 'I led a divided life. The true me at work, with Willis and my friends; another me with Jeffrey, continually yielding to his demands. If he didn't get his way, he became aggressive.'

Emmalyn surveyed her across the table, and then stood up to place an arm around Tamara's shoulder.

'You've been through a lot.'

'Emmalyn, I really didn't know Jeffrey was using the islands to make money fraudulently. I lived with a criminal. Do you ever think I'll meet a man who wants me for myself?'

'Tammy,' Emmalyn said forcefully. 'Look, can I give you a bit of advice?'

'Go on,' she wiped her tears with her paper handkerchief.

'Now, I don't want you to think I'm telling you what to do with your life, I'm just making a suggestion. Move on. Stop worrying about the past; and feeling sorry for yourself. Men aren't attracted to miserable women, even if they are beautiful. Start over again. Where's that bubbly, jolly Tamara everybody likes?'

Tamara looked up at her. She sighed. Her mouth became taught.

'This is a tiny island,' Emmalyn continued, 'but there's a whole world out there. You've got a job that will travel. Go and explore the world when Willis is at university.'

'But ...' Tamara started. She stared at Emmalyn again for a few seconds. 'God, why didn't I think of that? You know, that's excellent advice.' She squeezed her friend's hand.

Emmalyn returned to her seat, 'There's something I must tell you Tamara. It's ever so difficult, and may be upsetting to start with but ...'

~~~

'Hi Mom, oh hi Emmalyn, good to see you,' Willis strutted onto the decking, followed by a friend. 'We've come to use the pool. We might as well use it while we can,' he grinned. The friend waved.

Emmalyn noticed Tamara keep her head down, supposedly to keep her blotchy face hidden.

'Sure,' his mother said, 'a good idea. I'll go and get you some towels.'

Emmalyn's heart sank. Her opportunity had gone. She'd been ready to tell Tamara about Vincent, though on reflection, perhaps she was too distraught to cope with the revelation. And now with the boys around, it would be nigh impossible. She wouldn't want them to hear what she had to say. She watched Willis go to change into his swimwear and Tamara leave in search of towels. Willis' friend started swimming backwards and forwards in the pool.

It seemed it wouldn't be that day she'd impart the story about Vincent and her suspicions that jealousy had led him to kill Jeffery. Despite her anxiety, Emmalyn fixed a smile on her face while staring down at her feet. She'd make sure she cornered Tamara at work the following day and tell her then. The sooner Emmalyn went to the police the better. Vincent had to be locked up for as long as possible.

Mother and son returned. Soon there was a riot of shouting and antics coming from the pool, as the two boys took full advantage of it.

'I haven't enjoyed myself like that in years—not a care in the world,' Tamara commented.

'You will again Tammy,' Emmalyn assured her, though she knew the same could be said about her.

'So, what were you about to tell me before we were interrupted?'

Emmalyn so wanted to share her own horrors of her life, but the right moment had gone. It would have to wait until tomorrow. She smiled to herself and decided to convey another piece of her news instead: something positive.

'It's about Mr Jackson.'

'Oh yes,' Tamara returned the smile.

'I just wanted to say that, after the success of our first date, Mr Jackson has asked me to go to dinner with him at The Waters' Edge. You never knows what life's gonna bring, do you?'

Other Books by Cynthea Gregory

Cookbooks (in French, published by Editions CPE)
Le Chèvre en Folie
Poire et Coings
Le Fromage de Chèvre

Novels
A Little Slice of Paradise (written under the nom de plume
Cynthea Ash)

www.cynthea.gregory.com

Printed in Great Britain
by Amazon

85802729R00210